She did not resist.

As she felt herself drawn against the earl's hard chest, there was a roaring in Suzanna's ears. Then that roar became sweet music. As though obeying the compulsion of that wild music, she lifted her face to him.

Their lips met with the force of a thunderclap. No longer was Suzanna sure where she was or who she was. It was not important. All that mattered was that Brandmere was holding her and kissing her with a single-minded thoroughness. She wanted to be kissed for the rest of her life. It was almost as though—

It was almost, Suzanna thought dazedly, as though she were in love with Brandmere. . . .

LADY IN SILVER

Rebecca Ward

FAWCETT CREST • NEW YORK

To Lynn and Bert,
Sandra and Mark,
and to newlyweds everywhere.

A Fawcett Crest Book
Published by Ballantine Books
Copyright ©1990 by Maureen Wartski

Library of Congress Catalog Card Number: 90-93041

ISBN 0-449-21805-8

Manufactured in the United States of America

First Edition: September 1990

Chapter One

"Hello, hello, *hello*," crowed Peter Vries, "there sits the hero of the hour."

Anthony Harte, Fifth Earl of Brandmere, scarcely glanced up as his young cousin thrust his plump and perspiring countenance around the door of the morning room. He merely nodded and continued with his breakfast and a perusal of the morning paper.

Undisturbed, Peter entered the room, tripped over a Louis XV sofa, caught his heel in the Aubusson carpet, and nearly knocked over a lamp before subsiding into a chair by the marble fireplace.

"Stap me if all of London ain't talking about you this morning, Brand," he exclaimed. "It's only natural—mean to say—it was the race of the century. After all of Kirkland's boasts, you and your bays left his nags standing still. Privilege to have sat beside you in your curricle, give you my word!"

Brandmere waved a languid hand in the direction of the toast. "Breakfasted yet?" he questioned, but Peter was still lost in memories.

1

"D'you remember when the road divided and that accommodation coach and that wagon came at us from both sides? Couldn't believe it when you dropped your hands and let the bays shoot. Stap me if we didn't clear that wagon with a bare inch to spare." He paused to shake his head before adding, "You're the finest whip in London—and the coolest. But then, I suppose that a man who has fought on the Peninsula needs to have nerves of steel."

An indescribable look flickered briefly in the young earl's eyes, but he remained silent.

"Tell you what, Brand. Kirkland won't have the stuff to challenge you again, but there's Maxell. Just bought a pair of Welsh-bred grays, and he thinks they're high steppers. He'll be at Lord Chiltern's ball tonight. If you say the word, he'll jump at the chance of racing you."

Brandmere tossed down his napkin, yawned, and leisurely stretched his six feet two inches before rising from his cane-backed chair. As he strolled toward the window, September sunlight burnished his fair hair, then angled across a proud bridge of nose, hard line of cheek and chin, and the fine line of an ironic mouth.

The window of the earl's town house overlooked St. James Square. On the street below, a pair of fine bays were harnessed to a curricle. A tiger, dressed in spotless livery, waited beside the horses. Brandmere glanced at them dispassionately before announcing, "I'm not going to Chiltern's."

His cousin's slightly protuberant blue eyes turned anxious. "Are you feeling quite the thing, Brand?"

"Bored, old fellow." An unexpectedly sweet smile softened Brandmere's features, and eyes of a near midnight black lightened momentarily. Then they darkened again. "I'm damned bored," he corrected himself.

Peter swallowed. "Bored with Chiltern? But he's not such a bad fellow. Sets a good table, too. I should have thought—"

"I'm tired to death of feeding and boozing and of the same faces, the same conversation, the onslaught of simpering debs and their mothers." Brandmere turned his back on the window. "I'm played out."

Peter lifted his quizzing glass from his striped waistcoat, buffed it on the sleeve of his bottle-green coat, and eyed his tall cousin. There was an unmistakable sheen of health in Brandmere's sun-darkened cheeks and no sign of sickness about his athletic body. Humbly, Peter admired the broad shoulders flawlessly encased in dark superfine, the fawn riding breeches that fitted muscular thighs and long legs like a second skin, the glossy Hessians crafted by Hoby. No matter how much he primped before the mirror, no matter how skillfully his tailor padded his shoulders with buckram, he could never manage the je ne sais quoi that Brand achieved so effortlessly.

He began, "But I should have thought that after yesterday's triumph—"

"A game hardly worth the playing. I knew I could best Kirkland's commoners with one arm tied behind my back."

An odd expression had begun to suffuse Peter's round pink countenance. "So you're tired of racing, too," he said. "What about Boodle's and White's and—and sparring at Gentleman Jim's? You excel in the ring."

Brandmere yawned.

"Stap me, but that's excellent news!" Peter ex-

5

claimed. "Wonderful, in fact. Now I know you'll come to Devon with me next week."

Brandmere raised his fine brows. "Devon in September?" he drawled. "You're bamming me. I can't think of anything worse."

"But you're tired of London, ain't you?" Peter demanded. "Just heard you say so."

"Not as fatigued as I will be in Devon."

"But, Brand, I *need* you to come to Grapewood with me." Peter dropped his quizzing glass and gazed imploringly into his cousin's countenance. "Sir Malcolm Traherne will be there, and—and so will his daughter."

The light of understanding filled Brandmere's dark eyes. "Aha," he murmured. "Anabel the fair."

Peter's round cheeks grew pinker. His eyes held the far-off look of a ruminative sheep. He ran plump white hands through hair that had until now been modishly arranged à la Titus.

"I wouldn't have the nerve to go there alone. I need you to give me moral support. You see, I love Miss Traherne." As his cousin began to grin, Peter added fervently, "I know what you're thinking, but stap me if Miss Traherne isn't the love of my heart."

Brandmere considered rather cynically that it could also be a love of the pocket. Anabel Traherne was the only daughter of a wealthy nabob who had just returned from India, where, it was rumored, he had amassed his fortune. Peter, on the other hand, had very little with which to feather his expensive London nest.

Unfortunately for the earl's young cousin, many other featherless birds of the *ton* had the same idea, and Anabel Traherne was besieged by a flock of admirers and offers.

4

"You've seen her. You know that she's like a goddess. Venus is nothing compared to her." Peter began to walk up and down the room until a collision with a Chippendale daybed forced him to stop. "She has so many admirers and yet, she—she smiled at me. Brand, that smile transported me to paradise! To get another such smile, I would gladly be torn apart by lions."

"No," Brandmere said.

"But I would. Cheerfully."

"I meant," said the earl, "that I won't go with you to Devon. It's a curst flat place and besides, we haven't been invited."

"Doesn't matter," Peter shot back swiftly. "We'd be paying guests."

Brandmere stopped in mid-yawn and blinked. "I beg your pardon?"

Glad to have his cousin's complete attention, Peter explained. "Grapewood used to belong to Sir Bartholomew Campion. Never heard of him before, but his was supposedly a name to conjure with in Devon. Sir Bartholomew pegged out this year. Grapewood's heavily mortgaged. The present heir—a younger brother, name of Richard—is trying to keep the place up by inviting paying guests who'd enjoy the thrill of staying in a haunted manor. From what I hear, the first group of guests are converging on Grapewood next week."

Brandmere remarked coldly that he had heard of Richard Campion. "My father referred to him as a bad hat who lost his inheritance on cards and horses and shady speculations. He lost other people's money, too. When he left for the Continent a few years ago, creditors were nipping at his heels. The man is a regular Captain Sharp."

"Oh, I say," Peter exclaimed.

"Now you say he's back in England and turning his late brother's home into an inn." Brandmere's fine lip curled disdainfully. "Paying guests and a bogus ghost. The kind of trick you'd expect from a man like Campion."

In a subdued voice Peter said that there really was a ghost. "That's why Sir Malcolm's going. He's hipped on spirits and things that go bump in the night. Comes from living in India, I expect. Stap me, Brand, I didn't know about this Campion fellow. Even so, we wouldn't have to associate with him. We—"

He broke off, as there was a discreet knock on the study door, and the earl's manservant, Marlin, entered. He proffered a letter on a silver tray. Brandmere took it and opened it.

"Good God," he muttered.

"Something wrong?" Peter wondered.

"My sister Honoria is coming to London next week." Brandmere's stricken eyes met those of his valet, and that unflappable individual actually paled.

"My lord," he stammered, "may I be so bold as to inquire whether Lady Danbury's children will accompany her?"

"Yes. All five of the brats."

Peter could not repress a shudder. He admired Brand's control. If he, Peter, had received word that Honoria and her horrible brood were descending on his London quarters, he would have been howling like a bedlamite.

Marlin was asking, "Her ladyship and the children, are—are staying here, my lord?"

"Yes, damn it. My sister wants to discuss family

6

business with me. She adds that things will be easier now that 'dear Percival' has started to talk. And she is glad to inform me that Augustus has not tried to set fire to the house for several weeks."

There was an awful silence broken by Peter, who croaked, "Well, what are you waiting for? No time to lose. Do a bolt to Brandmere—or to one of your other properties."

The earl shook his head. "No use. She's bound to follow me and run me to earth. We are in for a siege, Marlin."

The valet took the news with the cool blood of one who had been the earl's batman at Salamanca.

"Very good, my lord. I will inform the servants of her ladyship's arrival."

As Marlin left the room, Peter seized the opportunity fate had presented him. It was now or never.

"Honoria wouldn't follow you to Grapewood, Brand," he murmured. "There'd be no children there at all. None of your shirts would be ruined by sticky little hands. And your boots—didn't you say that one of your nevvies punched holes in your boots during Honoria's last visit?"

"The oldest, Jeremy. The little beast wanted to try out his pocket knife."

"Your boots will be safe at Grapewood, Brand."

The earl gave his cousin a long, hard look. Then he shouted, "Marlin!" As if by magic, the manservant materialized at the door. "Pack up, man. We're going to Devon. I will write my sister and inform her that since we will not be in town next week, her visit is out of the question."

Color seeped back into Marlin's cheeks. "Yes, my lord," he said joyfully. "I will see to it immediately."

Brandmere turned to the grinning Peter. "You

7

needn't look so pleased with yourself, either. It's a mutton-headed idea, and I'm going under protest. I warn you that anything that's connected with Dickon Campion's bound to smell like last week's fish."

"This is the most mutton-headed, ramshackle idea you have ever had."

Suzanna Campion pushed back an errant lock of black hair and glared at her uncle. The severity of the glare was somewhat weakened by the smudge of dried mud along her cheek. The mud, along with an enormous starched apron, gave Suzanna the look of a ten-year-old.

"I never thought to see the day," she continued bitterly, "when a Campion would go into trade. *Paying* guests coming next week—as though Grapewood were a common inn. Poor Father must be spinning in his grave."

Her uncle pursed his lips judiciously. "Not Barty," he said. "Barty never spun. Slow and stately, that was his style. Never knew a man with more starch than Barty, God rest him."

"Uncle, it will not *do*."

"On the contrary, I think that it will do very well."

Dickon Campion rose gracefully from the shabby but comfortable armchair in which he had been ensconced. He was a man in his forties, of middle height and weight and with a young man's quickness, and though he shared his niece's coloring, they were completely unalike.

Suzanna's gray eyes seemed almost too large for her heart-shaped face and were as open and as clear as an early morning sky. Dickon Campion's eyes, on the other hand, were keen and sparkled with wit and often with malice. His hooded lids seemed to hide many secrets.

There were other differences, too. Suzanna's small, straight nose was amply freckled from being outdoors in all kinds of weather. Dickon, proud of his fair complexion and fine hands, shuddered at exposing himself to the sun and often used lead to whiten his skin. And while Suzanna's dark hair was thick and curly and constantly escaping from the no-nonsense bun at the back of her small head, Dickon liberally powdered his own smooth, straight, carefully coiffured hair.

Dickon Campion, moreover, wore clothes in the kick of fashion. Today he affected white silk stockings embroidered with clocks, stockinette trousers of canary yellow, a ruffled cambric shirt, a square-cut yellow coat, and a cravat arranged in the waterfall style.

He shook his head over Suzanna's appearance. There was a tear in the sleeve of her blue house-dress, and various splatterings of mud marred the hem.

"Deuce take it," he grumbled, "you look like a hoyden. What will our guests think of you?"

"I do not care what they think. I do not want them here at all," Suzanna countered.

Dickon changed his tactics. "I collect that you were outside just now in the, ah, barn? How are Porcina and that ancient goat of yours?"

"Porcina will have her piglets very soon, and all will be well with her, but Ione is failing." Suzanna's eyes grew shadowed as she added, "She is so old, Uncle Dickon. No doubt she dreams of her youth."

Dickon briefly wondered whether goats dreamed. Then, modulating his voice to tenderness he crooned, "It is for Porcina and Ione that I am trying to preserve Grapewood."

9

"Stuff," retorted Suzanna.

Dickon winced. Unlike his stiff-rumped older brother, Suzanna was as game as a pebble, and he had always been fond of her. But he could not get used to her forthright ways. Her regrettable frankness, Dickon mused, must spring from her unorthodox upbringing and from her preoccupation with the useless beasts and the impossible servants with which Grapewood was populated.

"I know that the manor is heavily mortgaged," Suzanna was continuing. "I realize that we may lose it if something is not done. But I would far rather do honest work—go as a governess, say—than welcome a series of paying guests. It is not only degrading but impractical."

She looked about her as she spoke, seeing the furniture that had been there so long as to almost take root, the faded carpet, the scratched woodwork, and nondescript watercolors on the wall. She loved this room, this house, but she knew well how other eyes would see it.

"Who would want to visit this shabby old place much less pay to come here?" she demanded.

"Sir Malcolm Traherne would."

Suzanna cried indignantly, "That is because you wrote to him and told him those whiskers about the Silver Lady."

Dickon said in an injured tone that the Silver Lady of Grapewood was no Bambury tale. "When your father and I were lads, our nurse used to frighten us into obedience with tales of Lady Blanche who during the sixteenth century was murdered and thrown into a well. I merely told Sir Malcolm that she sometimes 'walked.' Can I help it if he is interested in the occult?"

He rubbed his white hands together. "Sir Malcolm has a beautiful daughter. Together, they will be an excellent draw." Seeing that his niece looked bewildered, he explained. "I mean that the Trahernes will bring other guests to Grapewood. This very morning I received a card from the Earl of Brandmere. His lordship and his cousin will arrive next week."

Suzanna's shoulders slumped in despair. "Worse and worse. From all that I have read of him, Brandmere has a great deal of money and the haughty manners that go with such wealth. He has so many country estates to choose from that I am sure that he has lost count of them. If he is coming here, it is probably to ridicule us."

"He's coming because he has heard that Miss Traherne is to be our guest." Smiling broadly, Dickon continued. "Brandmere is only the first to take the bait. In the days that follow, you will see that there will be other cards. Young bloods will flock to hold court at the feet of the rich and lovely Anabel. And, naturally, news of Brandmere's coming to Grapewood will get about and cause mothers to rearrange their plans." He paused. "Deuce take it, my dear girl, do you *know* what a matrimonial catch the earl is?"

Suzanna's anxiety took another turn. "How many people are you expecting?" He told her, and she exclaimed, "Cook will collapse if such demands are made on her. And Margery will hand in her notice, as she always does when she is vexed, and Little John will be terribly cross."

Dickon frowned. "You allow those servants too many liberties, Suzanna. That fellow Little John especially does not treat me with the respect I deserve. He must come to heel." He paused and then added in his most persuasive tone, "You are thinking that this is a gamble, which it is. But I know that Grapewood will *take*. If our first week goes well, we'll become an *on dit* in London. Once we are fashionable, we will never need to worry about money again." He reached out and took Suzanna's hands. "That is why we must please the Trahernes and Brandmere at all costs."

In the back of her mind Suzanna could hear the late Sir Bartholomew sneering that his younger brother was a ne'er-do-well, a thatchgallows who could not be trusted. At the same time, the way he clasped her hand recalled a bleak time after her mother's death. While her father had ignored her and sent her to live with her Dorset cousins, Uncle Dickon had come to see her sometimes and had dried her homesick tears. He had once taken her to a county fair, where he had bought her a singing bird and a red ribbon. She had let the bird go almost at once, but she still had the ribbon.

Suzanna sighed. Dickon Campion was slippery and untrustworthy. He was also the man who had been kind to her when she needed kindness the most, and he was the only relative she had left. As she listened to her uncle spinning his dreams, she wished with all her heart that she could believe him.

"I know how you feel about this place," he was saying. "Deuce take it, I love it, too. And besides, consider the alternatives. If Grapewood is sold, what will happen to the servants? And to Ione and, ah, Porcina and the rest?"

From his niece's expression, Dickon knew that he had her where he wanted her. He almost felt ashamed of the ease with which he could manipulate Suzanna. The girl didn't have a devious bone in her body.

But after all, he reasoned, he meant most of what he said. He *did* want to settle down at Grapewood for some time. After his recent hand-to-mouth existence on the Continent, the prospect of living peacefully on the old estate was actually pleasant.

He smiled at Suzanna, whose searching eyes looked deep into his.

"If your scheme falls through, as I am persuaded it must, Grapewood will be lost anyway. Unfortunately, you are Father's heir and will do as you please." She paused before adding forcibly, "As for the Earl of Brandmere, I refuse to worry about him. Once he sees how provincial we are, I am certain that his lordship will run straight back to London—and good riddance to him!"

Chapter Two

"Stap me if this ain't the most godforsaken place in the world," Peter Vries complained. "Only fools would want to live here."

Silently, Brandmere agreed. Since leaving London some days ago, he had several times questioned his own sanity. The night they had spent at his estate in Gloucester was all very well, and the inn at Bridgewater had been tolerable. Now, however, they had left green downs and farmlands behind and were following a road that hugged the desolate north Devon coast. Even on this fine September day, the wind was raw and bitter.

Peter shivered violently. "Shouldn't wonder if I catch cold," he grumbled. "My throat feels raw."

"From talking too much," his unsympathetic cousin suggested.

"Been thinking," Peter continued, "that I should have brought my new blue evening coat with me. Man has to make a good impression, dash it all." He paused to glance over his shoulder. "I hope nothing's happened to our luggage. I can't see the chaise following us."

The chaise containing valets and luggage had evidently been left far behind. Peter continued to worry as Brandmere turned his curricle inland and followed a route that eventually took them to the top of a wooded combe.

"Grapewood at last," Peter exulted.

Brandmere reined in his bays and surveyed the valley below them. The manor which had been built in this sheltered place had a certain charm. It looked old, perhaps sixteenth century, and its stone walls had mellowed to a creamy gold. Late afternoon sunlight sprinkled more gold across the chrysanthemums and late-blooming roses in a pleasant country garden. On the south side of the house spread the grape arbor that gave the place its name.

But this good impression did not last. When Brandmere's curricle began its descent into the valley, the shabbiness of the old manor became evident. The grape arbor looked as though it had been cared for, but the garden was badly in need of weeding, the roof of the house needed repair, and the stable and carriage house that stood in back of the manor had seen better days. A decrepit building, apparently some sort of barn, looked ready to tumble into ruin.

Brandmere guided his bays into the courtyard. No groom hurried from the stable and no footman appeared at the door of the manor. "Where the devil is everyone?" Peter huffed.

The earl's tiger leaped from his station at the back of the curricle and ran to hold the horses' heads. As the young gentlemen dismounted from the curricle, there was a chorus of shouts nearby.

"Stop her, Little John," a clear female voice cried.

"Don't let her get past you. Oh, dear—now we are in for it!"

Both the earl and his cousin stared as a hideously fat pig careened around the corner of the stable.

"Oh, I say," bleated Peter. "Stop—shoo! Stap me, Brand, if that porker ain't coming this way!"

Grunting and squealing, the pig lowered its snout almost to the ground and made straight for the earl.

"Stop Porcina. Please stop her!"

A young woman had erupted into view. Her hat was off, her muddied skirts were bunched in her hands and gave a view of very neat ankles. Her appearance distracted Brandmere at a crucial moment, and he did not manage to sidestep in time. In the next moment, his arms were full of outraged pig.

"Oh, well done," the girl shrieked.

Finding itself held fast, the animal squealed and surged ahead, knocking the Fifth Earl of Brandmere into the mud.

Three hundred and fifty pounds of outraged pork waddled forward. As Brandmere was dragged through the mud, he heard the girl's exhortations mingling with shouts of a gray-haired individual who had come onto the scene and who was now closing on the pig.

"Hurry, damn you," Brandmere gritted.

" 'Old on, then, sir." A rope was slipped around the beast's neck. "There—we've got 'er fast," the newcomer bellowed. "Quick thinking, that were. Couldn't 'ave done better meself."

Brandmere got to his feet and glared at the speaker. He was a living caricature, being over six feet tall and as lean as a stick insect. An apron was tied around his waist, and the sleeves of his much-mended shirt had been turned back. Faded but fierce blue eyes under a thatch of gray eyebrows took the earl's measure.

Meanwhile the young woman had gone down on her knees beside the pig. "Porcina," she soothed, "you must not exert yourself, my dear. Thank you, Little John," she added in a loud voice, "take her back to her pen, if you please, and latch it securely. Can you manage?"

"I can *manage*, mum," the old man retorted, "but to my way o' thinking this 'ere pig aught to be made into bacon. Maybe you'll take my advice one o' these days."

Had he landed in Bedlam? Brand studied the wild-looking female. Her rosy cheeks were caked with mud. Her sun hat dangled by a ribbon around her neck, and her thick, curly black hair, which had escaped a flyaway net, cascaded down the back of a well-worn day dress. Only her eyes were in variance with the rest of her. Clear and gray and alive with rueful humor, they dominated her heart-shaped face.

"I apologize for Porcina," she was saying. "Someone left the latch to her pen undone and she took fright and bolted. You were so clever and quick—and strong, too—to catch her before she did herself harm."

"Did *herself*—" Brandmere sputtered into speechlessness.

Suzanna watched the expression on his hard-featured face darken further and felt suddenly at a loss. Everything had happened so quickly that she had not taken time to think that this muddy gentleman must be one of Uncle Dickon's guests. She got to her feet and said rather lamely, "I am so *very* sorry that you were knocked down."

"Pray don't mention it."

She took his quelling words at face value. "But if

you had not stopped Porcina, she may have done herself and her piglets a great injury. She is almost too old to be carrying a litter. This may well be her last."

Peter's mouth hung open in shock. Ladies of his acquaintance would have fainted at such frank talk. He himself was near fainting at the sight of his normally fastidious cousin.

"You ain't taken an injury, Brand?" he wondered.

Suzanna's gray eyes widened. Could this big man with the blond hair and angry dark eyes possibly be—"*You* are the Earl of Brandmere?" she gasped.

He nodded coldly. "This is my cousin, Mr. Peter Vries. I believe we are expected."

As he spoke, there was the sound of carriage wheels. "Oh, my God," Peter exclaimed. "Stap me if it ain't Miss Traherne."

Suzanna wanted to take to her heels but found that her legs were shaking too hard for movement. She could only watch helplessly as the stately traveling carriage that belonged to Sir Malcolm rumbled into the courtyard, followed almost immediately by the chaise that contained Sir Malcolm's valet, Miss Traherne's abigail, dresser, and the Trahernes' baggage.

Suzanna glanced at the house. Nothing was going right. Uncle Dickon should have been here to greet his guests and Little John aught to be present to let down the step of the carriage so that the guests could descend. But Little John was still conducting Porcina back to the barn, and Uncle Dickon was nowhere in sight.

Squaring her shoulders, Suzanna stepped forward and opened the carriage door herself. "Welcome to Grapewood," she said.

A sandy-haired man of middle age with a florid,

mustached face stared at her in surprise. "What's this, eh?" he exclaimed.

"Welcome to Grapewood, Sir Malcolm," Suzanna repeated determinedly. "I am Suzanna Campion."

Behind her, Suzanna heard an odd sound. Without venturing to look at the Earl of Brandmere, she continued. "My uncle will be down immediately to greet you."

She broke off as Little John came flying down the stairs. He had removed his apron and was tugging on a threadbare coat as he came. With his gray hair blowing in the wind and his fierce eyes, he looked like an antiquated bandit.

Sir Malcolm appeared to share the same thought. With a loud "Hey!" he hopped out of the carriage and struck a defensive posture. As he did so, a dulcet voice spoke from inside the carriage.

"Papa, stop. It is only a servant."

By comparison to the exquisite young lady who was leaning out of the carriage, Suzanna felt like a hedgerow drab. Miss Anabel Traherne was not only lovely but was also beautifully dressed. Suzanna admired Miss Traherne's saucy blue hat that matched perfectly a velvet, ermine-lined pelisse.

Blue eyes, shaded by golden curls, sparkled with amusement as she inquired, "Have we come at an awkward time?"

Suzanna shook her head. "No. I beg your pardon, truly. But our sow escaped, and unfortunately knocked the earl into the mud."

Sir Malcolm, who had been handing his daughter down, turned and gaped. "The Earl of *Brandmere*?"

Brandmere had never felt so out of temper. His usually glossy boots were spattered with mud. His impeccably cut traveling coat and breeches were drip-

19

ping with the stuff. When he bowed, several leaves that had been clinging to his cravat fluttered to the ground.

Beside him, he heard a sound that was suspiciously like a chuckle. He turned to glare at the wretched Campion girl and saw that her gray eyes were brimful with laughter. Brandmere realized that she was laughing at herself as well as at him, and his own sense of humor returned. The entire situation was too ridiculous for words.

Meanwhile, Peter had shot forward to greet the Trahernes. The effect of his elegant bow was lost when he dropped his hat in the mud. He turned bright red with mortification but then realized that Anabel was not even looking at him.

"My lord," she exclaimed, clearly addressing the earl. "How—"

She was interrupted by a dapper, middle-aged man who came running down the steps of the house. He was fashionably attired in a green jacket, striped waistcoat, and yellow corduroy trousers. His hair was powdered and neatly arranged, and his hands sparkled with rings.

The smile that had hovered on Brandmere's lips disappeared. *Campion,* he thought.

"My lord earl—Sir Malcolm, Miss Traherne—and Mr. Vries. I am desolate that I was not here to, ah, to ah—"

The well-oiled machinery of Dickon's greeting faltered as he stared at the mud-spattered earl. He flicked a horrified glance at his equally muddy niece before stammering, "You are very welcome to Grapewood, my lord. You honor us."

The earl inclined his head frigidly and folded his hands behind his back.

Inwardly groaning, Dickon did his best to mend matters. He apologized again, made a graceful leg to Anabel, and respectfully pressed the hand that Sir Malcolm held out to him. This done, he turned to his niece. "Has Miss Traherne's chamber been prepared, Suzanna?"

Suzanna replied in the affirmative and asked Miss Traherne to please follow her.

As Anabel stepped forward, she teetered on her delicate kid shoes and almost lost her balance. Automatically, Suzanna held out a hand to help. Anabel recoiled.

"Watch what you are doing," Dickon spat at his niece. "Can't you see that your hands are muddy?"

Unexpectedly, Brandmere came to Suzanna's defense. "Don't refine on it, Miss Campion," he said. "Mud washes off."

Suzanna was surprised to see that the earl was actually smiling at her. It was as though he understood how she felt and was trying to make her feel better. His surprisingly sweet smile transformed the harsh lines of his face and made him appear friendly.

Now, that was kind of the earl, Suzanna thought. It was especially thoughtful since it was largely due to her that he was covered with mud. She sent him a quick, answering smile before turning to lead Miss Traherne toward the house.

Dickon was apologizing again. "My lord earl, I can only surmise that in some deplorable way my niece has been responsible for your discomfort. I cannot say enough—"

"Don't regard it."

Brandmere spoke absently. He was thinking that Suzanna Campion's eyes turned almost to silver when she smiled. He was also wondering what she would look like with the mud washed away from her face.

Suzanna rested her elbows on her dressing table and looked hopefully into the oval mirror.

She was so tired. Her legs felt stiff, her back ached, and her cheeks felt tight from smiling. Uncle Dickon had been right in saying that Brandmere and Miss Traherne would draw other guests to Grapewood, for the afternoon had brought many such. Like bees clustering to a honeypot, young bucks of the *ton* had appeared: the foppish Honorable Augustus Stanhope and his friend Lord Freyden, and the almost too-handsome Mr. James Parrett, who was rumored to be a fortune hunter.

The gentlemen had no sooner been settled into their rooms when other guests had arrived. Suzanna sighed inwardly as she thought of the commotion that had accompanied the appearance of the Marchioness of Clavendell, her two unmarried daughters, and her younger brother, Lord Doherty. Immediately thereafter had come Colonel and Mrs. Bender and *their* daughter, Aramantha.

It had taken much work to see that the needs of these guests were met. This did not simply entail comfortable rooms, food, and drink, for Suzanna had also to make certain that Grapewood's staff—namely Mrs. Horry, the cook, the temperamental chambermaid, Margery, and Little John, got along with the haughty valets, lady's maids, and dressers who had accompanied their employers. What with the demands made upon her to send up tea trays, Mrs. Horry was puffing and blowing like a bellows, and Margery felt so put-upon that she had given her notice. As to Little John, he had threatened to horse-whip Lord Freyden's simpering valet.

That matters were not worse was due to Dickon Campion. Even while disapproving of what he was doing, Suzanna had to admire the way her uncle had taken charge. He had welcomed his guests and flattered them. He had smoothed the marchioness's feathers when she discovered that her room did not have a view of the grape arbor. He had affected a bonhomie with the young London blades and, in the next breath, had become bluff, soldierly, and sportsmanly with Colonel Bender. With Sir Malcolm, Uncle Dickon was all gravity. He murmured phrases such as "psychic manifestation" and "incandescent aura" as if he really had seen the Silver Lady.

Amid all of this he had found a moment to speak to his niece. "I don't know why it was necessary to cover Brandmere with mud," he had scolded, "and I don't want to know. But, deuce take it, come down to dinner looking like a lady."

Suzanna had done her best. She had put on the silvery-gray China-crepe dress that was her only decent costume. She had lost weight since her father's death and most of her clothes were too loose to wear, but the China-crepe had been made six years before her London come-out. It had a high waist and a froth of Alençon lace at the neck. With her dark hair braided about her head and with her late mother's pearls around her neck, Suzanna hardly resembled the muddy hoyden of the afternoon.

She winced as she remembered that scene. She also wondered a little. She had thought that Brandmere would be like the other London dandies. Instead, there was this hard-muscled man who conveyed purpose and determination—and humor, too. It was the humor that intrigued Suzanna most.

The asthmatic wheeze of the clock on the second-floor landing reminded her that it was getting late. The guests must have assembled in the drawing room by now. Suzanna hastened out of her room and down the faded carpet of the grand staircase.

Little John, in his capacity of general factotum, was standing beside the drawing room door. "Everybody is down, Miss 'Zanna," he said loudly. "Excepting Sir Malcolm and Miss Traherne."

She sighed. "Then I am late, and Uncle Dickon will scold me."

"The man's been nipping at the port.'E won't notice nothing," Little John retorted.

On the point of saying that Dickon Campion was now master of Grapewood and should be shown more respect, Suzanna checked herself. If her uncle had begun drinking, there would be a problem. Dickon liked spirits but had a very weak head, especially on an empty stomach.

And this thought brought up another worry. "How is Mrs. Horry bearing up?" she asked.

"As well as can be expected, mum." Little John grumbled. He was feeling quite fierce. The disgrace of seeing Grapewood opened to paying guests was nothing compared to the insults that he had been forced to endure belowstairs. Little John swelled with outrage when he thought of how Lord Federby's valet had questioned his status in the servant's hierarchy.

Little John had actually considered giving his notice but had not done so because Miss 'Zanna needed him. He glanced at her tired face and his brows jutted farther in a frown, but there was nothing he could do to help her. So he preceded her to the door and shouted, "Miss Suzanna Campion," as if he were announcing the Queen of England.

It was very noisy, so nobody noticed her entrance. As she looked about the drawing room, her first impression was of color. Grapewood's guests had come down to dinner dressed to the teeth.

Gentlemen wore padded coats of brilliant blue, green, and canary yellow, with gorgeous waistcoats and breeches fastened with ribbons at the knee. Their variously tied cravats were architectural masterpieces.

The young ladies were as splendid as the gentlemen. They had been primped, pomaded, and curled to within an inch of their lives. The marchioness's pretty daughters bloomed in pink and amethyst silks while Aramantha, the colonel's daughter, had covered her Junoesque frame in aquamarine satin. Even the older ladies were garbed like peacocks. The marchioness was a commanding figure in puce bombazine and Vandyke lace while Mrs. Bender's bright green dress clashed violently with her husband's regimentals.

Among all this brilliance was a man in black. Brandmere stood with his back to the fire that had been raked up against the chill of the September evening. When he moved, a diamond flashed in the snowy folds of his simply but elegantly tied neckcloth.

As Suzanna watched, the earl took out a gold and diamond fob watch and looked at it. He then stifled a yawn.

Elsewhere in the room, tension crackled as the guests eyed each other suspiciously. Peter Vries, who sported a blue coat and skintight yellow breeches, was sizing up Stanhope, while Parrett was edging toward the door so as to be the first to greet Miss Traherne.

Marchioness Clavendell was talking to Sir Malcolm but at the same time kept a weather eye on Lord Freyden, who was conversing with her older daughter. Aramantha Bender was pretending to listen to what Dickon was saying about horticulture whilst at the same time trying to catch the earl's eye.

Knowing that she should mingle with her uncle's guests, Suzanna turned to her left, where the colonel was talking to Lord Doherty about a particularly bloody hunt. She hastily turned to her right and heard Sir Malcolm hold forth on haunted castles.

"Miss Campion," a deep voice said.

Brandmere had left the fireplace and was strolling across the room toward her. You look transformed," he continued.

"So do you, my lord," she replied frankly.

The earl felt some of his crushing boredom ease as he regarded his hostess. With the mud washed away from her face and in that silvery dress that caught the exact color of her eyes, Suzanna Campion was striking. Her black hair and the light dusting of freckles across her upturned nose might be deemed unfashionable, but Brandmere thought they gave her a certain charm. Also, the girl's straightforward ways were amusing.

Suzanna watched the earl's lips twitch into a smile and thought that he was really quite agreeable. He was also definitely the best-looking man present. He resembled a black swan among a gaggle of geese.

The drawing room door now swung open and Little John bawled, "Sir Malcolm and Miss Traherne."

Instantly, the attention of the room shifted. All eyes were focused on the stocky, sandy-mustached man and the lady on his arm. And it was little wonder,

Suzanna thought. Anabel Traherne was dazzlingly beautiful.

Fully aware of the effect she was causing, Anabel paused for a moment in the doorway. Her hair was dressed in the Greek style, with soft golden curls cascading down her snowy white neck. Her dress of spider gauze embroidered with gold thread glinted over a slip of creamy silk. Roses braided with pearls crowned her head while more pearls, cascading over her white bosom, gave the illusion of dewdrops lying on the petals of a flower.

Peter Vries gave a deep sigh. In the silence that had fallen over the room, it sounded very loud. Peter went crimson, started forward, stubbed his toe against a settee, and fell forward on one knee.

Stanhope snickered. The marchioness raised her lorgnette. Anabel lifted her pretty eyebrows. Suzanna bit her lip in sympathy and was grateful when clever Dickon cried, "A fitting tribute to a lovely lady, Mr. Vries. We men can greet Miss Traherne only on our knees."

The young men immediately surged forward to encircle the Trahernes. The young ladies, hiding their chagrin, clamored sweetly to be the first to kiss Miss Traherne's cheek. Their mothers looked sour. Suzanna, in the background, saw the earl frown at his scarlet-faced cousin, who was attempting to edge Stanhope out for Anabel's attention.

"You must not be out of charity with Mr. Vries," she said. "He admires Miss Traherne so much that he feels lightheaded." Brandmere raised a quizzical eyebrow and she continued earnestly, "I know how he feels. Whenever I am trying to put my best foot forward, I always make some horrid blunder. Only think of Porcina this afternoon."

Brandmere winced, then laughed. "You may be right," he said.

Dinner was now announced. The earl, in view of his exalted rank, escorted the marchioness. The others followed in suitable order with Peter escorting the elder of the marchioness's daughters.

Lastly came Dickon and his niece. "It's going well," he whispered.

Suzanna glanced doubtfully at her uncle. He was in high good humor, and his cheeks were suspiciously red. She whispered, "You know that it is unwise to go nipping at the port. What can you be thinking of?"

He looked offended. " 'Nipping' is not a ladylike word. I may have had a drop—to see me through the ordeal of dinner. Now, be a good girl and behave yourself."

Suzanna did her best to obey this command, but when she saw the way Stanhope and Lord Federby, who were seated near her uncle, kept urging wine on him, she became increasingly uneasy. She kept an anxious weather eye on her uncle while trying to put Peter Vries, who was seated next to her, at his ease.

"I was born fumble-fingered," Peter was sighing. "So far I've made a proper cake of myself. Falling on my knees like that—"

"You were nervous," Suzanna soothed.

"You're too kind, Miss Campion. Appreciate it. But," Peter added dispiritedly, "the truth is the truth. Mean to say—how can someone as lovely as Miss—how could any lady overlook my clumsiness? I wish I was like Brand. That man has ice water in his veins."

Suzanna glanced at the earl, who was seated diagonally across from her. His eyes were half closed and he looked ready to fall asleep on the instant.

"He fought Boney on the Peninsula," Peter went on, "and was commended for bravery several times. Stap me if I know why he sold his colors. He was wounded, of course, but a man like Brand laughs at things like that."

At the head of the table Dickon began to giggle. Suzanna wished that she were close enough to kick her uncle in the calf. She tried to catch his eye, but he did not look in her direction and instead allowed Stanhope to refill his glass.

Suzanna knew that she had to engage her uncle's attention and make him stop this disastrous behavior. As she was racking her brain to think of what she could do, Colonel Bender began to boast.

"I don't say that it's the same as riding with the Quorn, but I do maintain a sizable stable. Good hunters. Best hounds in the country. I'm after a particular fox, and I don't mind telling you that I'll take pleasure in seeing that little beggar torn to pieces. He's given me a run for my money."

Forgetting about her uncle for the moment, Suzanna exclaimed, "Good for the fox."

Everyone's eyes swung around to her. Suzanna saw her uncle glare at her and glared back. She pantomimed with her wineglass and shook her head—*no more*. Defiantly, Dickon raised his glass and drained it.

And again that horrible young Stanhope filled it. He was grinning as though at a joke, and Suzanna wanted to box his ears. Meanwhile, Colonel Bender was asking coldly, "You do not care for the hunt, Miss Campion?"

With her eyes on her uncle, she shook her head.

The colonel harrumphed. "Nonsense. Nothing as invigorating as a hunt. I tell you, it's the only sport."

"It may be sport for you," Suzanna cried, "but what of the fox? I am persuaded that it cannot be at all pleasant to kill a very small animal that is running for its life."

The marchioness raised her lorgnette and stared at Suzanna. The gentlemen exchanged glances of horror or ridicule. Miss Traherne laughed and said, "Oh, fol rol. I do not think that we females know much about such things."

"That is true," Suzanna admitted. "But I know I do not care for fox hunting. If you were a fox—"

"Miss Traherne," Dickon interrupted, "ish not a foxsh."

Suzanna heard the slur in his voice and was horrified. Her uncle was thoroughly bosky!

"It does a lady credit to have a tender heart." Brandmere's voice cut through the disapproving hum that had begun to circulate around the table. He raised his glass and added, "I drink to your humanity, Miss Campion."

For a moment his dark eyes smiled across the table into Suzanna's. Then he turned to Sir Malcolm. "I understand, sir, that you are a hunter of another kind. Spirits bring you to Grapewood, I think?"

Sir Malcolm eagerly launched into a ghost story. It concerned a ruined Indian temple, chanting monks, and a malevolent ghost. "I saw it with my own eyes," he concluded. "If I hadn't done so, I would have sworn the tale to be a pack of lies. 'There are more things in heaven and earth.' Eh?"

Dickon Campion interrupted the ripple of delighted horror caused by Sir Malcolm's tale. "Here'sh another ghost shtory. A shtory about the very manor house in which we shi—in which we sit."

He began to relate the history of the lovely Lady

Blanche Campion, who had been found *in flagrante* by her husband, who murdered her. It might have been an entertaining tale except that the teller was very drunk indeed.

"She was thrown into the well, and her shcreams— her screams could be heard throughout the manse," Dickon slurred. "After that, strange things occurred. Blood spots appeared on the walls. There were ghosh—ghostly manifestations. One of my ancestors awakened from a dead sleep and found the Silver Lady standing next to hish bed. His hair had turned white overnight."

The marchioness sniffed through her high nose and observed that it was time for the ladies to retire.

Dickon hiccuped. "Not before the pudding, ma'am," he protested. "It's a family treasure, that pudding. And that reminds me. Heard about the buried treasure of Grapewood?"

Suzanna tried desperately to interrupt her uncle. She failed. Impervious to the scornful looks that were bent on him, Dickon continued to stumble on.

"Treasure—'at's right, treasure," he hiccuped. Wagging his finger almost under Sir Malcolm's nose, he went on. "There's treash—ure here. Buried someplace by Lady Blanche and her lover. Needed it to set themselves up, y'see? Needed it, but never got to use it." Dickon paused to add, "Gimme more wine."

As he drained his glass again, Anabel Traherne shrugged her pretty shoulders and said satirically, "La, Mr. Campion, treasure *and* a ghost? I am glad we came to Grapewood."

Dickon Campion leered with drunken imperti-

31

nence. "So'm I," he agreed. "Have—have a drink, ma'am."

"Disgraceful," Mrs. Bender was heard to hiss.

Sir Malcolm cleared his throat and looked uncomfortable. "My daughter doesn't share my belief in the unknown," he rumbled. "Eh? Now I, for one, believe that the Silver Lady will walk."

"If she does, I will be very much surprised." Anabel nodded at Suzanna and added jokingly, "This is like to be the only lady in silver we see tonight. How clever of you to dress for effect, Miss Campion."

Brandmere did not join the ripple of amusement that greeted this sally. He saw the unhappiness and embarrassment in Suzanna's eyes and though he had nothing but contempt for Campion, pity stirred for the girl's humiliation.

"It is," he remarked calmly, "a very pleasant effect. The color becomes you, Miss Campion."

Anabel frowned a little. Suzanna sent the earl a grateful look and stiffened her spine. Somehow, in spite of Uncle Dickon, she must get through this horrible dinner.

Smiling upon Sir Malcolm, she requested another story about India. The nabob was only too eager to oblige, and Suzanna was about to lean back in relief, when there was a cough at her elbow.

"I'm sorry, mum," Little John said in a carrying whisper, "but there's been a muddle in the kitchen."

Suzanna's heart sank. "What has happened?"

"Mrs.'Orry," Little John replied in that same loud whisper, " 'as collapsed. And none of us know what to do about the pudding, mum."

Avoiding the many pairs of eyes on her, Suzanna rose from her seat and followed Little John out of the dining room.

Since Uncle Dickon had made them innkeepers, she thought, she might just as well play the part of an innkeeper's niece. The problem was that she knew very little about cooking. What, she wondered, *did* one do with a pudding?

Chapter Three

The spiral of smoke from Brandmere's cigar rose over the dark, deserted garden. Everyone else at Grapewood had long ago gone to bed, and for this he was grateful.

With uncharacteristic vehemence he cursed his sister, his cousin, and himself for having been such a fool as to leave St. James Square for this down-to-heel manor with its shabby furnishings and its incompetent staff.

Nor were the guests at Grapewood inspiring. With the possible exception of Sir Malcolm and his daughter, they were a singularly lackluster crowd. And as for Campion—Brandmere's mouth twisted in disgust as he recalled how, egged on by such fribble as Stanhope and Freyden, Campion had recounted tales of horror and melodrama that would have caused him to be booed off the stage. The man's ravings had been silenced only when the pudding was served. It had been a pudding the likes of which he had never tasted before, but that was to be expected in a place like Grapewood—

Brandmere's thoughts broke off as the French windows fronting the garden were flung open. Through them hurtled a shadowy figure which immediately stumbled, cursed, and fell over a rosebush.

"Peter?" Brandmere exclaimed.

"Brand—thank God I found you!" Hastily picking himself up, Peter limped across the garden toward his cousin. "I've seen her, Brand!"

"Well, that's what you came up here to do, isn't it?"

Peter's eyes seemed to be on the point of popping out of his head. "Not Miss Traherne," he babbled. "I just saw that damned ghost."

For a moment Brandmere stared. Then he roared with laughter. His cousin moaned, "It's true. Stap me if it ain't. Gave me gooseflesh, Brand. Covered with the stuff!"

Brandmere stopped laughing and drew thoughtfully on his cigar. "Just where did you see this specter?"

"On the first-floor landing." Peter pulled out a handkerchief and swabbed at his damp forehead. "Couldn't sleep, Brand. Excitement at seeing Miss Traherne again, I expect, though it could've been the pudding. Awful pudding that, heavy as a millstone. Stap me if I ever ate anything like it before."

"You walked down to the first-floor landing?" Brandmere prompted as Peter became lost in culinary reflection.

"Well, not exactly. I felt restless, and when I thought I spotted you nipping outside to blow a cloud, thought I'd follow you." Horror returned to Peter's round eyes as he breathed, "But when I'd come down the stairs, I saw *it*. It was all silvery and it—it floated, Brand. Floated up to the blasted landing."

"Did it say anything?"

Peter goggled. "Didn't stay to talk to it—did a bolt." With an attempt at dignity he added, "Proper cake I'd have looked jawing with a ghost, Brand. Have to draw the line somewhere."

The earl tossed his cigar into the chrysanthemums and led the way back toward the house. Peter followed cautiously as his tall cousin stepped through the French doors and into the empty ground-floor anteroom. "There's nobody on the landing now," Brandmere observed.

"No *thing*, you mean," Peter muttered. He glanced around him apprehensively as they mounted the stairs. Here night candles burned in wall sconces and cast a feeble light along the corridor. The doors of the library and the great hall were closed.

Brandmere picked up a many-branched candelabrum from a table, lit the candles, and proceeded to open the doors. "Empty, as you see," he remarked.

Peter looked sulky. "You don't believe I saw her."

"I believe you saw what you were meant to see." Brandmere mounted threadbare stairs to the second floor, where he opened the doors to the drawing room, morning room, dining room, and the picture gallery. The door hinges to the picture gallery squealed horribly.

"Hinges need oiling," Brandmere commented. "It gives a ghostly affect. Campion probably did this on purpose to impress Sir Malcolm."

"Do you mean to tell me that that ghost was Campion in disguise? No such thing, Brand," Peter protested indignantly. "I may not have much in my brain box, but I can tell a man from a woman."

By now he was feeling somewhat sheepish at his headlong flight. "Where d'you suppose it's got to?" he wondered.

"Back to bed, no doubt." Peter was surprised to see how grim his cousin suddenly looked. "Best you do the same, old fellow. And this time, go to sleep."

As Peter meekly obeyed, Brandmere looked down the long row of pictures and statuary. The statues were clothed in a layer of dust, and dispirited Campion ancestors looked down from cracked gilt frames. One heavily bearded individual—a cavalier in the time of Charles I—appeared so disgusted that the earl felt a pang of sympathy.

"No doubt you'd *like* to walk," he murmured, "with all that's going on."

"Is someone there?" a clear voice asked.

Suzanna Campion was standing in the doorway. By the light of the candle she held, Brandmere observed, her dress shimmered like silver.

He was conscious of an inexplicable disappointment. There had been no other possible explanation, of course, but he hadn't wanted to believe that Suzanna had been playing ghost. She had appeared so honest. "But I see that the apple has not fallen far from the tree," he commented.

She blinked at this incomprehensible speech. "I beg your pardon?" she said.

"No, madam. It is I who should beg yours," Brandmere retorted.

"I don't understand."

"I am keeping you from your duties," Brandmere explained. "I'm certain that you have important business to attend to."

Flickering candlelight brought out the harsh planes of the earl's face. His mouth was hard, his eyes cold. "After your departure from the dinner table tonight," he continued, "you have been very busy."

Enlightenment came to Suzanna. "Oh, dear," she sighed, "so I am unmasked."

She actually was brazen enough to admit her perfidy—perhaps even to boast about it. "Did you not expect to be?" Brandmere demanded harshly.

"I must plead my case. I have not had much practice, you see." As Brandmere stared incredulously, Suzanna continued. "Was my effort so poor?"

"It was good enough to fool my cousin. He was convinced that he had seen the Silver Lady."

It was now her turn to stare at him. "Who said anything about the Silver Lady? I thought we were talking about the pudding I had served up."

He gritted out, "I warn you—don't try to trifle with me."

Suzanna heard the leashed menace in his voice. Involuntarily, she took a step backward. The earl continued. "I don't give a damn whether you dress up in a burial shroud and prowl the halls. Give Sir Malcolm his money's worth by all means. But I will not have you frightening my cousin."

Suzanna shook her head as though to clear it. "Do you mean to say that you believe I was pretending to be Uncle Dickon's ghost? You mean to say that your cousin saw me and thought I was the—the S-Silver Lady?"

She burst out laughing. Brandmere could have sworn that her whoops were genuine. She was clever, he thought grimly.

"It must be on account of the dress," Suzanna choked. She wiped her eyes, adding, "I am sorry, really, for scaring poor Mr. Vries. I will apologize tomorrow."

"And ruin the effect of your little charade?"

At his sarcastic tone, her amusement died. "Surely, you do not think that I did it on purpose?" Her gray eyes narrowed. "But I see that you do. You actually believe I would rattle around dressed as a ghost. What utter fustian!"

Her scorn stung. "I believe," he said coldly, "that we've said quite enough."

"*You* have, you mean. I have not said anything, my lord earl—yet!"

Brandmere's bow was so scornful that Suzanna itched to box his lordship's noble ears. In what she hoped was a calm voice she said, "I left the dinner table because Little John told me that Mrs. Horry had been taken ill. The effort of cooking for so many people had brought on a collapse. We have not many servants, as you have no doubt observed, and not one of them can cook, so I was summoned to produce the pudding. Unfortunately, I had never made a pudding in my life."

"That I can well believe!" They glared at each other a moment before Brandmere continued. "None of this is an explanation for what my cousin saw."

"I am not giving you an explanation. I do not owe you any explanation," Suzanna retorted. "I resent your horrid insinuations. Do you actually believe I have nothing to do but clank about in chains? If you must know, I was bathing our poor cook's forehead and trying to calm her. The poor dear knows she must be up to preparing breakfast in the morning."

She paused to draw breath. In that silence she heard him say, "I don't believe you."

The noise in Suzanna's ears became the roar of drums and cannons. "You can believe what you please," she shouted. "And you can go to Jericho!"

Head high, she whirled on her heel and swept out of the picture gallery. She was so angry that she could hardly feel the ground under her feet. Who was Brandmere that he should accuse her of lies and of trickery?

"Detestable man," she muttered, "I hope you *do* go to Jericho—and the sooner the better."

Suzanna did not sleep very well that night. At first she was sleepless because she was angry, but sometime toward morning anger faded and common sense took hold.

That was when the trouble started. Logic told her that Brandmere's reaction had not been unreasonable. A pampered aristocrat could hardly be expected to believe that the lady of the manor would stay up half the night nursing a mere servant. And she had told him to go to Jericho. She had actually told a guest under her roof to go to *Jericho*!

As soon as dawn lightened the sky, Suzanna dressed. She put on stout leather shoes and an apron and went to find solace from the friends who had never failed her. The servants were still abed, but in the barn Suzanna's animals greeted her with love.

Ione looked stronger this morning, and this lifted Suzanna's spirits. Next she came to Porcina's pen, where she exclaimed in delight.

"Porcina—fourteen piglets! What a dear, good pig you are."

Porcina preened herself. She gave little grunts of appreciation as Suzanna scratched between her ears. Then she allowed her beloved mistress to come into the pen and examine her offspring. "Not fourteen— sixteen," Suzanna cried. "At your age, too. You may think yourself very clever, my dear, but how are you going to manage?"

There was reason for concern. Though fourteen of the piglets were busy with their breakfast, two tiny forms rooted disconsolately about the straw. Suzanna watched for a moment, then hurried back to the house.

Sometime later, carrying a jug of milk and a soft cloth, she returned to the pen. Lifting out the two runts, she carried them outside to a wooden bench near the barn. Then, dipping the cloth into the milk, she commenced feeding the piglets.

As the piglets sucked eagerly on the milk-soaked cloth, Suzanna felt a measure of peace return to her. With all her heart she wished that people were more like animals. Animals did not lie to each other or laugh at each other. They did not urge each other to get drunk and make fools of themselves. And they did not look down their aristocratic noses as Brandmere had done.

There was a footstep on the gravel nearby. Suzanna looked up and was horrified to see Brandmere walking toward the carriage house. His riding crop was tucked under one arm, his Hessians were glossy with polish, and his beautifully cut gray riding coat and doeskin riding breeches were immaculate.

The earl could not fail to see her. Suzanna's heart gave a hen-hearted quaver as she tried to tuck her head deeper into her shawl. Perhaps he would pass by without recognizing her.

"Miss Campion?"

"My lord," Suzanna muttered. Hastily, before the earl could resume last night's hostilities, she added, "Are you driving your curricle this morning, sir?" she asked.

"I am." It was said with icy civility. Then his tone changed. "But what have we here?"

He had seen the piglets on her lap. Suzanna felt mortified.

"Porcina has had her litter," she explained. "There are sixteen of them, so I am helping to feed them."

His footsteps scrunched closer. "Yorkshires, I see." Sensing her surprise at his knowledge, he added, "We breed them at Brandmere."

His neutral tone emboldened her to take the plunge. She looked him in the eye and began, "My lord, I must tell you how sorry—"

She was interrupted by a loud squealing from both piglets, and she hastily broke off her apology and began to feed them again. As he watched her, Brandmere was conscious of a tug of conscience. Last night when she had talked about her duties at Grapewood, he had not believed her. He had spent the greater part of the night in fury, first with her and then with himself for having lost his temper. Now he realized that Suzanna Campion *did* have more to do than play ghost for her uncle.

With her head bent over the little pigs she was saying, "I am very sorry about last night. I should not have lost my temper and told you to—to—it was very wrong of me, and I beg you will forgive me."

Her voice was subdued and she finished the sentence in a breathless rush. When she glanced up at him, he saw that her cheeks were scarlet, and the look in her eyes made her seem very young. Brandmere was caught between a baffling wish to shake her for making him lose his temper and the desire to put a comforting arm around her.

He began to say, "There's nothing to forgive,"

checked himself, and said in a milder tone, "I suppose I was insufferable."

"Yes, but I understand *why* you were so odious," Suzanna replied. "And if I had been you, I should have boxed my ears."

Amused by her honesty, Brandmere relaxed. He watched her for a moment then accused her, "You are not giving enough feed to the fellow on the left."

"That is because the one on the right is much greedier. I wish that I had two pairs of hands." Suzanna stopped feeding the piglets and asked hopefully, "Perhaps you could help me—just for a moment?"

Later, he wondered how it came about. One moment he was preparing to go for a drive. The next moment found the Fifth Earl of Brandmere seated on a rough wooden bench and holding a squirming pink piglet.

He regarded it with a frown. "What am I supposed to do with this?" he asked.

Suzanna explained. Under her direction Brandmere dripped milk into a wide-open mouth. The piglet looked ecstatic, and Brandmere could not help grinning.

"A litter of sixteen, you say?" he asked.

"Yes. We will keep one hog and some of the sows and sell the rest when they grow to be a good weight."

"They'll reach that weight soon. I've never seen anything eat so much."

"Then you did not watch Colonel Bender at table last night." Brandmere laughed at her matter-of-fact tone, and the sound startled the piglets. They began to squeal, and Suzanna got to her feet.

"They have had quite enough for one morning. I cannot thank you enough for your help, but now I must take the little pigs back to their mama." She hesitated. "Would you like to see Porcina again? In her pen, this time?"

"Why not?" Brandmere followed Suzanna into the barn, which was populated by clucking fowls, an old milk cow, and a goat that bleated feebly as Suzanna approached.

"Ione is blind," Suzanna explained. "She knows me by scent." She began to stroke the goat as she continued. "Uncle Dickon feels that it is foolish to keep useless animals, but Ione has been my friend for many years."

With some surprise Brandmere realized that he understood how she felt. Watching Suzanna and her ancient goat had made him remember a lamb he had had when he was a boy. The animal had followed him everywhere, and he had prevailed upon his father not to have it slaughtered. Old Falstaff had had the run of the estate for years, fathered hundreds of wooly lambs, and finally died of overeating while Brandmere was at Oxford.

Strange that he should have remembered the old ram after all these years. Brandmere looked around him and noted that in spite of the fact that the barn appeared ready to collapse, the place was spotless. He wondered who did the mucking up.

"I do," Suzanna replied, and he realized he had voiced the question aloud. "Little John has enough work as it is."

The earl covered his surprise by saying that this was an odd name. "His name is Little John, really. When I was a child, I thought him to be a member of Robin Hood's band," Suzanna explained. "I am afraid it has become a habit to call him Little John."

Grapewood was certainly not what he was used to on his own vast and well-ordered estates. Brandmere owned himself intrigued enough to help Suzanna feed her beasts. She accepted his help gratefully, told him the history of each animal, and reflected that she seldom had such a sympathetic listener. Her father had ignored her animal friends. Dickon was contemptuous, and even Little John, usually her staunch supporter, spoke of "the beasts" as though he were already tasting pork pies, roast beef, or chicken pasties,

The earl was different. Suzanna could sense that he was interested in what she had to say. And as they walked out of the barn into the morning sunshine, she asked him about his estates.

He looked surprised, then a little vague. "Tottenham is in Shropshire, which is sheep country. Brandmere produces grain. Or so it did when I was up at Oxford. At harvest time I sometimes used to go into the fields with the men."

Suzanna noted that the earl spoke of his estates in the past. "I believe that my uncle said you lived in London?" she queried.

"Yes. It's a decision I made after returning from the war," Brandmere replied.

Something in his tone told her that he was leaving much unsaid, but before she could refine upon it, there was a halloo in the distance, and a scarecrow figure was seen shambling toward them.

"Oh, dear," Suzanna exclaimed. Raising her voice, she called, "Little John, you must not run. You know that running is bad for your sciatica."

The footman clapped a hand to his ear. " 'Ey, wot's that?"

"Running is bad for you," Suzanna shouted.

The old man looked quite fierce. "Can't 'elp it, Miss 'Zanna. It being almost time fer breakfast, and there being the Quality complaining that they're used to 'aving trays sent to their rooms, which can't be done at Grapewood. And then your uncle 'as the wobblies. 'E sent me out to get you."

Suzanna had no doubt that Uncle Dickon had "the wobblies." It served him right, she thought. "How is Mrs. Horry?" she asked.

"Walking about wi' a cold cloth round 'er 'ead, she is, and acting like she's ready fer 'er funeral. And that there old fool, Margery, is slamming around and swearing she's going to leave yer service, and them Lunnon val-lays is giving theyselves airs." Little John paused to draw breath. "So, are you coming, then?"

He shambled off, and Suzanna rolled her eyes. She glanced apologetically at her companion and explained, "I know he is a caution, and he pretends to be deafer than he is, but he has been with the family for centuries and is really so devoted. I hope you are not too astounded at our peculiar manners."

Brandmere shook his head. "*Nothing* about Grapewood," he said, "would surprise me."

Domestic duties kept Suzanna busy for a good part of an hour after her return to the house. She helped the cook as best she could, then aided Margery in preparing the morning room for an influx of sleepy and bad-tempered guests. Then, with a few scant minutes to spare, she sped to her third-floor bedroom to dress.

By the time she had changed into a serviceable checked-muslin day dress, most of the guests had descended. Suzanna entered the morning room at a run and nearly collided with Colonel Bender, who was standing by the breakfast table and helping himself to a plateful of eggs and kidneys. He said, "Excuse me" in a dismissive way and continued to pile food on his plate.

Suzanna glanced quickly around the morning room. The young men were still abed, but the marchioness was there, keeping an eye on her daughters and gossiping to Mrs. Bender. Dickon Campion was attempting to carry on a conversation with a glum-looking Sir Malcolm while Miss Traherne sat prettily enthroned on a chair by the fire.

It was actually an unheard-of hour for Anabel to rise. She had sacrificed her sleep because she had guessed that Brandmere would be an early riser. Since she desired the earl's interest, Anabel had spent much time on her toilette and looked very lovely in a high-necked muslin gown of robin's-egg blue, decorated by streaming blue ribbons. As footsteps echoed in the hall, she turned expectantly toward the door, but it was Peter Vries who burst into the room.

He stumbled over the threshold, caught himself, and made his way to Anabel's side. "Miss Traherne, your most obedient," he gabbled. Then he blushed and added, "Hope you slept well, ma'am."

"Indeed I did. And you, Mr. Vries?"

But even as Peter stammered an answer, Anabel's attention wavered, for Brandmere had entered the room. The earl had changed into garments that were a tribute to Weston's tailoring. His fair hair had been brushed to glossy gold. Anabel preened herself on the smile with which he greeted her but then saw that Brandmere's eyes were straying toward Suzanna Campion.

A small pucker marred Anabel's forehead. She was not used to sharing center stage with any other woman, and she could not understand why the dowdy Suzanna should command the earl's attention. But before she could turn that attention to herself, Campion stepped forward.

Today Dickon had no need of lead paint to whiten his skin. Ten thousand demons danced behind his eyes, and even his teeth ached. Only the discipline acquired through years of living by his wits held Dickon upright as he said, "Good morning, my lord. You have been up early, I see."

"Yes," Brandmere said.

Dickon winced at the earl's repressive tone. He knew that his behavior the night before had been inexcusable, and he cursed himself for being such a fool as to drink with those useless dandies. He cast around for a diversion.

"Does not Miss Traherne look like an angel this morning?" he whispered.

Disgusted by Campion's familiarity, Brandmere turned his back and strolled over to the breakfast table. "Tell me, Miss Campion, did you cook any of this?" he asked Suzanna.

She shook her head. "You are safe. But I should warn you against the chicken cutlets. Ernestine was a *very* old hen."

"What's the joke, Brand?" Peter questioned as his cousin threw back his head and roared with laughter.

Peter himself found little to laugh at. Grapewood, to his way of thinking, was proving to be a curst flat place. The food was mediocre, the company dull, and he felt like a fool for being routed by the "ghost" last night. Worst of all, Miss Traherne seemed to have eyes only for Brand, who had apparently shaken off the killing ennui that he affected in London.

"Took the bays out this morning, did you?" Peter continued.

"I'd meant to, but I did not do so. I spent the morning being instructed on animal husbandry."

"On what?" Peter demanded. Then he added sourly, "You must be bamming me. If you got up at the crack of dawn to look at a pack of animals, I'd think you had bats in your cockloft."

"More like piglets," Brand corrected, deadpan.

Suzanna turned away to hide a smile, and Anabel's chagrin deepened. She hid it with her most enchanting smile and cooed, "You are an early riser, my lord earl."

Desperate for his goddess's notice, Peter cried, "Gets up before the sun, give you my word. Must be because he used to be a military man. Third dragoon guards, you know."

Anabel's long lashes fluttered. "I do so enjoy hearing about the deeds of brave men," she murmured.

"Alas," Brandmere replied, "I have no such deeds to relate."

"The earl is being modest," Colonel Bender suggested. He smoothed the folds of his uniform about his ample middle as he added complacently, "I believe your regiment was at Salamanca, sir."

"Indeed, yes. The earl was decorated by no less a personage than the Duke of Wellington," Dickon put in. He congratulated himself on finding the perfect way to ingratiate himself with the earl, since all military men preened themselves on their exploits.

But Brandmere was not pleased. He looked about the morning room and thought that none of the people present cared a ha'penny about the war. Colonel Bender belonged to a regiment that had seen little actual action, and the rest of them knew nothing about the reality of conflict. To them, Salamanca was merely a topic of conversation.

He felt shaken with a sudden, overwhelming sense of disgust. What, he wondered, was he doing in this dismal place surrounded by these fools?

He pretended to hide a yawn. "Your interest is very flattering," he said, "but unfortunately I have no time for reminiscences. I'm afraid that my cousin and I must leave you."

Peter looked astounded. "Oh, I say. When are we going?"

"Immediately," Brandmere said.

Dickon stared in dismay. If the earl left, the other guests were sure to follow. He began to protest volubly. "But, sir, you have not had time to sample Grapewood's many pleasures—"

"I have pressing duties," Brandmere interrupted.

At these words Sir Malcolm roused himself and spoke of departing also. "The psychic vibrations at Grapewood are not all I expected," he complained. "My daughter and I will return to Somerset this afternoon."

For a moment Dickon looked stricken. Then he rallied. "I understand," he said. "Who better than I? The Presence in your manor must be far more intriguing to you than the Silver Lady."

"Eh, how's that?" Sir Malcolm wanted to know.

Dickon pretended to be astonished. "But surely you know that Reed Hall has the reputation of being haunted? It is a hotbed of psychic activity."

Sir Malcolm's mouth hung open. "No, by God," he breathed. "I didn't know that."

Cynically, Brandmere watched Campion slip his arm through Sir Malcolm's and draw him aside. The loose fish, he thought, had more tricks up his sleeve than a conjurer. Campion's duplicity made the earl more than ever eager to leave this place.

Then, as he waited for Peter to take his leave of Miss Traherne, Brandmere glanced toward Suzanna.

She looked unhappy, and Brandmere also felt a tug of regret. He immediately repressed this. Though he had been convinced that Suzanna was innocent of playing ghost, he was now not so sure. Campion was a charlatan, and Suzanna *was* his niece.

Watching the earl, Suzanna saw his expression harden. His thoughts were not hard to read. After watching Uncle Dickon at work, Brandmere had returned to his theory that the Campions were tricksters and liars. And the worst of it, Suzanna thought, was that this time she couldn't blame him.

Chapter Four

With his usual light hand, Brandmere guided his bays down a street in London's fashionable West End. The late afternoon sun was warm on his back as he halted his curricle near an imposing town house, tossed the reins to his tiger, and climbing the steps rapped on a heavy, brass-bound door.

"Duchess home, Cushing?" he inquired of the dignified individual who answered his knock.

The butler's bow was one reserved for a select few. Advised that Her Grace was in the Green Saloon, Brandmere strolled up the stairs to the first floor, paused to admire a new chinoiserie figure, and entered a chamber where a middle-aged lady was reading by the fire.

She looked up, dropped her spectacles, and shrieked, "Anthony! I had given you up for lost!"

Smiling, Brandmere kissed the lady's cheek. "Bad pennies always turn up, Cousin Clarice."

The Duchess of Claddington hid her glasses in a convenient pocket.

"I have been trying to find you for the past two weeks, but you had dropped out of sight," she scolded. "That idiotish boy, Peter Vries, told me that you were in Gloucester, but no one can credit what *he* says."

"He's right as it happens. I was at Brandmere."

The duchess wished her eyesight were better and that she could see her favorite cousin more clearly. Her third cousin actually, for Her Grace was more than twenty years older and had known Brandmere since he was in leading strings.

"I also heard that you let Peter talk you into going off to Devon," she scolded. "A more maggoty idea I have never heard."

Brandmere laughed, but as he turned away toward the fire, the duchess watched him with some concern. Outwardly, the young earl looked to be in top form. His muscular, athletic body almost vibrated with health, and his cheeks still carried the glow of a week in the country. But there was a restlessness in his eyes that the duchess did not like.

Abruptly, she asked, "Anthony, are you sorry that you returned to civilian life?"

Brandmere did not answer. He was gazing deep into the fire. It seemed to him that the flames in the ornate marble fireplace had become other flames, and that the crack of the wood changed to rifle fire and the whine of shrapnel. He drew the singe of battle smoke into his lungs, and he thought he heard anguished voices. "I'm hit, Major! Water, sir, I beg you! Oh, Lord, Brand, they've done for me!"

A log snapped in the grate and he jerked back into himself. Salamanca was gone. The stench of battle was gone. His men and the friends who had died in his arms were long in their graves.

Brandmere drew a deep breath as he looked back

across the ornate room at his cousin. "No, I don't," he replied calmly. "Why do you ask?"

"You seem so different these days. When you first came to London you seemed to be full of spirits. Almost feverish with energy, I thought. Now—oh, I don't know." The duchess frowned a little as she added, "Claddington remarked the other night that you seem bored near to death, and you know, my dear, how little Claddington notices."

She paused and waited hopefully, but her cousin merely shrugged.

"Well, never mind," she resumed. "Now that you are here, I insist that you stay and dine with us. We have invited Lady and Lord Stewart, and Mrs. Waye and her protégé Mr. Leeland, who will give us a reading from his new verses."

The earl looked somewhat alarmed and said that he had another engagement. He then added, "Claddington's right. I *am* bored. That's why I went to Brandmere."

"But there is nothing there but sheep and cows."

"There's the spirit of Falstaff," Brand murmured.

The duchess whipped out her glasses, settled them on her nose, and regarded her tall cousin anxiously. "Are you sure you are feeling quite the thing?" she was asking when there was a knock on the outer door and the muffled sound of voices. "Don't concern yourself," she said. "I have told Cushing that I am at home to nobody."

There was a crash in the hallway and a familiar voice was heard to say, "Don't try to gammon me, Cushing. Know Her Grace is in. Know Brand's here, too, because I saw his tiger holding the bays."

The duchess groaned. "It is that silly boy again. It is not his fault, really. His mother was one of the

Scottish Argulls—and you know that family is queer in the attic." As she spoke, an indignant Peter Vries burst through the doorway.

"Knew you were in," he exclaimed.

He strode forward to kiss his cousin's hand, upsetting an Oriental lacquer chest in the process. "Not easy to walk around here with all these piles of furniture," he complained. "Stap me if it ain't a demmed obstacle course, Cousin Claddington."

The duchess marshaled a smile and murmured, "Pray sit down, dear, and compose yourself. Why have you called?"

Peter sank into a chair. "Didn't mean to call on you precisely—trying to find Brand. Hard man to find. Mean to say—this is an emergency."

Brandmere asked with real concern, "What scrape have you got yourself into?"

Peter leaped out of his chair and seized Brandmere by the lapels of his coat. "Did you get the invitation?"

Impatiently, Brandmere removed the clutching hands. "What in hell—I beg your pardon, Clarice— what the deuce is so important about some invitation?"

"The Trahernes sent it," Peter babbled. "It *must* have been waiting for you when you got back to London."

"The invitation to the Trahernes's house party, do you mean? I chucked it into the fire without reading it. You know I abominate house parties."

"Chucked—oh, stap me, that's the outside of enough." Peter became very red in the face and commenced to tug at an envelope that rested within his breast pocket. In the process he dislodged a button the size of a saucer, which rolled across the floor and came to rest at the duchess's feet.

"Here's my invitation," Peter puffed. "Read this."

Brandmere glanced at the duchess, who rolled her eyes and made significant corkscrew motions near her temple. He then pulled out the single sheet from within the envelope and looked it over. "No," he said. "Absolutely not."

"But, Brand—"

"Under no circumstances whatsoever will I go to Somerset. If you want to languish at Miss Traherne's fair feet, you must go to Reed Hall alone."

"But—!"

"No."

It was a tone of voice Brandmere seldom employed, and even Peter knew he was beaten.

"Know you're hipped with me, Brand," he said gloomily. "Don't blame you. Stap me if I knew Grapewood would be such a curst flat place. That Campion—you were right, he *is* a rum touch. And on top of that to be knocked head over pins by a pig and be fed that awful pudding—it don't bear thinking on, that's all."

The shadow of a smile haunted Brand's fine mouth. "I don't think I will ever get over that very interesting—pudding."

The duchess's eyes were not poor enough to miss that smile. In a rallying tone she asked, "Do you stand there and tell me that they keep a pig at Grapewood and that it knocked you down, Anthony?"

Brandmere roused himself enough to give a comical description of his meeting with Porcina. The duchess laughed until she got the hiccups and had to ring for a restorative. "That settles it," she exclaimed. "I am going to Somerset."

She smiled mischievously at the men's astonishment. "Our invitation was delivered last week. Claddington met Sir Malcolm at his club, and Miss Traherne was made known to me at Lady Sommer's ball. A very pretty girl, I thought."

Peter put a hand to his heart. "She is a goddess!"

"Claddington will not like to leave London," the duchess continued, "but I will persuade him. Sir Malcolm has invited a great many people to Somerset, including these Campions, whom I would not miss meeting for the world."

"He's invited *Campion*?"

The duchess wondered why Anthony looked so black and ready to fly up into the boughs. From what he had said about the pig and Campion's niece, he had appeared diverted by these odd people.

Peter was saying, "You remember, Brand, that Campion was nattering on about there being ghosts at Reed Manor. Specter of the Hooded Monk, I think it was. Best way to get into Sir Malcolm's good books, don't you know. Sir Malcolm's got ghosts in his noggin."

He paused to draw breath. "Wish you was coming, Brand. Don't mind admitting to you that I'm no dab hand with the ladies. Whenever Miss Traherne looks at me, I feel like a flat."

But Brandmere reiterated his desire to stay far away from Somerset. He soon took his leave of the duchess and Peter and drove back to St. James Square, where his valet informed him that he was in danger of being tardy.

"Tardy for what?" Brandmere demanded. When told, he groaned and said, "Oh, my God. I'd forgotten about that early supper with Lady Humby. Didn't I cry off?"

"No, my lord."

Looking resigned, Brandmere strode to his dressing room, where his evening clothes had been laid out. He dressed mechanically, then sat down at his dressing table.

With a flourish Marlin presented a box embossed with the family's coat of arms. Brandmere took it and snapped it open. For a moment he gazed into its velvet recesses, then snapped it shut and placed it on his dressing table.

"I won't need my watch tonight, Marlin," he said.

"Very good, my lord."

The valet did not trouble to disguise his surprise. He could not recall when the earl had dressed for a formal occasion without donning the watch that Charles I had given to the Third Earl of Brandmere. Wearing the diamond and gold heirloom was a tradition in the family.

But the present earl had more than tradition on his mind. Dismissing his valet, he reached for the box again and flicked it open. As before, the box was empty.

Swiftly, his mind went back over time. He had not worn the watch at Brandmere, for they were less formal in Gloucester. The last time he could recall donning the heirloom was at that wretched dinner at Grapewood.

"Of course," the earl muttered.

He leaned back in his chair and stared into the glass, seeing not his own hard-planed features but Campion's shrewd fox's face. It was hard to believe that even Campion would stoop low enough to rob a guest, but there was no other possible explanation.

For a moment Brandmere thought of alerting the Bow Street runners so that Campion could be arrested, but further reflection told him that this would not do. He had no proof, and Campion would have by now fenced off his booty. "And now," Brandmere mused, "he's managed to get an invitation to Somerset."

A flush of anger rose in the earl's suntanned cheeks. He would write and warn Sir Malcolm at once, and then he would tell Clarice that on no account must she go to Reed Hall. Brandmere started to ring for writing materials, but then paused as another thought occurred to him.

Campion had stolen something that meant a great deal to him. It was a personal affront that required personal intervention—and satisfaction. Brandmere's dark eyes narrowed as he decided that he would go to Reed Hall himself. He would catch Campion at his dirty work and personally see the scoundrel hanged or sent to Botany Bay.

This pleasant prospect made the earl smile. Then, just as suddenly, he frowned. He had remembered Campion's niece.

Instantly, vividly, Suzanna's face rose before his mind's eye. Thick, dark hair tumbled across a high forehead, and clear gray eyes that dominated a heart-shaped face seemed to look searchingly into his.

The mental image was inexplicably disturbing. Brandmere rose from his chair and began to pace up and down his room as he considered the facts. Suzanna Campion might well be her uncle's accomplice, or she might be innocent. Either way, he would know soon enough.

And either way, he could not allow Campion's niece to distract him from his purpose. In fact, Brandmere decided, while at Reed Manor he would avoid her like the plague.

* * *

"Heart up, Suzanna, it is almost the end of our journey."

A strange sound, between a cough and a gasp, emanated from the shadowy figure beside Dickon. He glanced at her sideways and almost put an arm around her shoulders before deciding against it. Sympathy at this moment would no doubt cause Suzanna to dissolve into tears.

"There is the Parrett River," he said in a rallying tone. "We will soon reach Reed Hall."

A moist sniff was his only answer. This would never do, Dickon thought. Red eyes and a nose swollen with weeping would do nothing toward making a good impression on the Trahernes.

He took out his watch—a cheap, gilt affair he had bought in Spain after being forced to pawn the gold one left him by his father—and frowned at it. "Eight o'clock," he complained. "We are very late. However, people of distinction do not keep country hours, so we may not have missed dinner."

Suzanna muttered that she didn't care if she never ate again. "We should not have come," she added.

Dickon sighed. "Don't tell me that you are going into mourning for a *goat*. Collect, my dear, that it could not have lasted much longer."

Suzanna swallowed determinedly and said, "It—it's not just because of poor Ione. We really do not belong at Reed Hall."

"We were invited, remember."

"Only because you gammoned Sir Malcolm about a bogus apparition," Suzanna replied with some vehemence. "We are not well connected or rich. We will be looked upon as interlopers."

"Fol rol," Dickon snorted.

Complacently, he stroked the silken folds of his

neck-cloth, which was arranged in the waterfall style. He flicked a particle of dust from the sleeve of his dove-gray coat and smoothed back his hair. He looked elegant. The chaise, hired for the purpose of conducting them to Reed Hall in style, looked equally the thing.

Though his first attempt at turning a profit at Grapewood had failed, Dickon was far from discouraged. With the Trahernes to give him countenance, Grapewood could still become popular with *ton*nish Londoners. And the bored, rich aristocrats that Sir Malcolm had invited to Somerset would be just the people necessary to make Grapewood flourish.

If only Suzanna would cooperate. Dickon winced as he recalled her rudeness to Colonel Bender about hunting. And when he thought of her comparing Miss Traherne to a fox . . .

"Suzanna, my dear," he said in his most persuasive tone, "we must put our best foot forward. Remember how important it is to make a good impression on Sir Malcolm's guests."

Half expecting his niece to retort in her usual frank way, he was relieved when she remained silent. Perhaps, he considered, it was a good thing that the wretched goat had chosen this time to expire. Grief might serve to keep Suzanna subdued and out of trouble.

Sir Malcolm's estate had by now come into view. It was a tremendous contrast to Grapewood. The gracious old house was set in a carefully manicured, rolling green acreage bordered by the Parrett River on one side and by woodlands on the other. The entire place had the look and smell of money.

Dickon rubbed his lead-whitened hands. "How delightful to be a nabob from India," he exclaimed. "How wonderful to be rich!"

They drove into the courtyard, and a natty groom materialized to take the horses' heads. A brace of gorgeously liveried footmen shot through the door to lower the chaise's step.

"This," Dickon said, "is more like it." He settled his coat, offered his niece his arm, haughtily instructed the footmen to see to the luggage, and strolled up the marble steps toward the house. "Think, Suzanna. With a little luck and a great deal of blunt, Grapewood could be like this."

Suzanna knew how impossible this was but forebore to say so. Reed Manor was a stately edifice built of red brick, and its interior had been arranged in the old style. But here similarity to an English country home ended. Exotic wood, and brass and silver carvings from India decorated the walls of the ground-floor anteroom, and a huge elephant, worked in ebony, ivory, and semiprecious stones stood by the door. Opulent Persian and Indian rugs flowed over the stairs that led up to the second floor.

The sound of music and dancing wafted down from this floor, and Dickon grumbled, "Deuce take it. We've definitely missed dinner."

At this moment Sir Malcolm appeared at the top of the stairs. He shook hands with bluff heartiness, saying, "Good of you to come, Campion. Servant, ma'am."

Dickon explained their delay on the poor condition of the road. "The government's to blame," Sir Malcolm agreed. "I told Claddington so this evening at dinner. He's a duke, and he's in the House of Lords, so he should do something about the roads. Eh? But it's the same everywhere. Same in India, same in Tibet, same in Timbuktu."

He paused, and added, "You'll be joining us in the dancing, eh? But first you'll want to see your rooms. Brought your servants with you?"

When Dickon said that their personal servants had contacted an ague and had remained behind, the nabob waved expansive hands. "No problem at all. We've got servant-wallahs to spare—any amount of them. They'll take you to your rooms now."

But Dickon had been thinking that since food was out of the question, the next best thing was to engage Traherne's attention. He affected a thoughtful air and murmured, "I beg your pardon for mentioning it, Sir Malcolm, but as I came through the door I felt a *chill*." He added significantly, "It was not an ordinary chill, sir, but the coldness of the *grave*."

Sir Malcolm brightened. "Noticed it already, eh? Thought so, but couldn't be sure. You were quite right that something's afoot here, Campion."

He drew Dickon aside, leaving Suzanna to follow a curtsying maidservant to the third floor of the house. Here a life-size Indian statue with many arms was sticking its tongue out in the hall, but Suzanna was relieved to find her bedchamber was much less exotic. It was decorated in the English style with over-stuffed, chintz-covered chairs, watercolors, and a vase full of autumn asters.

"Would you like me to unpack, ma'am?" the maid asked.

"No, I thank you. I am particular and wish to do it myself," Suzanna said primly.

Not for anything could she allow a servant of this wealthy household to see how poor the Campions were. But, Suzanna noted bleakly, servants could always smell poverty. She glimpsed a patronizing smile on the maid's face as she eyed the one shabby box that had been brought up to the room.

The woman's smirk depressed Suzanna, and she wished that she did not have to go downstairs tonight. She did not want to watch people dancing and preening themselves, and she did not want to see Uncle Dickon at his tricks. She recalled that Sir Malcolm had mentioned the Duke of Claddington and winced at the thought of her uncle trying to persuade His Grace to come to Grapewood as a paying guest.

If only her uncle had listened to her arguments against accepting Sir Malcolm's invitation—but Dickon had turned a deaf ear. He had planted the idea of a Reed Hall ghost in Sir Malcolm's mind and was now ready to reap the harvest. Even when Ione had suddenly taken sick, he had refused to give up the idea of attending the house party.

Suzanna began to unpack. This did not take long. A white linen nightgown with a single band of lace, an unadorned nightcap, a muslin day dress that had seen better days but was brave with new ribbons—that was all. That, and her silver evening dress.

Suzanna shook out this dress and tried not to mind that Miss Traherne would surely recognize it. No doubt she would be too kind to say anything, and besides, there was no use worrying about things that could not be helped.

She dressed, braided her hair anew, and coiled it about her head. There remained only to add her mother's pearls, and she was ready. With much trepidation Suzanna stepped out of her room and into the hall.

Laughter and music rose to greet her. It grew louder as she descended to the second floor. Suzanna approached the door to a room where two gorgeously liveried footmen stood at attention and looked inside.

The room dazzled her eyes. It had been hung with silver cloth and festooned with flowers of every description. It blazed with many candelabra and chandeliers. Along the wall, mirrors had been placed so that the guests were reflected many times over. The effect was that there appeared to be a hundred people in the room.

Some of the older ladies, including the Marchioness of Clavendell, Mrs. Bender, and a handsome dowager with a blaze of diamonds about her throat, were sitting along the sides of the rooms gossiping. A cluster of gentlemen stood together at the far corner of the hall, and she recognized the colonel. Near him stood Stanhope and his inseparable companion, Lord Federby. No doubt the young men had come to court Miss Traherne once again.

All the other guests were dancing. One young gentleman, dressed in a salmon-pink coat, caught her eye. As he hopped about with his partner, he turned his head, and Suzanna was startled to see that it was Peter Vries.

The earl's cousin—and that meant that Brandmere must also be here. Suzanna glanced swiftly about the room and saw the earl dancing with Miss Traherne.

Tonight Brandmere was dressed in a dove-gray jacket of the finest cut. His breeches of double-milled stocking accented his hard-muscled thighs. A ruby flashed at his throat as he danced.

The ruby complimented Miss Traherne's round-dress of rose-colored jaconet, which was banded with French lace and cut low to emphasize her white bosom. There was a small coronet of silk roses in Miss Traherne's hair, which she wore in the Grecian style.

She looked, Suzanna thought, like a princess out of a fairy tale, and she danced with the earl as if she had partnered him all her life.

Rapidly, Suzanna backed away from the door. Not for anything would she take her weary self and her much-worn dress into that room and mingle with those glittering people. But as she turned to go upstairs, the music came to an end, and there was a hum of talk and laughter.

Fearing that some of the dancers would pass the open door and see her, Suzanna looked quickly about and spied a side door that was half ajar. Without pausing to think, she whisked through it and closed the door behind her.

At first blush it seemed as though she had stepped into a garden, but this was illusion. Suzanna saw that she had entered a large chamber ringed about with potted trees and bushes. Parrots and cockatiels squawked from cages that had been hung at intervals, and orange trees filled the air with their scent.

Along the sides of the chamber were chairs and small tables, and in the center of the room was a table covered with edibles. Suzanna's eyes widened. Even in Grapewood's heyday she had never seen so much food.

There were chops. There were platters piled high with paper-thin slices of ham. There were oysters swimming in sauce, and quails done to a turn, and chicken arranged in succulent pyramids. There were also mountains of exotic-looking fruits and tarts and pasties and truffles. Presiding over all was an imposing cake of marzipan molded to resemble an Indian temple.

Suzanna's stomach gave a very unladylike growl. Because she'd been so upset at Ione's last illness, she had hardly eaten these past two days. Now she realized that she was starving.

Did she dare take something to eat? But Suzanna checked this rag-mannered impulse immediately. In a house like this, food would have to be eaten with ceremony. At a prearranged time, Sir Malcolm would give the signal for gentlemen to escort their ladies in the proper hierarchal order. It would be unmannerly to take even the smallest piece of crusty brown chicken.

The music had started up again, and Suzanna backed away toward the door. Here she stopped and looked yearningly at the table. Her stomach gave another gurgle, longer and louder than the last, and her mouth began to water. Would it matter, she wondered, if she took one *small* piece of chicken? And there were such lovely apples on that table. Such luscious, red, juicy apples.

Suzanna took several steps forward and felt the aroma of food overpower her good sense. She took a drumstick from the enormous plate. She nibbled it. It tasted heavenly.

Suzanna finished her drumstick and took another. And another. Not knowing what to do with the bones, she held them in her hand as she munched. Then, with the edge of her appetite stilled, she reached out to take one of the marvelous apples.

That was when she heard footsteps coming toward the room. Discovery would be terribly embarrassing, and Suzanna looked around her for someplace to hide. There was no place of concealment except for the trees.

She crossed the room and slipped behind the largest and thickest of these just as the door creaked open and a man came in. Peering through concealing branches, Suzanna saw a tall figure with his back to her. To her horror, she recognized Brandmere.

Go away, she prayed silently.

Instead of obliging, Brandmere approached the table, took a handful of grapes, and began to eat them.

Suzanna held her breath while the earl finished his grapes. Now would he go away? But instead, he turned and looked idly about him. His gaze seemed to linger on the tree behind which she was concealed, and involuntarily, Suzanna stepped backward. This unsettled the bones she was holding, and one of them slid out of her hand and thumped onto the fine Aubusson carpet.

"Who's there?" Brandmere demanded.

He crossed the room swiftly and shoved aside the concealing branches. Next moment, Suzanna was staring into his hard, black eyes.

"Eve with her apple," the earl said.

Chapter Five

"What have you got there?" Brandmere continued sharply.

Suzanna looked down at the apple in her hand. As she did so, more concealed chicken bones fell to the floor.

She bent to retrieve the bones. So did he. Their heads collided with a sharp crack. Through the stars that were floating before her eyes, Suzanna heard the earl exclaim, "Good God—bones."

Mortified, Suzanna scooped up the bones and dumped them into the pot of the tree behind which she had been hiding. She then put the apple back on the table and turned to face Brandmere.

He was rubbing his temple. "You have a hard head, Miss Campion," he observed.

"So do you, sir," she retorted.

A rueful smile curved his lips. "That is what my sister Honoria tells me. When did you arrive at Reed Hall?"

Suzanna explained that she and her uncle had been

delayed. "My uncle wished me to come down and be presented to Sir Malcolm's guests, but when I did as he asked, I realized how tired I was."

He raised a quizzical eyebrow. "And that is why you decided to hide in this room?"

"It is difficult to explain," Suzanna sighed.

Her voice was troubled, and Brandmere felt a twinge of remorse. When he had found her hiding with some unknown object clutched in her hand, he had assumed that she had something to hide. He soothed his conscience by telling himself that under the circumstances he was justified in being suspicious of the Campions.

"You see," she was saying, "it was my fault that we were so delayed. I could not leave Grapewood until—Ione died this morning."

She swallowed hard and lowered her eyes to mask her tears and so missed the change in his expression. "I'm sorry to hear that," Brandmere said.

Suzanna did her best to smile. "You must think me goosish to grieve for a goat, but as I told you, Ione is—was an old friend. After Mama's death, she was such a comfort."

Brandmere forgot his resolve not to have anything to do with Campion's niece. "Surely," he exclaimed, "there was someone to comfort you. Your father—"

"Papa was grieving terribly and so had little time for me. Little John and Mrs. Horry tried to help, but many guests came to Grapewood, and their hands were full."

"But where was your governess?"

Unexpectedly, Suzanna chuckled. "Miss Minchin was fond of the bottle and went on the toodle very often. When she was bosky, she would sing songs that had been taught her by her sweetheart, who was a naval man. One was about a one-eyed sailor and a mermaid."

Brandmere was torn between amusement at Suzanna's frank speech and the appalling thought that the bereaved child's only consolation had come from a goat. "So you are in mourning for Ione," he said. "Is that why you didn't want to join the dancing?"

"Not really. You see—" She hesitated for a second and then said frankly, "I cannot dance, my lord."

There was something wistful in her admission. "Weren't you taught how?" he asked.

"Oh, yes. After Mama died, Papa sent me to live with Aunt and Uncle Linwood in Dorset. My oldest cousin was having her come-out, and my aunt hired a dancing master. I was included in the lessons until I kicked him in the ankle."

She looked rueful, but there was a glint of mischief in her eyes. "What happened then?" Brandmere asked.

"He yelled and hopped about and swore I had lamed him forever. The doctor had to be called, and servants ran about with pails of salts and water—at any rate, my aunt told me that I was much too clumsy ever to learn to dance."

At that moment the band in the Great Hall struck up a waltz. "No doubt she was wrong," Brandmere consoled her. "Because a sap-skulled dancing master made a mull of things does not mean that you are hopeless."

Doubtfully, Suzanna shook her head. "It is kind of you to say so, but I think I am *very* hopeless."

It was Brandmere's intention to wish Miss Campion a good night and return to the dancing. Instead, he was shocked to hear himself suggest, "Suppose we try and see?"

Suzanna looked horrified. A shade of red crept into her cheeks, and she put her hands behind her and backed away from him.

"I did not mean—I was not thinking—" Her words ended in a little gasp as he stepped forward and slid an arm around her waist.

She did not protest but went very stiff in the circle of his arm. "I will most probably kick your ankle, too," she warned somewhat breathlessly.

"Is that any way to begin a lesson? All you need do is step to the music. *One* two three. *One*—" The earl broke off as she trod hard on his toes.

"You see?" Suzanna wailed.

Brandmere frowned. "Ma'am, you have battle nerves," he accused.

"I beg your pardon?"

"Your cheeks are flushed. Your eyes have a certain wildness. Raw young recruits look exactly so before a charge. And they turn into blocks of wood, just as you have done."

Suzanna was mortified, and yet she did not want to leave the circle of his arm. That firm pressure about her waist was producing the oddest sensations within her—sensations that caused her heart to pound hard and the blood to sing in her ears.

"Take a deep breath," the earl ordered. "Close your eyes. Relax, and let the music guide you."

Unthinkingly, she obeyed. Her long eyelashes swept down and lay like dark half-moons on her cheeks. Standing so close to her, Brandmere could see the silky bloom on those cheeks and the dusting of freckles along the bridge of her small nose.

One or two wayward curls were lying against Suzanna's forehead. Brandmere felt a wholly inappropriate desire to brush back the soft black silk.

Hastily, the earl began to move with the music. *"One* two three," he encouraged his partner. *"One* two three. That's it. You're doing famously."

Suzanna remained stiff at first, and several times she made mistakes, but the earl was a good and surprisingly patient teacher. His arm about her waist guided her so expertly that after several turns around the room, she realized that she was no longer treading on his toes. A few more turns, and she began to relax.

Dancing with her eyes still closed, Suzanna allowed the music to take her over. She had the uncanny sensation that her heels had sprouted wings, and though Brandmere held her the regulation twelve inches away from him, she felt as though his strong, athletic body was moving in perfect unison with hers.

Suzanna could not believe that she had ever been afraid to dance. Now she wanted to go on dancing forever.

She smiled at this thought, and watching that smile, Brandmere wondered at the change in his partner. Suzanna had been transformed. Far from being a block of wood, she was now light and graceful in his arms. Miss Traherne, with whom he had danced earlier this evening, was an accomplished dancer, but Suzanna's grace was somehow different.

"Am I waltzing?" she breathed.

"You are, and very well." She opened her eyes at that, and he smiled down at her. "What do you think of dancing now?"

Breathlessly, she replied, "It's a little like flying, isn't it?"

Brandmere laughed and swung her about the room again. He tried to ignore the elusive fragrance of flowers that seemed to emanate from her. Suzanna's perfume and the heady scent of orange blossoms was causing him to feel inexplicably light-headed. Involuntarily, his arm tightened about her.

"Good heavens, so this is where you are," a surprised voice exclaimed.

Brandmere stopped in the middle of a turn, and Suzanna promptly trod on his toes. Together they turned toward the doorway where Anabel Traherne was standing.

"The duchess sent me to find you, Brandmere," she explained. "Her Grace was sure that you had found the party tedious."

"Not at all. As you see, I have been giving Miss Campion a lesson in the waltz."

As if noticing Suzanna for the first time, Anabel purred, "My dear Miss Campion, it is good to see you. And you are wearing your silver gown again. How sweet."

Still somewhat dazed from waltzing, Suzanna could only stammer, "I beg your pardon for being rag-mannered. I should have come to greet you as soon as we arrived."

"Oh, fol rol, do not regard that," Anabel said airily. "It is not every day that a lady has dancing instructions from an earl. I, too, must beg for such an honor."

"But you already dance exceedingly well. Miss Campion is only a promising beginner." Brandmere smiled at Anabel while extending his arm to Suzanna. "Well, ma'am? Shall we show the assemblage how to waltz?"

Suzanna glanced uncertainly at Anabel's set face. She felt a recurrence of nerves and said, "I do not think it would be wise."

"Nonsense." Still smiling, the earl whisked her out into the hallway. As he escorted her toward the Great

Hall, he directed, "No more battle nerves, remember. Take a deep breath and relax."

He would have said more except that just then he spotted Campion. Without so much as a thought for his niece, the man was hobnobbing with the other guests. He had infiltrated a group consisting of Colonel Bender and Claddington and was crowing with laughter over some joke.

With loathing, Brandmere noted that Campion was dressed in the kick of fashion. Every hair on his head was in place. His cheeks and hands had been whitened with lead, and a diamond flashed on his finger. Probably that diamond had been stolen, too.

The earl thought swiftly. On a whim he had undertaken to teach Suzanna to dance, but perhaps that whim could serve a different purpose. Instead of ignoring Suzanna Campion as he had originally planned, he would be very attentive to her.

As frank as she was, Suzanna would surely say or do something that would help him expose her thieving uncle.

The dancing lasted late into the night, and next morning Sir Malcolm's guests remained in their beds until a fashionably late hour. It was only after they had breakfasted on the sumptuous trays that were sent up to their rooms that they began to trickle down into the morning room to see what their host had arranged for their diversion.

They found Sir Malcolm eager to embark on a boating expedition.

"The Parrett runs through my land," he explained. "Beautiful river for boating. And since the day is warm, I've arranged for a picnic on the riverbank." Then, seeing that Stanhope and Lord Federby looked alarmed, he added reassuringly, "No need to turn a finger. Eh? There's plenty of servant-wallahs to do the rowing."

"Perhaps some of the gentlemen wish to exhibit their skill with the oars," his daughter suggested. "The dear duchess tells me that Mr. Vries, for instance, is quite an oarsman. He apparently excelled in the sport at Oxford."

Peter turned crimson with surprise and pleasure. He knew that so far he had not acquitted himself well. Last night during the French quadrille, he had stepped on Miss Traherne's feet. Later, while trying to impress her with his *savoir faire*, he had spilled ices on her dress. His performance had caused his rivals great glee, and that odious worm, Stanhope, had sneered in a way that made Peter itch to call him out.

It just went to show, Peter told himself blissfully, that a fellow's luck could turn as quickly as March weather. This morning he had been on the point of despair—and now here was Dame Fortune tipping him a winning card.

"Splendid idea, ma'am—would like it above all things. Privilege to row you anywhere," he stammered.

Immediately, Lord Federby and Stanhope clamored for the honor of rowing their hostess to the ends of the earth.

Angelically, Anabel smiled at her admirers. "Papa, perhaps it would be intriguing if these gentlemen did the rowing instead of the servants." She placed a hand on Peter's arm and added archly, "Mr. Vries, I wish you to take special good care of the lady in your charge."

Peter nearly swooned with joy, and Dickon, standing behind his niece's chair, thought that the young tulip looked like a sheep ready for slaughter.

Dickon was pleased with himself. He had spent most of the night with their host, walking the corridors and discussing spiritual vibrations. He had repeated his tale of the Monk of Reed Hall, and the nabob had swallowed every mendacious word. Further, Sir Malcolm had believed Dickon's lie that the Silver Lady had been sighted at Grapewood and had immediately booked a week's stay for himself and his daughter.

All this would have made Dickon rub his hands with glee except for one thing. "I don't like boating," he told Suzanna under cover of the conversation. "Never trusted a boat—nor water, either. Deuce take it, I wish there were some way to cry off."

He checked himself as Anabel lifted her voice to ask, "Do you have something warm to wear on the water, Miss Campion? It will be cold on the river. If you have not brought something suitable, I will be glad to lend you anything you require."

Several guests turned their heads to see what woman would be so foolish as to travel in September without adequate clothing. Suzanna was embarrassed but answered frankly, "Thank you, I have a heavy wool shawl that has seen me through several winters."

Dickon saw the marchioness's fashionable daughters raise their eyebrows at each other and watched the Duchess of Claddington surreptitiously produce her spectacles in order to study Suzanna. When, Dickon wondered disgustedly, would his niece ever learn to hold her tongue? Naturally no lady would *ever* admit to having such an ancient garment.

The duchess was not shocked but intrigued. She

had been interested in this Campion girl even before she came to Reed Hall, and her curiosity had been further piqued when Anthony presented her and then danced attendance on her for most of last evening.

She glanced at the earl, who was standing a few feet from her. He was supposedly deep in a political conversation with Claddington, but he was actually watching the Campions, and he did not look at all bored. Well pleased, the duchess decided that she would go on this tedious boating expedition just to see whether Anthony would take Miss Campion out on his boat.

When the party left Reed Hall later that morning, all the ladies except Suzanna had changed into fashionable walking dresses. Noting that Anabel now wore a half-dress of peach-colored cambric embroidered with poppies and a modish gauze hat trimmed with silk flowers, Suzanna wrapped herself even deeper into the recesses of her shawl.

Dickon did not help. As he fell into step beside her, he demanded peevishly, "Suzanna, why didn't you bring something decent to wear? Deuce take it, that shawl looks like the one Cook wears when she does the marketing."

It was, indeed, Cook's shawl, but Suzanna did not tell her uncle so. "It is a perfectly good shawl," she retorted. "I cannot see why we should waste money on unnecessary fribbles."

Dickon rolled his eyes at this imbecilic statement. Then he looked anxiously up at the sky. "There are clouds on the horizon," he grumbled. "I hope it's not going to rain."

Suzanna shrugged, and Dickon felt his irritation rise. "I wish," he said meanly, "that you would not make such a guy of yourself. Look, the duke is staring at you."

Suzanna's cheeks turned warm as she saw the contemptuous look that that florid, choleric-looking gentleman was giving her.

"I tell you, clothes are more important than anything," Dickon went on.

As he spoke, Brandmere came strolling over toward them. He lifted the brim of his beaver to Suzanna and approved, "It was very sensible of you to bring that shawl along. Just the thing for an outing on the water."

Dickon dropped back a few paces and watched the earl smile down at Suzanna. He noted the way his niece's eyes brightened as she returned that smile. He was also aware that Miss Traherne, who was walking between her father and Peter Vries, suddenly looked as if she was sucking lemons.

Dickon pursed his lips and whistled soundlessly. "Oho," he murmured to himself. "Now, what game is being played here?"

The group had reached the banks of the Parrett River. It was swollen with autumn rain but looked placid enough as it wound between its green banks. On one bank a canopy had been spread over Persian rugs, and tables and chairs had been set out. Several servants stood at attention beside baskets of delicacies and wine while other domestics waited beside decorated boats.

Sir Malcolm assigned these boats to various personages. He himself was to row the duke and duchess in the largest boat. The colonel, his lady, and daughter were given a vessel cushioned in military scarlet.

"And that blue one with those two servant-wallahs in attendance is my daughter's," Sir Malcolm continued. "Brandmere, would you favor my girl by accompanying her?"

Peter, who had been working himself into a state of nervous exaltation, almost choked. "But I thought that I was to row Miss Traherne!" he protested.

"Dear Mr. Vries, you are to row Mr. Campion and his niece," Anabel directed sweetly. "You will take particularly good care of them, will you not?"

Peter blinked and said rather wildly, "But I had hoped—that is, I mean to say, I want to row *you*, ma'am!"

The other guests were watching and listening with obvious interest. Stanhope and Federby were grinning widely. To spare his young cousin further humiliation, Brandmere put a hand on Peter's arm. "Our hostess has spoken," he said. "We must obey."

With an air of calm detachment, he bowed and offered Anabel his arm and strolled off with her.

Peter did not join in the conversation and laughter that ensued as the guests boarded their boats. His normally pink countenance had paled, and he fairly quivered with misery. Feeling very sorry for him, Suzanna said, "We have a fine boat, Mr. Vries. Do you not think so, Uncle Dickon?"

Dickon shuddered.

The crafts were pushed into the water. The gentlemen manned the oars or leaned back in the boats and allowed servants to propel the crafts forward. Ladies snapped open their little parasols and trailed their fingers in the water. On the bank, an orchestra began to play.

Peter tried to ignore the fact that the boat containing his tall cousin and Miss Traherne was gliding nearby, but he could not shut his eyes or ears. He saw that a stalwart servant was propelling Anabel's boat and that she was laughing prettily at something Brandmere had said. Peter fairly gnashed his teeth with frustration.

Suzanna did not know how to cheer him. She tried to sustain a conversation but was not very successful. Peter was too dismal to do more than mumble monosyllabic answers, and Dickon had closed up like an oyster.

In fact, Dickon's sole contribution was to ask how deep the river was. He then shut his eyes, clung to both sides of the boat, and resigned himself. But when they had rowed some little way downriver, he started and gasped, "Deuce take it, I felt a raindrop!"

Suzanna looked up at the sky and saw that it had turned gray with low-lying clouds.

"Rain," Dickon repeated in tones of alarm. "My clothes will be quite ruined. Get us back to shore at once, Mr. Vries."

His words carried to the duchess, who exclaimed, "Good heavens, he is right. It looks as though it is going to pour in a moment. Sir Malcolm, we must turn about."

A wind gusted up and gave emphasis to her words. "Turn the boats about," Sir Malcolm commanded. "*Hari bai*—I mean to say, be quick about it! Never fear, your grace," he added cheerfully. "Once back at shore we can refuge under the canopy."

Rapidly, the little fleet came about. Peter attempted to follow suit but in his hurry fumbled his oars and lost one of them.

He made a grab for the lost oar which floated out of reach. "Mr. Campion, get that oar," Peter yelped.

Galvanized by Peter's cry, Dickon let go of the side of the boat and leaned over the side. "Take care!" Suzanna cried.

But Dickon's fear of boats was nothing to his horror of having his new coat ruined. He made a grab at the oar, lost his balance, and toppled into the water. He sank like a stone.

"Uncle Dickon!" Suzanna shrieked.

Peter attempted to bring the boat alongside Dickon, but the craft was caught in the river current and began to drift toward the bank. Try as he would, Peter could not control the boat with only one oar.

Dickon rose to the water's surface and sputtered, "Help me! I can't swim!"

Peter began to rise to his feet then subsided. "Forgot—can't swim neither," he moaned.

He started to shout for help, but no one heard him. The other boats had pulled some distance away, and in the general confusion, no one had noticed Dickon's mishap.

Suzanna gave a despairing look around and decided that there was no help for it. "Hold the boat steady," she commanded.

Kicking off her shoes, she took a deep breath and jumped into the river.

The cold water enfolded her and took her deep, and swimming underwater, Suzanna kicked her way toward her uncle. She had managed to get an arm around him when he seized her in a stranglehold.

Dickon had never been as terrified in his life. He was sure his hour had come. Not realizing what he was doing, he tightened his hold on Suzanna. She struggled, but she could not break free from her uncle's death grip. Her lungs felt as though they would surely burst.

Suddenly, Suzanna felt her uncle being ripped away from her. Another swimmer had seized Dickon by the hair and was dragging him upward. Freed, Suzanna also surged toward the surface.

For a moment she could do nothing but draw air into her lungs. Then she realized that her rescuer was Brandmere. "Can you swim to shore?" he was shouting.

Where had *he* come from? Suzanna wondered, but she nodded.

"Good," the earl cried. "Follow me."

With swift, powerful strokes, he pulled ahead of her with Dickon in tow and created a wake in which she could swim more easily. In a few moments they reached the shore. Brandmere unceremoniously dumped Dickon onto dry ground and turned to help Suzanna.

"Are you all right?" He demanded.

His eyes were almost black with concern, and as his hard hands smoothed the hair from her face, Suzanna forgot how badly her muscles ached. She forgot that she had had a near brush with death. Feeling safe and inexplicably happy, she nodded wordlessly.

"How did this happen?" Brandmere continued. "If I hadn't heard Peter shouting for help, I might never have seen you jump into the river."

His words recalled the horror of what might have happened. Suzanna swallowed and tasted river water. "Mr. Vries lost his oar and Uncle Dickon went after it and fell into the river," she explained in a low voice. "He cannot swim, but I can. I tried to help my uncle, but he was so frightened that he caught hold of me and wouldn't let me go."

With her dark hair plastered about her face and her teeth chattering with cold, Suzanna looked very fragile. The thought that she could well have drowned made Brandmere feel a terror such as he had never before experienced. He wanted to strangle Campion for endangering her. He also wanted to put his arms around Suzanna and draw her chilled body against his. At the same time, he wanted to box her ears for her foolhardiness.

These conflicting emotions roughened his tone as he demanded, "You aren't strong enough to break his hold—you might very well have drowned, too."

Suzanna blinked at the change in Brandmere's voice and somewhat defensively said, "But I am a good swimmer."

"Not so good as to save a man much heavier than you," he pointed out.

He was interrupted by a halloo sounding nearby. The lead boat, with the duke, the duchess, and Sir Malcolm, was making for the shore. Behind this large craft came Anabel's.

"Fell in the river, eh?" Sir Malcolm was bellowing. "Are you all right, Campion?"

Dickon sneezed repeatedly. The noise he made was not loud enough to drown out another sound. In her beribboned boat, Anabel was laughing.

Suzanna could not believe her ears. Convinced that she had made a mistake, she stared at Anabel and realized that no, she had not erred. Miss Traherne *was* laughing.

"I am sorry," that lady giggled. "I truly am. But you do look so wet and comical."

Unfortunately, Brandmere chose this moment to say, "It was idiotic of you to attempt such a thing."

Hot, bracing indignation surged through Suzanna. Striving to keep her voice even, she replied, "Perhaps I was wrong, but my uncle is my family. We take care of each other."

"Do you indeed!"

His sneer was the last straw. Her frazzled nerves snapped. Eyes blazing, Suzanna shot to her feet.

"Indeed, you are the most odious man," she cried. "I did not ask you for help. I do not *want* your help. And," she concluded fiercely, "I would not take your help if you were the last man on earth, my lord."

Chapter Six

Wrapped in borrowed shawls, rugs, and table-cloths, the Campions sloshed back to Reed Manor.

Rain was still falling, but they were too miserable to care. Dickon's only consolation was that he need not face Sir Malcolm's guests, who had elected to shelter under the canopy on the riverbank and wait out the storm. Suzanna felt no such comfort. She was too agitated to be relieved that Brandmere had stayed back to speak to the duke and duchess, and that except for the apologetic Peter Vries, the Campions walked alone.

The young man had insisted on escorting Suzanna and her uncle to Reed Hall. He was almost incoherent with remorse. "Clumsy of me—I was cockle-brained to go and lose that oar," he groaned. "Stap me if I'll ever forgive myself."

Dickon sneezed violently.

"Fact is that I've been fumble-fingered since I was born. Despair of my parents." Peter ran agitated hands through his already disordered hair. "How could I have been such a—such a—"

"Nincompoop?" Dickon suggested unkindly.

Through chattering teeth Suzanna said that losing an oar was something that could happen to anyone, but Peter was not consoled. "No, it couldn't. It happened to me. And Miss Traherne was watching. How she must have laughed."

Remembering Anabel's giggles, Suzanna said nothing further, and they approached the house in sodden silence. A servant had run ahead with news of the mishap, and the Campions were met by a small army of maids and footmen bearing blankets and towels. Sir Malcolm's stately butler announced that baths were already being filled and added that hot chocolate as well as brandy had been conveyed to Mr. and Miss Campion's rooms.

A short while later Suzanna was soaking in almost scalding water. Unfortunately, as her numb body thawed her memory sharpened, and every word that Brandmere had said to her returned to torment her.

Her only consolation was that she had given as good as she got. She had caught a look at the earl's face when she slogged past him, and he had resembled a thundercloud. She was sure that, wet as he was, he had not returned to Reed Manor because he wanted to avoid even looking at her.

Well, she didn't want to see him, either. He was an odious, infuriating, interfering man. Water sloshed over the lip of the porcelain tub as Suzanna squirmed and kicked in impotent fury. "Why does he not just mind his own business?" she muttered.

Then she heard Brandmere's deep voice on the stairs. A moment later he passed her door on his way to his room. The earl's walk was that of a very angry man, and a few seconds later his door down the hall slammed shut.

Suzanna had not realized she was holding her breath. She let it out now in a ragged sigh. "He should mind his own business," she repeated, but this time her voice lacked conviction.

The awful realization was dawning that she had done it again. And this time she had flown into a fury at the earl just after he had risked his life to save her uncle.

"When will I ever learn to hold my tongue?" Suzanna lamented. "I will have to apologize to him. *Again*."

It wasn't going to be easy. Suzanna thought of the last time she had seen Brandmere and knew she didn't have the nerve to meet him face-to-face. While she dried herself and dressed and brushed out her hair, she tried to think of how she could manage to convey an apology while avoiding a confrontation with the earl.

Perhaps if she wrote him a note? Now, that was a thought. A note of apology could be slid under Brandmere's door or handed to his valet. The other houseguests had by now returned, but the ladies were no doubt resting in their rooms before changing for the evening, and the men would be smoking and drinking port. No one would see her if she went down to the library, where no doubt there would be writing materials.

But Suzanna found herself singularly reluctant to leave her room. Supposing she should happen to meet Brandmere in the hall?

She gave herself a hard mental shake. "Oh, for heaven's sakes," she told herself, "the man will not *eat* me. I don't care a ha'penny if I do meet him."

Head high, Suzanna pulled open the door and glanced down the hall. It was empty. She had taken a few steps down the corridor when she heard an agitated voice shriek, "Misery—oh, misery me!"

Suzanna gave a jump that nearly took her out of her skin. She turned her head quickly but saw nothing. The voice now spoke in an even louder tone.

"I tell you, Your Grace, they are nowhere to be found."

The voice was a woman's and was emanating from the suite that was occupied by the Duke and Duchess of Claddington.

"I have been in Your Grace's service for twenty-five years and nothing like this has ever happened before," the woman wailed. "Oh, madam—"

Unwilling to eavesdrop, Suzanna stepped back into her room and closed her door. Even so, she could hear the woman's voice rising and falling in a threnody of woe. A few moments later there were heavy footsteps en route to Their Graces' suite, a murmur of voices and Sir Malcolm's loud exclamation.

"Your Grace has misplaced your diamonds?" Sir Malcolm cried.

Suzanna remembered the stones that had blazed around the duchess's neck. If they had been misplaced, no wonder Her Grace's maid was panic-stricken. She wondered whether she should offer to help search for the jewels, but then decided that such an offer might be inappropriate. She had just decided that it were best to remain in her room, when there was a knock on her door.

A shaken-looking Sir Malcolm was standing in the hallway. "I apologize for interrupting your rest," he said, "but something has come up. If you'll be so kind as to step across the hall to Their Graces' suite, ma'am, perhaps you can shed light on the matter."

Bewildered but willing, Suzanna followed her host. As she did so, her uncle emerged from his room at the far end of the hallway. Apparently, he had been summoned by Sir Malcolm's butler, who was hovering pallidly in the background.

In spite of the fact that he wore a velvet dressing gown over his clothes, Dickon still looked cold. He sneezed several times before exclaiming, "Sir Malcolm, what's amiss?"

Before the nabob could answer, the duke looked out into the hall. His normally florid features had gone quite pale, and his pugnacious jaw was set like a bulldog's. Eyes, red-rimmed and angry, fastened themselves on Suzanna.

"Miss Campion," the duke growled, "please to come in here. You, too, Campion."

Suzanna stepped into a large room hung with gold silk curtains and carpeted with a beautiful beige and gold Kashmiri rug. Paintings by Dutch and English masters hung on the wall.

The duchess was sitting on a lacquered daybed by the fire. She also was pale, but she attempted a smile.

"Miss Campion, Mr. Campion, forgive me for summoning you in this way. You are so obliging. I need to ask a question of the utmost delicacy, if you please."

Suzanna dipped a knee. Dickon executed a leg, excused his appearance in a graceful speech, and begged Her Grace to command him in anything.

"Get to the demmed point," the duke interrupted impatiently.

Somewhere in the back of the room there was a sob.

Suzanna saw the duchess's elderly maid near the window. Tears were rolling down her cheeks.

"It was my fault, all my fault," the woman moaned.

"That will do, Porter," the duchess said. In a kinder voice she added, "No one is blaming you, you goose. I myself saw you put away the case." She turned back to the Campions. "This is an awkward question, but— did you see anyone in the hallway when you returned this afternoon?"

Uncle and niece exchanged puzzled glances. "No, Your Grace," Suzanna said.

"You're sure of that?" The duke's jowls fairly quivered as he added, "You came back earlier than the rest. Must have seen someone."

"Mr. Vries was with us," Dickon pointed out. "Perhaps he saw something we did not."

"I do not think so. Peter did not enter the house but rejoined us immediately after leaving you at Reed Hall. Only the two of you were upstairs when—" The duchess broke off to ask, "You saw no one in the hallway—no one on the third- or second-floor landing?"

As Dickon shook his head, there was the sound of hurrying feet, a thud, and a curse. A moment later Peter limped through the door.

"Tripped on that confounded statue in the hall," he announced as, rubbing his hip, he hobbled over to the duchess. "Here I am, Cousin Claddington. What's this about your diamonds being stolen?"

Dickon started as if he had been stung. "Your Grace's diamonds have been *stolen*?"

"So you are familiar with those jewels?"

Everyone in the room turned to look at Brandmere, who was standing in the open doorway of the suite. In his well-fitting gray coat and fashionably tight breeches he looked as if he had done little all day except to stroll through the orangery, but there was tension in his stance. An odd mixture of revulsion and triumph flickered in his eyes.

Dickon sneezed, excused himself, and bowed to the earl. "I have not yet thanked you, sir, for saving us this afternoon. My own life is insignificant compared to the safety of my niece. I pray that at some future day I can be of service to you and show—"

"You are familiar with Her Grace's diamonds?" Brandmere repeated.

Dickon looked astonished. "Naturally. Her Grace wore them last evening. I admired the gems—as did everyone else present, I am sure."

"So they should have done," the duke grated. "Bought those demmed stones last year and they cost me a demmed fortune. And now some demmed thief has got ahold of them." He turned a baleful look at his duchess, who had sunk back on the daybed and closed her eyes. "Aye, you may well look faint, madam. I beg you to remember that I never wanted to come to Somerset in the first place. That was your idea."

The duchess half rose on the daybed and said with energy, "We do not know if there *was* a theft. Pray do not prose on and on, Claddington." Ignoring the rude noise her husband made, she added, "Unfortunately, it is true that the diamonds are missing. Porter put them away in their case last night, and we placed them in a chest by my bedside. I locked the chest and pocketed the key. Today the case is empty."

It was curious, Brandmere thought, how history repeated itself. He watched Campion blow his nose with a delicate scrap of handkerchief and waited for the man to cover his tracks by blaming the servants.

"Has Your Grace considered the, ah, servants?" Dickon asked.

Sir Malcolm was the one to answer this. "I've ordered Mackerson—my butler—to convene the servant-wallahs. Eh? I'm going to interrogate them now. I'd appreciate it, Brandmere, if you'd come along and listen to what they have to say."

The earl agreed and followed Sir Malcolm out of the door. Dickon sneezed again. "I regret that I am not feeling quite the thing," he apologized. "With Your Grace's permission, I will retire to my room."

Suzanna went out into the hall with her uncle, and Peter followed them. He then shook his head and reflected that Dickon was looking pale. "Shouldn't wonder if you were coming down with the grippe," he continued. Then, as Dickon began to cough, he added helpfully, "Heard of a fellow who died from being dunked in the river. Frightfully unhealthy stuff, river water."

Dickon's coughs worsened precipitously. Suzanna ordered her uncle to bed and rang for some hot tea before recalling that Sir Malcolm's staff was being interrogated. She decided to get the tea herself and on the second-floor landing met Sir Malcolm and Brandmere.

"I can't credit it, Brandmere," Sir Malcolm was saying. "But that's the way it is. Eh? 'Cherchy la femmy' as the Frogs say."

"You have found the diamonds?" Suzanna wondered.

Sir Malcolm shook his head. Coldly, not meeting her eyes, the earl said, "One of the housemaids *appears* to be missing."

Suzanna did not miss Brandmere's emphasis. He

did not believe that the housemaid was the thief, but apparently Sir Malcolm did.

"What else would explain her disappearance?" he demanded. "The girl ran off this afternoon without anyone knowing where she was going. I've ordered the parish constable to get on her trail."

With his eyes on Suzanna's face, Brandmere said that he had little faith in the local constabulary. "The girl will reach London and disappear, and so will my cousin's diamonds. *If* she has them."

Sir Malcolm looked astonished. "Eh? You don't believe the wench stole that necklace?"

"Who then could be the thief?" Suzanna added.

Thieves, Brandmere thought cynically, were master liars. Campion's surprise over the missing diamonds had seemed almost genuine, but he was as guilty as Cain. And it was almost certain that Suzanna had acted as her uncle's accomplice.

Brandmere reflected that the Campions had been alone at Reed Manor for a quarter of an hour. This was more than enough time for Suzanna to distract the duchess's maid while her uncle made off with those diamonds.

He was angry with himself. Not only had he not warned Clarice about a thief in their midst, but he had also softened toward Suzanna. There had even been a moment when he had been terrified for her safety. Now he believed that Campion had engineered the accident to give him the opportunity to steal unhindered.

He had been a fool, but there was still hope. Thinking himself safe, Dickon might now become bolder and overplay his hand. Brandmere thought of telling Sir Malcolm about his plan to trap Campion but decided against it. This was a duel of wits between himself and that scoundrel.

Sooner or later, my lad, you'll make a mistake, he thought. *And I'll be waiting for you.*

Suzanna did not have a chance to write her note of apology, for following their interview with the duchess, Dickon began to feel feverish. "That young fool, Vries, might have the right of it, for once," he sniffled. "Man of my years could die of a cold."

"That is nonsense," Suzanna cried, but Dickon continued to act as though he were a ninety-year-old invalid. Toward evening he looked so ill that Malcolm had the local doctor stop in. Unfortunately, the man did nothing but shake his head and talk about fatal infections that were caused by river water.

Suzanna was worried. Flushed and shivering and with his dark hair concealed under a striped nightcap, Dickon's resemblance to her father was uncanny. And it was also ominous. Just so had Sir Bartholomew looked in his last illness.

She requested that a dinner tray be sent up to Dickon's room, and when he professed himself too ill to eat, she spooned the soup for her uncle. Then she sat by his bedside and bathed his hot forehead and finally watched him sink into a troubled sleep.

Evening shadows lengthened into night, but Suzanna kept her vigil. Downstairs, dinner was concluded, and she could hear the ladies leave the gentlemen to their port. Anabel stopped by to ask if there was something she could do, and later Sir Malcolm came by to see how Dickon did.

He walked up to the bed and frowned at the sleeping invalid. "Fever's nothing to laugh about. Seen enough of it in India. Eh? But I have just the thing.

Roots and herbs given to me by a *hakkim* in Myerspore. I've had it myself and I know it'll do your uncle more good than those potions the doctor ordered."

Suzanna was doubtful about the effectiveness of this concoction, but she was ready to try anything that might help. She was touched when Sir Malcolm himself brought up a powder which he mixed in brandy. Then he woke Dickon and held the potion to his lips.

Dickon sputtered and complained that the medicine tasted vile. Some of it spilled, and Suzanna went to get a cloth to mop up the mess. Meanwhile, Sir Malcolm coaxed the rest down the patient's throat.

"He'll do now," the nabob said. "Don't you worry, Miss Campion. His fever will break."

Dickon slept again. Sitting by her uncle's bed, Suzanna listened to his harsh breathing. She heard the guests coming upstairs to bed, the servants' subdued voices, and shuffle of feet. Then, Reed Hall settled down for the night.

Eventually, she fell into a doze. Suzanna did not realize how much later it was when she suddenly started up, saw that the fire had burned low and that her candle was almost down to its socket. She also saw that Dickon now slept peacefully. She touched his forehead and rejoiced to find it cool.

Sir Malcolm's medicine had done the trick, and now she could go to bed with an easy heart. Weary but grateful, Suzanna left the sickroom and walked down the hall to her own chamber. The corridor was almost in darkness, and she was grateful for the remains of her candle. But as she passed the multiarmed Indian statue near her door, the flame flickered and went out. In the semidark, Suzanna saw one of the statue's arms move.

She dropped the candle and opened her mouth to scream, but before she could do so, Brandmere spoke. "Good evening, Miss Campion," he said.

"What are you doing lurking about in the shadows?" Suzanna gasped.

"I could ask the same question."

She checked the retort that rose to her lips. It would never do to brangle with the earl a *third* time.

"I must have fallen asleep in the chair beside my uncle's bed," she said coldly. "His fever has broken."

"Of course—that convenient fever," he murmured.

Suzanna frowned at the earl's sardonic tone. "There was nothing convenient about it. Uncle Dickon is not a young man, and he sustained a shock when he fell into the water. It is not unnatural that he became ill."

The earl picked up Suzanna's candle, struck a match, and relit it. He then set it on one of the god's upturned palms and turned to face her. "He could have had worse."

"You mean he could have drowned."

Suzanna straightened her shoulders, lifted her chin, and looked the earl straight in the eye. "I am very thankful to you for having saved Uncle Dickon's life," she said.

He shrugged his broad shoulders and drawled, "Pray don't mention it."

Her eyes narrowed at his tone, but then she shook her head. "Oh, no. I have yet to apologize to you for the *second* time I raked you over the coals. I will not break straws with you again before I say that I am sorry for having been rag-mannered."

With her stormy gray eyes and the curl of her lips, she did not look in the least bit repentant, and in spite of himself, Brandmere was amused. He said, "Why should you be sorry when you were the soul of courtesy? All you said was that you wouldn't accept my help if I were the last man on earth."

Suzanna gritted her teeth. "I collect that I was entirely abominable to you, but it is your fault, too. It is not very easy to apologize to you, my lord earl. You have a way of looking at someone as if that person were an insect."

His lips had begun to twitch. "Is that what I do?"

She nodded but added generously, "I daresay you cannot help it, just as I cannot seem to hold my tongue when I should." She drew a deep breath and smiled uncertainly. "Will you forgive me—again?"

Brandmere felt her tremulous smile in some deep and hitherto unknown part of his being. It made him feel as though he were standing on an active volcano. Incredible, unasked-for thoughts and sensations whirled through his mind, and without conscious thought he reached out and gathered Suzanna into his arms.

She did not resist. As she felt herself drawn against the earl's hard chest, there was a roaring in her ears. Then that roar became sweet music. As though obeying the compulsion of that wild music, she lifted her face to him.

Their lips met with the force of a thunderclap. No longer was Suzanna sure where she was or who she was. It was not important. All that mattered was that Brandmere was holding her and kissing her with a single-minded thoroughness. She wanted to be kissed for the rest of her life. It was almost as though—

It was almost, Suzanna thought dazedly, as though she were in love with Brandmere.

At that incredible thought, some instinct for self-preservation surfaced in her befuddled brain. Involuntarily, she put her palms against Brandmere's chest and pushed.

The feeble pressure recalled Brandmere to himself. *My God,* he thought, *what am I doing?*

He dropped his arms and stepping back stared at the girl he had just been kissing. She looked back at him wide-eyed, and he felt befuddled. It was a state of mind with which he was not familiar.

Brandmere had been in military campaigns and had led charges. He was famous for his cool blood, even in matters of the heart. He had fancied himself in love several times, but he had never before had the sensation that the ground on which he stood had dissolved and that the air around him had turned to champagne. Even now, knowing that what he had done was as reprehensible as it was absurd, he still wanted to sweep Suzanna back into his arms.

The look in the earl's eyes was both exciting and frightening. Suzanna began to say, "Brandmere," but then stopped in confusion. Her soft red lips parted.

It was an invitation few men could resist. Brandmere gave his roving mind a savage shake and hauled himself back from the edge of disaster.

This, he reminded himself, was Campion's niece. Besides that damning truth, it was a fact that Suzanna had neither social position nor the accepted social graces. She spoke with a lamentable frankness and constantly infuriated him with the things she said and did. Also, she was addicted to that old ruin of an estate and antiquated beasts and servants.

Suzanna Campion was simply not the kind of woman that a man in his position could take seriously, yet she made his heart race.

Brandmere couldn't help it. His arms reached out

for Suzanna just as she blindly took a step forward toward him.

There was the sound of a door creaking open followed by footsteps. The earl jerked up his head and saw that Campion had emerged from his room and was walking slowly down the corridor.

The turmoil in Brandmere immediately subsided to a less confusing but much less pleasant emotion. He should have felt triumph that he had been right about Campion, but was conscious only of a bad taste in his mouth.

Suzanna had also turned her head to look over her shoulder, and her eyes widened in alarm. "Uncle Dickon," she exclaimed.

Brandmere spoke through clenched teeth. "Naturally, it is your uncle." Then, as she started to walk toward her uncle, he ordered, "Wait—stay where you are and let him come."

Bewildered by his peremptory tone, Suzanna protested. "But he could do himself an injury. Do you not see that his eyes are shut?"

Both the earl and Suzanna watched as Dickon, clad only in his white nightshirt and striped nightcap, negotiated the hall. Dickon's eyes were shut tight, his hands extended, and he walked like a marionette. Cynically, Brandmere thought that the man was no fool. Knowing that he was discovered, Campion was pretending to be sleepwalking.

"He has never done this before," Suzanna continued worriedly. "It must be that medicine Sir Malcolm gave him."

As she spoke, a door down the hall opened and Sir Malcolm, wrapped in a striped burnoose, peered out. "Good God," he exclaimed. "Sleepwalking, eh?"

"So it appears," Brandmere replied dryly.

Suzanna looked uncertainly at the earl. He had changed from the man who, a moment ago, had held her in his arms and kissed her so passionately. She did not like his tone or the hard glitter in his eyes.

But she had no time to refine on this. Going up to Dickon, she pleaded, "Uncle, please wake up."

She would have put her hands on his shoulders, but Sir Malcolm prevented this. "Dangerous thing to wake sleepwalkers," he warned. "I saw native *shikhari*—a tracker, you know—sleepwalking in Myserbad once. Beggar walked right through a patch of cobras. The snakes were coiled and ready, but they didn't strike. Then one of his mates raised a halloo and the fellow woke up—got bitten—and died. Eh?" He shook his head. "Never wake a sleepwalker."

"What shall I do?" Suzanna asked helplessly.

Dickon snored. Brandmere reflected that it was a pity the man had not turned to the stage instead of to crime.

"We'll have to guide him to his bed," he said. "If you'll take one arm, Sir Malcolm, we can turn him."

Together they guided the supposed sleepwalker to his room. Picking up her candle, Suzanna followed. She watched nervously as the two men deposited Dickon onto his four-poster and drew the covers over him.

"That's all right, then," Sir Malcolm exclaimed. "Now, Miss Campion, if you'll fluff up your uncle's pillows, he'll sleep till morning."

Obediently, Suzanna shifted the pile of pillows under Dickon's head. As she did so, she saw something glitter amid the folds of cloth. "What in the world?" she exclaimed.

She leaned forward, but Brandmere was much quicker. His hand shot out, reached inside the pillowcase, and drew something out. All at once the room seemed to blaze with light.

"I believe," Brandmere drawled, "that we have found my cousin Claddington's diamonds."

Chapter Seven

"**I** don't believe it!"

As Suzanna cried out, Dickon opened his eyes and blinked at the three faces ringed around him.

"Wha'sa marrer?" he slurred. "Is the house on fire?"

Suzanna put her hands on her uncle's shoulders and shook him none too gently. "Uncle Dickon, pull yourself together. You are being accused of stealing those horrid diamonds."

Wordlessly, Brandmere held up the necklace. Dickon stared at the gems as if hypnotized. "What," he stammered, "where—"

"They were found under your pillow, where you hid them," Sir Malcolm barked.

Suzanna rounded on him. "You mean where *someone* hid them. My uncle is not a thief."

She looked wildly at Brandmere, whose expression of contempt cut her to the quick. "He didn't do it." She wanted to shout, but the words came out in a hen-hearted whisper.

"I'm going to send for the constable," Sir Malcolm said.

Dickon covered his face with his hands. "I didn't do it. I swear I didn't do it."

Sir Malcolm strode toward the door and found Suzanna barring the way. "There must be some explanation," she pleaded.

"I already have all the explanation I need," Sir Malcolm growled. "Out of my way, girl."

Suzanna shook her head, and something in that mute defiance moved Brandmere to say, "A constable may not be the answer."

"Eh?" Sir Malcolm exclaimed. "What's that?"

"If the newspapers get wind of this wretched business, we'll all become three-day wonders," Brandmere pointed out. "My cousin won't thank you for that."

Sir Malcolm bit the ends of his mustache. "Something in that," he owned.

He glared at Dickon, who babbled, "If the diamonds are replaced, nothing need be said. Isn't that so? Gentlemen, I'm innocent of any wrongdoing. I swear—"

He was interrupted by the door banging open to reveal an irascible figure swathed in a purple dressing gown. "How can a man sleep with all this demmed noise?" Claddington wanted to know.

Dickon hopped out of bed, crying. "Your Grace, I can explain everything."

But Claddington was not looking at him. "By Gad," he breathed, "that's my wife's necklace!"

Brandmere handed the diamonds over. While the duke examined them, both Dickon and Sir Malcolm burst out with conflicting explanations. "Shut up!"

the duke roared. "Stop this demmed argle-bargle. Here, Brandmere, you tell me what's going on."

The earl obliged, and Claddington's countenance became suffused. His eyes narrowed to baleful slits as he regarded Dickon. "Take him out and hang him," he ordered.

Dickon blanched, and Suzanna cried, "But, Your Grace, my uncle did not steal those diamonds. He—"

Before she could finish her sentence, the duchess rustled into the room. She had obviously risen in some haste and was still belting her dressing gown of amber satin. "Whatsqoniuth?" she demanded.

Her husband held up the necklace and shook it. "Do you remember these, madam?"

The duchess detached a linen chin-strap that she wore nightly to preserve the youthfulness of her chin. "I beg you, Claddington, not to be sheep-brained at this odious hour," she said impatiently. "Where did you find my diamonds?"

In the midst of the tumult that followed her question, Anabel Traherne made her entrance. Even at this hour of night she was a vision of beauty in her embroidered silk dressing gown trimmed with swansdown.

"I heard shouting," Anabel said. "Has Mr. Campion taken a turn for the worse?"

Only Peter, hurrying down the corridor at this moment, heard her. Everyone else was too busy talking. Dickon was volubly protesting his innocence. The duke was reiterating that hanging was too good for Campion. His duchess was vowing that from now on she would not let the diamonds out of her sight. Sir Malcolm was bemoaning the fact that a crime could have been committed in his house.

In the midst of the commotion, Brandmere and Suzanna alone remained silent.

Suzanna was feeling physically ill. She wished desperately that she could faint dead away and so escape this horrible scene. There seeming to be no likelihood of this, she put her back against the wall and tried to think of some explanation for those wretched diamonds.

"You look ready to faint."

Brandmere had crossed the room and was pushing a chair forward. When she shook her head, the earl spoke coldly to counter the uneasiness that had begun to plague him. "You had better sit down."

"You believe my uncle to be a thief," Suzanna whispered. "I tell you he is not. If he were, he would not be so mutton-brained as to leave the evidence under his pillow."

Before Brandmere could reply to this, the duke bellowed, "I want this demmed villain taken to Newgate."

Dickon fell on his knees and clasped his hands in supplication. "You cannot condemn an innocent man," he wailed.

"Oh, can't I?" Claddington transferred his glare to Sir Malcolm and growled, "Well? What are you waiting for? Call the demmed constable."

Suzanna wrung her hands, and Brandmere frowned. Though Campion thoroughly deserved the fate that awaited him, he couldn't help pitying anyone condemned to Newgate. It was an accursed place where a prisoner could rot away in one of many dark, damp, subterranean cells. Very few who entered the prison's portals escaped except by way of the nubbing chit—as the denizens of the underworld called the gallows.

And if Campion were not hanged, he would most probably be transported to Botany Bay. That would be happy release, for the prison hulks were incredibly filthy and full of every conceivable disease and privation. Jail fever would probably finish Campion before he set sail for Australia.

Correctly interpreting the look on Brandmere's face, Suzanna felt true despair. She fell on her knees before the duchess.

"Please, Your Grace, listen to me."

When she looked into Suzanna's imploring face, the duchess's kind heart was touched. However, she had suffered a great deal of anxiety, and she would not soon forget the thundering scold that Claddington had given her about her carelessness.

She averted her head as her irascible husband barked, "Listen to you? Be demmed to that, madam. I'll wager my wig that you're Campion's accomplice." He wagged a beefy finger, adding, "You're going to Newgate along with your precious uncle."

Intent on the duke and Campion, no one saw Brandmere start. Claddington continued. "You'll both go to Australia, and good riddance. Now, Traherne, where's that demmed constable?"

"But supposing Campion and his niece leave England?" Brandmere asked.

Everyone turned to stare at him. Claddington's eyes bulged. "Have you taken leave of your senses?" He gasped.

Brandmere shook his head. "I'm trying to spare you a great deal of unpleasantness. I don't believe you would enjoy having your name and Clarice's bandied about by the press?"

Peter spoke for the first time. "Brand's right. They'd have a heyday. 'Duchess's diamonds nicked.'

Or, 'Peerless thieves prey on peer.' You know the sort of rubbish they print."

The duchess looked horrified. Seeing this, Brandmere heaped on more coals. "And it goes without saying that you'd be chaffed in the House of Lords, Claddington." As the duke winced, Brandmere continued. "You've got the diamonds back, and no harm has been done. If you wished, I would attend to the matter and make certain that Campion left the country."

The duke considered. "Demme me if I want to be the butt of jokes," he huffed after a moment. "And you're right about one thing. If it's puffed in the papers, there'll be a lot of talk. Perhaps you're right, Brandmere."

"But surely, one could not be *certain* that the Campions would leave England," Anabel exclaimed.

She stepped forward and let a disdainful look encompass both Suzanna and her uncle before addressing the duke. "Persons like these are full of trickery, Your Grace. Though Brandmere might think they had left the country for good, who could prevent them from returning secretly?"

"Once a thief, always a thief," Sir Malcolm agreed.

"Demmed if you don't have the right of it, ma'am," the duke growled. "Only place for criminals is behind bars."

Peter wished he could say something helpful. He didn't care a rap for Campion, but he was sorry for Miss Campion, who had always been kind to him and who was now looking so white and desperate. Peter wished Brand would say something in her defense, but the earl was apparently enthralled by Miss Traherne.

Anabel was saying, "I put it to you, Brandmere.

Can there be honor in thieves? Did they not also steal from *you*?"

Suzanna saw by the earl's set expression that he agreed with everything Anabel said. She despaired as the duke cried, "Well, Brandmere, what do you say now?"

As though tired of the subject, the young earl shrugged. "Miss Traherne is quite right. Prison is the only place for thieves."

The Campions were allowed little time to ready themselves for prison. During this short interval, they were guarded as though they were desperate and dangerous criminals. Two hostile chambermaids watched the dazed Suzanna's every move as she packed her few things. They then marched her down to the ground-floor anteroom, where a stout and grizzled constable awaited his prisoners.

Near this denizen of the law stood her uncle. He cut a sorry sight. His hands were chained together, his hair was disarranged, and his neck-cloth was askew. He sneezed repeatedly until told by the constable to shut his face.

"Gentry as goes bad is the worst of the lot," the constable said to Sir Malcolm who, together with the duke and Brandmere, had come to see justice carried out. "Rotten apples need to be warched off the tree, sir."

"Demmed if the fellow don't have the right of it," the duke agreed. "Now the woman, constable."

"Stop for a moment." Brandmere put his hand on the duke's arm and drew him aside, saying in a low tone, "Think carefully what you are about, Claddington. A pretty woman being arrested for this sort of theft will cause an uproar in the press. There may be speculations about your character, too."

The duke looked astonished. "My *character*, Brandmere?"

"This is something I couldn't discuss before the ladies, but you could well be assailed as a womanizer. The press may accuse you of keeping the Campion girl as your light-skirt." A look of alarm shot across the duke's countenance as Brandmere added, "Nonsense, of course. But if enough mud is flung, some of it may stick."

The duke was thinking of the pretty young ladybird that he kept in a house on Baker Street. He also thought of his previous *amours*. If the press should discover them and they should come to Clarice's ears . . .

The duke shuddered visibly. Hastily, he said, "Well, perhaps you have something there. There's no real proof against the girl, besides which, Clarice has a kind heart. She don't want the girl put in prison."

There was a cough behind them. "Well, your honors," the constable asked, "do I arrest the mort— I means, the young woman, too?" He looked disappointed when the duke shook his head but added briskly, "Right. I 'ave one thief to deliver to Jojo Hamper at Carchet-on-Water."

"But I want this demmed villain in Newgate!" Claddington cried.

Sir Malcolm explained that since London was some distance away, local criminals were housed at the jailhouse at Carchet-on-Water. "Don't concern yourself," he added reassuringly. "He'll be quite safe there. Hamper has quite a reputation."

Feeling too dazed to be grateful for her own escape, Suzanna followed her uncle and the constable to a rickety cart hitched to a pair of wheezing old horses. It had turned raw and a slight rain was falling as the constable's assistant drove the cart toward Carchet-on-Water. They reached this town an hour later and drew up before a ramshackle building that had been built on the riverbank.

"That's for convenience, like, so that prisoners can be loaded onto prison 'ulks," the constable explained. He added with a grin, "Australia's where yer going, my lad, *if* yer escapes the nubbing chit."

Dickon gave a groan, and Suzanna felt a desperate and unfocused anger. Dickon was not guilty of theft—she was sure of it. He was going to prison for a crime committed by someone else. But who had gone to all the trouble of stealing the diamonds only to let them be discovered again? Who had such a grudge against her uncle? Suzanna could not make any sense of it.

The constable was meanwhile hammering on the jailhouse door. When it opened, the odors of damp earth, filth, and peat smoke assailed them. Suzanna shrank close to her uncle as the constable explained matters to a youth with a flat, foolish face. This individual, who was apparently the assistant turnkey, grasped Dickon by the shoulder and hauled him into the jailhouse's dark interior.

As Suzanna followed her uncle, the few hopes she had clung to died. Just inside the jailhouse door was a small room with a cot, two chairs, a table, and a smoldering peat fire. There was also a heavy locked door.

Nothing but darkness yawned beyond that door, but there were sounds. As the assistant turnkey produced a key from his belt and opened the padlock on the doors, men's and women's voices were heard pleading, lamenting, or merely cursing. Dickon was shoved through the door, and a man snarled, "Get off me bleeding feet!"

"I beg your pardon," the terrified Dickon mumbled.

Suzanna's eyes had become accustomed to the dark. She now saw that ragged men and women were lying on the floor of the cell or sitting up along the walls. Some were coughing. Others shivered uncontrollably. The bare earth was muddy from the river and the wooden walls were damp and slimy with mold.

Dickon lifted his bound hands in mute appeal, but the assistant turnkey shook his head and grinned. "It costs three pennies to 'ave those taken off," he said.

Suzanna dug in her reticule for the coins, and the chains were removed. "Now, you settle down an' be good," the youth sneered, "and we'll call the gentleman ter 'is breakfast. If there is breakfast."

Seeing how pale Suzanna had become, Dickon tried to look hopeful. "I won't be here long. Deuce take it, girl, I didn't do anything wrong—the charge won't stick."

But she could tell that he didn't believe his own words. With the combined word of so many aristocrats against his, Dickon didn't stand a chance.

He lowered his voice. "Listen to me. Bribe the fellow in charge. A few amenities—a blanket, perhaps, and some decent food—can usually be obtained for a few coins."

She didn't have much money, but she did have her mother's pearls. Determined to do her best for her uncle, Suzanna requested to see Mr. Hamper. Obligingly, the constable said he would fetch him on his way out.

It took some time for Jojo Hamper to appear. When he did, Suzanna was not reassured. The turnkey was

112

a heavyset individual with a bulging stomach and tufts of hair slicked across the forehead. He stared at Suzanna and snarled, "What d'yer want?"

Affecting a briskness she didn't feel, Suzanna stood firm. "My uncle requires a blanket, if you please," she stated.

The turnkey put his head on one side. "A blanket. Anything else I can do fer you, miss?"

Heartened by his respectful tone, Suzanna continued. "My uncle is not well. He needs decent food. Beef, perhaps, or—"

A roar of derisive laughter cut her short. "Oh, la-de-*dah*." Jojo Hamper jeered. "The lady wants her uncle to have beef. And she needs a blanket. Perhaps your ladyship would rather 'ave a bleeding feather-bed fer 'is nibs?"

The assistant turnkey was laughing so hard he collapsed onto a chair. Behind them, the dark cell also erupted into guffaws. "Now, then," Suzanna heard a man sneer, "we've got a bleeding gentry mort 'ere. Let's see if 'is coat fits me."

There was the sound of scuffling and blows that muffled Dickon's cries. Neither the jailer nor his assistant moved to interfere. Suzanna ran to the prison door, grasped the bars, and rattled them impotently. "If harm comes to my uncle," she cried, "you will be to blame."

Hamper was tiring of his joke. "Look, missy, who cares what 'appens to yer uncle? If they doesn't 'ang 'im, they'll send 'im to bloody Australia, where 'e'll be flogged every day. That's if 'e survives the 'ulks. Them ships," he added meaningfully, "is powerful uncomfortable."

Something snapped in Suzanna's brain. She no longer felt afraid, only angry and desperate. Her eyes blazed as she marched up to the turnkey and pushed her face within inches of his. "How dare you speak to me in that way?" she shouted.

Such was her fury that Jojo Hamper actually retreated a step. Suzanna stepped forward and waved her finger under his nose. "You will give my uncle a blanket," she ordered, "and some decent food. And you will stop those brutes from manhandling him. Otherwise—"

"Otherwise, wot?" the jailkeeper sneered.

"Otherwise you will have to answer to me."

The new voice was deep and cracked like a whip. At the galvanizing authority in it, the assistant turnkey sprang up and stood at involuntary attention. Hamper himself turned ponderously about and stared at the gentleman who had appeared as if by magic.

Brandmere was dressed in black—a black coat and waistcoat and tightly fitting pantaloons that showed off the hard muscles of his thighs and legs. A black cloak lined with fur hung from his shoulders.

Suzanna gave a shriek of relief. Forgetting that Brandmere was the one who had found the diamonds under her uncle's pillow, she ran to his side and put an urgent hand on his arm. "Brandmere, thank heavens you have come. This man has incarcerated my uncle in that loathsome place, where he is being robbed of his clothes."

The earl leveled a cold and searching look at Hamper. Then he gently disengaged Suzanna's hand, strode to the barred door, and rapped sharply against the bars with his riding crop. "Stop that noise," he roared.

There was an instant silence. Calmly, almost negligently, Brandmere turned to the jailer. "You are a disgrace to your calling," he said. "I will have you replaced."

The jailer became voluble in his defense. He was only a humble public servant. Was it his fault that the young lady's uncle had been accused of a crime and arrested?

Coldly holding Hamper's eyes with his own, the earl drew a gold coin from his waistcoat pocket. He flipped it in the direction of Master Hamper, who caught it and tested it between his teeth.

"I shall have you replaced unless you find different accommodations for Mr. Campion," the earl continued.

Jojo Hamper was suddenly transformed. He showed yellow, broken teeth in a smile that would have done justice to a crocodile and assured His Honor that all would be arranged at once.

"Wot're you awaiting fer, stoopid?" he then hissed at his underling, who hurried to open the barred door and gesture Dickon out. There was respect in that gesture. Anyone who had a rich lord for a protector had to be treated with kid gloves.

As Suzanna made certain that her uncle had not been hurt, the assistant turnkey seized the lantern and flew out of the jail door. "We'll have Mr. Campion comfy in a few moments," fawned Jojo Hamper. " 'Twill be like 'is own mawther was seeing ter 'is comfort."

The earl nodded, but as Dickon began to stammer his thanks, he turned his back. The contemptuous gesture did not bother Suzanna, who was too busy being grateful. *Thank God he came when he did,* she thought.

Now that she had had time to reflect, it was incredible that Brandmere had come at all. Suzanna remembered the look he'd given her when Anabel had dissuaded him from letting uncle and niece leave England. Why was he here now? she wondered.

Hamper's assistant had reentered the jail and was whispering something to his master. "Will Yer Honor come this way?" Hamper gushed. "Mrs. 'Amper 'as found a room fer the gentleman which she is desirous as you should approve of, your magnificence."

Brandmere stood aside so that Suzanna and Dickon could precede him through the prison door. They emerged into a gray dawn that partially lit the yard that lay between the jailhouse and an adjacent dwelling. Here, on the second floor, a tiny woman in a dressing gown and nightcap was making up a bed.

She dipped her knee and chirped, "I 'ave took care of important prisoners in this room before this, Yer Honor. And I will go now and strangle a fowl fer the gent's breakfast."

Dickon brightened. Suzanna looked around her and saw a small but neat room, a good fire, a comfortable bed, some odd pieces of furniture, and a washbasin with thick towels. This was a considerable improvement on the barred cell.

More gold changed hands. Jojo Hamper looked positively radiant and nearly bowed himself in two. Dickon once more began to pour forth his thanks which Brandmere again ignored. Without even glancing at the man he had rescued, the earl strolled through the door and went downstairs.

Dickon turned to his niece. "Go after him," he cried. "Thank him. I'd be torn to pieces by now if it weren't for him."

Suzanna sped after their benefactor and caught up to him in the yard. "Sir," she began, "I must thank you—"

"I would rather you didn't," he replied.

But her emotions had to have some release. "Thank you for speaking up for us back at Reed Hall and for persuading the duke not to have me arrested, too," she cried. "And thank you for arriving in the nick of time just now. We owe you so much, my uncle and I."

"I've told you that there is no need for thanks," he replied. "No purpose would be served by having Campion die of jail fever. He should have a proper trial before being convicted."

She bit her lip. "But if you think he is guilty, why are you going through all this trouble to help us?"

Instead of answering, he said, "Shall we walk? I need to speak to you, and it is hardly pleasant conversing in front of this jail."

She took the offered arm, and they walked along the river road. The road was muddy and full of potholes in which an unwary walker could catch a heel, and avoiding these kept Suzanna busy until they had come to the village proper. Then Brandmere broke the silence that had fallen between them.

"What will you do now?" he asked.

"I had not thought that far. But I collect that I must take the accommodation coach back to Grapewood and bring some of my uncle's effects to him. Of course I will want to be near him until his case comes before the magistrate. There must be a local hostelry where I can stay."

As she spoke she saw a sign that read The Pipe and Dragon. Brandmere followed the direction of her eyes and demurred. "It may be some time before your uncle is brought to court. An inn isn't a suitable place for an unprotected young woman. Besides, it will be expensive."

Suzanna sighed. "Money. I had forgotten about that."

Brandmere watched the conflicting emotions fill her eyes and saw the dark smudges under them.

"Have you breakfasted?" he asked suddenly.

"I am not—"

"Your stomach," he pointed out, "is growling. What do you fancy? Eggs and kidneys? Plates of muffins? A rabbit pie?"

Suzanna could not believe the change in Brandmere. The haughty aristocrat was gone and in his place was the kind gentleman who had saved Uncle Dickon from a wretched fate. The man, who, moreover, had taken her in his arms. Hastily, she repressed such thoughts.

"I am already in your debt," she reminded him.

The smile that could transform his face softened his lips. "Do me the favor of breakfasting with me. I'm devilishly hungry myself, and we have much to talk over."

Suzanna allowed the earl to conduct her to The Pipe and Dragon. Here he bespoke a private parlor, a fire, and breakfast, and Suzanna forgot her past fears and her present problems as she warmed herself and tackled a large dish of mushroom fritters, goose and turkey pie, eggs, and ham.

But the edge was scarcely off her hunger before she pushed away her plate. Brandmere paused in his own hearty breakfast to ask if something was wrong with the food.

Suzanna shook her head. "But it is really too bad that with my poor uncle in jail, I can eat an enormous breakfast like this."

Privately considering that her poor uncle deserved jail more than most men he knew, Brandmere reminded Suzanna of the fowl that Mrs. Hamper was plucking for Campion's breakfast.

"I do not mean his breakfast. I am afraid of what will happen when he comes before the magistrate." Suzanna's natural optimism, brought back by warmth and good food, had begun to dim. In a low tone she added, "I collect that you believe him to be the greatest villain, and you are not alone in that view. My father thought that of him, and sometimes my uncle does things that make me wonder, too. But he has been kind to me. Now that he needs my help, I cannot do anything for him."

Brandmere had been watching her face as she talked. Now he leaned back in his chair and casually remarked, "But there is something you can do."

"What can that be? I would do any—"

"Would you sell Grapewood to me?" Brandmere interrupted.

Suzanna frowned. "That is not amusing," she exclaimed.

"I have no intention of being amusing. I'm making you a business proposition," Brandmere replied.

But he was having trouble concentrating on the business at hand. Brandmere could not help but remark on how the early morning sun caught the coppery glints of Suzanna's dark hair or the way it touched the curve of her soft mouth.

That mouth quivered a little now as Suzanna protested. "But you must be roasting me. Why would anyone want to buy Grapewood?"

He shrugged. "The place interests me. Besides, I enjoyed treasure hunts when I was a boy."

"That," retorted Suzanna, "is utter fustian. You do not believe Uncle Dickon's Bambury tales about buried treasure any more than you believe that the Silver Lady walks."

"You do your uncle an injustice. I've done some research into the subject, and there are documented historical reports that tell of money and jewels that disappeared around the time of Lady Blanche's murder. It's generally believed that the lady stole from her husband so that she and her lover could make their way to France. The booty was never found. It could be hidden somewhere at Grapewood."

Suzanna wrinkled her forehead. "It is the first I have heard of it," she said, "and I doubt that there is any truth to what you read."

A silence fell upon the private parlor. In that silence they could both hear the talk of guests in the common room, the chink of cutlery, and the landlord's cheerful voice. These homely, ordinary sounds brought a sharp little pain to Suzanna's heart.

She was homesick, she realized. She yearned to hear Little John grumbling and Mrs. Horry fussing at Margery in the kitchen. She wanted to hold a bunch of sun-ripened grapes in her hands and hear Porcina's piglets squeak their welcome.

"I do not want to sell Grapewood, my lord," she whispered.

Brandmere named a sum that took her breath away. Wide-eyed, she stared at him. But at the same time she knew that to her Grapewood was worth much more.

Suzanna remembered her mother carrying her into the grape arbor. She thought of playing hide-and-seek in the garden. She recalled a birthday celebrated in the morning room. Mama and Papa had both been alive and happy then, and there had been sunshine and laughter and the warmth of unconditional love.

Now everything was changed. Mama was dead, and Papa, too, and Grapewood was in ruins. The grounds had gone to seed, the gardens were overgrown with weed, and the house was shabby and worn and mortgaged to the eaves. And yet the memories it held were without price.

"I cannot sell it," Suzanna repeated firmly.

"You are forgetting," Brandmere pointed out, "that you are not the one to make the final decision. Your uncle is the inheritor. Naturally, you will discuss my offer with him."

But for the earl's kindness, "the inheritor" would still be in that terrible barred cell. Suzanna frowned as she realized that she could not continue to be beholden to Brandmere for Dickon's keep. Where was she going to get the money? The huge breakfast she had consumed—Brandmere had paid for that, too—suddenly felt like lead in Suzanna's stomach.

Had the earl put her under obligation to him because he wanted Grapewood? The thought brought Suzanna to her feet. Brandmere also rose, and they stood facing each other across the breakfast table.

As calmly as she could, Suzanna spoke. "I will repay you. I give you my word that I will. As to Grapewood—"

"You will talk to your uncle about my offer?" the earl interrupted.

His eyes still held hers. Was it her imagination, Suzanna wondered, or was there really a ruthless glint in those dark depths?

With an effort she kept her head high. "I am very much obliged to you for all that you have done, but I am sorry. I cannot sell Grapewood to you or to anyone."

* * *

Suzanna did not bring the matter up to Dickon that morning. She told herself that this was because her uncle needed time to adjust himself to his new way of life, but as she rode the accommodation coach back to Devon, she knew that this was not the real reason for her silence.

She was afraid that Dickon would want to sell. She knew that, and of course Brandmere knew that, also. Suzanna felt devious and dishonest and the coach rattled and bumped along the road, and it did not help her mood that a storm was brewing and a chill rain falling. Wind-whipped waves chewed at the north Devon coast, and Suzanna huddled into Cook's cloak and shivered dismally.

No welcome awaited her at journey's end. Since no one knew she was coming, no one was there to meet her. Suzanna hefted her luggage and tramped the mile from the posting inn in the village to Grapewood, where Little John met her at the door.

He was carrying a pan in one hand. When he saw her, he nearly dropped it. "Miss 'Zanna!" he yelled.

He half dragged her in, scolding and fussing like a bony mother hen. "What was you thinking of, walking all the way? And why are you 'ome so soon? You wasn't expected till tomorrow at the earliest." Little John peered over Suzanna's shoulder into the rain and added, "So, where is 'e?"

Suzanna ignored the fact that as usual Little John refused to defer to the new owner of Grapewood. "Is the drawing room ceiling leaking again?" she asked.

The old retainer's eyes smoldered. "It is, and the dining room has more 'oles than a sieve. I've used up every pan in the 'ouse."

"There must be new leaks in the roof. Please, will you start a fire in the morning room?" Then, as Little

John's mouth screwed up, she cried, "Do not tell me that the morning room is also leaking."

"Then I won't tell you, but there's a puddle by the old master's chair." Little John paused but then added, "I'll make up a fire, but best you change first, Miss 'Zanna, or you will catch yer death."

Nodding, Suzanna went up the stairs. Pots and pails and a soup tureen had been positioned at various points, and an umbrella stand had been pushed under a large leak on the second-floor landing. Suzanna glanced into the drawing room, where several other pots and pans were collecting rain. Then she opened the door to the morning room, went to the fireless grate, and knelt down beside it. As she arranged the scattered remnants of coals in the grate, Little John appeared.

"You leave that alone," he lectured. "You're not a servant 'ere, Miss 'Zanna, are you?" Then, as he built up a small fire, he added, "'*E* must be wanting in the noddle to let you come 'ome on yer own like this."

"My uncle was detained," Suzanna said coolly.

Little John made a sound that sounded like a snort. "By a pack o' cards, probably," he muttered.

Inwardly, Suzanna sighed. Old servants were hard to deal with because they were so often right. Disregarding the leather armchair with the milk pail beside it, she sat down on a faded settee and held her hands to the fire. "How is Mrs. Horry?" she asked.

"Not well, Miss 'Zanna. She worked 'erself silly when all those nobs from Lunnon came out 'ere. And," Little John added darkly, "my joints ain't been too good, neither, though I'm not one to complain."

"I told Margery to buy some liniment for your sciatica," Suzanna exclaimed.

Little John's long face lengthened still more.

"Margery's 'opped it, mum. Finally done what she said she'd do fer years and left yer service. Good riddance is what I says. And you shouldn't give 'er no character, neither."

So now there were just two old servants and a leaky old house that was mortgaged to the hilt. "How are Porcina and her piglets?" Suzanna asked desperately.

The old man's face lightened a trifle. "Them pigs are getting fat and big. They'll soon be big enough to eat."

Suzanna repressed a shudder. Naturally, Porcina's progeny must be eaten or sold so that the family could be warm over the winter. But they could not be sold for enough money to keep Dickon comfortable.

"Though I'm thinking 'e will have some other way of making money off they pigs," Little John was adding sarcastically.

"That will do," Suzanna said sharply, and when the old servant raised his hand to his ear, she added, "And do not pretend that you cannot hear me, if you please. You have said quite enough for one day. You may go."

Growling beneath his breath, Little John took himself off. Suzanna stretched her hands to the meager blaze, and as she listened to the dreary thud of rain, she tried not to think of Uncle Dickon a prisoner in the Hampers' house. He *could* not have stolen those diamonds, and she knew it, but no one else would believe him, not even his own servants.

"What shall I do?" Suzanna asked the disspirited little fire.

A drop of moisture was her only answer. Suzanna turned her eyes upward and saw that a new fissure had appeared in the ceiling. Through this crack dripped water that plopped onto her face and trickled down her neck.

It was more than flesh and blood could stand. "That does it," Suzanna screamed.

She leaped to her feet and shook her fist at the ceiling. "Have it your own way, you horrid old house. I *will* sell you to Brandmere!"

Then she burst into tears.

Chapter Eight

"His lordship is engaged in business with his solicitor, sir. He has left instructions that under no circumstances is he to be disturbed."

Marlin's respectful tone was firm. Peter scowled and gave his knobbed cane a twirl, thereby unbalancing an umbrella stand that stood in the hallway of his cousin's London town house.

"Dashed inconvenient," he complained. "I need to talk to my cousin, Marlin."

The valet suggested that Mr. Vries might care to wait. With darkling countenance Peter agreed. "But," he added feelingly, "it ain't any way to treat one's own flesh and blood. Stap me if it is."

Marlin deftly caught a vase that Peter's progress had dislodged, opened the door to the morning room, and seeing the earl's cousin safely bestowed in a chair by the fire, departed to bring restoratives.

So busy was Peter with his own thoughts that he did not see the valet leave the room. "Awkward business," he muttered. "Very awkward. Stap me if I ever thought it'd come to this."

Muffled voices were now heard as the door to the earl's study opened. "See to it, then," Peter heard Brandmere say, "and report to me when you're back in England, if you please. It is a matter of great interest to me, Flint."

"You may safely leave this matter in my hands, my lord." The speaker then lowered his voice and, try as he might, Peter could hear only an interminable mumble.

"Long-winded old bubble," he grumbled. "He'll probably keep jawing for hours."

He shifted in his seat, thereby dislodging a cushion. The cushion tumbled to the floor and knocked over the andirons by the fire. The clatter of the falling andirons caused the talk in the hall to subside. A moment later Brandmere was heard to say, "I'll wish you good hunting on the continent, then."

A moment later the earl came striding into the morning room. "At last!" Peter cried.

He shot to his feet and exclaimed, "Sir, I demand satisfaction of a gentleman."

Just then Marlin came in with glasses and decanters. "Sherry or claret?" Brandmere wondered.

"Don't want any damned sherry. Nor claret neither. I want—"

"Excuse me for a moment, old fellow." Brandmere turned to his valet and asked, "Has my curricle been brought around to the door?"

The valet's carefully bland face still managed to express a certain disapproval. "Yes, your lordship. And your bags have been made ready. However, if I may make so bold, I wish that you would allow me to accompany you."

The earl shook his head. "On this campaign I travel fast and light. I'll leave at once."

This was too much for Peter, who burst out, "Stap me if you're going anywhere till you've heard what I've got to say."

Brandmere raised his eyebrows and enquired mildly, "Well, what *do* you want to say?"

Peter stared significantly at Marlin, who made a discreet exit. He then drew himself erect and arranged his face into what he hoped were martial lines. "Brandmere," he announced, "I'm calling you out."

The earl burst out laughing. Peter turned a bright crimson and shouted, "Stop that, or I'll—damn you, Brandmere, will you listen to me?"

Abruptly, the earl stopped laughing. "You're serious," he exclaimed.

"I have never been more serious." Peter struggled to regain his earlier pose, gave it up, and cried, "You've played a scurvy trick on me, and I'm calling you out."

He seized his gloves and advanced upon the earl with the intention of flinging them in his face. Unfortunately, he caught his toe in the Aubusson carpet, tripped, and fell forward.

His cousin caught him by the arms. There was no mirth in his eyes now, and his face was stern as he demanded, "What injury do you think I've done you?"

"Don't think—I know!" Peter pulled himself free of Brandmere's grasp and glared at him. "You've been poaching on my preserves, Brand. Trifling with the woman I love."

Brandmere's face cleared. "Aha," he muttered.

"Don't you 'aha' me, neither," Peter flared. "I ain't one to wrap plain facts in clean linen. You pretended to hate the idea of going to Reed Hall, but once there you monopolized Miss Traherne's attentions. And you can't make me believe you ain't been dancing attendance on her since."

Brandmere sank into a chair by the fire. He crossed his muscled, booted legs and looked up into his cousin's agitated face. "Go on."

"When Miss Traherne returned to London, she was invited to Lady Jersey's crush," Peter spluttered. "So was you, and you *went*. And you danced with Miss Traherne. It was the same thing at Cousin Claddington's rout last week."

"You seem to have made a study of my movements," Brandmere drawled. "A great detective was lost in you."

There was a dangerous glitter in his eyes, but Peter was beyond caution. "There's worse." His voice rose to a squeak as he added, "Stap me if you didn't go to *Almack's!*"

The damning accusation hung between them like a poisonous cloud. "You *never* go to Almack's, Brand. You've said all along that you abominate the place, and the dancing and the dowagers, and the tepid lemonade." Peter paused to gulp air before plunging on. "You went there only because you wanted to see Miss Traherne. And now you're making for Sussex and Lady Fraby's second-daughter's come-out party because Miss Traherne will be there, too."

As Peter panted to a stop, his tall cousin spoke quietly. "I'm going to Devon, not Sussex."

Peter scowled. "You'll catch cold trying to gammon me."

"Are you saying I'm lying?"

Under his tall cousin's level gaze the young man became flustered. "Stap me, Brand, but it's shabby. I didn't think it of you." A plaintive note crept into his tone as he added, "You know I love her, yet you're going to offer for Miss Traherne. Everybody's laughing at me."

He threw out both arms, which caught the sherry decanter, and sent it flying. It crashed onto the hearth, spewing golden liquid everywhere. Disregarding this destruction, Brandmere said, "Sit down."

"I won't sit down. I've come to tell you—"

Very calmly, Brandmere interrupted. "Sit down, Peter."

Quelled in spite of himself, Peter sat.

"It ain't," he said mournfully, "as though I had much chance with Miss Traherne. But *your* courting her when you knew I have a *tendre* for her has made me look like a fool. Man shouldn't do that to his own flesh and blood, Brand."

"I would not do anything to hurt you." Brandmere locked Peter's eyes with his own as he added, "I give you my word on that."

Peter had never known his cousin to tell an untruth. Yet there was the evidence of the past few weeks.

"Brand, I don't want to brangle with you. But, I mean to say, it looks dashed smoky," he sighed.

"Things are not always what they seem." On the point of saying more, the earl seemed to think better of it. He got to his feet. "Have you given up the idea of shooting me?" Dispiritedly, Peter nodded, and Brandmere patted the young man's shoulder. "Good. I can't stay to explain, but it will come clear. Now I must be off to Devon."

Bewilderment replaced the indignation in Peter's eyes. "Why Devon, of all places? All that way with those uncomfortable inns and that wretched road.

You couldn't wait to get out of there last time we was down."

Brandmere smiled and explained. "I've bought Grapewood. Flint arranged the sale last week."

Peter's eyes threatened to pop out of their sockets. He made a strangled sound in his throat but could not produce a word. Taking advantage of this momentary silence, Brandmere strode to the door. "Good of you to call, old fellow."

Peter leaped to his feet, tripped on the carpet, and fell over a settee. While struggling to regain his feet, he heard the front door close behind his cousin. "Bought *Grapewood*?" he muttered.

He considered this idiocy for several moments and then shook his head. "Never thought to say it of Brand," he sighed, "but he's acting queerer than Dick's hatband. In fact, the man's gone clean off his chump!"

"Anyone who would want this place must be stark, raving mad," Suzanna sighed.

She put down her quill pen and stretched her back, which ached from hours of labor. In preparation for the arrival of Brandmere's land steward, she had all morning and early afternoon been trying to balance the ledgers that pitted Grapewood's expenses against its assets. It was a thankless task. Grapewood was definitely in the red.

Even listing Porcina and her offspring as assets hadn't helped, and at any rate, this was a lie. The pigs ate much more than they were worth. So did the hens, though they were temperamental layers and too tough to eat, and milk and cheese produced by the old cow still did not amount to much.

"Brandmere will send the cow to be slaughtered,"

Suzanna sighed. "And the old cart horse will go to the knacker's." Her voice faltered, but honesty forced her to admit that the earl would be a fool otherwise.

And Brandmere, though possibly insane, was no fool. He was rich and powerful and she was in his debt. Without him Uncle Dickon would be by now rotting in that terrible cell. "And," Suzanna told herself, "what must be, must be."

She comforted herself with the thought that she would at least be able to pension off Little John and Mrs. Horry. That is, she could do these things if there was any money left after the mortgages on Grapewood were paid and Dickon's creditors satisfied. On the old desk before her lay a stack of dunning letters from these creditors. Suzanna picked up a tailor's bill and tried to understand how a man could have paid two hundred and fifty pounds for a coat with large buttons. She was still studying the bill when she heard the sound of wheels in the courtyard.

That would be the earl's land steward. Suzanna returned to her unfinished ledgers and did not look up when Little John came shambling up to the morning room door.

"The Earl of Brandmere's come, Miss 'Zanna," he shouted.

Suzanna whipped around in her chair. "It cannot be Brandmere! His solicitor told me that he was going to send the land steward."

"Well, 'e didn't," Little John retorted irascibly. "The earl's waiting in the drawing room as big as life."

Did Brandmere mean to take immediate possession of his estate, perhaps even to reside here? Suzanna's legs felt rubbery as she rose to her feet. She felt even more unsteady when Little John remarked,

"All o' us 'ad better be looking for a new place to live, seemingly."

"It may not come to that," she began, but when she saw the unhappiness in her old retainer's eyes, her hopeful lies died unspoken. "I'm sorry," she whispered.

Little John's eyebrows beetled together, and his watery blue eyes became fierce. "You 'ave nothing to be sorry about, Miss 'Zanna," he growled. Then, pulling himself to his full, scrawny height, he added, "Whatever 'appens, I am proud to 'ave been in yer service."

Very stiff and proper, he preceded Suzanna down the stairs. Grieving, she followed. Late October sunlight was streaming through the landing windows, exposing the faded and torn places in the once-fine carpet, the chips, and the marks in the furniture. And there were water stains everywhere. In fact, the earl was standing close to the stone-cold drawing room hearth and surveying a huge stain on the ceiling.

He smiled at her and said, "An eagle, that's what it is."

Suzanna blinked. "I b-beg your pardon?"

"The stain on the ceiling looks like an eagle." Seeing her bewilderment, the earl explained. "When we were children, my sister and I would look at clouds and shadows and try to see what they resembled. Did you never play that game?"

Miss Minchin had not believed in games. Suzanna cleared her throat and said formally, "I did not expect you, sir. I had thought your steward would come in your stead."

He shook his head. "I'd some business this way and hoped it would not inconvenience you to show me my property."

He wasn't going to take possession of Grapewood today. Suzanna felt as if a mountain had rolled off her shoulders. For a little while longer she and the servants and animals could remain in their old home. She tried to keep her voice steady as she offered refreshments, but the earl said he was in a hurry and eager to see Grapewood while the light lasted.

Stopping only to pick up a shawl that was hanging in the hall, Suzanna led the way outside. Here a brisk autumn wind carried the scent of hay, woodsmoke, and the leaves Little John had been burning. Brandmere breathed deeply of these earthy odors.

"Nothing like country living," he observed cheerfully.

He picked an apple from a stunted tree. "It is probably wormy," Suzanna warned. "We have been using the fruit to feed the pigs."

"In that case, I'll take this to Porcina as a gift. How is she?"

He walked briskly to the barn, scratched Porcina's ears, and pointed out the runts of the litter. "I have a particular affection for those two," he said.

Suzanna swallowed hard. "What do you propose to do with them?"

In spite of her steady voice, Brandmere could sense her agitation. He was sure that under the folds of her thick shawl she was trembling. In a deliberately casual voice he replied, "Why, that depends on you." She looked up swiftly as he added, "It's my hope that you will remain here. Kittering's a good land steward, but much too busy with my other estates, and I haven't the time to look for a suitable chatelaine for Grapewood."

Her eyes had widened in sudden hope. "Then the servants," she stammered, "these animals—"

"That would be entirely in your hands."

Suzanna's face brightened. "I would like that above all things. But," she added painfully. "I thought you would want to make a clean sweep. Neither the servants nor the animals are particularly useful."

Her honesty made him smile. "I'm not concerned with such things."

Suzanna reminded herself that the earl was interested only in the so-called treasure. She knew she should again warn him that it did not exist, but she could think only of Little John and Cook safe and the animals reprieved. She was so grateful that she wanted to hug the earl.

Repressing this idiotish notion, she held out her hand. "Thank you *very* much," she cried.

There was a callus under the first finger of her right hand. There was a scratch on the back of it. Brandmere contrasted this capable, hardworking hand with the delicate white one that Anabel Traherne had just a few days ago offered him to kiss.

Obeying an impulse he could not analyze, he bent and touched his lips to Suzanna's hand. She withdrew it at once and looked uncertainly up at him.

"Miss Campion," he said, "It's I who am in your debt. Your staying here will free me to pursue other matters." He then added, "I'm eager to see the grape arbor. Since it gives the place its name, it must be particularly fine."

Suzanna's agreement was subdued. She was feeling quite out of patience with herself. It was not at all like her to tremble or feel close to both tears and laughter, but Brandmere's lips on her hand had made her remember another kiss.

With all that had happened, Suzanna had managed not to think of that incident. Now, with the earl standing beside her, memories were inescapable. Why had he taken her in his arms that night? Why had he kissed her and then a moment later helped prove Uncle Dickon a thief? And why did her heart still feel skittish when he was near?

Nothing that had happened since Reed Hall made any sense. Suzanna glanced apprehensively at the earl and saw that he was looking briskly about him. Brandmere appeared to have completely forgotten that incredible incident.

And she, too, must forget. Giving herself a stern mental shake, Suzanna led the earl through some untrimmed yew hedges toward a path that sloped downward to the grape arbor.

Because it had been built lower than ground level, the arbor was cut off from the wind. It was quite warm, and some grapes still hung among the yellowing vines. In the center of the arbor, a marble seat had been positioned so as to catch the afternoon sun.

"It's a pleasant spot," Brandmere observed.

Suzanna agreed. "It used to be my favorite place." She walked toward the stone bench and, seating herself, looked about her. "Papa did not enjoy sitting out here, but Mama and I came here every day, even in winter. After she died, I continued to come here until—"

She stopped abruptly, and Brandmere prompted, "Until?"

Suzanna hesitated. Then, with a little shrug she said, "I do not know why I thought of it. It was just that one night I could not sleep, so I slipped out of bed and came to the arbor. But when I came down the path I could hear Miss Minchin giggling."

She broke off, and silently Brandmere damned Miss Minchin. By bringing her sweetheart to the arbor, she had destroyed the child's refuge. He did not need to ask whether Suzanna had ever come to the arbor again—he could see that she had not.

He sat down on the marble seat beside her. "I also had a special place," he said. "Even my sister was persona non grata there."

Making an effort to shed painful memories, Suzanna asked why this was.

"Honoria hated water, and my kingdom was in the middle of the mill pond. One had to swim to reach it." Brandmere grinned reminiscently. "The shore was covered with interesting pebbles, and inland there was a mossy stone and blackberry bushes. A toad that lived under a stump. I called him Jabez."

Suzanna looked interested. "I once knew a toad. When I brought him bits of cake, he let me stroke his head." She added enviously, "Your island must have been a perfect place."

Her eyes had become dreamy and had a faraway look as if she, too, were looking at that enchanted place. Impulsively, he said, "Someday I would like to take you there, Suzanna."

Even as he spoke, Brandmere realized that he had addressed her in an unbecomingly familiar way. He knew he should apologize, but when she looked like that, apology was the farthest thing from his mind. What he *wanted*, Brandmere realized, was to take Suzanna into his arms and kiss her.

His intense expression was making her feel breathless. Suzanna drew a bracing breath, and was invaded by the earl's clean, vital scent. Suddenly she knew that she wanted nothing more than to be in Brandmere's arms.

Such madness frightened her. She edged a little distance away from him on the garden seat and attempted a rallying tone. "But," she said, "we are no longer children, my lord."

With his eyes still upon her, he replied, "Even so, we need a place that means something to us. A place that holds a part of our hearts."

Sadly, Suzanna reflected that to her Grapewood would always be this kind of place. "Does London hold a part of your heart?" she wondered.

"Not my heart, no. But I thought that the activity, the liveliness, the noise of the city, would divert me."

He spoke in an even tone, but she could sense his tension. "Divert you from memories of the war, you mean," she murmured. "It must have been terrible for you."

His dark eyes seemed suddenly to look into her deepest self. "What do you know about the war?" he demanded.

"You must have felt like a hunted fox, running with all the hounds at your heels. But for you the hounds were memories."

He drew a deep breath that was almost a sigh. "So many died at Salamanca. So many of my men—and many of my friends, too."

Some instinct told Suzanna that Brandmere had never spoken of this before. She listened intently as he went on. "Their death was something I wanted to forget, so I ran like the fox you spoke of. Only, London could not make me forget for long. The life I found there was meaningless and damnably tedious."

Though he attempted to lighten his tone, he could do nothing about the look in his eyes. That look went straight to Suzanna's heart. Impulsively, and without thought, she put both her hands around his and held them tightly.

That wordless gesture cut through Brandmere's reserve. But as he turned eagerly to her, she spoke again.

"Forgive me for having reminded you of such terrible things. Uncle Dickon is right when he says I talk too much."

Brandmere started as if he had been stung by a wasp. "Ah, yes," he murmured. "Your uncle."

Suzanna saw the earl change before her eyes. Warmth and candor disappeared as though wiped away by a damp sponge and were replaced by a masklike detachment. Abruptly, he disengaged his hand and rose to his feet.

"We had better get on with our tour of Grapewood," he told her. "The light will not last."

Then he turned his back on her and began to walk away up the path. Suzanna felt as if she had been slapped awake from a dream.

Brandmere had come to Grapewood not to see her and exchange confidences with her. He had arrived to take inventory of his property. She meant nothing to him—no, she meant much less than nothing.

Bleakly, Suzanna remembered that the earl considered her uncle a thief. And he most probably thought her to be Dickon Campion's accomplice.

Chapter Nine

"But if Brandmere's at Grapewood, what are you doing here?" Dickon asked his niece. "It seems rag-mannered of you not to have met him."

Suzanna removed her traveling cape and hung it on the hook by the door. "I doubt if the earl will care one way or the other."

"You can't hold a grudge against the man for buying Grapewood," her uncle pointed out. "We must all make the best of things."

He leaned back in his fireside chair and sipped his morning tea. On the table beside the tea tray lay a pack of cards and some dice with which he and Jojo Hamper had been gambling last night. When he moved, Dickon's pocket fairly jingled with the turnkey's losings.

"Yes, we must all make the best of our lot," he repeated complacently.

Suzanna noted that her uncle had put on weight since his incarceration and that a comfortable roll had begun to gather around his middle. "Your lot seems better than most," she remarked.

"We were talking about Brandmere," he reminded her. "Why didn't you stay at Grapewood to greet him? You are acting as his housekeeper at Grapewood, after all." Dickon's hooded eyes became keen. "Do you perhaps have some reason for *wanting* to avoid the earl?"

"Fustian," Suzanna retorted, but her cheeks felt warm. "If I thought that my visit would be unwelcome to you," she added sternly, "I would have stayed home. It took a great deal of trouble to set out on this journey, for Little John was determined I should not travel alone. He insisted on engaging Mrs. Horry's grandniece to act as my abigail, and the girl had no traveling clothes, so they had to be bought. And the accommodation coach in which we traveled last evening was certainly not comfortable."

As though soothing a ruffled hen, Dickon made clucking noises. "Don't fly up into the boughs. You know that I enjoy your visits. But," he added earnestly, "we must keep on Brandmere's good side. When I am brought before the magistrate, a word from the earl will carry weight."

Thinking of the way Brandmere had looked the other day when Dickon was mentioned, Suzanna shook her head. "There is no use hoping that Brandmere will help us. He bought Grapewood because of your Bambury tales about buried treasure, and when he finds out that there is none, he will be angry. I collect that words from an *angry* earl will bear even more weight."

Dickon waved an airy hand. "You worry too much. Besides, you are a pea-goose. Obviously, he comes to Grapewood because he likes your company."

An ache had developed in Suzanna's chest. "I wish you would not say such things," she retorted. "He comes to Grapewood because he has bought the place, and he allows me to stay there only because it is convenient to him. How could he enjoy the company of a thief's accomplice?"

There was such unhappiness in his niece's voice that Dickon felt an uncharacteristic twinge of remorse. Getting up, he crossed the room to put an arm about her shoulders. "Deuce take it, girl, what maggot have you got in your head? Brandmere can't possibly think that of you."

Her voice sounded muffled. "Why not, pray?"

"He didn't strike me as a man wanting in the cockloft, and no one but a fool could ever suspect *you* of anything even remotely wicked." He gave her shoulders a squeeze. "You couldn't be an accomplice if your life depended on it."

She rested her cheek against his shoulder for a moment. "You make it sound as though that were an insult," she sighed.

"As the world turns, child, it is. But I'll admit that I'm puzzled. Is it treasure our handsome young peer is after, I wonder? Or is he playing a hidden hand?"

Looking thoughtful, Dickon returned to his seat by the fire. "Brandmere has been a busy man of late," he continued. "That fellow Hamper tells me that the earl has taken to visiting Reed Hall whenever the Trahernes are in residence. *And* wherever Sir Malcolm and his daughter are invited, there is the earl."

The ache in Suzanna's chest worsened. It made her feel irritable. "You should not spread such gossip," she exclaimed. "You said yourself that the earl was welcomed everywhere."

"I *said* that he was a great matrimonial catch. Apparently, that goes for the daughters of rich nabobs. Ah, well. I suppose it's only natural that the fair Anabel aspires to being a countess."

When Suzanna was silent, Dickon added that his news did not come from one source only. "That fellow the constable goes everywhere and gossips like a mother's meeting. I learned a great deal about Brandmere's affairs from him when we last sat down to cards—ahem—I mean, when he stopped by to visit me the other day. I'm only surprised that the earl's engagement hasn't been puffed in the newspapers by now."

Before Suzanna could react to this, there was a clatter of horse's hooves and the squeak of wheels in the courtyard. Fearing that some poor wretch had been brought to the jail, Suzanna tried to ignore the sounds until a voice bellowed, " 'Urry up, then. I don't want to stand 'ere all day in the rain."

"That's Little John ," Suzanna exclaimed.

A wide-eyed girl now came running into the room. She dipped a knee and cried, "It's Mr. Little John, ma'am, and 'e's come ter fetch us in the carriage."

"What carriage? What are you talking about?" Suzanna hurried out of the room and leaned over the landing. She saw Little John standing just inside the door and called, "What has happened at home? Has Mrs. Horry been taken ill?"

The old man shook his head. " 'Is lordship 'as sent me in 'is carriage ter bring yer back to Grapewood. Forthwith, was what 'e said, Miss 'Zanna."

Brandmere wanted her back at Grapewood? Suzanna started to ask his reasons but checked herself when she saw Mrs. Hamper's avid face peering out of the shadows in the hall. She did not want to discuss family affairs in front of outsiders.

Little John apparently shared her feelings. "Best you be coming along with me now, mum," he rumbled. "I'll wait outside."

Suzanna explained matters to Dickon, who agreed that she must leave at once.

"I don't understand what sent you on a bolt to Somerset in the first place, Suzanna," he added, "but it's got something to do with Brandmere, that much I know."

Pretending to draw on her gloves, Suzanna turned away. Her uncle's sharp eyes saw too much for comfort.

"Since you won't tell me what has happened," Dickon continued, "I can't advise you. But keep your head. Watch. Listen. Think before you say or do anything that may land you in the suds."

Suzanna kissed her uncle's cheek and then went outside to where the earl's richly appointed carriage waited. Her abigail had already been dispatched to the inn where they had taken a room and was now panting up with Suzanna's small trunk.

Suzanna would have liked to have Little John ride in the carriage with her, but he was outraged at such an idea. "That sort o' thing ain't done, Miss 'Zanna, which you knows. The girl can ride inside wi' you, but I'll stay with the driver, as is proper. Now, you get in that carriage and wrap that rug around you."

"If you are going to be so stiff-necked as to remain outside in this weather, *you* will take the rug. But tell me now—what *is* happening at home?"

Little John rolled his eyes. "E's digging."

"Digging what, for heaven's sakes?"

The old servant cupped his hand around his ear. " 'Ey, what's that?"

Knowing that she would get nothing more out of

him, Suzanna climbed into the earl's carriage. But as she and her abigail settled themselves against the comfortable cushions, she felt an uneasiness that bordered on fear.

Dickon was right. She *had* bolted when she learned that Brandmere was coming to visit Grapewood again. But Dickon had not guessed that his niece had fled because she could not forget the last time she and the earl had been together.

The ache in Suzanna's chest became a gnawing pain as she recalled her talk with the earl. As they exchanged confidences in the grape arbor that day, something had shimmered between them. Though she very much wanted to deny it, there had been one moment when all creation seemed to stop. And in that shining heartbeat of time, Suzanna had realized that she was in love.

It was incredible that she should fall in love with Brandmere. It was irresponsible and ridiculous considering the circumstances that had brought him to Grapewood. But even so, it had seemed to Suzanna that Brandmere, too, had been caught in the magic and the madness. Then, at mention of her uncle, everything had changed.

Suzanna squirmed in the comfortable carriage. If she lived to be a hundred, she would never forget the expression on Brandmere's face. It had forced her to see her uncle as the earl saw him, and it was this knowledge that had driven her to take the accommodation coach to Somerset the previous evening.

Now he had summoned her back to Grapewood. As his housekeeper, she was bound to respect his wishes. But, Suzanna promised herself, she was going to make sure to keep out of his way as much as possible.

Suzanna was not conscious of time or of the miles

covered by the earl's swift-moving horses, but morning turned to afternoon and then to twilight before the carriage bowled into the courtyard at Grapewood. Even so, there was light enough to see the two deep trenches that had been dug near the barn and by the rose garden.

"I warned you," John told his mistress as he handed her down. "And there's changes in the 'ouse, too."

Suzanna looked about apprehensively and saw that several workers were engaged in erecting an awning over the front steps of the house. She picked up her skirts and walked swiftly past these men and through the front doorway. Here she paused and stared.

Grapewood had been invaded. Everywhere she looked there were people. Some were washing windows, others polished the floors or whitewashed the walls. Still others were ripping out the faded carpet, and a pounding from above announced that unseen workers were mending the roof.

"Who are all these people?" she asked faintly.

Since the servants' entrance had been temporarily blocked, Little John had entered behind Suzanna. He informed her that the earl had brought in his staff and a multitude of workers. "They're doing Grapewood over," he explained.

He was interrupted by two footmen who were carrying an enormous potted plant toward her. "Beg pardon, m'lady," one of them puffed as he staggered by her, "but 'is lordship wants this put down in the 'allway."

Suzanna closed her eyes and shook her head violently. When she opened her eyes, all this would surely disappear like a bad dream and the familiar, shabby old house would present itself.

"Are you making a wish?" a deep voice inquired.

146

Brandmere was standing on the second-floor landing. Apparently, he had been working, for he had removed his coat, and his shirt-sleeves were rolled up to the elbow. Before Suzanna could reply, he looked over his shoulder and called, "Take that outside and burn it."

Two more footmen had appeared on the landing. Between them they were carrying the leather chair that had been her father's. Following these men came two more with the faded daybed from the morning room.

That daybed had been her mother's favorite resting place. Suzanna bit her lower lip and lowered her eyes so as not to see it being taken away to be burned.

"I see that you are refurnishing the house," she managed to say.

"I'm making some changes." He broke off to call another order and then added, "Come upstairs, Miss Campion. I have some matters to discuss with you."

Her footsteps echoed on the bare wooden stairs, and the landing now lacked the wheezy old clock. As she passed the picture gallery, Suzanna caught a glimpse of servants who were removing paintings, dusting, and cleaning with a vengeance.

"In the morning room, I think?" Brandmere suggested.

The morning room looked more familiar. Apart from the missing leather chair and daybed, and with the addition of an elegant Persian rug, the room remained almost the same. Suzanna felt some relief which evaporated as the earl said, "Perhaps you did not get the message that I was coming to Devon? When I was settled at the Blue Boar last evening, I sent Marlin to the house to tell you of our arrival. I was surprised to hear you had gone to see your uncle."

"I did not know you required my presence."

Brandmere didn't miss Suzanna's stiff tone or the way she straightened her back and squared her shoulders. His voice softened as he said, "Your presence is very necessary. You see, I'm giving a house party."

Mindful of her uncle's advice to listen and watch, Suzanna nodded silently and waited.

"It will be held in three days' time," Brandmere continued.

She was startled into exclaiming, "You must be joking! Three days is hardly time enough to write invitations and order the food, let alone—"

"I've my reasons for haste," he interrupted. "Sir Malcolm and his daughter are about to go abroad on holiday. But there's no need to worry. I've brought down my staff from Brandmere, and they will attend to everything."

She looked alarmed at this. As if reading her mind, he added, "Foote is an excellent butler and will be careful not to tread on Master Little John's sensibilities. As to the other arrangements, the caterer has been selected, the menu arranged, and the musicians have already been hired."

It sounded like a military campaign. And all of this had been done because the Trahernes were going abroad. Suzanna reflected that Master Hamper and the constable had been well informed and reminded herself that the earl's matrimonial plans had nothing whatever to do with her. Still, she felt that she had to point out certain facts.

"Your guests may not be able to accept your invitation on such short notice," she warned. "Many of them will be in London and will have other engagements."

"Almost everyone I invited has accepted. My cousin Mr. Vries is coming, as are Stanhope and Freyden." The earl's lips curled in distaste. Suzanna was wondering why he would invite people he so apparently held in contempt, when he added, "Colonel and Mrs. Bender and Miss Bender accepted with pleasure, as have the Marchioness of Clavendell and her daughters. Doherty will act as their escort."

Brandmere paused. "And my cousin the duchess and Claddington will also be present."

Brandmere had invited the very people who had witnessed her uncle's and her own humiliation. Hoping that he was joking, Suzanna searched his face. He was not. In fact, he looked as he had that day in the grape arbor.

She swallowed hard and managed to say, "I see now why you wanted to speak to me. I agree that my presence would offend your guests, so I will stay away."

"You misunderstand. I want you to greet my guests at the door as though you were employed for that purpose."

"But why?" Suzanna cried.

"I need your help to bait a trap." When she looked bewildered, he added, "I plan to catch a clever thief."

"A *thief*?"

Suzanna's eyes widened. She looked as though she were about to faint. Brandmere moved forward with the idea of steadying her, but before he could reach her she ran across the room and threw her arms around him.

"Oh, thank you," Suzanna cried. "*Thank* you."

Instinctively, he clasped her tightly. She was

laughing and crying at the same time, and Brandmere felt her tremble in his arms. He could also feel the agitated beat of her heart against his, and the urge to protect her welled up in him until there was almost no room for thought or reason. And it was then that realization hit him with the force of a lightning bolt.

He loved Suzanna Campion.

He had loved her from the first moment he saw her across the bulk of Porcina. She had made him laugh, she had astonished and infuriated him, and she had forced him to examine his life. She had made him want to box her ears and at the same time ache to hold her as he was doing now.

Infuriating, exasperating, unconventional, and so dear—the earl's arms tightened further about Suzanna as he realized that love for her had driven him to try to clear Campion. It was for the niece that he had gone to these lengths to save a man he despised.

But as this truth touched his mind, Suzanna drew a little away. She looked radiant with relief, but tears sparkled in her eyes. Brandmere very much wanted to kiss those tears away but warned himself that this was not the time for declarations of love.

With an effort that was almost physically painful, he dropped his arms from around her and stepped back. "Are you all right?" he asked.

She did not notice the unfamiliar huskiness in his voice. "I *beg* your pardon," she was saying. Then, with a laugh that was also half a sob she added, "It was shocking of me. I hope you will forgive me. But I am not rainbow-chasing, am I? You *did* say that you wished to trap a thief. Does that mean you think Uncle Dickon is innocent?"

"I don't believe he stole those diamonds, no."

His dry tone did not dampen her enthusiasm. "Who is this thief?" He shook his head and she continued. "You suspect someone but cannot prove it. *That* is why you are inviting everyone who was at Reed Manor that day."

"It is as you have said. Well, Miss Campion, will you be my accomplice?"

His mouth softened into the smile that melted her heart, and it took some effort for Suzanna to remind herself that the earl was in love with Miss Traherne. Hurriedly, she moved some distance away from him.

"I would do anything," she said earnestly. "You know that I would. But I do not know whether I would be any good as an accomplice. My uncle says that I am shockingly transparent."

Brandmere grimaced. That was exactly what a loose fish like Campion might say. Unfortunately, in his niece's case, the man was right. Suzanna was much too honest to conceal anything—which was why he could not afford to tell her all his plans.

"It won't be easy," he warned. "In fact, it will be wretched for you. My guests will cut you shamefully. I am asking too much, perhaps."

He almost hoped that she would agree with him, but she did not hesitate for a moment. "I could bear anything if it would clear Uncle Dickon. And besides, I am suspected of helping to steal those diamonds. Miss Traherne said so at Reed Hall, and she was speaking for everyone."

"Not everyone," Brandmere could not resist saying. At his warm tone, Suzanna felt her heart begin to sing. Without meaning to, she took a step toward him. On his part, Brandmere leaned toward her.

"Suzanna," he murmured.

There was an apologetic cough at the door. "I beg your pardon, my lord," Marlin said.

The earl took several steps backward and collided painfully with a marble jardiniere. "What *is* it?" he demanded.

"My lord, Lady Danbury has arrived."

Suzanna saw a stricken look leap into the earl's eyes. "*Honoria* is here?"

"Yes, my lord."

"Hell and all its devils, man—what's she doing here?"

A nerve quivered in Marlin's cheek. "Her ladyship explained that she went first to London, where she met Mr. Vries. From him she learned that you were at Grapewood. She has informed me that she plans to remain here for several days."

Loudly and without restraint Brand damned his cousin's loose tongue. He broke off as a projectile flew through the air and whizzed past Marlin's cheek. Marlin did not flinch, but Suzanna gave a faint shriek as a toy soldier narrowly missed her before landing at her feet.

"Her ladyship's children are with her, my lord," Marlin added.

Brandmere glanced with loathing at the toy soldier. "Who threw that toy?" he barked.

A tow-headed urchin appeared at the door. He was very small and had blue eyes, a snub nose, and a rosebud mouth. He could not have been more than five or six. Behind him crowded three more boys of varying sizes but of almost identical appearance. The oldest, Suzanna conjectured, was perhaps eight. Brand glared at the boys. "The next man jack of you who throws anything won't be able to sit down for a week."

The boys looked back at him innocently. "Where's your mother?" Brandmere went on.

The oldest one acted as spokesman. "She's with Elizabeth and nurse, Uncle Anthony. Nurse," the boy added scornfully, "is having spasms. Again."

Footsteps on the stairs now announced a tall lady in a violet pelisse. A matching turban crowned her dark hair and gave her even more height.

"Lady Danbury," Marlin announced.

Handing her pelisse to Marlin, Lady Danbury sauntered into the room. She eyed her brother with languid disapproval, saying, "Really, Anthony, we have not set foot in the house for over a minute, and you are already shouting at the children. And glowering like a thundercloud, too."

"Honoria, *why* are you here?"

Paying absolutely no attention to the earl's quelling tones, Lady Danbury walked over to him and presented her cheek for his kiss. Suzanna now noted that brother and sister wore similar, obstinate expressions.

"You are a very hard man to find, Anthony," Lady Danbury accused him. "It is really too bad the way you flit about. It shows a lack of mental balance. As dear Papa used to say, a rolling stone cannot gather moss."

"Why—are—you—here?" The smallest of the boys had climbed up on a chair and was beginning to jump up and down. The earl walked up to him, lifted him up by the scruff of his jacket, and gritted out, "So. We meet again, Augustus."

"That is not Augustus. It is Percival. *This* is Augustus, and this is Lancelot. And here is the future Danbury—Jeremy, make your bow to your uncle." Lady Danbury paused to add feelingly, "You have been away from your family so long, you cannot even recognize your nephews. That is a disgrace."

Brandmere dropped his nephew to earth and turned his back. It was a mistake, since the other three boys immediately began to scuffle among themselves. Their mother watched them dotingly whilst pointing out, "I collect dear Mama saying that gentlemen required time to settle down, but you are nearly thirty. It is high time, Anthony."

As Suzanna listened in tongue-tied astonishment, she saw something move outside the door. A small girl was creeping along the floor on her stomach. Suddenly, the child sprang up and jabbed a sharp object into Marlin's left calf.

The valet started violently and shouted, "Godalmighty!"

Lady Danbury turned her turbaned head and surveyed Marlin. "Anthony," she spat out, "that man has just used profane language in front of females and young children."

Brandmere was conscious of a great wave of fellow feeling toward his valet. "Ah, Marlin," he commanded, "see that tea is served to the children in the nursery."

But the scarlet-faced Marlin's sangfroid had completely deserted him. "The nu-nursery, my lord?" he stammered.

"The nursery, man. The place," Brandmere added significantly, "to which my nephews and niece can be removed."

Suzanna spoke for the first time. "The blue room on the third floor used to be my nursery. It is a large and *sturdy* room."

Marlin sent her a look that fairly quivered with gratitude. Lady Danbury also turned to Suzanna, and lifting a quizzing glass that hung around her neck, scrutinized her languidly.

There was a cough upon the stairs, and a gaunt, harried-looking female appeared on the scene. "Ah, there you are, Nurse," Lady Danbury remarked. She dropped her quizzing glass and smiled at her offspring, saying, "Nurse will see to your tea, my darlings."

"Come, my dears," the newcomer sighed. Nobody paid her any attention. The little girl was poking at the walls with the penknife in her hand, and her two older brothers had commenced to race about the room. The smaller boys meanwhile flung themselves on the carpet and began to kick each other.

Brandmere confiscated the penknife. He then grasped his two older nephews by their collars, held them several inches above the ground, and bellowed, "Stop!"

His roar caused the windowpanes to rattle. All activity ceased. The older boys hung helplessly in their uncle's grasp, the little girl stared with her mouth open, and the small boys on the floor stopped rolling about.

Lady Danbury's eyes narrowed ominously. "Anthony," she began.

Ignoring his sister, the earl spoke in the same compelling voice. "The last child to leave this room will have no tea. Not even one cake or biscuit. Not even one crumb. And no dinner, either."

It was the voice he had used on the battlefield. It was effective. The children looked at each other, then stampeded for the door. The marble jardiniere went one way, a gilded-wood armchair another.

"Marlin," Brand commanded, "do your duty."

Bowing, the valet limped away. Lady Danbury

looked after him in profound disapproval. "I would not," she announced, "allow that man to come within a mile of my children. A servant who *swears*, Anthony. It is the outside of enough."

There was the sound of a muffled shriek. "Elizabeth's fallen down the stairs," a gleeful voice announced. "Augustus pushed her."

Instead of rushing outside to see what had become of her progeny, Lady Danbury strolled to a cane-backed chair by the fireplace and settled herself upon it. She spread out her skirts and folded her hands in her lap. This done, she turned to Suzanna and regarded her complacently.

"You are, of course, Miss Campion?" When Suzanna curtsyed, her ladyship continued graciously. "I am pleased to meet you. I have wanted to meet you this long while."

"M-ma'am?"

Lady Danbury smiled. "I shall explain. I collect that it was after he visited Grapewood that my brother was seized with the desire to visit his ancestral seat at Brandmere. He has not set foot on that property for over a year, and I had begun to despair that he would ever again have any family feeling of any kind. His going to Gloucester was your doing, Miss Campion."

"Honoria," Brandmere interrupted, "how long do you intend to stay?"

As if he had not spoken, Lady Danbury rambled on. "Miss Campion, my brother does not favor *me* with his confidences. However, that sap-skulled cousin of ours, Peter Vries, told me that it was only after a visit to Grapewood that Anthony recalled his neglected duties as the heir to our ancient name." She shot a significant look in Brandmere's direction and added, "Under your direction, Miss Campion, it seems that Anthony became interested once more in animal husbandry. I am deeply in your debt, since it is undoubtedly you who awoke better feelings in my brother's breast."

Finding her voice at last, Suzanna murmured, "Ma'am, I beg you will not think that I—"

Her ladyship raised a hand. "Say no more. I know what I know."

"And *I* know," Brandmere exploded, "that your visit is damnably inconvenient. There's going to be a house party here in three days' time, and I won't have those brats raising hell with the staff or with my guests. If they put pepper in the men's snuffboxes or soap in the cream, I will drown the little beasts."

Lady Danbury stiffened. "You would offer violence to innocent babes?"

"Indeed I would. I would offer the most barbaric violence possible."

They glowered at each other for a moment. Her ladyship then put a hand on her heart and sighed melodramatically.

"So be it. I will instruct Nurse to keep my angels in the nursery during your house party. However, I trust that *I* may appear in society?" She matched her brother's glare with her own and then turned to Suzanna. "Come, my dear," she said loftily. "I beg you will escort me to my chamber. That is, if a clean room can be found in this bear garden. I do not blame *you*, of course, knowing what kind of man my brother is. *Really*. To redecorate the house just before a party is the outside of enough."

Her ladyship rose and perambulated toward the door. As she opened it, there was the sound of a crash in the near distance and a howl of childish laughter.

Suzanna turned to look at Brandmere and saw wrath struggle with rueful humor in his eyes.

"Carry on, Miss Campion," the earl said.

Chapter Ten

Grapewood was under siege.

Any ghosts wishful of haunting its corridors were routed by a procession of caterers and musicians and the earl's well-trained staff. Brandmere's butler, Foote, led his battalion of chambermaids, housemaids, footmen, and grooms in making ready for the impending house party, and such was his efficiency that within forty-eight hours it seemed as if Grapewood had always been a gracious, well-ordered household.

Neither the cook nor Little John felt slighted. In fact, Cook swelled with pride that she could oversee the work of two male *sous* chefs, a scullery maid, and a pot boy. Little John, given mastership over two underfootmen, complained less and sometimes even hummed under his breath.

Suzanna was consulted at every turn. It was she who decided the placement of the guests. She also arranged last-minute changes in the menu and orchestrated the deposition of new pieces of furniture.

And if this were not enough, there was the problem of Lady Danbury and her offspring.

Brandmere had originally intended to put up at the Blue Boar nearby. After his sister's arrival, however, he removed to Grapewood, where he managed to keep Lady Danbury's five children reasonably quiescent. An uneasy peace lasted during the first forty-eight hours of her ladyship's stay, but on the third day the earl had business to attend to. He drove away and took his valet with him, and as soon as the dust had settled behind their uncle's curricle, the children went into action.

Augustus and Percival played tag through the house. Elizabeth lurked behind furniture so that she could leap out and scare the servants. Lancelot slid down the banisters and collided with Little John, who threatened to give his notice then and there.

"It's more than flesh nor blood can stand, mum," he complained to Suzanna later. "Those imps 'ave terrorized the 'ouse'old."

Suzanna went in search of the children's mother and found her sniffling over a romantic novel. Lady Danbury listened to Suzanna placidly then commented, "They are high spirited, that is all. Children should not be held back from their natural inclinations."

"But those inclinations have reduced the staff to tears," Suzanna argued. "The servants are on the point of revolt. Lancelot has been putting spiders in the pantry, and the youngest housemaid swears that Percival made such a face at her that she nearly swooned. And just this morning Marlin complained that his tea tasted salty. Apparently, Jeremy had put salt into the sugar bowl."

Lady Danbury narrowed her eyes. "Do not talk to

me about that man. He uses the vilest language in front of females and young children. I cannot understand how my brother keeps such a creature in his employ. By the by, Miss Campion, do you know where Anthony has ridden off to?" When Suzanna shook her head, her ladyship frowned. "He *flits* too much."

She closed her book and looked meaningfully at Suzanna.

"I had hoped," she said, "that my brother might be ready to settle down when he returned from the wars. But what must he do but racket off to London, where he leads a life of frivolity and associates with fribble who have nothing but sawdust in their heads."

Recalling the bleak look on Brandmere's face when he had spoken of his lost friends, Suzanna murmured, "Perhaps he has reasons for acting as he does."

Lady Danbury sniffed. "Gentlemen," she said repressively, "always have *reasons* for behaving like perfect blocks. However, I must admit I had hopes when he came to Grapewood." She saw Suzanna's startled look and explained. "It is here that he met the Traherne girl. It has been an *on dit* lately that he seems to go everywhere Miss Traherne goes. I have not seen the girl, but I am told she is a nonpareil. Is she?"

When Suzanna agreed that Miss Traherne was the reigning beauty of the past two Seasons, Lady Danbury tapped her book thoughtfully. "I should have thought that Anthony was not a man to dangle after a pair of handsome eyes. What is the girl's character like? That is what I should like to know."

Loud screams from outside interrupted her ladyship at this point. She looked vaguely toward the window, made some comment about high spirits, and added, "Do you see what is occurring, dear Miss Campion. I am persuaded you will soon set things to rights."

Leaving Suzanna to investigate, she returned to her novel. Suzanna went downstairs, where she discovered that, despite the awful din, none of the staff had gone outside to see what was the matter. In fact, the servants seemed to be in hiding, for she met not one of them on her way out of doors.

It was late afternoon. By the sunlight that lay thick and golden over the grounds, Suzanna saw four of Lady Danbury's brood circling one of the trenches Brandmere had caused to be dug. Fearing that the imps had trapped some victim, Suzanna hurried toward them, calling, "Has someone been hurt?"

The four children eyed her with silent suspicion, but the screams increased in volume. Suzanna reached the lip of the hole and saw that Lancelot had been buried up to the neck in damp earth.

"Let me out, me hearties, let me out," Lancelot was shouting. "Blackbeard never forgets them as harm him!"

Suzanna looked at Jeremy. "I think that you had better explain."

Lady Danbury's oldest looked sulky. "We are playing pirates. Lancelot is Blackbeard and has broken the rules of the brethren of the coast. He must suffer for what he has done."

Suzanna remembered a time when she was very young and had tried to get Ione and Porcina to play a game of pirates. It hadn't been a success. "What are you going to do to Lan—to Blackbeard?" she asked.

"We're going to leave him buried on this sandy beach so that the tide will drown him and the crabs will eat him."

"But there is no tide," Suzanna pointed out, then winced as she saw several large buckets full of water.

"We couldn't find any crabs," Elizabeth explained, "so this box of spiders will have to do."

Suzanna smiled. "I see that you have thought this out very well."

Lady Danbury's brood looked at Suzanna with new respect. She was, they decided, an unusually reasonable person for an adult. Jeremy unbent so far as to tell Miss Campion that she could stay and watch Blackbeard's execution.

"Thank you. I would like that above all things." Suzanna sat down on a stone near the trench, then offhandedly asked, "Of course, you have got the map out of Blackbeard?" The children turned to look at her. "I mean the map to Lady Blanche's treasure."

Elizabeth took the bait. "D'you mean that the ghost has a treasure?"

Suzanna began to spin a gory and dramatic tale that eclipsed any that Dickon had ever invented. By the time she had finished, her audience was spellbound.

"I heard Uncle Anthony talking to Mama about a treasure," Augustus piped up. "Mama said it was a whisker, but Mama doesn't know *anything*. Is there really a buried treasure?"

"I don't believe it," Jeremy said stoutly. He was the oldest and felt he had to assert his leadership. "I bet Uncle Anthony don't believe it, neither."

Suzanna shrugged her shoulders. "Why else would he have caused these ditches to be dug? But of course you may be right, Jeremy. It must be a farradiddle that the treasure is buried under an old oak that had been struck by lightning."

Elizabeth stiffened like a foxhound on the scent.

"There's a tree like that on the other side of the house," she yelped.

Followed by her three brothers, she skimmed off. Lancelot bellowed to be helped out so he could go, too, but was ignored, so Suzanna clambered down into the ditch and rescued him.

The muddy little boy emerged, scrambled out of the ditch, then paused and looked down at Suzanna. "You done me a good turn," he told her gravely. "Blackbeard always repays his debts, me hearty. You see if he don't."

Suzanna kept a straight face till Lancelot was out of earshot. Then she leaned against the side of the ditch and had the first laugh she had had in several weeks. She laughed till her sides ached.

"Don't tell me that the brats have driven you stark, raving mad!"

Suzanna looked up and saw Brandmere standing on the lip of the trench. She wiped her streaming eyes and said weakly, "Not at all. I have just rescued Blackbeard the Pirate."

He lifted his eyebrows at this but said only, "You look as if you could do with some rescuing yourself."

Suzanna glanced down at herself and saw that her skirts were muddy, her shoes a ruin. When Brandmere extended a hand to help her out of the ditch, she shook her head and protested, "I will cover you with this stuff."

Brandmere leaned down, caught her hands, and with one swift movement swung her over the lip of the ditch. Caught by surprise, she lost her footing and stumbled and fell forward against him.

Hastily, Suzanna drew away. "Oh, dear. Now I have got mud all over you."

"It isn't the first time. Dare I ask for an explanation about Blackbeard?" She told him, and he grinned. "Those ruffians. My fault for not having the ditches filled in, I suppose, but they must remain as they are for now."

"For what reason? I assume you were looking for that bogus treasure, but since it was not found—"

"It's lucky for Lancelot that you found him when you did," he interrupted. "The staff wouldn't have lifted a finger to save him from being drowned and eaten by crabs. Neither would I, come to think of it."

Her eyes brimmed with merriment. "I am persuaded that you do not mean that. Just think—Lancelot could have contracted a cold and the entire household would have had to wait on him hand and foot. That would have caused a few megrims. And your sister would have blamed you for a lack of family feeling."

Brandmere winced. "I can imagine how they terrorized the household while I was gone. I'm sorry I deserted in the face of enemy fire, but there was a matter that needed to be seen to."

"Something concerning tomorrow?" He nodded, and she cried, "I am eager for tomorrow to come."

The earl looked into Suzanna's clear eyes and felt a sudden qualm. For the first time, he had doubts about involving her in his scheme.

"I met my cousin Clarice while I was in London. Claddington was with her and made no bones about the way he feels toward your uncle—and about you." She could not help wincing, and he spoke in a different tone. "It won't do. You must leave Grapewood before they come."

"But you told me—"

"I know what I said, but it will not *do*. They will

cut you to ribbons. You must leave Grapewood to-night and visit your uncle."

He put both hands on her shoulders and looked searchingly down at her, and Suzanna had the strangest sensation. It was as though her bones were melting under his touch and that the rest of the world had disappeared into thin air. Grapewood no longer existed. Dickon ceased to matter. Only she and Brandmere had any reality.

She held her breath as he spoke in a voice she had never heard him use before. "I can't let you go through with this, my dear. You see, I—"

His words were sheared away by a blood-curdling whoop that was followed immediately by yells and hoots of laughter. Next moment there was a jarring thud and the sound of Marlin's curses.

The commotion was coming from the carriage house. Letting go of Suzanna, Brandmere strode off in that direction. Suzanna ran after him, but he out-distanced her, and when she caught up to him near the carriage house, the earl was helping his valet to stand up. Suzanna observed that the red-faced Marlin was clutching a metal box.

He spoke in a mortified voice. "I beg that you will not concern yourself, my lord. I am sorry that I disturbed you with my—I'm very sorry, my lord—and madam."

Marlin glanced apologetically at Suzanna as he spoke. Recalling that he had been about to divulge the whole of his plan to Suzanna, Brandmere was not sure whether he was glad or sorry that Marlin had "disturbed" their conversation when he did.

He said, "No need to tell me what happened. The brats ambushed you."

All of Marlin's training could not prevent a shudder. "They caught me off guard, so to speak. I had just come from the inn, where I'd left—"

"Quite so," Brandmere interrupted.

Marlin glanced at Suzanna again. He coughed and resumed. "I had returned to Grapewood and had a word with the grooms, my lord. I was walking to the house when the young persons leaped from the shadows. I suspect that they were playing at being Mohocks."

Brandmere announced that he would speak to Lady Danbury, but Marlin demurred. "I beg you will not do so, my lord. If anything, that would only encourage the young persons, and they may do something that would spoil the—ah, that is, they may act in an untoward way. It is my own fault for letting down my guard. It has been many years since the Peninsula. One forgets."

Marlin drew himself up and spoke no longer as the earl's valet but as his batman. "Next time," he vowed, "I will be ready."

For a moment Suzanna thought that the valet was going to salute. Instead, he bowed and withdrew, clutching the metal box even closer to him.

"He is right, you know," she said.

Engaged in watching Marlin's retreat, Brandmere spoke absently. "What do you mean?"

"You must not be afraid that my feelings will be hurt," Suzanna replied. "I am not so hen-hearted as to spoil your plans by leaving Grapewood now." She met his searching gaze and added staunchly, "I promise that I will be there to greet your guests tomorrow, and that I will be ready for *anything*."

It was afternoon by the time a carriage with a ducal crest bowled into Grapewood's courtyard. From her station on the top outer step. Suzanna watched as Brandmere's groom held the horses' heads and his underfootman bent to lower the carriage step.

Claddington alighted first, leaned on his cane, and glared at the earl, who, hands in pockets, was strolling down to greet him.

"Demmed roads," he growled. "Government should do something about 'em. And the inns—pah! Racked up at a wretched little posting inn with demmed shocking food." The duke banged his stick on the ground and added peevishly, "I'll tell you to your head that it's a maggoty idea having a house party at this time of year. Wouldn't have come if Clarice hadn't insisted on it."

The duchess leaned out of the carriage and exclaimed, "For heaven's sakes, Claddington, stop spluttering and assist me down." When he had done so, she offered Brandmere her cheek to kiss and looked about her. "I confess I came because I was curious to see the changes you had made, Anthony. It could be a charming place if only—"

Her Grace's words died away as she spotted Suzanna. The duke, noticing his wife's fixed stare, turned to look over his shoulder. As Suzanna sank into a deep curtsy, he snorted and turned his back.

Mentally, Suzanna shrugged her shoulders. She had prepared herself for this sort of behavior. But the duke had not finished. In a loud voice he demanded to know what the trollop was doing here.

"Miss Campion has been employed as my servant," Brandmere explained. "Poetic justice, don't you agree?"

It wasn't what he said, it was *how* he said it. Forewarned as she was, Suzanna still felt as if Brandmere had slapped her.

"Servant?" the duke repeated. "Oh—I see. Demmed clever of you, my boy." Chuckling, he poked the earl with a beefy finger. "Law mightn't be able to touch the doxy, but you can make her squirm, hey?"

Coolly, Brandmere removed the duke's prodding finger. "How perceptive of you, Claddington."

He was *acting*, Suzanna told herself, but the scorn in Brandmere's voice sounded so real that she felt quite chilled.

The duchess glanced at Suzanna's white face and hastily averted her eyes. It was not, she thought, like Anthony to be deliberately cruel. The Campions were thieves, but even so . . .

Unhappily, the duchess reminded herself that the Good Book called for an eye to replace an eye.

"But it's a dangerous game, hey?" the duke was saying. "Demmed hussy may steal us blind."

Claddington did not trouble to lower his voice, and his remarks were heard by the underfootmen, the groom, and by Foote, who was standing just behind Suzanna. These personages also heard Brandmere reply, "Do you take me for a fool? She's being carefully watched. I don't want a repeat of what happened at Reed Hall."

As though frozen to the spot, Suzanna watched their Graces mount the steps to the front door. The duchess did not look at her, but the duke's insolent eyes made her want to slap his florid face. Brandmere strode past her without a look or word.

Suzanna was bewildered. Brandmere had warned her that his guests would try to humiliate her. What she hadn't expected was that he himself would speak of her with such disgust.

He was *acting*, Suzanna repeated. She tried to hold to this thought as other guests arrived. To each newcomer Brandmere gave the same explanation. The Campion girl was a servant in what had once been her home. She deserved to be humiliated because she was a thief's accomplice.

During the next two hours Suzanna was subjected to one insult after another. She bore Stanhope's amused titters and Lord Federby's languid insolence. She held fast under Lord Doherty's speculative stare. She stood it when the Marchioness of Clavendell bade her daughters move away from "that woman" as if to touch her was contamination. She said nothing when Colonel Bender remarked acidly that in the regiment, thieves were given short shrift and a long rope. She bore it all, but Little John had had quite enough.

He made a fist and shook it at the departing colonel's back. "That old bugger—I feel like punching 'is 'ead," he snarled. "There's no need for you to be 'urt like this, Miss 'Zanna."

"I have to go through with it. I promised."

Hurt throbbed in her low voice, and Little John made a strangled noise. His hands itched to clasp themselves around the earl's throat. "It isn't *right*." He rasped. "I won't stay in a house where you're insulted, Miss 'Zanna. I'll give my notice and tell all these twiddlepoops to go to 'ell."

Though he spoke fiercely, there were tears in the old man's eyes. Suzanna longed to lean against his bony shoulder and weep. Instead, she squared her shoulders and admitted, "I did not know it would be so bad. Even so, the play must go on."

Little John stared at her as if she were demented, and Suzanna bit her lip. She wished that she could explain *why* Brandmere was saying those terrible things about her, but she knew that for Dickon's sake, no one must know that the earl was only pretending.

There was another rumble in the courtyard. Looking out of the window in the anteroom, Suzanna's heart sank. She had recognized the Trahernes' carriage.

"Get ready, Miss 'Zanna," Little John growled. " 'Ere come some more Quality."

Brandmere strolled down the grand stairs while the old man was talking. He steeled his heart to ignore the hopeful look Suzanna sent him and asked, "Are you ready to greet Sir Malcolm and Miss Traherne?"

Suzanna was stricken dumb for a moment. Then she managed to rally. "Yes, my lord. I am ready."

It is necessary, Brandmere told himself sternly. "Straighten your shoulders," he ordered aloud, "and smile. I want no Friday faces from you, Miss Campion."

Then he strode out of the door to greet the Trahernes. In a turmoil of doubt and misery, Suzanna noted that Brandmere did not trouble to disguise his pleasure at seeing Anabel. So eager was he to reach her side that he nearly bowled over the underfootman who had been setting down the carriage step.

Suzanna blinked her eyes clear of a sudden inexplicable mist. When that mist cleared, she saw that Anabel was preening herself. Though used to being admired, she could not help but be flattered by the attention of such a man as Brandmere. As the earl handed her down from her carriage, she allowed him to squeeze her hand.

Then she protested, "I beg you will not look too close at me, Brandmere. I have been cramped in that

171

odious carriage so long that I am persuaded that I look a fright."

"Fright" was not an accurate description. Bleakly, Suzanna took in the fashionable hat that Miss Traherne wore. Her ruched and braided velvet cloak lined with ermine kept away the November chill from her person, and the hand she extended to the earl was gloved in the softest leather, dyed blue to match her tiny shoes.

Brandmere gallantly bent over Anabel's hand. "Ma'am, you have only to command me to go away and I will do so—even though that would break my heart."

Anabel dropped her long lashes and murmured, "Oh, my lord, you say *such* things. I am not sure that they are proper."

"Stuff and nonsense, girl." Bluff Sir Malcolm had emerged from the carriage and was beaming at his daughter and the earl. "Brandmere, you're too sensible to be gammoned by what my baggage says. Eh? No wonder she looks fetching. Primped in front of a mirror for two hours and reduced her dresser and her abigail to tears, that's what she did."

"Oh, Papa," Anabel pouted. "I beg you will not listen to a word my father says, my lord—"

She broke off, and a small frown creased her forehead. She had recognized Suzanna.

"Shall we go up to the house?" Brandmere asked. He offered Anabel his arm, and with her eyes still on Suzanna, she took it.

As Brandmere and the Trahernes started up the stairs, Suzanna sank into a deep curtsy. Steeled for any rudeness or slight, she was astounded to realize that Anabel was smiling at her.

The tightness in Suzanna's chest let go like an unclenching fist. After all she had endured today, Anabel's smile was like a ray of sunshine. Gratefully, Suzanna's own lips parted in an answering smile.

"Oh, la," exclaimed Anabel, "the forward creature is smiling at me."

Suzanna's smile died on her lips. Anabel went on. "This woman and her uncle made us suffer great embarrassment. Why is she here, Brandmere?"

"She is being made to suffer for causing you pain." Brandmere's glance flickered over Suzanna's stricken face as he added indifferently, "I thought you would enjoy the joke of seeing Miss Campion act the servant in her own home."

Anabel's brow cleared. She smiled happily and said, "You are devious, Brandmere. I will enjoy telling everyone of this creature's humiliation."

She swept by and left Suzanna stricken. Nothing, not even the most cutting remarks she had endured this morning, hurt as much as this. Up until now Suzanna had been able to believe that the earl was acting a part. She had trusted him and been sure that her suffering would help to clear her uncle's name.

Now she wasn't sure of anything. Perhaps Brandmere had really schemed to humiliate her in order to please his beloved Anabel.

A small voice, nearly lost in her tumultuous emotions, cried out that Brandmere could not be so cruel. But, after all, what did she know about him? Suzanna thought of her uncle's remarks about the earl playing a hidden hand and felt physically ill.

" 'Ere's another one," Little John groaned.

Suzanna saw that a smart landaulet had stopped in the courtyard and that a well-dressed gentleman was clambering out of it. He began to walk up the stairs, tripped on the third step, and promptly fell on his face.

"Oh, Mr. Vries," Suzanna exclaimed, alarmed. "Are you hurt?"

She ran down the stairs toward him, and Peter watched her arrival with an unhappiness that had nothing to do with his mishap.

He said, "It's too bad, stap me if it ain't."

"It certainly is," Suzanna soothed him. "There is a nasty crack in the step. You must have caught your toe in it."

Peter shook his head. "It ain't that. I came a few minutes earlier and I heard what was said to you. Miss Traherne shouldn't have insulted you, ma'am. Can't think what got into Brand, neither."

Suzanna turned away but not before Peter had seen her eyes brim with tears. "It does not matter," she said, but Peter knew that it mattered a great deal.

People were always laughing at his clumsiness and making jokes about him. They didn't think he minded, but he did. Only two people had never laughed at him—his cousin Brand and Miss Campion, who had just now invented a nonexistent crack in the steps to help him salvage his dignity.

His throat swelled with indignation at the way she was being treated. "Mustn't refine on what Brand says," he advised. "Man's been acting as queer as Dick's hatband recently. My feeling is that he's gone off his chump. ''Tis true, 'tis true, and pity 'tis—' forget the rest, but it natters on and on like that. And it *is* true, dash it. Not a word of truth in what Brand says now. Poor fellow ain't responsible.

While listening to this disjointed speech, Suzanna helped Peter to his feet. She did not mind that he then dropped his hat, which rolled into the garden and had to be retrieved, and then stepped on her toe. The young man's words had steadied her and made her resolve to play out the game, if game it was, and let the cards fall as they would. No doubt, she told herself, the guests had already gotten rid of their venom. The worst was surely over.

Lost in these reflections, she followed Peter up the stairs. But as they entered the front door, a gurgling scream brought her back to reality. Both Suzanna and Peter stared as a lady's maid, her starched cap askew, raced down the stairs screeching that there were "henormous, 'airy spiders" in Miss Traherne's room.

"Them is crawling everywhere!" she yelled. Then, turning to Little John, she added, "*Do* somefink, you! My poor lady is 'aving 'isterics."

Not troubling to hide a broad grin, Little John began to mount the staircase. As he did so, there was a heavy thud upstairs. It was followed by a bellowed curse.

A small boy came sliding down the banister, hopped onto the floor, and vanished out of doors. In hot pursuit came Sir Malcolm Traherne. The nabob was red in the face, his mustaches were bristling in every direction, and he was waving a hairbrush.

"Wait till I get my hands on you, you young scalawag," he howled. "Come back here! I'll teach you to trip me!"

Sir Malcolm, too, disappeared out of doors.

Peter goggled. "Spiders?" he questioned feebly. "Don't like them above half meself. Are there many around Grapewood, Miss Campion?"

But Suzanna was laughing too hard to answer. She was human enough to relish the way in which Blackbeard the Pirate had settled his debt to her.

Chapter Eleven

From the third-floor landing Suzanna watched the busy scene below. The caterer's underlings were scurrying about with plates of dainties and trayfuls of wine and cordials. Others busied themselves with preparations for the formal dinner scheduled to begin at ten o'clock. Footmen moved furniture, housemaids arranged pillows and smoothed the folds of curtains. Inspecting and directing, Foote wended his way through this organized confusion.

"I won't be made a fool of again," Suzanna declared. "I will not go down there."

She would not do it. Nothing would induce her to stand at the drawing room door and curtsy to Brandmere's odious guests. She was going to retreat to her room, and if the earl wanted to humiliate her further, he would have to drag her downstairs by force.

But even having decided this, Suzanna stayed where she was. Grapewood's transformation fascinated her. As though awakening from a long sleep, the house glowed with the light of many-branched candelabra. It thrummed to music and was redolent with the fragrance of hothouse flowers and good food. This was how the old house deserved to look, Suzanna had to admit.

An underfootman hurrying toward his post at the door of the drawing room glanced up and saw her on the landing. He goggled at her and then said something to a passing housemaid, who also sent a questioning glance upward.

Suzanna tried not to mind that the servants were talking about her. She surmised that the earl's remarks had circulated belowstairs, and though she could not know that Mrs. Horry had slapped an impertinent chambermaid or that Little John had come to blows with Lord Freyden's valet, she realized that everyone was well aware of her humiliation.

And, after all, what good had that humiliation accomplished? She was no longer sure whether Brandmere had lied to her about setting a trap for a thief. For all she knew, the earl was laughing at her this very moment.

There was a step behind her, and a familiar voice demanded, "Why are you standing here?"

Slowly and with loathing she turned and faced the earl. She resented the sartorial elegance of his black silk evening clothes, his intricately tied neck-cloth, and his emerald stick-pin. She hated the assured way in which he repeated, "Why are you here? The guests will be coming down soon."

"Let them come!" Suzanna snapped.

He frowned. "You must remember what you promised to do."

"I collect that I am to give your guests another opportunity to humiliate me. I will not do it."

Her attempted sneer ended in a sob, and Brandmere was alarmed. It would not do, he thought. He must take the risk of telling her now.

"Suzanna," be began, "I must explain why—"

A musical voice broke in. "Look, Papa, we are not too early after all, for here is Brandmere."

Preceded by a footman carrying a five-branched candelabrum, the Trahernes were walking toward the landing. Tonight Anabel's hair had been arranged in the Roman style and cascaded in golden ringlets from a knot at the side of her head. Her flowing dress of amber silk was embroidered with roses and decorated with pearls, and its new short length called attention to her shapely ankles.

Suzanna saw the grim look leave the earl's face as he eyed Miss Traherne. Instead, he looked very pleased—*smug,* Suzanna thought bitterly. As Brandmere moved forward, she fought an urge to trip him and send him sprawling at his lady's feet.

"Miss Traherne," the earl was saying, "will you desert your father and allow me to escort you down to the dancing? You will make me the envy of every man present."

"Fol rol," Anabel protested prettily, "You are full of compliments, my lord."

She was now convinced that the earl was in love with her. Her father had been sure of it for weeks, but Anabel had remained unconvinced, for some feminine sixth sense warned her that there still was a rival in the field.

She had not forgotten her first visit to Grapewood or the way Brandmere had treated Suzanna. He had laughed with Suzanna, championed her. And even when the Campions had been exposed as thieves, the earl had managed to keep Suzanna out of prison.

Anabel had been suspicious when Brandmere

bought Grapewood, and the news that Suzanna had not been turned out of doors irked her tremendously. When she and her father were invited to Brandmere's house party, she had been on her guard. But now that she saw the way Brandmere treated Suzanna—Anabel smiled.

No, there was no rival here. Complacently, Anabel gave her hand to the earl. "Shall we go down?" she suggested.

With his eyes on Anabel, Brandmere addressed Suzanna perfunctorily. "I have made my wishes plain. See that you comply with them."

With a look of undisguised triumph, Anabel swept past Suzanna, who closed her eyes and counted to ten very slowly. Then, since there was no help for it, she began to descend the stairs.

A gusty sigh echoed behind her, "Brand's ready for the parson's mousetrap," Peter lamented. "I might as well go home."

Gloomily, he fell into step beside Suzanna. "He'll offer for Miss Traherne tonight—see if he don't. Stap me, but everyone will say they make a handsome couple."

Suzanna glanced at Brandmere and Anabel, who were walking toward the drawing room. Their heads were almost touching. Hastily, she averted her eyes.

Peter sighed. "I've been in love with Miss Traherne for months, but there wasn't a prayer for me." Inconsequently, he added, "Did anyone ever trap those spiders, Miss Campion? Where did they come from, I wonder?"

"I really cannot say," Suzanna said.

He seemed not to notice her abstracted tone. "Honoria's brats brought them in, I'll be bound. Last time I was in the same house with those monsters, they put pepper in my snuffbox." Peter glanced around him somewhat nervously. "Ah—where are they tonight?"

Suzanna explained that the children were in the nursery. She did not add that Sir Malcolm had nearly had an apoplexy chasing Lancelot and that following this Brandmere had had a lengthy interview with his nevvy. Now, cajoled with promises of sugar cake by their mama and threatened with dismemberment by their uncle, the children had been bestowed in the nursery.

"Here comes Cousin Claddington," Peter remarked, and Suzanna braced herself as she awaited the duke and duchess's arrival. They greeted Peter cordially but ignored the curtsying Suzanna.

"I might as well be invisible," she murmured.

"Don't refine on it, Miss Campion. 'Struth, Claddingtons don't have much in the upper works." Peter paused. "Oh, I say. Here comes Honoria."

In leisurely fashion Lady Danbury was descending the stairs. She wore a turquoise brocade dress decorated with silver acorns, and her matching turban was crowned by a curling ostrich plume.

"Miss Campion, how well you look," she commented. "That shade of gray brings out the exact color of your eyes." She nodded at Peter, adding, "See, however, that you do not dance with my cousin here. I, alas, have done."

Indignantly, Peter protested, and Lady Danbury fixed him with an unfriendly eye. "The last time we stood up together, you stepped on my feet until I was forced to soak them in salts. And Jeremy upset the water and Danbury was furious because the Portuguese petit-point carpet with the design of hounds and hunters was ruined. Make sure you do not come any-where near me once the dancing starts."

With a friendly nod at Suzanna, she sauntered into the drawing room. Peter quivered with affront. "She didn't tell you that she kicked me in the ankle. Stap me if I wasn't lame for days. Mean to tell her so."

He trotted off in pursuit of Lady Danbury, and Suzanna ventured to glance into the drawing room. She saw that Brandmere's guests had formed groups. Lady Danbury had settled herself by the duchess, with whom she was preparing to gossip. The duke, deep in conversation with Colonel Bender and Sir Malcolm, was thumping his fist on a marble-topped *bas d'armoire.*

Anabel was ensconced near the new, gold silk curtains. She was attended by Stanhope and Lord Freyden, and though Brandmere stood a little distance apart, Suzanna noted that he could not keep his eyes off Anabel.

What would happen to Little John and the cook and all the animals when Miss Traherne became Brandmere's countess? Suzanna felt her heart sink as she read the future. The old servants would be sent away. The useless animals would go to the knackers. And she, Suzanna, had been the Judas who had sold Grapewood to Brandmere.

Suddenly, a voice pierced her misery. "Do come here," Anabel was drawling.

Suzanna raised her head and saw that Anabel was looking directly at her. She twitched an empty wine-glass in her hand and commanded, "Be so good as to take this glass away."

An underfootman started forward. Anabel waved him back. "Campion," she said, "do you not hear me? Take my glass, if you please."

For an instant Suzanna stared. Then, anger flamed. How dared the woman? How *dared* she—

"You are so slow." Seeing that Brandmere was watching, Anabel continued. "I thought that the girl was a servant. Could I have misunderstood?"

Her smile was guileless, but Brandmere correctly read the challenge in her eyes. With an effort he replied, "You did not misunderstand. Thieves must be punished."

He tried to catch Suzanna's eye as he spoke, but she was staring at Anabel. And now Claddington made a bad business worse. "Has that demmed blackguard Campion been sentenced yet?" he demanded.

"The thief will get his desserts, Claddington," the earl replied calmly. "I promise that justice will be done."

It was too much, Suzanna thought. She would tell Brandmere what she thought of him and his beloved Miss Traherne.

"La," Anabel exclaimed, "the creature is still haughty."

Stanhope tittered with laughter. Lord Freyden snickered. Suzanna glared at Brandmere and was astonished to see one of his eyelids lower in a wink.

It took a moment to take in the meaning of that wink. Then blood began to race through Suzanna's starved veins. Brandmere *was* playing a part. He was playing it with such skill that even she had been deceived. Suzanna felt sick as she realized that she had nearly spoiled everything.

"I'm sorry, ma'am," she said meekly.

She came forward to take Anabel's glass, and Brandmere ordered, "You may collect the empty glasses of the other guests."

Again their eyes met, and again there was that fractional wink. "Yes, my lord," Suzanna whined.

As she turned to do his bidding, she nearly collided with Peter. The young man did not bother to excuse himself. Striding past Suzanna, he tugged at his cousin's sleeve. "Brand," he said. "Have to talk to you."

"Not now," the earl replied.

But Peter was not to be denied. "You can't treat Miss Campion like a servant. It ain't right. Stap me, Brand, but it ain't like you. I won't stand by and watch—"

He yelped as he staggered backward, narrowly escaped falling into Lady Danbury's lap, and landed on the carpet. Brandmere hauled him upright.

"You pushed me!" Peter accused.

"Be quiet, you young fool," Brandmere gritted out, "or you'll give the game away."

Before Peter could demand an explanation, the orchestra struck up a waltz. Leaving Peter where he stood, Brandmere walked across to Anabel and, bowing to her, led her to the floor.

"Not like you at all," Peter gloomed. Disconsolately, he watched his cousin and Anabel dancing. Then, shaking his head, he wandered out of the room.

Lady Danbury watched him go. "Infamous," she muttered.

"What did you say, Honoria?" the duchess asked. When there was no reply, she added, "It seems that Anthony has at last been smitten."

"Anthony," Lady Danbury replied, "is a totty-headed nincompoop."

The duchess raised her eyebrows. "Why have you flown into the boughs, pray? The Traherne girl will bring a sizable dowry with her, and she *is* a beauty."

"Handsome is as handsome does, and Anthony is

rich enough. He does not need to dangle after a fortune." Lady Danbury lifted her quizzing glass and surveyed her dancing brother and his partner. "Did you observe the Traherne girl's vile treatment of Miss Campion just now?"

The duchess, who had been thinking the same thing, murmured that thieves needed to be punished.

"Stuff," Lady Danbury replied. "Suzanna Campion's uncle is a loose fish, but that has nothing to do with her. Precious few of us can shake the family tree without dislodging some scaff and raff. Look at our uncle Malcolm, who gambled away his fortune and ran off with that opera dancer—Mademoiselle Zizi, I think she was called. There is also Claddington's great-aunt, the duchess of Partidge, who likes to steal silverware, and—Clarice, *look* at the way that minx is gloating and smirking!"

The duchess whipped her spectacles out of her reticule and balanced them on her nose. "You are right," she breathed. "That odious young woman believes she has Anthony in her pocket."

The dowagers exchanged speaking glances. "I cannot like the woman," Lady Danbury announced. With uncharacteristic vehemence she added, "Just this afternoon she called Lancelot a horrible little boy. And that brute, her father, actually threatened my son with bodily harm." She swelled with anger for a moment and then added, "But Miss Campion has an understanding of children. I must tell you that Jeremy thinks her to be 'a great gun.' "

Before the duchess could react to this, the waltz ended and a cotillion began. Brandmere nodded to the bandleader, who immediately stopped playing.

"I have an announcement to make," the earl said.

Everyone stared at Anabel. The Marchioness of Clavendell and Mrs. Bender sniffed loudly, their daughters looked pained, and the young gentlemen gritted their teeth and kissed the nabob's fortune good-bye.

Brandmere let speculation and interest build for a few moments. "My announcement," he then said, "has to do with buried treasure."

"Oh, come—you don't believe the hogwash that Campion told us," the duke protested.

"On the contrary, Claddington, I conducted a systematic search for the treasure. You may have seen the ditches I ordered dug."

The earl snapped his fingers, and Marlin marched into the room. Under his arm he carried a metal box.

As though performing a military drill, Marlin carried the box to his master, bowed, and retreated. "Here is the Silver Lady's treasure," Brandmere announced.

Colonel Bender blessed himself. Lady Danbury was heard to declaim to the duchess, who once again had put on her spectacles, that this was better than a novel.

"Well? What are you waiting for, man, what's in it?" Claddington demanded.

But Brandmere was bowing to Anabel. "Miss Traherne, would you do me the honor of opening Lady Blanche's treasure?" he asked.

As she glided forward, Anabel felt triumphant. It was obvious that the earl was going to present his treasure to her as a betrothal gift. Complacently, she lifted the metal lid. Then she started, and a stricken expression filled her eyes.

"Your watch, Brandmere," she gasped. "But—but that's impossible. We have—"

Sir Malcolm made a hissing sound. Anabel broke off and turned pale as Brandmere reached into the casket and drew out a handsome fob watch.

"No, Miss Traherne, this is not my watch, but a replica I had made in London. As you were about to say, *you* have my real watch."

He turned to the waiting Marlin and said, "Show in the Baron de Foucald."

A newcomer was ushered into the drawing room. A slender man in his thirties, he was dressed with an elegance that was slightly foreign. In a heavily accented voice he declaimed, "*Serviteur, Mesdames et Messieurs.* I am Baron Henri de Foucald."

Sir Malcolm had turned as pale as his daughter. "I've had enough of this foolishness," he grated out. "Come, Anabel, we're leaving."

The baron held up a hand. "Before you go, Monsieur Mabraye, may I 'ave ze ring you stole from me? It is, I see, on your daughter's finger."

Anabel put her hands behind her back. Sir Malcolm, who had begun to walk out of the room, stopped dead in his tracks.

"So you recognize me," de Foucald said.

"Never saw you in my life!" Sir Malcolm blustered.

Ignoring him, the baron began a graceful speech in which he explained that his family had once owned much land outside of Paris. Unfortunately, the terror had forced them to flee to Austria. "It was zere, at the 'ome of Count von Hessenberg, that I met ze Mabrayes," he said. "Zey were so charming, but after zere departure, it was seen that jewelry had also departed—including my ring."

The baron added that the Mabrayes had gone by many names. "Zey are well known on ze Continent. Zey call zeirselves Mabraye in Austria, Kirk in Spain,

Sebastian in Portugal. Always zey were so rich. Ze fazzer was always a nabob from India, ze daughter so beautiful an heiress. Always, zey attend many fashionable parties, balls, 'ouse parties—and always, jewels and money disappear. Zen, after zey have stole from everybody, zey move on to anozer country."

Brandmere picked up the baron's narrative. "After the events at Reed Hall, I began to follow the Trahernes' movements. I went wherever they went and saw that, as the baron pointed out, money and jewels disappeared in their wake. Some unfortunate servant was always blamed." He paused for a moment, then added, "I had suspicions but no proof, so when I learned of the baron, I sent my solicitor to persuade him to come to England in order to identify the thieves."

"Lies," Sir Malcolm sputtered. "Filthy lies! Surely you don't believe some Frog we've never clapped eyes on before? I never met him before, I tell you. I never even saw his ring. And, what do you mean, 'the events at Reed Hall'? The diamonds were found under Campion's pillow."

"You put them there," Brandmere said sternly, "because you saw that I wasn't convinced that a servant had stolen the diamonds. You wanted to deflect suspicion from yourselves."

Sir Malcolm had turned magenta. "You've gone mad," he shouted. "To think of accusing us!"

"Your daughter accused herself the night that Claddington's diamonds were stolen. She reminded me that Campion had stolen something from me." Anabel began to speak, but Brandmere cut her short. "Madam, I had not told anyone—not even my valet— that my watch was missing. It was something only the thief could know. Again, I couldn't prove my suspicions, so Miss Campion agreed to help me trap you into making a confession."

With a snarl Sir Malcolm seized a brass candlestick from a chair. "Get out of my way," he yelled. "I'll brain the first man who tries to stop me."

Colonel Bender made a grab for the nabob and was knocked down. "Stop that man!" Claddington bellowed.

Little John and the underfootman tried to do so, but Sir Malcolm eeled himself out of their grasp and together with his daughter raced out of the drawing room.

As they came to the second-floor landing, Peter emerged from the picture gallery, where he had been contemplating his woes. He goggled at the fleeing Trahernes, stumbled over a toy soldier that had been left on the floor, and fell heavily forward. Instinctively throwing out his arms to break his fall, he found them full of Sir Malcolm.

For a moment the two men teetered on the edge of the second-floor landing. Then they crashed backward. Anabel screamed again and again as the two men rolled and bumped down the stairs.

Brandmere was the first to reach the foot of the stairs, where Peter was lying across the stunned Sir Malcolm. "Well done, old fellow," he exulted. "Well done, Peter. You're the hero of the hour!"

The protesting Sir Malcolm was restrained, and an underfootman was dispatched to fetch the constable. On the stairs Anabel wailed, "I am innocent. He made me do it. Brandmere, you must believe me—"

"Madam, the play is ended."

Brandmere looked at Suzanna as he spoke. He wanted nothing more than to stride over to her and take her into his arms and tell her he loved her, but her bewildered expression checked him.

Suzanna needed time to understand what had happened. Brandmere told himself that he must allow her time to regain her balance before telling her what was in his heart.

He turned to Lady Danbury. "Honoria, will you see to my guests? M. de Foucald and I must go with the constable and see that this precious pair is locked up."

Suzanna listened to the earl speak and fought an urge to pinch herself awake. She still could not believe all that had happened. Dazedly, she looked from the Trahernes to the grinning Peter, who was being made much of by all the ladies.

Suzanna felt a rush of thanksgiving. It really *was* over! But before this thought could take hold, she heard Claddington's growl.

"That's all very well, but you can't convince me that Campion's innocent. Man's a thatchgallows if I ever saw one."

There was vigorous agreement from Colonel Bender, his wife, and the marchioness. Suzanna felt her heart sink.

The Trahernes had been apprehended and her uncle would be now set free, but in the eyes of the world, Dickon Campion would always be suspected of being a thief—and so would his niece.

Chapter Twelve

Arm in arm with his niece, Dickon strolled through the garden. Chrysanthemums," he declared, "and Michaelmas daisies, too. Asters. What could be finer than autumn at our Grapewood?"

Forbearing to point out that Grapewood was no longer theirs, Suzanna said, "I am so glad that you are free."

Dickon gave her arm an affectionate squeeze. "You're a good girl, Suzanna. Game as a pebble. I still can't believe how you and Brandmere hoodwinked those Trahernes."

Remembering that night and Claddington's damning words, Suzanna winced.

"What do you plan to do now?" she asked.

"I shall probably go abroad. You should accompany me, for travel improves the mind." Complacently, Dickon continued to stroll along a garden path that had been weeded and cut back by newly hired gardeners. Other gardeners labored in the flower beds, and underlings were clearing and pruning everywhere.

"It's a mild day for November," Dickon continued. "Let's rest awhile on this bench so that I can conserve my strength. That terrible jail has taken its toll on me."

"Your so-called prison was much more comfortable than Grapewood," Suzanna pointed out. "At least, it did not leak."

"Well, Grapewood doesn't leak now. Brandmere has seen to that." Dickon carefully parted his coat-tails, sat down on the stone bench, and clasped his hands on his now-comfortable middle. "I wonder why he did it?"

"You forget that Grapewood is his now."

"I wasn't talking about Grapewood. I meant that Brandmere went to a great deal of trouble to expose the Trahernes and clear my name."

"They had stolen his watch," Suzanna began.

"It wasn't just for his watch that Brandmere exerted himself." Dickon shot his niece a speculative look and added, "The lengths he went to to prove me innocent boggles the imagination, especially since he doesn't like me above half."

Suzanna was silent. "It also astounds me that you were such a good actress," Dickon continued. "That old curmudgeon Little John told me how you allowed Miss Traherne to humiliate you while all the time setting a trap for her."

"Most of the time I was not acting, for Brandmere did not tell me all his plans."

Dickon sucked in his cheeks. "The man is not a fool. If he'd told you everything, you'd have given the game away, my girl. As it was, the hurt look on your face reassured the fair Anabel that Brandmere no longer had a *tendre* for you."

Suzanna rounded on her uncle. "Will you stop saying such things?" she cried. "They are untrue and wicked, and—"

At this point Little John's loud voice interrupted her. "The earl 'as returned from Lunnon and requests to see you Miss 'Zanna."

Testily, Dickon demanded, "Must you always yell?"

Little John cupped a hand to an ear. " 'Ey, what's that?"

For a long moment Dickon glared at the old servant. He then winked at Suzanna. "He's just returned from London and wants to see you. Well, well. I wonder why."

Studiously ignoring her uncle, Suzanna asked where his lordship was.

" 'E is out walking in the grape arbor, on account of the 'ouse being full of those young'uns playing 'idean'-seek," Little John informed her. "So, are you going, then?"

Dickon settled himself more comfortably on the garden seat and stretched his legs. "Go, Suzanna. I will sit here and commune with nature."

Suzanna walked briskly away until she was out of her uncle's sight. Then her footsteps began to lag. She had realized that she did not know what to say to the earl.

Brandmere had left for London immediately after the Trahernes' arrest. He had absented himself from Grapewood for the past few days, and Suzanna had not yet had a chance to thank him for all his help.

She thought of this as she slowly walked down the sloping path toward the arbor where the earl was waiting for her. He was standing near the stone bench where they had sat together. Suzanna's heart gave a little jolt as she noted how the sun turned his hair to gold and glinted over the breadth of his shoulders, strong back, and powerfully muscled legs.

He greeted her with a slight bow and said, "Miss Campion."

Brandmere's hands were clasped behind his back. He stood with his booted feet a little apart like a man who had resolved to do something and was impatient to do it. Reminded that she also had something she must do, Suzanna walked up to the earl and held out her hand to him.

"I have not yet thanked you for my uncle and for myself," she said. "Our good name means everything to me."

As he took the hand she offered him, Brandmere felt strangely at a loss. The fine speech he had been rehearsing while waiting for her had gone clean out of his mind.

Suzanna continued. "Of course, we must return the money you advanced on my uncle's behalf, but that is nothing. Your time, your personal efforts—we will always be in your debt."

Brandmere cleared his throat. "I'm here because I have a favor to ask you," he managed to say.

He did not recognize his own voice, nor did he know what to do with the emotions that were seething through him. Sternly, the earl warned himself that it would not *do* simply to gather Suzanna into his arms and kiss her. He must show her he was entirely serious by obeying the proper forms. He must ask her uncle for permission to pay his addresses to her.

The thought of having to ask Dickon Campion for anything was so unpleasant that Brandmere's lips twisted in distaste. Suzanna's heart sank. Brandmere looked, she thought, like a man who had to swallow some bad-tasting medicine.

She withdrew her hand from his and said, "Do you wish me to remain as your housekeeper here at Grapewood? I will be happy to stay on for a while—until a suitable replacement has been found."

"There can be no replacement for you," he replied.

"But—but, you see, my uncle will wish to go abroad, and I—"

"Oh, damn and blast Campion," Brandmere cried. Seeing her shocked expression, he added hastily, "Miss Campion, I request the honor of your hand in marriage."

It wasn't the way he had wanted to say it, but at least it was out. Brandmere watched the emotions that filled Suzanna's eyes—incredulity, then blinding joy. Filled with happiness and relief, he held out his arms to draw her to him, but to his astonishment she stepped back out of reach.

"Please don't," Suzanna whispered.

She had gone so pale that the band of freckles stood out on her small nose. Her eyes were so wide that they seemed to dominate her heart-shaped face. Brandmere was shocked to see that despair had taken the place of the happiness he had seen in her eyes.

"You must not say those things to me," she continued in that same shattered whisper. "I can't marry you. I won't."

"But what—"

She interrupted him by whirling on her heel and taking flight. For a moment Brandmere was nonplussed. He started to follow her, then was checked by a horrible suspicion.

Suzanna must never have cared anything for him.

She had been interested only in clearing her precious uncle's name.

Brandmere stopped in his tracks. "You bloody fool," he named himself.

Anger and hurt were like a tight, hard band around Brandmere's chest, and for a moment he could hardly breathe. Then, gradually, the pride of his blood asserted itself. He straightened his traveling coat and began striding back toward the carriage house. He would not stop to see Honoria, he thought, but would drive back to London immediately. His business at Grapewood was over.

Meanwhile, Suzanna was busy running away from Brandmere. She had no idea where she was going and did not much care.

The unthinkable had happened. Brandmere had offered for her. As she listened to him a few moments earlier Suzanna had known the greatest joy in her life and the most profound despair.

She knew that she could never be Brandmere's countess. Not for anything could she expose the man she loved to the cutting looks, the insults, and the rebuffs that she herself had endured. Suzanna could still hear the Duke of Claddington's sneering remarks about her uncle. This was the sort of thing that Brandmere would have to endure if he married her.

"Nothing will change," she told herself miserably. "They will always look on my uncle as a thief. And they will wonder why the Fifth Earl of Brandmere with all his wealth and his centuries-old title had to stoop to marry a Campion. Ridicule and suspicion— what a fine dowry I would bring him!"

Tears began to trickle down Suzanna's cheeks. She didn't have a handkerchief, so she swabbed at her eyes with her sleeve.

She tried to brace herself with the thought that she need not see Brandmere again. She and Uncle Dickon would soon leave England, and when she returned, she would find the earl affianced to some noble lady. This thought depressed her even more. Suzanna realized that she didn't want to go to the Continent or anywhere else. She wanted to stay at Grapewood—and she wanted Brandmere.

So lost was she in her misery that she did not at first heed the babble of voices in the near distance.

"Stop them—'ead them off—Bill, yer great lummox, why din'yer 'old 'er?"

"Now, tha's done it. Tha's done it!"

"Oh, look Jeremy—the pigs are getting away!"

On the heels of that childish treble came a loud grunting and squealing. Suzanna jerked up her head as a massive, determined shape came plunging through the bushes.

"Good heavens," Suzanna exclaimed. "Porcina!"

Porcina was in a stamping bad temper. Her swill this morning had been late in arriving, and to add insult to injury, instead of food had come five small, human creatures who had wanted to play with her piglets. They had opened the door to her sty and, hungry and disgusted with everyone, Porcina had made a dash for freedom.

After her streamed her piglets, and behind the piglets raced Jeremy, Augustus, Percival, Lancelot, and Elizabeth and an assortment of grooms, gardeners, and undergardeners.

Lancelot caught sight of Suzanna and waved a grubby hand. "Oh, Miss Campion, the pigs are running away," he crowed. "Isn't it famous?"

"Porcina, come back this instant," Suzanna commanded, but the sow paid no attention and continued to roll forward.

Suzanna began to run after her. "Head Porcina off," she shouted over her shoulder. "If she is caught, the piglets will come to her—"

There was a yell from the garden as the sow detoured and knocked Dickon off his garden seat. Then she began to make for the grape arbor.

Brandmere was just leaving the arbor when he heard the commotion. He turned to look over his shoulder and saw Porcina bearing down on him. Acting instinctively, he threw out his arms and found them full of indignant, squealing pig.

"Hold her—don't let her go," Suzanna shrieked. She burst into the grape arbor, fell on her knees beside the sow, and cried, "Porcina, stop this foolishness. It is Suzanna come to take you back to your nice pen. Porcina, you are being very naughty indeed."

Hearing Suzanna's familiar voice, the sow stopped struggling. The piglets gathered about their mother and commenced to loudly grunt and squeak.

Ignoring them, Suzanna looked up at Brandmere and was horrified to see that his traveling clothes were covered with black, clinging mud. "I *beg* your pardon," she stammered. "I had no idea that you were still here."

On the point of making an icy rejoinder, Brandmere looked full at Suzanna's face. "Good God," he exclaimed, "you're crying. Are you hurt?"

"Of course I am not hurt." Suzanna desperately wished she could turn her head away, but she couldn't do so without letting go of Porcina. Helplessly, she felt more tears scald her cheeks.

Brandmere got down on his knees so as to be level

with Suzanna. "Why are you crying, my love?" he asked.

His tender tone was her undoing. Suzanna laid her cheek against Porcina's side and wailed, "Because you are going away and I will never see you again."

The earl let go of Porcina, reached across the sow, and gathered Suzanna into his arms. "That's wonderful. Don't cry, my darling—I love you so much."

Suzanna lifted her face to speak. She never uttered a word, for Brandmere's lips found hers. In the magic moments that followed, neither of them realized that Porcina, released, had turned about and was lumbering back the way she had come. In a few seconds the yells of her pursuers also changed direction, and squeals, snorts, shouts, and gleeful shrieks dwindled into the distance.

Blissfully unaware of any of this, Brandmere and Suzanna remained fused together until lack of air forced them to draw apart. Then, shaking with breathlessness and emotion, they separated a few inches and gazed at each other.

"You *love* me?" Suzanna wondered.

"Idiot. Of course I love you." Brandmere commenced to kiss the tear marks from her cheeks. Between kisses he added, "Why else would I have asked you to marry me?"

He continued to kiss her fervently, but Suzanna was regaining possession of her senses. "No—*please* stop. Anthony, I mean, my lord earl, you know I cannot marry you."

Brandmere told her forcefully that he knew nothing of the kind. Suzanna drew a quivery breath and stated, "My uncle is considered a thief. Even with the Trahernes apprehended, he is in disgrace. How can I marry you?"

"I am not marrying Campion," Brandmere pointed out. "And you can very easily marry me. Simply say yes."

Suzanna trembled. She wanted nothing more than to sink into the earl's arms. But the memory of aristocratic snubs and sneers were too fresh in her mind.

"Please," she whispered brokenly, "do not say these things. You might believe you love me *now*, but later you will come to regret marrying me. That I could not bear."

She broke off as footsteps rustled down the path and, looking up, they saw Lady Danbury perambulating toward them. She did not appear surprised to find them both kneeling on the ground with their arms about each other but smiled calmly and said, "I have been searching all over for you both. I have *news*."

Suzanna scrambled to her feet. Brandmere also rose and said, "Really," in a tone that would have quelled anyone but his sister.

"The stolen valuables, including your watch, Anthony, have been recovered," Lady Danbury reported. "Unfortunately, those Trahernes have escaped en route to Newgate."

"Escaped!" Brandmere exclaimed.

"No doubt they bribed the constable and are on their way to the Continent at this very moment." Lady Danbury paused to smile at Suzanna. "However, this is good news for you, my dear. Their escape will be taken as an admission of guilt. Naturally, all suspicion will be lifted from your uncle now."

"Do you hear that?" Brandmere demanded. "*Now* will you marry me?"

Before she could answer, an aggrieved voice said, "Really, Suzanna, that confounded sow of yours is the outside of enough. She should be converted into bacon."

Dickon came limping into the arbor. "That beast," he complained, "bowled me over and gave me a spasm in the right leg from which I doubt that I will ever recover. I should think—"

"Uncle," Suzanna said, "go away!"

Dickon looked outraged. "Go away when you have just been made an offer of marriage?" He turned to the earl. "I take it, Brandmere, that you *do* intend to marry my niece."

"Yes," said Brandmere.

"No," Suzanna cried.

Lady Danbury sank down on the stone bench and shook her head at her brother. "Did you make a mull of things, Anthony? I am not surprised."

A faint sound suggested that the earl was grinding his teeth. Dickon said cheerfully, "Well, well. Dame Fortune did not smile upon your suit, Brandmere. But heart up, for there are compensations. You recall the diamond shares that we discussed, do you not?"

Suzanna started as though stung by a wasp. Brandmere gazed hard at Dickon for a moment and then said heartily, "Ah, yes. Investments in—what was it again?"

"Diamond mines, my boy. Just the thing. And since you are committing a large portion of your fortune, you cannot fail to make money."

Suzanna fairly screamed, "Indeed, you must not do any such thing, Brandmere. Those shares are surely bogus!"

"Nonsense. I am satisfied that if I turn over a hundred thousand pounds to Campion here, my fortune will be made."

Brandmere folded his arms across his broad chest

and smiled at Dickon, who smiled back and laid his finger against the side of his nose.

For once Lady Danbury's composure deserted her. Rising hastily, she drew her brother aside. "Anthony, have you gone quite mad? You told me yourself that you consider this Campion a loose fish and a thatch-gallows. The man is not to be trusted."

"Uncle Dickon," Suzanna threatened, "if you don't stop this at once, I will—I will box your ears."

Dickon tutted. "You see what a shrew she is, Brandmere. Let that be a lesson to you, my boy, where you engage your affections." He flicked a piece of grass off the sleeve of his elegant, puce-colored coat and added, "I am glad that you won't marry Brand-mere, Suzanna. Deuce take it, it's not every day that fortune sends me such a ninny—I mean, such a worthy partner."

Suzanna clenched her hands into fists, but her uncle had begun to hobble away. "I am going back to the house," he called over his shoulder. "I need to make plans for a long and costly holiday in southern Italy."

Lady Danbury shook her head so strongly that her bright orange turban was threatened. "Preposterous, Anthony! This will never do. Miss Campion, I beg you will listen to my brother's suit."

She took Suzanna's hands in both hers. "I will not peel eggs with you. I realize that Anthony is far from the ideal. However, not many gentlemen come up to snuff. Consider, if you please, young Peter Vries. He has always cut a poor figure in polite circles and yet all at once he is being hailed as a hero. The daughters of the marchioness are throwing sheep's eyes at him. He has been invited to Colonel Bender's home. Really, if there is hope for Peter, there must be hope for my brother."

As her ladyship paused to draw breath, Suzanna glanced at the earl. He shrugged and smiled the sweet smile that she had grown to love.

"You have made Anthony take his duties more seriously," Lady Danbury continued warmly. "Moreover, my children are fond of you. They consider you 'a great gun.' I beg that you will also marry my brother for my sake, Miss Campion."

"For *your* sake, ma'am?" Suzanna stammered.

Lady Danbury shot a dark look at Brandmere. "I have endured much for Anthony's sake. Many times a year I have made exhausting journeys to see him. I have attempted to awaken him to his better self. I have tried to wean him from his frivolous ways. But, Miss Campion, if *you* become his wife, I shall know that Anthony is in good hands. I would not then be required to subject myself and my dear angels to wearying journeys."

There was a shriek from the direction of the house, and Jeremy was heard to exclaim, "Let's find the ghost and throw it out of the window!"

Lady Honoria's maternal instincts were aroused. "Throwing things out of the window may be dangerous. Where is that fool of a nurse?"

She began to amble up the garden path, and Brandmere took Suzanna's hands in his. "Have pity on me," he begged.

He was straight-faced, but imps of mischief danced in his eyes. "I do not know that you need pity," Suzanna tried to say sternly, but her own lips had begun to tug upward. "I think you are a shocking fraud," she sighed. "You are as bad as Uncle Dickon."

"Just because I want to lose my money in a nonexistent diamond mine? Besides, you heard Honoria. My love, how can you condemn me to future visits from my sister and her brats?"

Suzanna began to chuckle. He laughed, too, and slid his arms about her waist. "You see," he said, "it is your duty to marry me."

"This is blackmail, Anthony."

His name sounded so sweet on her lips that he could not prevent himself from kissing her. The experience was pleasant, and he kissed her again. "Your uncle would say that blackmail is a very good thing," he told her.

Suzanna made one more heroic effort to bring the earl to his senses. "You realize that if we are married, Uncle Dickon will become *your* uncle, too?"

But even this fact did not disturb Brandmere. "I must confess that the rogue has virtues that I didn't suspect," he admitted. "Besides, he does tell the truth sometimes." He drew Suzanna closer and added tenderly, "There *is* a Silver Lady at Grapewood, and I am very much in love with her. Suzanna, you are adorable when there is mud on your cheeks."

Suzanna made no further protest. Her smile was as radiant as the sun. As Brandmere bent to kiss her again, she murmured, "In that case we had better invite Porcina to our wedding, hadn't we?"

BLOODY
SHAME

CAROLINA
GARCIA-AGUILERA

BERKLEY PRIME CRIME, NEW YORK

BLOODY SHAME

A Berkley Prime Crime Book / published by arrangement with
the author

PRINTING HISTORY
G.P. Putnam's Sons hardcover edition / 1997
Berkley Prime Crime mass-market edition / January 1998

The Putnam Berkley World Wide Web site address is
http://www.berkley.com

ISBN: 0-425-16140-4

Berkley Prime Crime Books are published
by The Berkley Publishing Group, a member of Penguin Putnam Inc.,
200 Madison Avenue, New York, NY 10016.
The name BERKLEY PRIME CRIME and the BERKLEY PRIME CRIME
design are trademarks belonging to Berkley Publishing Corporation.

PRINTED IN THE UNITED STATES OF AMERICA

10 9 8 7 6 5 4 3 2 1

THIS BOOK IS DEDICATED TO
MY THREE DAUGHTERS,

Sarah, Antonia, and Gabriella,
the loves and passions of my life,
and to Cuba,
mi patria.

¡VIVA CUBA LIBRE!

ACKNOWLEDGMENTS

I feel honored to call my literary agent, Elizabeth Ziemska, of Nicholas Ellison, Inc., my friend. As I often do when I speak with her, I would like to thank her again for all the efforts she has put forth on my behalf. From the very beginning of our association, she has had total faith in me, and has unfailingly encouraged me to write my stories. Celina Spiegel, my editor at G. P. Putnam's Sons, has also become a valued friend. In addition to being an outstanding editor, Cindy is open to my ideas, allowing my creativity to flourish. I am indebted to her in countless other ways as well. Quinton Skinner deserves many thanks for his help and his magical way with words.

As always, I wish to acknowledge the importance my family has in my life. My husband, Robert K. Hamshaw, is a continuing source of support and strength to me; my mother, Lourdes Aguilera de Garcia, deserves thanks for her constant backing of my work—not to mention her bullying her friends into buying books; my sister, Sara O'Connell, and my brother, Carlos Antonio Garcia, have always asked about the books and their progress; and I'm also indebted to my nephew, Richard O'Connell, for always bragging about his *tia*.

But, inevitably, it is to my daughters, Sarah, Antonia, and Gabby, that I owe the biggest debt of all. I want to thank them for the pride I hear in their voices when they say, "My mother, she's a writer—she writes books." That will keep me going for a long, long time. *Gracias, gracias, gracias*.

BLOODY
SHAME

ONE

I GLANCED AT my Mercedes' speedometer to make sure I wasn't over my self-imposed limit—twenty miles an hour above the posted speed on South Dixie Highway—then checked the rearview mirror to see if any cops were following me. I've been stopped so often my Allstate agent has me programmed on his speed-dial.

I wasn't seriously worried, though. Chances were I would deal with a male cop if I was stopped—which meant I would probably get off with a warning and a dinner offer. A female cop meant my luck was up. All my tickets were from female cops. Most women don't like me much, a fact of life I realized and came to accept a long time ago. For that reason I treasure the few women I can truly call friends. Among them was Margarita Vidal, my closest female Cuban friend. I pressed down on the accelerator a little harder, because I was late for our South Beach lunch date.

Although I loved Margarita, I knew she would lecture me mercilessly if I was even a couple of minutes late. Margarita had an English grandfather who had instilled in his entire family the Anglo values of punctuality—values whose only real purpose is to make everyone else's life miserable.

Margarita and I met for lunch about every two weeks, one of my few regular customs. We always met at South Beach, though it was inconvenient—her company, MMV Interiors, was in the Miami design district, while my investigative office was in Coconut Grove. The hassle and drive time were made worthwhile by the free therapy sessions we tended to conduct on one another over our meals. There was little we didn't know about each other's lives.

Traffic grew heavier as I reached South Beach, and as usual I was agitated. I cursed at the red lights, squealed my brakes, tailgated, sweated bullets, and generally made a mess of myself. Finally I found an open stretch of road and floored the Mercedes. Ah, I love those Germans! With a quick burst past an Oldsmobile full of confused tourists, I reached Ocean Drive with minutes to spare.

I groaned when I saw Margarita already seated at an outdoor table at the News Café. My only consolation was that I was able to "TV park"—to find a perfect open space, like a detective on a TV show—on Ocean Drive directly across from the restaurant. In my haste to cross the street I collided with a camera-wielding, red-faced tourist who was gawking at all the half-naked Rollerbladers.

I strode over to Margarita's minuscule table and kissed her. She had already ordered designer water for me.

"That was some tackle you made out there," she said, smiling ironically. "Other than that, *chica*, you look good. Anything going on I should know about?"

"Not really," I said. "Working too much, not sleeping enough. Dating the same guys. The usual."

Margarita laughed, displaying her perfect white teeth. "The single life!" she said. With a touch of bitterness, she added, "I remember that. The good old days."

I didn't know what to say, so I drank my water and looked over my friend. As always, she looked chic. She had the kind of Hispanic coloring that was almost a cliché: black curly hair, dark brown eyes, coffee skin, and a voluptuous body—all emphasized by the vivid colors she wore. Though

Margarita wasn't a naturally beautiful woman, she gave the impression of being one. She achieved this partly through the knife and cosmetics, but mostly she had an inner beauty and a sort of glow about her.

Though I decided to let her comment pass, I had some idea what was souring her mood. "So," I said, "how's Rodrigo?" Rodrigo was her husband. I didn't really care how he was doing.

"Fine." She didn't elaborate.

"Good," I responded. In truth, I was ecstatic to receive a one-word answer. Too many of our lunches revolved around his lousy behavior. I didn't like the guy, and listening to Margarita go on about him was sometimes more than I could bear.

The waiter came and took our orders. For once, we'd been together for ten minutes and our beepers hadn't gone off. This coincidence was aided by the fact that I had shut mine off.

This was a big day for me, and I couldn't wait to tell Margarita about it.

"How about you, Lupe?" Margarita stared out at the street. "How's your work?" She had always been interested in my occupation, probably because it was as different from hers—interior decorating—as possible. I always told her about my latest cases, while being careful not to divulge anything legally kept in confidence. This time, though, I had something really good to tell her.

"Remember how many times I've bitched that I need a vacation?" I began. "Well, the day after tomorrow I'm getting out of town. Tomorrow I'm going to clear my desk, write reports, and return all my calls. I'm going to get Leonardo squared away so he can take care of all our back billing. Then I can really relax."

"You mean you guys are behind in sending out your bills?" Margarita said in astonishment.

"That's how busy we've been," I answered. A few years before, this state of affairs would have been unimaginable. "But I'm heading for the Keys and going incommunicado.

The most pressing decision I'll have to deal with is what bathing suit to wear to the beach.''

The food arrived midway through my speech. I must have been a little overexcited, because the young waiter looked at me as though I might be dangerous. His fear didn't keep him from brushing against my shoulder when he put my plate in front of me, however.

"Lupe, *querida*, I'm so proud of you!" Margarita said, digging a fork into her salad. "I have to confess, I never believed you would take any time off. How long has it been?"

So long that I really had to think before answering. In the seven years Solano Investigations had been in business, it seemed the workload always steadily increased, even though I had help in the office. My work took up so much of my time and energy that I tended to neglect myself. I couldn't complain, though: I was making my own way in the world, and it sure beat pulling a Maytag repairman and waiting for the phone to ring, as in those TV commercials.

"Shit. I really can't remember my last vacation," I said. Defeated, I took a bite of my cheeseburger. It was then that I realized Margarita's salad wasn't a warm-up; it was her main course. That was strange. I'm no slouch in the food department, but she consistently outordered and outate me.

"Aren't you hungry?" I asked, eyeing her rabbit food.

Margarita shrugged delicately. "It must be the heat. I haven't had much of an appetite lately." I noticed she looked a little pale.

We sat quietly for a while, eating and watching the scene on the street. Our terrace table was high off the sidewalk, with an excellent view. That afternoon was quintessential South Beach, with beautiful young bodies marching around the sidewalks like they were in a decidedly risqué parade. Margarita and I were both twenty-eight, but by South Beach standards we were about ready to apply for Social Security benefits. It was hard not to feel voyeuristic, and a little self-conscious, about the procession of flesh and skimpy clothing passing from all directions.

The News Café was just across the street from the wide

strip of sand leading to the ocean. The palm trees swayed lazily in the breeze, heat waves simmered off the sand, spray from the waves danced in the near distance. It all seemed a bit surreal. Drape a few melted clocks over the palms and Salvador Dalí would fit right in.

As a Miami native, I had become accustomed to South Beach long before it turned hopelessly trendy. When my sisters and I were children, my mother would bring us here to sit by the ocean, where she would tell us about the breathtaking beaches in Cuba. When she later lay dying in the hospital, her only regret was that she could no longer see and smell the ocean water. Of her three daughters, I was the only one to inherit her love of the sea.

In later life my visits to South Beach were less innocent. As teenagers, Margarita and I would sneak into the clubs using fake IDs. We looked even younger than our years then, and we were turned away more often than not. Sometimes, though, a bouncer would take pity on us, lift the magical red velvet rope, and allow us in—with the condition that we didn't try to order a drink.

Margarita didn't appear to be enjoying herself, so I gave her a nudge. "Remember when we went clubbing here?" I asked. "When we were kids?"

My ploy seemed to work. Margarita looked at me as though I had just painted a mustache on the Mona Lisa. "You bet I remember," she said. "Remember that first fake ID you had—the one we got at that gas station on Calle Ocho, the one that said you were twenty-five when you were fifteen? And that your name was Mary and you were from Ohio?"

"Yeah, well, what about yours—'Candace Olafsen'?"

We laughed so loudly that the other lunchtime diners started to stare. Then Margarita's beeper went off. It was too good to last.

"Damn," I said.

Margarita squinted over her beeper display. "I can't stay," she said. "I have to meet a client in forty-five minutes."

That was that. Margarita would rather chew off her foot

than be late for a meeting. It seemed that the older we became, and the more immersed we were in our work, the shorter our lunches were.

I paid the check, since it was my turn, and tucked my credit card back in my purse. "Come on, I'll walk you to your car," I said.

When we reached Margarita's Lexus she hugged me, hard and without warning. I'm never very physically demonstrative toward women, and Margarita knew it. I was a little taken aback.

"Is there anything you want to tell me?" I asked.

When Margarita pulled away, her eyes were shiny. "No. I'm just glad to have such a good friend. Is there anything wrong with that?"

She was bullshitting. "Don't give me that. We've been friends for twenty years, and you never got weepy over it. Talk, girl."

Margarita turned off her car alarm and climbed inside without answering. When she rolled down her window, she gave me an exasperated look. "I'm *fine*, Lupe," she said. "Don't be so suspicious."

I thought for a moment, and decided she was right. "I'll call you when I get back from vacation," I said.

She blew me a kiss, smiling now, and pulled away. I watched her turn the corner, my mind already elsewhere. I should have insisted she tell me more. It might have changed things.

TWO

"LUPE, *QUERIDA*, COME on. Just think about it."

The voice on the other end of the line was so seductive that I was almost tempted to give in. Almost. "You'll love this one," he said. "Murder Two, right up your alley. You know you're the best investigator in Dade County, and I need you. Say you'll do it."

Tommy McDonald was trying every trick he knew to talk me into taking a case I had absolutely no interest in. I switched him onto the speakerphone and finished off my double chocolate-brownie ice cream with sprinkles. Thank God I didn't gain weight easily, or I'd be drinking Ultra Slim-Fast instead. Nothing in the world would convince me to take the case, but I politely let him ramble on. After all, it was nice to hear the most successful criminal defense attorney in Miami beg for my services. I'm not above accepting flattery.

"Tommy, honey, you know I need some time off," I finally interrupted. "And you almost finished me off with the last case we worked. I want to go someplace without phones, faxes, or beepers—in other words, heaven. I'm going to the Keys to vegetate. I'm sure you understand.''

He didn't seem to hear me. "Lupe, angel," he pleaded. "This one is a quickie, I promise. Interview some witnesses, run a little background. Maybe a couple of other things. That's all, I swear.''

"According to you, Tommy, they're all quickies.'' I finished off the ice cream, scraping the sides of the Styrofoam cup with my white plastic spoon, making sure I got every last bit. If I was going to have a thousand-calorie breakfast, well, I wanted all of it. I swung my legs off my desk and aimed for the garbage can in the corner.

"*Mierda!*'' I yelled when I missed the shot.

Tommy was silent for a moment. I could almost hear the gears turning. "Does this mean you'll take the case?'' he said. I had to give him credit for persistence. "Look, I'll have the file couriered over to your office immediately.''

"Sorry, sweetie,'' I said. "I just missed wide on a free throw. Tommy, I'm only going to tell you this one more time: As soon as I finish writing a few more reports, I'm out of here. Tomorrow night, I'll be walking in the sunset. Remember relaxation, Tommy?''

"No problem,'' he said. "We can have you on the beach by tomorrow.''

I sighed. Tommy was growing tiresome. "Why don't you call someone else to work it for you? Do you want me to give you some names?'' I asked helpfully. And just a bit teasingly.

"Okay,'' he said. "Why don't I pick you up for an early dinner tonight, and I'll tell you a bit about the case. Just give me that. We'll go someplace nice and quiet, and we'll talk.''

No. No. I knew what *that* meant, and so did he. That's the problem with dating clients—they always want to take me off to someplace quiet. It wasn't a bad strategy, in Tommy's case, because he had the routine down pat. He'd take me someplace sexy for dinner, ply me with champagne, and by morning I'd be the investigator of record on the case. It had never been otherwise in the last seven years.

This time, I was determined not to be a pushover. "No

way, Tommy. I'm packing tonight and leaving tomorrow, and that's that. I'll call you when I get back to Miami. Good luck with the case.''

Feeling very proud of myself, I hung up the phone just as Tommy began another line of attack. I knew he wouldn't be mad at me, at least not for long. Aside from work, we always understood one another.

I opened my office windows and closed my eyes for a moment, feeling the warm humid air and listening to the parrots squawking in the backyard avocado tree. Then I forced myself to return to my desk.

It took me an hour of paperwork before I could see the wood surface and desk calendar. The volume of paper in my office, and the speed with which it accumulated, was staggering. And writing up cases was never one of my strengths; I tended to keep case facts in my head or on scraps of paper, a lousy habit that I never managed to break for long. I plowed through the folders on my desk like a robot, but my mind kept returning to Margarita. I made a mental note to give her a call before I left for the Keys.

Just when I thought I was in the clear, I found a legal pad that hadn't been touched in six months. I knew the writing was mine, but it looked like I would need a hieroglyphics expert to figure out what I had written.

Luckily, my assistant, Leonardo, barged in the door. As usual, he was dressed in workout clothes with Teva sandals. For my part, I wore jeans and a blue T-shirt. Solano Investigations does not have a stringent dress code.

''Lupe,'' Leonardo said, ''this just came for you.''

I could barely see him behind the enormous flower arrangement he carried—an ostentatious mess of white roses and orchids surrounded by a halo of baby's breath, displayed in a white straw basket. The smell was intoxicating, and my eyes widened when I saw two bottles of Dom Pérignon coyly peeking out from the center.

It was a good thing Leonardo was into weight training, because that creation looked heavy. Letting him keep a health club's allotment of workout machines in the office's spare room seemed like an even trade-off at that moment.

But finally the burden was too much even for him and, before he lost his balance, he staggered over to my spare table in the corner and put down the basket. Files, pens, and legal pads flew everywhere as he lowered the display to its final resting place.

Leonardo stepped back and wiped his dark curly hair from his brow. "Wow," he said.

I joined him, and we just stood there and stared at it. Such a gigantic arrangement was more suitable for a hotel lobby than a small investigative firm. And it brought out Leonardo's creative side; once his shock wore off he started fiddling with it, turning it around and moving flowers so the best side faced the room. With a flourish he handed me a gold-embossed card impaled on a green stick.

I groaned when I read it: "Have a good rest. I'll miss you. All my love, Tommy." On the back was another message: "P.S. My client will be fine in jail until you get back from vacation. I'll make sure he takes his medicine."

If I hadn't already had breakfast I could have eaten the card out of anger. "I can't believe Tommy would sink so low," I said.

Leonardo gave me a look. Actually, we both could believe it. Tommy could pull off some pretty sleazy stuff, especially in the courtroom. His clients loved him for it, as well they should have, and they always paid his exorbitant bills without complaint.

"He's going to talk you into it," Leonardo said. He dropped into one of my guest chairs and adjusted the weights he had strapped to his calves. "You've got that look."

"I do not!" I cried out.

He knew me too well. In addition to being my assistant, Leonardo was my cousin. But this time he was mistaken about me.

"I don't care if he sends me ten baskets," I said. "There's no way I'm postponing my vacation."

"Whatever you say, Lupe." Leonardo shook his head, unconvinced. Through his thin muscle shirt I could see the heart monitor he had recently taken to wearing. For a twenty-five-year-old, he was almost maniacally worried about his health. He had his nutritionist's, acupuncturist's, and reflexologist's phone numbers all memorized. In the seven years he had worked for me, I never saw him ill once.

He got up and fussed with the flowers, like an old lady preparing for a garden show. He took one of the bottles of Dom Pérignon from the basket and turned to me like a little boy hinting for a piece of cake.

I shrugged. "What the hell."

"It's unhealthy," Leonardo said, patting his taut belly. "But it's also Dom Pérignon."

I checked my watch. Ten in the morning. "Well, I know it's a crime to do this to good champagne, but why don't we mix it with orange juice and have mimosas?"

Leonardo's eyes lit up, no doubt at the prospect of consuming vitamin C with his alcohol. I put together a tray with a silver ice bucket we kept in the office, while Leonardo ran across the street to buy freshly squeezed juice from the corner stand. Finding first-rate orange juice in Coconut Grove was never a problem.

When he returned, we went to the back porch and settled into white wicker armchairs. We drank mimosas from chilled tulip glasses and listened to the birds.

"Here's to self-employment," I toasted.

"Here's to your vacation. You've earned it," Leonardo said sweetly. He took off his heart monitor and set it aside. "No point in setting off the alarms," he said.

By the time Tommy McDonald showed up we were well into the second bottle. We had run out of orange juice and had started drinking the champagne straight, our afternoon spent listening to Leonardo's New Age exercise music. I hated the stuff, but as time wore on, it didn't sound half bad. A part of my brain shouted out in dismay as I took Tommy in my arms and led him in a slow dance across the porch.

My judgment was shot. Taking a Murder Two seemed like the most natural thing in the world. Tommy always had exquisite timing.

THREE

I DIDN'T MUCH care for the stale mango juice from my office refrigerator, but it was good enough to wash down aspirin—the fourth I'd taken in the last fifteen minutes.

After a last gulp of juice I tried to stand very still, to make the room stop spinning. It was no good; I was still drunk. An hour before, Tommy had dropped me off on the way to his office. I had intended to pick up my Mercedes and drive home, but I was in no shape to travel.

Giving in to the inevitable, I walked into the spare room, found the black leather bench Leonardo used for his free-weight workouts, and collapsed. I wished it were possible to detach my head surgically from the rest of my body for a few hours. My mouth felt as though it housed the contents of an overheated radiator in the middle of the Mojave Desert. Each blink caused me pain. I hadn't suffered a hangover like this since my cousin Inez's *quince* party ten years before. At least this morning I had awakened in a familiar place: Tommy McDonald's bed.

Leonardo still hadn't shown up for work. I was able to piece this together because his car wasn't in the lot when I arrived. And because I set off the alarm when I let myself in. The alarm blared, my heart rate doubled, my eyes crossed, and I was barely able to call the alarm company with the password before they sent the cops over. The alarm was usually Leonardo's job.

I tried to reconstruct the events of the last twenty-four hours, but the details were fuzzy and painful. Only one thing consoled me: I hadn't screwed myself up completely. Instead of taking on Tommy's entire Murder Two case, I had stopped at agreeing to a jailhouse interview and subsequent report. I realized I was fooling myself. I should have been on the road south already, with a clear head and the radio blaring. Instead, I looked like a candidate for a rest home.

After trying once to get up and finding the nausea too strong, I lay back down again and waited for the room to settle. The next thing I knew, I heard the phone ringing.

"It's now or never," I sang, but my own voice made my head hurt. I made my way from the gym room to my office, holding the wall the entire time, and managed to grab the receiver before the service picked up.

"Lupe, *querida*, how are you?" Tommy whispered sweetly in my ear. He sounded as though he were underwater. "I thought I'd call and see how you were doing. You didn't look so hot when I dropped you off."

"You bastard!" I shouted. "You have some nerve, calling me after what you made me do!"

"Wait a minute, honey." Tommy laughed. "It was you who insisted we party all night! I just went along with you."

"I'm not talking about that," I said crossly. "I'm talking about tricking me into taking that case. You played dirty with me."

"Lupe, come on. You're a big girl," he said. "You can't blame me for wanting you to take the case. Why shouldn't I want the best investigator in town?"

"And why do you sound so damned chipper?" I asked. Tommy had matched me drink for drink. "I feel like I'm going to die."

"Irish constitution," Tommy said. "Anyway, it's just one jailhouse interview. Honest, Lupe, that's all I ask. I know you deserve a vacation, and I'm grateful you'll delay it one day for me. I know you won't take the entire case, but I want you to talk to this guy. You have a nose for bullshit, and that's just what I need with my client.''

While I still objected to his underhanded methods, I couldn't really argue with that. And in all fairness, I had to admit that I had gone along with his plot to get me involved. The first chink in my armor came when I took the first sip of champagne the day before, figuring that since I was going on vacation the next day, there was no harm in starting the celebration early.

''One interview and that's it, Tommy. I'm on vacation.''

''Excellent,'' Tommy said. I could tell he was grinning on his end.

''All right,'' I said. ''So let's get on with it.''

''My thoughts exactly.'' I could hear Tommy shuffling papers. ''I'm going over to the Stockade at three this afternoon to see our client.''

''*Your* client, Tommy.''

''Whatever. I'll need you to come along. I took the liberty of having Sonia prepare a file for you—including your notice as investigator of record—so you'll be all set. I know you're only doing one interview, but we have to make it official so they'll let you in.''

''Fine. Fill out whatever form you want—I'm done after the interview. Pick me up on your way over. You can tell me about the case during the ride.''

I hung up without even saying goodbye. Even in my addled state, I could tell Tommy would try every trick in the book to get me to see his case through to the end. ''Investigator of record,'' I said to the empty room. ''He must think I'm an idiot.''

The next item on my agenda, after I made sure I could stand up without falling, was to call Leonardo at home to see if he was still alive. He never drank much, so I knew he was probably even worse off than I was. My memory was still a little hazy, but I had a clear recollection of him the previous day, dancing in front of the floor-to-ceiling mirror in the office weights room, with music blasting away on

his boom box. It was the last I saw of him, and it didn't
bode well for his current health.

I cursed when I got his answering machine, cursed some
more on the message, and hung up. I prayed this meant he
was on his way over. With me alone there, it felt more like
a sick ward than an investigator's office.

I went to the bathroom and splashed icy water on my
face. Inventory time. In the mirror I saw that, amazingly
enough, I didn't really look as though I was operating on
two hours of alcohol-induced sleep. I was tempted to step
into the shower and clean off the night before, but I decided
against it. I remembered from my last shower at the office
that I was out of my favorite almond soap. I admit it, I'm
spoiled. I decided to go home to Cocoplum, where I had
supplies and where I could have a decent Cuban breakfast.
Anyway, I had time to kill until I went to the Stockade with
Tommy. I wrote Leonardo a note and left.

Backing the Mercedes out of the parking lot onto the
street, I felt lucky to have the kind of job in which staying
out all night wasn't unusual and didn't alarm anyone. Nice
Cuban girls from good families don't stay out until all hours,
even if they do carry a gun. Although I lived alone in an
apartment on Brickell Avenue, I spent a lot of time at my
family's house in Cocoplum. My father and my sisters
checked up on me a lot, but they rarely asked questions. I
had trained them well.

At that hour of the day there wasn't much traffic on Main
Highway, the road I usually took between my Coconut
Grove office and the house in Cocoplum, which was part of
Coral Gables. I hadn't quite reached full consciousness,
even though I was improving, so it seemed as though only
minutes had passed when I reached the guardhouse protecting the only entrance into Cocoplum.

I waved for the guard to lift the wooden barrier, thinking
for the millionth time how much I disliked living in such a
controlled environment. Still, I understood that the security
brought peace of mind to the residents—and they paid good
money for the luxury. It's no secret that, in today's Miami,

security and peace of mind are as much a development strategy as lot size and bedroom space.

I spotted the house from a block away. When he built it, Papi situated it so it faced southeast—toward his beloved Cuba. When Fidel Castro fell, or was removed from power, Papi wanted to be able to hop in his Hatteras with nothing in his way. He planned to motor out immediately with my mother's ashes secured in the cabin, where they awaited their burial in Havana.

We didn't talk about it much, but my sisters and I were starting to worry about Papi. He had recently taken to listening only to the call-in Spanish talk-radio stations, so that he could monitor the day-to-day political situation in Cuba. In the past he'd kept the Hatteras stocked with canned and dried staples for his trip across the Florida Straits, but lately he had begun to stock perishables as well. Personally, I didn't think Castro's fall was imminent. I knew it would happen in my lifetime, but Papi had become consumed with the idea that it would happen at any second.

The last couple of New Year's Eves, the anniversary of Castro's rise to power, Papi thought Fidel would fall during the night—Cubans are very cognizant of symbols and omens. In the morning, he would awake depressed to learn that nothing had happened—no revolution, no revolt, no assassination—and he would be depressed for days, the realization weighing heavily upon him that he would be forced to stay in Miami a little while longer.

When Mami was alive, she could control him, but now that she was no longer around, there was nothing to stand in the way of his obsession with returning to Cuba. Although he never specifically said it, I knew he wouldn't rest easily until he buried his wife in Havana. Actually, one side result of his fixation was positive: since Papi and Fidel Castro were almost precisely the same age, he kept himself in great shape in his determination to outlive the dictator. Papi was recently saddened to learn that Castro had given up smoking cigars, because this meant he too had to forgo one of his greatest pleasures. Everything being equal, my bet was on Papi in terms of longevity—he, at least, didn't have to worry about assassination attempts.

Pulling closer to the house, I winced at it even more than usual. I truly was in a delicate state. The place was a monstrosity by any standard, a pink hallucination of balconies and balustrades. Papi had trucked in dirt from Homestead to build the place on a hill; he claimed this offered better protection from the sea surges in case of a hurricane, but my sisters and I knew better. The Solano home was bigger, louder, and higher in altitude than any of its neighbors.

Granted, it's difficult to build a small, demure, tasteful ten-bedroom house, but Papi had gone completely overboard. He was a contractor, and could get materials cheaply, but that didn't explain it all. The house was a living nightmare of immigrant ostentation, and the neighbors all hated us for it. Even though it raised their property values considerably.

I took extra caution pulling the Mercedes into the driveway, not wanting to damage Osvaldo's lovingly planted garden. Well into his seventies, Osvaldo took incredible pains tending the grounds, dedicating countless hours doubled over this bush or that shrub. It was all worth it. In contrast to the house's showiness, the garden was tasteful and restrained. We had, by far, the best-landscaped property in Cocoplum.

Fortunately, I encountered no one, so I was able to step off into the kitchen and help myself to some of the coffee and freshly baked bread Aida had prepared for the family's breakfast.

I went upstairs and climbed into the shower, feeling myself come fully back to life. After a change of clothes I made my way out, ignoring Aida, Osvaldo's wife, calling to me from the kitchen. She had to know it was me and not an intruder—she habitually checked the monitor for the security cameras installed by the front door—and I knew she would delay me with questions about what I'd been up to lately. She was entitled to ask me almost anything she liked, really, since she had worked for my family since before I was born. As I hurried out, I caught a whiff of bacon frying.

As usual, Aida was cooking up a storm. I hoped there would be something left for me when I returned.

When I arrived back at Solano Investigations, I was pleased to see Leonardo's Jeep parked in its usual place. This freed me from spending the afternoon looking for him in emergency rooms. I checked my watch and saw that Tommy was due soon to take me to the Dade County Stockade.

"*Buenos días!*" I yelled, letting the front door slam behind me.

Leonardo lifted his head off his desk with a puppy dog look of sincere hurt. "Hi, Lupe," he said mournfully. "It's going to be a few minutes before I can get to work on the billing."

The poor guy. His face had achieved a greenish tint, broken up only by the red hue where the whites of his eyes should have been. I almost told him he was early for Christmas, but I held back. Never let it be said that I lack pity.

"Take your time," I said. "I'm off to the Stockade in a few minutes. And I just remembered something else I have to do."

Leonardo nodded sadly. "Whatever you say, Lupe."

I was almost out the door when Leonardo cried out for me. "Lupe, please," he said. "Help me remember something, from now on. Just one little thing."

"What's that?" I asked.

"Look at me," he said, framing his face with his hands. "The next time I want to drink, remind me of what I look like right now."

"Oh, you'll be in the weight room by this afternoon," I said. "Have a health food shake, or whatever you're taking these days."

I hurried into my office, because I had forgotten to call Margarita, as I had promised myself. I telephoned her office in the design district, on her private line. I succeeded only in reaching her machine, so I dialed her assistant, Leonora.

Leonora picked up on the second ring. "Oh, Lupe, hello," she said. "Margarita isn't here. She went to see a couple, prospective clients who just built themselves a mansion.''

From past experience I knew Leonora loved to talk when she thought she had a receptive ear, so I knew I would get more information out of her than I needed. I often told Margarita to speak to Leonora about this tendency, but my friend was fond of her assistant and was willing to put up with all sorts of minor transgressions.

''When is she due back?'' I asked, trying to keep it simple.

''Well, she's going to meet the Sanchez family. You probably know about them, they made a bunch of quick money in the carpet-cleaning business.'' Leonora chortled. ''Now they think they're so fancy, they're going to change their name to de Sanchez. Do you believe that?''

''Well, I'm sure Margarita will get the job,'' I said. ''Clients always hire her after they meet her in person. Would you please have her give me a call when she gets back?''

A moment after I hung up the phone Leonardo announced queasily over the intercom that Tommy had pulled into the driveway. I grabbed a pad and paper and got ready to go.

Still, I couldn't shake off an uneasy feeling within myself, one that revolved around Margarita. My mother always used to say we could have been sisters. Mami claimed we used to finish each other's sentences, and that when one of us got hurt the other would cry in sympathy. It would have given me peace of mind to speak with her. On impulse, I dialed her cellular phone, but it was turned off.

When I heard Tommy in the outer office, asking Leonardo what the hell was wrong with him, I almost called Leonora back. I don't know what I would have asked, maybe for the phone number at the Sanchez mansion. I told myself I was just being paranoid. What could possibly be wrong with someone as levelheaded as Margarita?

FOUR

"YOU DRIVE." TOMMY handed me the keys. "I'll read to you from the file on the way."

It wasn't every day that I got to drive a Rolls, so I was happy to comply. My Mercedes looked like it came from Rent-A-Wreck next to Tommy's Silver Shadow. The motor was so silent that when I turned the key, I had to strain to hear it start. I almost made Tommy put the top down, but controlled myself.

Tommy and I go way back. I met him seven years ago, during an excruciatingly dull deposition in a civil case. Tommy normally took only criminal cases, and he was doing a partner a favor by sitting in. It was a personal injury case involving insurance fraud, and because I was just starting out, it was important to me. Stanley Zimmerman, my family's attorney, referred me to Tommy as a favor.

Tommy wanted me to prove that the plaintiff was trying to defraud the insurance company by claiming a false injury. One of Tommy's partners, Marcel Parrish, was a prominent personal injury attorney in Miami, so I wanted to make a good impression. I really worked that case—with sworn witness statements and photographs proving the plaintiff was a liar. Tommy has trusted my work ever since.

"Here, let me give you the overview on the case," Tommy said. He took off his glasses and put them in a lovely Oliver Peoples black leather case, turning sideways to me as he spoke. Even in my impaired condition, I felt the pangs of desire. The air conditioner kept blowing the distinctive scent of his cologne my way. It was hard to concentrate on the road.

"The client's name is Alonso Arango, Sr. He's charged with killing a man named Gustavo Gaston," Tommy said. "Alonso owns Optima Jewelers—you know, that fancy shop on Miracle Mile in Coral Gables."

"I know the place," I said, hitting the horn as I swerved around a pickup truck puttering along in front of us.

"Our client's story is as follows: Gustavo Gaston came into the store and walked straight to the back, where they do gift wrapping, repairs, accounts, and so on. It's off limits to customers. Alonso was back there at the time, fixing a watch. He claims he saw Gaston come at him with a knife, so he whipped out his trusty Magnum and shot him."

"No conversation?" I asked.

"No questions asked," Tommy replied. "And no hesitation. And he didn't just blast him once, no, not our boy. Alonso shot him six times in under thirty seconds. The cops aren't buying the self-defense angle."

We had to stop for a red light, so I took the "A" form from Tommy and had a quick look at it. Coral Gables police officer Jesús Miranda's handwriting looked like that of a nine-year-old. The arrest report was too long to read at the light, but I saw that there were plenty of witnesses listed. Good. If Mr. Arango was telling the truth, there would be at least three individuals to corroborate his story.

"Can't you bond him out?" I asked as the light turned green.

"No way. The judge questioned the self-defense angle at the bond hearing. She said that one shot, maybe two would be enough to stop an attacker at such close range. Especially after the State revealed that Alonso Arango took a concealed-weapons course last year. I argued about five different ways, but the judge didn't buy it.''

"Who's the judge?''

"Shirley Markey,'' Tommy said, his voice barely a whisper.

"Ay, mierda!" I yelled, slapping the steering wheel. "We got Sparky Markey? Heaven help this Alonso Arango!''

Judge Shirley Markey was known in the Miami legal community as "Sparky Markey'' because of her love for sending defendants to "Old Sparky''—the electric chair at Starke Correctional Facility. Sparky Markey didn't believe in rehabilitation; she was a staunch supporter of pulling the switch and doing away with the criminal for eternity. On top of it all, she had an impeccable record as a jurist. In her thirty years on the bench she had never been reversed. Alonso Arango wouldn't fry for a Murder Two, but he was in trouble anyway.

"I'm no happier about it than you are,'' Tommy said, looking out the passenger window. "Anyway, I've only seen Alonso once before, at his bond hearing. That's when he agreed to hire me for the entire case. His English is pretty good, but he claims it tends to fail him when he gets nervous. You might have to do some interpreting for me.''

By then I was lost in concentration. We were approaching the intersection nearest the Stockade, and the traffic was hectic and confusing. Huge trucks roared by at reckless speeds, bound to or from the neighboring warehouse district. Six main roads and, for good measure, two railroad crossings intersected at that spot. The Stockade sat directly under a flight pattern heading into the airport, which only added to the distractions.

"How did you get this case, anyway?'' I asked, gritting my teeth and accelerating through the intersection. A van honked its irritation as I narrowly missed it.

"Wow, that was a close one.'' Tommy glanced back at the jammed intersection I had just sped through, clearly impressed. "My partner Peter represented Alonso's neighbor last year in a big personal injury case. You probably remember it—a wife was rear-ended at a stoplight by an Apex Concrete and Cement truck, and the driver blew a point thirty. The company settled for ten million."

"That was Peter's case?" I signaled a left, toward the Stockade. "I remember that one—the woman was the mother of seven, and was on her way home from dropping the kids off at school. So Peter got his usual forty percent contingency fee off ten million? No wonder he moved to Indian Creek."

"Yeah, and I used to make fun of Peter when he was starting out, for buying advertising on all those bus benches." Tommy shook his head as though in pain. "He sure as hell had the right idea."

With a deep sigh, probably thinking of money lost, Tommy put his papers into his briefcase. I parked as close as possible to the barbed wire fence near the walkway leading to the correction officers' hut.

After locking up the Rolls, I took out my driver's and investigator's licenses, putting my black leather Chanel bag in the trunk. Visitors to the jail weren't allowed to bring in personal belongings, other than pertinent files, along with pads of paper and writing utensils. I could have left my bag with the officers before going inside, but I didn't need the hassle of explaining the Beretta. Anyway, they wouldn't know how to properly care for good leather.

I also had to fix my look before we entered the compound. I learned long ago to dress appropriately for a jail visit, especially to the Dade County Stockade. This day I chose a two-piece navy-blue linen suit that covered most of my body. I tied my long hair back in a tortoiseshell clip, and wiped off my red lipstick.

Instead of my usual stiletto heels, I wore a pair of demure pumps. I never like wearing low heels, but I really hate it when I'm with Tommy. He's well over a foot taller than me, and with my height, I need every inch I can get. Tommy leaned on his car and watched my preparations with detached interest. We had been to the jail together before, and he knew the drill.

The Stockade layout required visitors to move across a

completely exposed walkway before reaching the interview areas. The walkway faced the cells, with a clear view either way, so the bored prisoners inevitably watched the visitors and were generous about sharing their thoughts. Their comments, whether delivered in English or Spanish, were so specific that I sometimes felt I was attending an anatomy professor's convention. Needless to say, after my first visit I learned to dress demurely before walking that particular gangplank.

I passed through without eliciting much comment, aside from the usual pedestrian vulgarities. I tried not to take it as a slight, though I felt a little disappointed. I always counted on the prisoners to give me the latest synonyms for men's favorite female body parts. I like staying up-to-date.

Tommy and I quickly reached the first of the correction officers' checkpoints, surrounded above and to either side by chain-link fences. When we got closer to the main hut, I saw three men dressed in the usual dark green uniform moving around behind scratched-up bulletproof partitions. We flashed our identification through the minuscule opening and signed in.

The officers kept our IDs, which was standard. There were two purported reasons why this was done: first, in case a prisoner was sprung, they wanted to know who was responsible; the second—more plausible to me given the quality of inmates in the Dade County prison system—was that they needed to know who to notify in case we were murdered inside.

While we waited for our clearance, I took the opportunity to call Margarita's cellular phone one last time from the pay phones outside the guard's station. The phone rang and rang.

Now I was worried. First the phone was turned off, now it was on but she wasn't picking up. What in the world was going on with her? I thought about calling Leonora again, but didn't. I'd already left one message, and I didn't want to get Leonora started on some side topic.

"Alonso Arango, Senior," an officer barked into his walkie-talkie. He made the name sound like a distasteful species of insect.

One perk—if you can call it that—of being a private investigator is that your license entitles you to visit a jail at any time, not just during regular visiting hours. After a garbled reply on the walkie-talkie, we were escorted to yet another office to await the arrival of our client. *Tommy's client*, I reminded myself.

Tommy settled himself into a beat-up metal chair in front of a chipped dark brown wooden desk, and began jotting notes on a legal pad. One of the guards was waiting in the room with us, and we both knew better than to discuss the case in his presence.

I tried to put Margarita out of my mind, just for the moment, and realized all at once that my hangover had eased up quite a bit. I figured some sugar would help me even more, so I made for the soft drink machine at the end of the hall, hoping for a Coke.

I was momentarily despondent to see that the machine was out of everything save for Orange Crush, but then the little black and white linoleum squares on the floor began to vibrate before my eyes. Who cared what it tasted like; I needed something sweet to wake myself up.

Just after I opened the can, a blaring voice made me jump. It was the facility's loudspeaker system, informing me that Alonso Arango was waiting in the inner interview room.

FIVE

ALONSO ARANGO, WITH a distinctly proud bearing, stood in the doorway of one of the several interview rooms branching off from the main area. He was handcuffed, in accordance with prison rules, but this didn't detract from his proud demeanor. Stockade prisoners were permitted to wear their own clothes, and Alonso was dressed in neat khaki pants, a pressed sports shirt, and a wool cardigan sweater that gave him a slightly professorial look.

A corrections officer removed Alonso's handcuffs, and the jeweler invited us into the small room designated for our interview. He gestured inside with a benevolent, courtly air, as though we were guests in his home. Before we stepped in, the officer showed us the bell on the wall, which we would ring when we wanted to be let out of the room. All three of us—client, attorney, and investigator—released a collective sigh of relief when the door finally closed behind us.

"Señor Arango, this is Miss Guadalupe Solano," Tommy said in his best professional voice. "She is the investigator I've hired to assist me on your case. We've worked together many times in the past.''

"It's a pleasure to meet you," I said. I dug into my suit jacket pocket for a business card and presented it to him.

Alonso Arango took the card from my hand and carefully examined it while I had a look around the room. It was the same as in all other jails: a small, windowless box, barely wide enough for a table and three chairs. I hoped Mr. Arango wasn't a pacer; there wasn't much room to move around.

"Miss Solano, thank you for helping me," Alonso said, tucking my card in his shirt pocket as we settled into our chairs.

As soon as he sat down, Alonso pounded the table and looked as though he might get back up again. "I'm not sure what I'm doing here," he said to me. "A man tried to kill me, and I shot him to defend myself. There are witnesses who saw it all! He came at me with a knife!"

He seemed to realize that he was on the verge of losing control. His dark eyes shone under his fine, close-cropped hair. A bright vein pulsed on his tanned forehead. "I am sorry to get excited," he said. "But can't a person defend his own life in this country, Miss Solano?"

Instead of replying, I snuck another peek at the "A" form Tommy had placed on the table. Alonso's date of birth was listed as 6/15/36, making him sixty years old. He was facing a Murder Two rap from the State. Tommy would try to get the charge reduced to manslaughter, but if he couldn't and the case was lost Alonso Arango could well spend the rest of his life in prison.

I didn't know what to say, so I resorted to pleasantries. "Please, call me Lupe."

"Okay," he said. "But only if I am Alonso to you." Now that he had calmed down, I could see that he was quite good-looking, especially when he trained his effortless smile on me.

Tommy watched our exchange with a smile of his own. He knew the effect I could have on men, especially those of a certain age. He also knew that I might be able to extract information from Alonso that he would never be able to get at. This was one of my strong points as an investigator—people liked to talk to me, and they inevitably ended up confiding in me things they didn't realize they knew.

"Mr. Arango, suppose you start by telling us about the shooting," Tommy began, staring down at his legal pad. "I already have your statement, but I'd like Lupe to hear what happened last Saturday. She might have more questions for you."

"Very well." Alonso sniffed, folded his arms, and stared at the wall behind me. "Saturday morning we opened up, as usual, at nine-thirty in the morning. We don't actually open the shop until ten, but we come to work a half hour earlier, to get the place ready for customers."

I started taking notes. For some unknown reason, years before, my mother insisted I take a speedwriting course. It seemed absolutely useless at the time, but this skill has served me well. I've found that people don't speak as freely with a tape recorder running during an interview. I stayed silent, allowing Alonso to get into the flow of telling his story. I would have questions for him when he finished.

"By ten-fifteen, all four employees were present," he continued. "We have three salespeople, two Cubans and one American. We also have a bookkeeper, Silvia Romero. Her office is in the back, next to mine, behind the counter we use for repairs, gift wrapping, credit card checks. You know, things like that. The back area is separated from the main store, and you can only reach it through a door that is normally kept closed. No customers come back there."

He paused and I looked up. Alonso stared into my eyes. "Please go on," Tommy said. "And let's get back to Saturday morning. We'll ask you about the setup later."

"So sorry," Alonso said. When he spoke again, his voice was lower. "That morning I was standing in the back, behind the counter, changing a watch strap for a Venezuelan woman who had dropped it off a few minutes before. She wanted it done in a hurry, because she was flying to Caracas that afternoon and she wanted to take the watch with her. She left it with George, my American salesman, and said she would pick it up in a half hour, after she ran some errands. So I was concentrating on that job, to get it done fast. The Venezuelan lady is a reliable customer. I wanted to be sure the watch was ready for her when she returned.''

Tommy fidgeted in the chair next to me, impatient for Alonso to get to the shooting. I kicked him gently under the table. There was no point rushing Alonso; he obviously was a man used to speaking in his own way, in his own time. Besides, he was paying us well. If the old man wanted to take his time, it was his right and privilege.

''I remember that I was alone in the back of the store,'' Alonso said. ''Silvia had run out to the post office to buy stamps. Then I felt someone in the doorway. I just sensed that they were there, but I didn't look up because I was concentrating on the watch strap. Whoever it was just stood there without coming in. I thought it might have been a client, so I finally did look up. I saw a man there.''

''That was Gustavo Gaston,'' Tommy said. He still stared down at his pad, tapping it with a pencil.

''I learned his name later. Also, that he's a rafter—he came from Cuba on a raft,'' Alonso said. ''But this Gaston was just standing there, looking at me. I said no clients were allowed in the back, or something like that. Then he came at me with a knife. I knew he was about to stab me, so I reached under the counter where I keep the Magnum. I told him to keep away. When he kept coming at me, I shot him.''

Alonso leaned back in his chair and took a deep breath. His hands rested perfectly still in his lap. I didn't have to worry about the size of the room—Alonso wasn't a pacer. Though I could tell he was distressed telling his story, he remained perfectly composed. It struck me as a little unusual.

''And did anyone else witness what happened?'' Tommy asked.

''Well, no, I don't think so. Not the shooting itself.'' Alonso brushed his hair away from his forehead. ''I was alone in the back. Silvia returned through the back door, though, just after the man fell on the floor. She said she heard the shots. And George came in from the front of the store, just a moment or so later.''

It was my turn. ''Before we go into the shooting in more detail, I'd like to know more about your other employees,'' I began. ''You said you have three salespeople—George, the American, and two Cubans. Tell me about them, starting with their first names and how long they've worked for you.''

''The two saleswomen are cousins, Elsa and Olivia Ramirez,'' Alonso said. His voice was impassive and emotionless. ''Elsa started first. She's been with me for, let's see, almost from the beginning. Maybe twelve years? I started Optima Jewelers in 1984, and Elsa has been with me the whole time. We worked together four years in another jeweler's. That's how I met her.''

I was on my third sheet of paper. ''Go on,'' I said.

''Olivia came to me without any experience at all. She needed a job after her husband left her and her two children. Elsa said she would train her—and she did. Beautifully. George Mortimer has been with us the shortest amount of time, just three years. He's young, and recently graduated from F.I.U. This is his first job.''

''And I can get their personnel records from your office?'' I asked.

Alonso nodded, then smiled. ''But I don't keep the best records, I have to warn you. I hire people based mostly on how I feel about them, not just because of their experience or references. I go by this.'' He tapped his heart with his index finger. ''It's worked for me always.''

I didn't care to respond to his theatrics. ''Tell us about Silvia Romero,'' I said. ''She's your bookkeeper, right?''

''Yes. She's Puerto Rican, a transplant from New York,'' Alonso said. ''She came in two days a week in the beginning, but business has been good and I took her on full-time. She does all the paperwork—billing, insurance, benefits, credit card charges. She's only been with us full-time for less than a year. If you count her part-time work, she's been at the store for closer to four years.''

With a quick peek at my watch, I saw that we had been

at the Stockade for a little over an hour. My rear end was beginning to hurt from sitting still for so long. Next to me, Tommy had started to perspire slightly, his fair hair sticking to his forehead. Alonso, on the other hand, seemed perfectly comfortable.

"And who does the cleaning?" I asked Alonso. "Do you have a regular service that comes in?"

"Oh, I forgot all about Reina Sotolongo." Alonso hit himself lightly on his forehead, making a muffled thud. "She's the cleaning lady who comes in at night. Reina has her own key—she comes in to clean after we leave, sometimes quite late at night."

"How long has Reina been with you?" I asked.

"Years and years, from the very beginning. I remember, she came in and asked for a job the very first day we opened. She's a very good worker; it takes her less than an hour to do the entire shop. She cleans a lot of other shops on Miracle Mile. She was around that Saturday morning, too, cleaning the bridal store next door. She heard the commotion and came to see what had happened."

This was all well and good, but there was no point continuing without asking the hardest question. I pointed at the police report. "Alonso, according to the Coral Gables police, the knife you say Gaston tried to attack you with was never found."

I felt Tommy straighten in his chair. He hadn't asked Alonso this question yet, and I knew he would be glad I did. It went a long way toward explaining why Sparky Markey had denied bail.

"Yes, that is what I was told," Alonso said, his voice clear. "I have no idea what happened to the knife. All I know is, I saw it. That man would have stabbed me with it. I swear he had it."

Tommy stood up and started gathering papers. "I think that's all we need to know for now," he said. "Please tell your wife and your sons we will need to speak with them soon, as well as your employees at the store. I understand your wife is taking your place at the jewelry store until you get out."

"She is," Alonso said, and he seemed to sink into himself just a little. Some of his polish vanished, and he looked his age. "She comes in and works a few hours, every day."

"Hey, take it easy." Tommy put his hand on the older man's shoulder and gently squeezed. "I know it's difficult, but hang in there. We'll do everything we can to get you through this."

Tommy rang the bell on the wall, and we all looked at the walls until an officer came to escort us out. When the thick metal door was unlocked, Alonso nodded gravely and stepped outside.

He was led back to his cell, while Tommy and I headed for the outside checkpoint. We didn't say anything until we were safely strapped into the Rolls. Tommy drove.

"Let's get a drink," I said. I needed one.

"All right."

"He's lying," I stated.

"Definitely."

Tommy and I drove over to the Grand Bay Hotel in Coconut Grove and walked up to the second-floor bar. I asked him to excuse me while I found a pay phone and called Margarita on her cellular phone. Nothing. It was turned off again. I tried her home number, and got only the machine. I left a message for her to call me, no matter what time it was.

Back at the bar, Tommy was waiting patiently, jotting notes on a pad. The hostess led us to one of the more discreet tables, in a back corner. After we settled into the plush leather seats and ordered a bottle of Dom Pérignon—on Tommy's corporate account—he started in on me.

"Why exactly do you think he's lying?" he asked.

I watched the waitress expertly twist the cork off the champagne bottle and searched for a good answer. "He's shifty-eyed," I said.

Tommy made a strange sound and drained his glass in a single gulp. "I'm paying you a hundred bucks an hour, and all you can tell me is that my client is shifty-eyed!"

"You're paying me to give you my impressions of your

client and his story," I replied. "I'm not working this case, remember? Tomorrow I'm leaving for the Keys. I went along with you today because I said I would, and I keep my word. The guy knows a hell of a lot more than he's telling you, it's as simple as that. I only need one interview to know that."

I sat back in the deep cushions and sipped my drink. In the corner a young woman belted out a fine rendition of "I Left My Heart in San Francisco," accompanying herself on the piano. I raised my glass to her when she looked our way. It was easy to slip into vacation mode.

I suddenly burst out laughing with the memory of a night in Little Havana a few years before. "Tommy, remember the night we went to that Peruvian nightclub to hear your client who was a singer? You remember the one—she was charged with Murder One for poisoning her lover with her homemade seviche?"

Despite himself, Tommy started laughing too. "I never thought the jury would go for it, but when I made them taste her cooking they let her off!"

I was laughing so hard my eyes watered. "Remember when she sang 'I Left My Heart in Lima,' and all those Peruvians stood on the tables, waving those little paper flags, crying and drinking pisco sours?"

Tommy slapped his thigh in amusement, then gave me a longing look. "Oh God, Lupe. We've had some great cases together, haven't we?"

"No way, don't start that one on me," I said, intercepting the hand that was headed for my shoulder. "After we're done here I'll go home and write up my impressions of the interview. I'll say what the next investigator should know about the case's weaknesses, but that's it. If you want, I'll even make a few calls and try to find you another investigator. But that's it, Tommy. It's over."

To my amazement, Tommy shrugged, poured us each a fresh glass, and changed the subject. He started talking about a boat he was thinking of buying, wondering how it stacked up against Papi's Hatteras. It surprised me to see him give in so easily, but I was grateful. I was tired of fighting with him.

When we finished the champagne we said goodnight. Tommy drove me over to my office to pick up my car and gave me a kiss on the cheek in the parking lot. "Enjoy your vacation," he said.

I started to drive home to my apartment on Brickell Avenue, but I changed my mind when I remembered that my sister Lourdes was coming to dinner at Cocoplum. She was just the nun I needed to see to help me maintain that vacation mood.

SIX

I GLANCED AT the bright green numerals on my bedside clock. It was close to midnight. The day had been a long one, not to mention the fact that I had gotten only two hours sleep the night before. Still, I wanted to finish the report I had been working on for the last three hours, so that in the morning I could give it to Leonardo to type up.

I yawned, stretched like a cat, and poured myself a glass from the bottle of Cristal bobbing around in melted ice in the silver bucket propped up next to me in bed. I had started on champagne with Tommy earlier and saw no reason to switch. Now I noticed with alarm that the bucket, wedged between pillows and blank legal pads, had formed a pool of cold water that was creeping toward me. Just as I began to soak it up with a T-shirt I pulled from the floor, the phone rang.

"Lupe, it's me. Were you sleeping?"

"Hi, Tommy. No, I wasn't sleeping. I've been working on the Alonso Arango report for you."

"Anything interesting?"

"Maybe." I paused. "It's too soon to tell. I don't know

much for sure, but there are some things you should check out.''

''C'mon, Lupe, give me a break. Don't torture me. What did you find out?''

''Later, Tommy. Bye.''

I had no pity for him. As far as I was concerned, he hadn't paid enough yet for tricking me into going to the Stockade with him. I knew he was counting on my becoming interested in the case, so that I would give in and work with him. I would have been tempted, if I wasn't resolute in my determination to leave the next day for vacation. Tommy, after all, was one of the best criminal lawyers in town, and working a case for him was inevitably educational. And he nearly always got his clients acquitted, which meant I could enhance my own reputation by riding his coattails to victory.

And even though Leonardo and I were backed up in sending out our bills, we could use the money. We shared a pure refugee mentality: we both feared, without ever saying so, that our business would dry up without warning, and we'd end up out on the street. We both knew this was unlikely, but we had struggled a lot in the beginning and we sure as hell didn't want to return to those lean years.

Papi had backed me financially when I started Solano Investigations seven years before, and I was proud that I had paid him back every penny of his investment. When I started out I had to take every case that came my way, but time passed and I earned a reputation for hard work, honesty, and—most important—not padding my bills. After some time I had the luxury of picking and choosing.

I remember how angry and upset I was when Papi made employing my cousin a condition of his initial backing. I hardly knew Leonardo—only by his reputation as the wayward son of my mother's sister—and he was three years younger than I was. To my surprise, we got along perfectly. Now I can't imagine not having him around, even if he drives me crazy sometimes with his New Age crap and his granola-eating friends.

It's a small price to pay for having him in the office.

Sometimes I have to draw the line with him—like the time he tried to convert our back room into a meditation chamber, complete with Sedona posters, candles, incense, and crystals. I could have tolerated most of that, but I went crazy when I found he had covered the floor with sand. His timing couldn't have been worse. I walked in on all this tired, hungry, and dirty after a twenty-four-hour surveillance—and completely lost it. I ran out about a dozen of Leonardo's friends, stopping them in midchant. When I came to work the next day, the back room was returned to its original state, housing our files and supplies. Leonardo and I never spoke about it again, which was fine with me. My only lingering question was what his friend meant about my red and purple aura, but I figured it wasn't worth the bother of asking.

I remember as though it were yesterday when Leonardo and I were secure enough to turn down a low-paying domestic case. We actually went out to celebrate. Domestics are the worst, without question. Florida is a no-fault state, so it doesn't really matter who's screwing who outside a marriage as far as the courts are concerned. But people being people, one spouse always wants proof that their wife or husband is cheating.

Some of them want photos or video—in color—or audiotape. I still have nightmares that my clients would show the videos to their kids, their relatives, or their friends, just to prove what a miserable excuse of a human being their spouse was. In my worst dreams, of the sweat-drenched variety, I saw my clients serving popcorn as they viewed proof of the adultery in the family room on a wide-screen TV.

Maybe I worked too many domestics, but marriage held no appeal for me. I was perfectly content to recycle my old boyfriends, rotating them as the mood hit me. I was comfortable with them, and they understood me. Maybe we were all getting older and set in our ways, I don't know.

I had just about finished the report and recommendations for Tommy when I heard a soft knock at the door.

''Come in,'' I said, finishing one of the final sections.

My older sister Lourdes poked her head into the room.

"Lupe, I saw your light was still on. You're really working late. Are you almost through?"

"I am now. Hang on while I put these papers away." I slipped the stack of papers into a manila envelope and wrote Alonso Arango's name on it.

Lourdes came into the room and flopped down on the bed next to me, just like when we were little girls. She gave out a cry when she landed square on the freezing wet spot left by my ice bucket.

"Sorry," I said, mopping up more of the mess. "Try where I was sitting. I warmed it up for you."

Lourdes rolled over on the other side of the bed, giving a giggle. "Well, I know you were here alone tonight, so I won't get grossed out about that wet spot."

Lourdes was pretty cool, particularly for a nun in the Order of the Holy Rosary. She had discarded the pink bath-robe and fuzzy pink slippers she wore earlier that night, stripping down to her Miami Heat boxer shorts and her fa-vorite T-shirt—the one with "I'm a Bitch" plastered proudly across the front. She had her long hair pulled back in a braid.

I have two older sisters, Fatima and Lourdes. Mami, with her usual religious fervor, named us after three apparitions of the Holy Virgin. I lucked out; Guadalupe can be short-ened to Lupe, but there's not much to be done with Lourdes and Fatima. Fatima is my oldest sister, and the only daughter to live in the family house full-time. Sometimes it seemed that after Mami's death seven years before, Lourdes and I returned so often that we might as well have never left. Papi, always considering himself a traditional macho Cuban man, would sooner die than admit he likes having a gaggle of women around the house all the time. But we all know he loves it.

It didn't start off that way. Lourdes first lived in a Little Havana house with three other nuns, and for a while Fatima had a house in Coral Gables where she lived with her twin daughters. I kept the Brickell apartment to maintain my au-tonomy and independence. I signed a lease on the place a few months after my graduation from the University of Miami, and it was exciting then for me to be out on my own. The ink still fresh on my diploma—I majored in advertising, so needless to say, no one beat down my door with a job offer—I took a job as an intern investigator at White and Blanco, a firm in northwest Miami.

I suppose I fell into my career by accident. I learned about the field when Julio Juarez, Fatima's husband at the time, was suspected of embezzling funds from Papi's construction firm to pay for his girlfriend's condominium. I helped out Hadrian Wells—the investigator hired by our family's attorney, Stanley Zimmerman—and found that I liked the work. I went on some more jobs with Hadrian and his boss, Esteban Morales, and started toying around with the idea of making the work a career. It caused quite a scandal in my home when I announced my intentions.

Working conditions at White and Blanco were appalling. They were lucky the health department never dropped in for an inspection. Of course the clients never saw "the pit," where the seven investigators and I slaved away. They saw only the plush, thickly carpeted outer office, where they were served tea and coffee in china cups and saucers.

Meanwhile, I was behind closed doors, the only female investigator and thus the only one who didn't fart, belch, scratch my crotch, or discuss my bodily functions in front of everyone. Any illusions I might have harbored about the opposite sex vanished within the first hour of my first day there. On the positive side, anything I ever learned about human nature was also revealed to me on that job.

The day I got my class C license—which meant I could work as an investigator without needing to be employed under the umbrella of an established firm—I had a thousand business cards printed up. I plunked down three months' rent on the cottage in Coconut Grove, and I was in business.

"Want to share your daydreams?" Lourdes asked from next to me. "Or should I let you space out in private?"

"Sorry," I said, realizing my thoughts had been drifting. "It's been a long day."

"Still planning to leave tomorrow for the Keys?"

"You bet," I said. We were lying side by side, staring

up at the ceiling. "I would have left today, but Tommy tricked me into interviewing a client of his at the Stockade. I was finishing the report when you knocked, but you'd be proud of me. I turned down the case. After I drop off the report, I'm completely free."

I sighed loudly. Alonso Arango was not my problem.

Lourdes turned to me. "So, you're done with your work for the day?"

"What's with you?" I asked, getting up on one elbow so I could have a good look at her. "You have a mischievous look in your eyes."

Lourdes reached into the pocket of her shorts. "Oh, it's nothing. I just thought you might want this." She produced a fat, tightly rolled joint, and waved it in my face. Just the smell of the thing was intoxicating.

"Theofilus?" I asked, referring to the Jamaican gardener who worked at her convent.

"Who else?" Lourdes said. Her eyes sparkled, as they always did when she was being bad. "He came back from Montego Bay yesterday and brought me this as a present. I immediately thought of you."

Lourdes reached out for a book of matches on my nightstand, lit one, and held it out for me. "I'm grateful, you know, but I warned him about bringing this stuff on planes," she added, watching me inhale the smoke. "I told him how much trouble he'd be in if he got caught."

It wasn't long before the room was filled with sweet-smelling smoke, and soon I had to get up and open the French doors leading to the balcony outside my room. When I came back, Lourdes was looking at the joint smoldering in the ashtray.

"Go ahead, *chica*," I kidded her. When she was younger she would have joined me, but her devotion to her calling had given her incredible willpower. "Take a hit, just a small one. No one is going to find out."

Lourdes shook her head, rolling her eyes toward heaven. "You're wrong. Someone will know."

She was quiet for a few minutes after I joined her on the bed. I wondered what she was thinking about, but I quickly gave up. I could never tell what was on my sister's mind. For all I knew, it was filled with saints, miracles, and apparitions. Whatever the case, it always seemed she was one step ahead of me, her advice always perfect for the situation. Her irreverence didn't detract from her profound dedication to her calling. She had the sort of mind that thrived on contradictions, but one thing that was completely without ambiguity to her was her faith.

"What are you thinking about?" she asked me.

"You," I said.

She giggled. "What about me?"

"How I can never tell what you're thinking."

"That's because I'm busy reading your mind," she said in a spooky-movie voice.

"Don't get weird," I said. "Anyway, if you can read my mind, why did you ask me what I was thinking?"

She paused, just for an instant. "Oh, you know, little sister. Just to make conversation."

That was it. Before she could stop me, I had taken a handful of water and ice from the bucket next to me, pulled on the neck of her shirt, and dropped it down on her bare skin. She roared with laughter and planted one of my feather pillows square in the middle of my face.

"I just remembered something," I said, lying back on the bed. Lourdes grabbed another pillow, watching me to see if I was trying to pull a fast one. "Margarita didn't return my calls. I was trying to reach her all day."

"What's up with Margarita?" Lourdes asked.

"I had lunch with her two days ago and she was acting weird. It left me feeling really worried about her."

"Does it have to do with Rodrigo?" she asked, her eyes narrowing with distaste. Lourdes shared my feelings about Margarita's husband.

"I don't know, but she just sat there and barely ate anything. I need to talk to her before I leave town tomorrow."

Lourdes yawned. "I should get to bed, anyway," she said. She looked at me strangely. "You're really worried, aren't you? Don't be. You two have been friends since you were in diapers. She'll tell you about her problems when she's ready. Everything will be fine.''

I smiled at my sister. "You always know the right thing to say.''

"It's part of the job. Give her a call and put your mind at ease.''

When Lourdes was gone I dialed Margarita's home number, even though it was past midnight. No answer, so I left another message for her and tried her cellular phone. It was turned off.

I told myself there was no point in worrying. I would talk to Margarita in the morning and straighten everything out. I shut off the light and closed my eyes. When the image of Alonso Arango came into my mind I willed it away. Nothing would stand in the way of my vacation.

SEVEN

———————◆———————

"JESUS, NORMA, YOU'RE fricasseeing me!"

I had just slid my feet into the plastic pan on the floor—and yanked them out again the instant the hot water scorched my skin and turned it a shade of deep salmon. It was Friday morning, time for my standing manicure and pedicure appointment. I was also using the time to check over the report Leonardo had just typed up before calling a courier to deliver it to Tommy's office.

As always, Norma paid absolutely no attention to my protestations of torture. She had been caring for my hands and feet for nearly ten years and had heard it all before. I admired her skill, and the way she continued to work no matter how much I squirmed and tried to escape.

When my pain subsided a little, and I looked down to make sure there was still skin on my feet, I lowered my toes back into the water and tried to concentrate on the Alonso Arango report. My notes raised a lot more questions than they answered, but I had written everything up clearly enough so that the next investigator would know where to start working on the case. When I awoke that morning, after sleeping like the dead, I was a little surprised to see how coherent my report was—given my condition the day before—but I'm nothing if not a professional. Now I was rested and feeling good—really good—because I had consumed three of Leonardo's lethal Cuban coffees within the last hour.

"Lupe, no more café for you!" Leonardo scolded from my office doorway. I held my fourth coffee with shaking hands, my fingers delicately splayed into a fan so I didn't smear my freshly applied blood-red nail polish. "You look like Miss Manners on speed! Norma, how can you work on her when she's like that?"

Norma shrugged, not even looking up. In all the years I had known her, I heard her say perhaps a dozen words. Every few years I would become frustrated with her unresponsiveness and leave her, but my forays into the harsh world of other manicurists were invariably disastrous. It would take my cuticles weeks to recover from the butchering.

By the time Norma had packed and left I was deep into the police report that was awaiting me when I arrived at work that morning, courtesy of Tommy. From the outer office I heard the familiar sound of Leonardo counting out Norma's payment from the petty cash drawer—after nearly a decade, she still didn't accept checks from me or from any of her other clients, or so I had heard. I hoped it was due to her aversion to the IRS rather than distrust of us. I had started to jot a few notes when my phone rang.

"Tommy, good. I was about to call you," I said. "How thoroughly did you read the 'A' form on Alonso Arango?"

"I glanced at it. Why?"

I had a sinking feeling this case wouldn't be the easy home run that Tommy usually expected. "Well, you should read it," I said. "And you should read it carefully."

From the police report I learned that no one had actually witnessed Gustavo Gaston come at Alonso with a knife. True, there were witnesses listed on the report, but none of them saw the alleged attack that prompted Alonso's "self-defense." Silvia Romero, the bookkeeper, was returning from the post office just as the shots were fired. She parked her car in the municipal garage behind the building, and heard the gunfire at the same moment she was unlocking the bolt on the back door.

None of the other employees actually saw or heard anything—again, until the shots were fired. To make it worse, no one saw Gaston enter Optima Jewelers that Saturday morning. The store was full of people, but none of them could corroborate Alonso's story. And the knife, the major problem, was still missing. The next investigator had a lot of issues to work out. I was tempted, but not tempted enough.

"Is Norma gone yet?" Tommy asked.

There are no secrets in this world, I thought with disgust. "Yes, Tommy, she just left. Anyway, what's up? I'm about to send you your report."

"I didn't sleep very well last night," Tommy said in a vulnerable voice. "I kept thinking about this case. I should be used to my clients lying to me by now, but I didn't expect it from a guy like Arango. Live and learn, I guess. Anyway, what's on your agenda for today?"

"Besides leaving for Key West when my nails are dry?" I asked innocently.

"Ah, Key West!" Tommy said. He sounded pleased with himself, as though he had solved a puzzle. "So I bet you're going to see that old boyfriend of yours? The one who dropped out?"

I ignored him and stuck to business. "Like I said, I'll call the courier as soon as we hang up. My bill will be included."

"Or course," Tommy said drearily.

"I'm warning you, it's going to be a big one. I put a lot of hours in on this case, even though I'm not taking it." I paused, trying to figure out how to word what I had to say next. "Listen, Tommy. I'm worried about this one. It's all wrong. It has more holes than a doughnut store. From looking closer at the police report, I'd say it's no wonder Sparky Markey denied bail. I would've, too. You've got to get this guy to come clean with you, or else you won't be able to help him.''

"I know. You're right. And I have a confession to make.'' Tommy used his sweet-talk voice. "I really didn't do much background on this case before I took it on. To be perfectly honest, I was counting on you to work it for me, like you usually do. After all, you're the best. We never lose when we work together. I just figured you'd take the case after you talked to the old man.''

"Of course you did. But you figured wrong, didn't you?'' I hung up on him before he could say anything more.

Just then my direct line rang. Thinking it was Tommy again, I almost didn't answer. I was glad I did.

"Margarita!'' I yelled into the phone. "Where the hell have you been? I called you a hundred times!''

"I've been in Palm Beach, and I haven't left yet,'' she said. "I'm sorry. I got all your messages, but I wasn't ready to talk to anyone until now. There's . . . there's a lot going on in my life, things you don't know about.''

Margarita's voice had become so soft I could barely hear her. I instantly forgot my anger with her. "Are you all right?'' I asked.

"Yes. No.'' She sighed. "I don't know. Lupe, I can't talk now. But I should be back in Miami in two hours. I'll talk to you then, all right?''

"Wait, don't hang up,'' I pleaded. She sounded distracted and distant. "Are you sure you can drive? If I leave now I can be there in just over an hour. Where are you in Palm Beach? Are you with those Sanchez people?''

"Lupe, please, it's de Sanchez since I got the account.'' Margarita laughed softly at her own weak joke.

"Where are you?'' I repeated. "I'll leave right now.''

"No, please don't. I'm fine to drive.''

"What's the matter? Can you tell me?'' I wanted to keep her on the phone as long as I could. She sounded less distraught and more focused the longer she talked to me. She needed to get her head together if she insisted on driving back to Miami. It was just over sixty miles, but the interstate traffic was always atrocious. She would need her wits about her. I was also overcome with curiosity; Margarita wasn't the type to just disappear. With my usual tact, I began to barrage her with questions.

"What's so bad that you couldn't call?" I asked. "Does it have to do with your work? Are you in some kind of trouble? Do you need me as an investigator? Is there anything I can do for you before you get back to town?"

"Lupe, please," she interrupted. "It has to do with Rodrigo and me. We're having problems—real problems. We haven't had sex in six months, and now he tells me he wants to have a baby. I'm really confused and I don't know what to do. I just needed some time to get away and sort out my thoughts."

"What? You didn't say anything about this before," I said, my feelings hurt. "How could you hide this from me?"

My oldest friend had failed to confide in me. This stung plenty, but my professional pride was also at stake. I get paid for extracting secrets from people, and though I had known something was wrong with Margarita, I hadn't had a clue about what it involved.

"Margarita, I planned to leave for the Keys today, but I'll wait for you. It sounds like you need someone to talk to."

Now I sounded as strange as she had a few moments before. I knew things weren't smooth between her and Rodrigo, but having never been married myself, I figured it was just one of those rough spots that all married people go through. I had no idea their relationship had deteriorated so much that they were no longer physically intimate. Margarita, I knew, always had a healthy libido, so things must have been serious. I thought about Rodrigo's response, and realized I shouldn't have been overly surprised. The old wisdom is usually true: when a marriage is in trouble, the couple usually decides to have a baby or buy a new house.

"It would be nice to talk to you some more," Margarita replied. "It's been hell trying to keep it from you, but I didn't want anyone to know how bad things were."

"For crying out loud, Margarita. Why?"

"I didn't want to tell you the truth because I know you never really liked Rodrigo."

She was right, though I had never explicitly told her so. "Well, now you know," she said. "I feel a lot better just having told you. There's more, but it can wait until we get together."

"Great," I said. "I'll see you in two hours."

"Lupe, you made plans to get away and I want you to keep them. Thanks for offering to stay for me, but I won't hear of it. You need your vacation." Suddenly Margarita sounded stranger than she did at the beginning of the conversation. I heard her blow her nose. "Are you going to see Sam?" she asked.

Despite my concern, I detected a sly tone in Margarita's voice that reassured me about her state of mind. This was more like the Margarita I knew and loved.

"Yes, I'm going to see Sam," I said. "But I could put it off one more day and it wouldn't make much of a difference. I was supposed to leave yesterday, but Tommy talked me into doing a jailhouse interview with him—this guy who owns a jewelry store on Miracle Mile hired Tommy to defend him on a Murder Two. He shot a rafter who came into the store and allegedly attacked him."

"God, Lupe." Margarita's voice became as grave as I'd ever heard it. "What is Tommy's client's name?"

"Alonso Arango. Why do you ask?"

"There's something you should know. Wait for me," she rasped. "I'll be in your office in an hour and a half. Don't go anywhere."

With this, she hung up.

EIGHT

THE DRIVE DOWN to Key West wasn't nearly as bad as I'd feared. I set out at the height of the after-work rush hour, when the two-lane highway usually crawls, doubling the three hours it takes to reach the southernmost point in the United States from Miami. That day, though, the Fates were kind. Traffic was smooth and cops were scarce. With each relatively painless mile that passed, I felt myself relax a little more.

I was driving so late because I did as Margarita had asked, and waited for her to return to Miami from Palm Beach. I sat around from noon until six without any word from her. At first I was angry, thinking she was avoiding me again, then I grew worried and almost left messages on her machines. But then I stopped myself. I now knew what troubled my friend, and though she was obviously distraught it was essentially a domestic problem. At six I sent Leonardo home and climbed into my Mercedes. Margarita would talk to me when she was ready.

The sun shone on the ocean and made it silver and shimmery. I played the radio loud. The vista around the Seven

Mile Bridge was particularly gorgeous, with pelicans swooping around both sides of the bay, the commercial boats heading out for their night fishing, and the sailboats drifting into the harbor for the evening.

The traffic dwindled as time passed, and I could feel all the embedded tension leaving my neck and shoulders. I began to anticipate seeing Sam Lamont, my old friend and ex-boyfriend. It had been more than a year since I last saw him, and that was definitely far too long.

Sam had moved to Key West from Miami five years before. He never returned to Dade County, so if I wanted to see him I had to see him there. I love Key West, so it wasn't a bad bargain. I also loved and respected Sam, and would have driven even farther if I had to.

Sam lived in a house that, to me, defined sheer cool—a Victorian gingerbread home he had renovated himself. A bit of a hedonist, he designed my favorite part of the house himself, the outdoor shower. It was a generous wooden stall built out of fragrant wood, surrounded by orchids, and when I was in it I imagined myself lost within a tropical forest. Sam rigged the showerhead to mist the water down in a fine spray.

Several years before, when Sam lived in Miami and made a killing as a crack polygrapher, we had had a fairly serious romance. But, as usually happens with me and men, I decided I liked him better as a friend than as a potential husband. Sometimes I thought my refusal to allow anything more serious to happen between us contributed to his sudden decision to leave Miami and his practice, but he always told me it wasn't so. Besides his tall, Nordic looks, his self-assurance, and his quiet, intelligent sense of humor, I think what I liked most of all about him was how he always welcomed me back into his life, no matter what and for however long, never making demands.

I passed Stock Island and the Key West Aquarium, and in a matter of minutes, I was there. When I pulled into the driveway Sam was on the porch waiting for me, sipping coffee while reclining in a cushiony wicker chair. He stood up and tucked his polo shirt into his jeans, a big smile on his face. I hadn't even called to tell him I would be delayed for a day, knowing he wouldn't care. Sam was out of the rat race, and it showed in his calm, easy manner. A day one way or the other didn't matter much to him, and for the next week, it wouldn't matter to me, either.

"Nice drive?" he asked, taking my shoulder bag. He put his free arm around me and pulled me close. We walked toward his house together.

"Very relaxing," I said as he held the front door open for me. Inside the front room I saw that he had made progress since I had been there last. Now the walls were painted a buffed white, and the staircase was finished in fine, varnished wood.

Sam started toward the stairs to take up my bag, but I stopped him. "I had a long day of waiting around," I said as I took his hand.

His tanned features slid into a charming smile. "You could probably stand to get cleaned up," he said.

"That's for sure."

"And it gets lonely in there with no one to wash your back . . ."

An hour later Sam and I settled into his patio for a dinner of freshly caught red snapper and a green salad. While the fish cooked Sam kneaded my shoulders. If it wasn't heaven, it was close enough.

"I can't believe how good it feels to get away from it all," I said. "Miami's only a few hours away, but I feel like I've left it behind. All the cases, all the investigation, all the lying—"

I cut myself off, sensing that I was drifting into dangerous territory. When Sam first dropped out and bought his dream house, he made a formal offer for me to join him. He had scrupulously saved throughout his career and was now effectively retired, and he said I could come along if I wished. I told him I wasn't ready and I didn't know if I ever would be. He answered that it was a standing offer.

Maybe Sam was reading my thoughts, which wouldn't have been difficult. Whatever the reason, he dug harder between my shoulder blades, sending me into a state of mixed pain and ecstasy.

Just then my beeper went off. Sam groaned. "You brought that thing along?" he asked. "I have a standing rule in my house—no damned beepers. No cell phones, either."

I turned around and saw him smiling. He was only half joking. An acerbic reply was about to slip off my tongue when I saw that the number on my pager was that of the house in Cocoplum, followed by the numbers 911. This was an emergency code which meant that I was to call back immediately.

"Hey, what's the matter?" Sam asked, resting his hand gently on my shoulder. I held the screen up for him to see, and he led me to the wall phone in his kitchen.

I froze before the dial, instinctively knowing that this had something to do with Margarita. My hands shook as I punched in the familiar sequence of numbers. I was so rattled that I had to try three times before I got the number right, my feeling of dread quickening with each attempt.

Papi himself answered on the first ring. He almost never answered the phone, unless something was wrong. The lingering aroma of cooking fish from the patio now turned my stomach.

I swallowed hard. "Papi? It's me, Lupe. What's the matter?"

"Lupe, *querida*, I have some very sad news for you."

The old man was trying to keep his voice steady, but he couldn't fool me. "Papi, what is it? Please, tell me now."

"My dear, it's your friend Margarita." He cleared his throat. "Rodrigo called. There's been an accident."

I slid down the wall until I reached the floor. I knew what was coming. "What kind of accident, Papi?"

"An automobile accident." Papi spoke to me very slowly, carefully enunciating each word. "She was driving back from Palm Beach late this afternoon, and her car . . . Well, she was speeding off the exit ramp for Coconut Grove. Her car turned over."

Margarita was speeding on the ramp that led to the Grove

because she was coming directly to my office. She had no other reason to be there. I could barely listen to the rest of Papi's news. I didn't have to.

"Rodrigo called us a few minutes ago." Papi's voice was deep, stiff, and formal. I knew this broke his heart too. "No one knew where you were, so I called Leonardo at home and had him call your beeper for me. I'm so sorry, Guadalupe, but she's gone. I know how close the two of you were. Your mother always said you could be sisters, even when you were just little girls."

Papi was trying to comfort me as best he could, but I so rarely heard him become this emotional that he only added to my grief. "Did Rodrigo say anything about the arrangements?" I asked. I had to focus on business; the real sadness would hit me later. That's the way it worked with me.

"No, he just called to tell us." I heard a strange noise and realized that Papi was blowing his nose. "Where are you, Lupe? I don't want to pry, I just don't think you should be alone."

Although I didn't think about it much, I was still in mourning for my mother, seven years after her death. I knew Papi was, too. "It's all right, Papi, I'm not alone," I said. "I'll call Tia Alina and see what the arrangements are. I'm fine, Papi, really. It's late, you should go to bed. Who's in the house with you?"

"Both your sisters are here," he said. "As well as the twins. Don't worry about me. Come back tomorrow, and drive safely. Do you promise?"

"Of course I promise, Papi. Goodbye." I gently put the receiver in its cradle.

I turned around and Sam was there in the doorway. He had been listening to the entire conversation. "Margarita," I said. "It was about Margarita."

Without a word he lifted me off the floor, carried me up to his bed, and just held me for a long time. He had never met Margarita, but he knew who she was and how much she meant to me. We lay on the bed for hours, speaking softly, Sam holding me, until we fell asleep. I left for Miami at dawn.

NINE

I LAY ON my bed in my apartment, still wearing the black dress I had put on for the funeral, and sobbed until my ribs ached. The notion that my friend was gone forever had come to me in degrees, and now it was a reality. I didn't move for at least an hour save to look at a photo of Margarita and me taken by my mother at the beach one summer when we were fifteen years old. That snapshot, in a silver frame, had accompanied me to my new apartment and had been on my dresser since the day it was developed.

I let myself settle deep into the blankets, my eyes closed, envisioning the scene at Caballero, the funeral parlor where the family had held the wake. Her casket closed because of her injuries, I was robbed even of a proper chance to say goodbye. I smiled at the thought that Margarita would have been pleased to see how many people showed up to pay respects—she always did attract a crowd.

Tia Alina, Margarita's mother, insisted I sit with the immediate family in the lead funeral car on the way to the cemetery, and she held my hand the entire way. She didn't let go of me until the graveside ceremony was complete, and even then it seemed she had trouble saying goodbye to me. I have to admit, I held on to her as well.

Late-afternoon shadows gathered on my bedroom walls, but I couldn't will myself to rise from bed. I went in and out of sleep all through the night, finally getting a few hours' solid rest around dawn. Then I got up, hung up my dress, washed my face, brushed my teeth, and slept a few hours more. It was as though every sleepless night over the last decade had caught up with me all at once.

When I woke up at noon, I had twenty messages on my answering machine. I didn't check them, but I did turn the ringer on. I wanted to mourn in privacy, but I couldn't hide forever.

Five minutes later, as I poured myself a cup of Cuban coffee, the phone rang again. I scanned the screen of my caller ID gadget and saw that it was Tia Alina.

"Ay, Lupe," she said. "Thank God you answered. How are you?"

"I'm fine," I said. All through the ceremony the day before, I had begun to think of her as a second mother. "And you?"

"Tell me, my dear, please answer honestly." Her tone shocked me; she was at once insistent and hurt. "Why didn't Margarita tell us she was pregnant?"

"Pregnant?" I asked, nearly dropping the phone.

"I'm sure she told you. She told you everything." Despite her grief, Tia Alina's tone verged on accusatory.

"How . . . how did you find out?"

"It is all so strange, Lupe," she said, her voice kinder. "The police run a blood test after such a bad accident, to see if the driver was drinking. They told me it's routine, that it's done in all cases such as Margarita's."

Tia Alina began to sob. I could almost see her dressed in black from head to toe, sitting in the parlor of her big house, probably looking through one of her vast family photo albums. "It's all right," I said, waiting for her to compose herself. "Tell me what happened."

"I was told that the technician who drew the blood made a mistake," she said. "Or maybe it was at the lab, I didn't quite understand. But they ran a pregnancy test on Margarita, as well as tests for alcohol and drugs. Maybe it was a mistake, maybe the technician suspected something—I don't know. And she was almost three months pregnant. Oh, Lupe, she was going to have a baby! I didn't just lose my daughter, I lost my grandchild.''

Tia Alina broke down sobbing. She kept talking, but her words were unintelligible.

My mind raced. Margarita said the last time I spoke with her that she went to Palm Beach to think—and that her relationship with Rodrigo had become so strained that they hadn't had sex in six months. Six months. She was very specific.

''What about Rodrigo, Tia Alina?'' I asked. ''What has he told you about this?''

''He acted strange after the police officer came to tell us,'' she said. ''We were all together here at home when we got the news. The officer really came to tell us that the blood tests confirmed that Margarita hadn't been drinking or taking drugs before the accident. Then he said he was surprised no one in the family had mentioned anything about her being pregnant when she died.''

''So they didn't mean to test her for pregnancy?'' I asked.

''No, no. The police officer came to apologize for having run the wrong test on her. He acted as though we already knew she was pregnant.'' Tia Alina sighed, and I could hear the fatigue in her breath. ''Rodrigo said he didn't want to talk about it to me. He got up and left the room. I wondered why Rodrigo hadn't told us, but he wouldn't let me ask him anything.''

At that moment Tia Alina blew her nose loudly. I felt my ear nearly explode and held the phone away from my head until she was finished. I didn't really know what to say to her. My last conversation with Margarita, before I left for Key West, ran through my head like a tape loop.

Margarita had left me with two distinct facts. She hadn't slept with her husband in six months. And the Arango name meant something to her. I wasn't one to discount coincidences—heaven knows, in my business they crop up often and usually mean something.

But still, these two facts seemed far too random to be connected. I rolled what I had just learned from Tia Alina over in my mind for a moment longer, then let it go.

TEN

I MOVED BACK to the house in Cocoplum for a few days following the funeral, craving warmth and company. I told my family I needed privacy and they respected my wish, generally leaving me alone. Once Papi came up to sit with me for a while, and Lourdes left a plate of Aida's cinnamon crisps outside my door one afternoon, but by and large they let me rattle around my part of the house alone with my thoughts.

When I was ready I came out one morning to have breakfast alone on the dock. I was watching the pelicans swoop in the cool morning air when Aida came out of the house to tell me that Rodrigo was on the phone and he wanted to speak with me.

My first instinct was to brush him off with whatever feeble excuse I could think of. After all, I never liked the man—as Margarita knew and correctly pointed out. He never cared for me much either, and he knew I disapproved of Margarita's decision to marry him. While I had to deal with him before, I saw no reason to tolerate him now that my friend was gone.

But I was too intrigued by Tia Alina's news about Margarita's pregnancy. Here was a secret waiting for me to discover it. So I took the portable phone from Aida's hand, thanking her.

"Hello, Lupe," he said. I could tell from his tone of voice that he was making an effort to be pleasant. "How have you been?"

"I take it a day at a time, Rodrigo. And you?" I watched a pelican glide off a wooden dock piling. He flew upward, took aim, and majestically plunged down into the blue bay waters to scoop a wriggling fish into his beak. I've always had respect for predators.

"The same as you. A day at a time," Rodrigo said, sounding a little too glib. "Listen, why don't you and I get together one day this week. If you're up to it, that is."

It was a little hard to hear what Rodrigo was saying. Papi had begun firing up the Hatteras engines in midsentence. He had heard there was an uprising of sugarcane cutters in the western Cuban province of Oriente, and he wanted to be ready to take off in case it sparked a revolution. He had been listening to Cuban radio stations full blast since dawn, driving everyone crazy. I hated to think how much fuel he was burning, idling the engines like that.

Margarita was barely cold in the grave, and Rodrigo was already on the phone to me—it almost sounded as though Rodrigo was hitting on me. I didn't know whether to feel curious or grossed out, but curiosity won the day—I owed it to my friend to discover what he was up to—so I agreed to meet him at Versailles the following day for lunch.

When I hung up, I scolded myself for being so suspicious. I wanted to give Rodrigo the benefit of the doubt. Maybe he was just worried about my well-being, without any ulterior motives. After so many years of distrust for him, it was hard to imagine.

Lourdes showed up at the house about fifteen minutes later, enjoying some home time before she had to enter a retreat that evening. She joined me on the deck with a steaming cup of coffee. When I told her about my plans to meet Rodrigo, her reaction was predictable. She stuck two fingers down her throat and mimicked throwing up. That brought me back to reality really fast. My vaguely charitable feelings for Rodrigo vanished in an instant.

"You're going to meet that pig?" Lourdes asked. "Margarita will come back to haunt you for sure. Lupe, why in the world would you agree to sit at the same table as that man?"

"I'm curious," I said. "I'll tell you all about it later."

Lourdes sat heavily in a chair and shook her head. She probably hated Rodrigo more than I did, now that I thought about it. She was even more observant than I was—it was part of her job, the same as me. I also knew that, as Margarita's best friend, I might have let my feelings be swayed one way or the other. Lourdes, on the other hand, was able to remain objective.

I knew that Lourdes was sensitive to all the times Rodrigo had insulted Margarita in front of us. Margarita would never have put up with any kind of physical abuse, but she shrugged off Rodrigo's often terrible emotional treatment of her. Lourdes spoke to me about it a number of times, trying to make me talk about it with Margarita. I never did. I felt that if my friend married a loser, well, that was her decision. No one forced her into the marriage, so she must have seen something in Rodrigo Vidal that eluded everyone else.

In addition to treating his wife badly at times, Rodrigo was a drain and a slug. He managed the family's two shoe stores in South Miami, and that was as apparently as far as he wanted to go in life. Not only did he lack ambition, but he often derided Margarita for hers—and for her success in business. The more successful she became, the greater the strain on their marriage. It's an old story.

Margarita put on a happy face to the world when it came to her marriage, but I always remembered what took place on her wedding day five years before. She had asked me to be her maid of honor. I disliked Rodrigo from the moment I met him and thought she was making a mistake—I even thought she would come to her senses and dump him before the ceremony at her family's palatial home in Gables Estates—but I agreed to support her choice, in action if not in spirit.

Half an hour before the wedding Margarita called to me from her bedroom and said she had to speak with me. I was ecstatic—she had finally come to her senses, I thought, and wanted me to go downstairs to call everything off. It didn't matter to me that hundreds of guests had arrived for the wedding. Tia Alina, though she didn't care for her future son-in-law, had turned their garden into a stunning outdoor chapel, with breathtaking white flowers and satin ribbons cascading from the trees. I would help Tia Alina take it all down, I thought.

I went into Margarita's room and closed the door behind me. She was sitting on her bed, already in her wedding dress, enveloped in yards of cream-colored tulle and lace. In her hand was a half-empty bottle of Dom Pérignon, and from the high color on her cheeks it wasn't hard to piece together what was going on.

"Lupe, I can't do it," she said, looking away from me. "I just can't."

Just what I was waiting to hear. "Fine," I said. "Great! I'll go down and tell Tia Alina."

I started to leave the room—I had my hand on the door-knob—when Margarita called out for me to wait.

"Stay here," I said quickly. "I'll just be gone a minute."

Margarita rose from the bed and slammed the door to seal us in again, almost catching my fingers. "Wait, it's all right," she said.

The door opened again—it was her aunt. Margarita waved her away, trying to smile, and pulled me into the bathroom, locking the door behind us. "Sit down," she ordered, shoving me down on the cold marble floor and taking a seat next to me.

Between us, we covered the entire floor with the fabric of our dresses. I was a vision in powder-pink taffeta—not my idea, of course, just part of Tia Alina's wedding frenzy. Margarita put the champagne bottle on the closed toilet seat after having a good long swig. "Lupe," she said again. "I just can't go through with this."

"I know. I'll be right back." I started to get up, a little impatient now. "Don't move," I ordered.

"What about the guests?" she asked plaintively.

"Your dad will deal with them," I said. "They came to party, anyway. They don't care one way or the other whether there's a wedding attached."

"What about the food? Mom ordered enough to feed an army!" She had another giant swig straight from the bottle. It reminded me of the good old days, when we'd get trashed on the beach.

"Don't worry about it," I said. "They'll eat it anyway, and what they don't eat they can take home in doggy bags. That's the least of your concerns. Just let me go down."

Margarita gave me a sad, tipsy wave goodbye. I found Tia Alina in the garden greeting the late arrivals. Before I could pry her away I heard the first faint strains of "Here Comes the Bride."

I groaned when I looked up to see Margarita appear at the top of the stairs, holding her father's arm. I saw her trip on the second step, her father just catching her before she tumbled down the steep, long staircase. I hurried over to take my place in the wedding procession, my heart broken. I had come so close.

Every so often I wondered whether Margarita ever regretted leaving that bathroom floor when she did. Whatever her feelings, she never brought them up, and it was as though the incident had never happened. I still had my maid-of-honor dress in my closet on Brickell Avenue, the champagne stains still staining the front. I never sent it out to be cleaned—it wasn't as if I would ever need to wear it again.

I ARRIVED AT Versailles the next day promptly at noon to meet Rodrigo. I never ate much that early, but I knew we would get better service eating before one o'clock—a more traditional Miami lunch hour. I wanted to get in and out quickly, because I didn't want to spend a minute longer with Rodrigo than I had to.

In the parking lot I looked around for Rodrigo's Lexus— a fifth-anniversary gift from Margarita—and saw it parked in the handicapped space. I looked around for Rodrigo and saw him inside speaking to the maitre d'. In the spirit of pure malice, I circled the block while I dialed the Miami police nonemergency number to report a Lexus parked illegally in a handicapped space at the Versailles restaurant. Then I drove back, parked, and walked in.

Rodrigo was seated at a table far from the restaurant entrance, giving him a view of the room, but he could still see the parking lot. So my first words to him were to ask that we switch seats, claiming that the air-conditioning vent was aimed directly at me. He could have pointed out that there were no vents anywhere near the table, but instead he graciously agreed.

"You look well, Lupe," he said. He offered what Lourdes referred to as "that shit-eating grin of his."

"Thanks. You do, too," I lied.

I glanced around the room while we waited for a waitress to arrive to take our order. When I turned back to Rodrigo, who was immersed in the menu, I saw over his shoulder a cop ticketing his Lexus.

The company I was keeping aside, I always loved Versailles. The restaurant was a Miami institution. When my sisters and I were little girls, Mami and Papi took us there every Sunday night for dinner after seven o'clock mass. The food was savory, cheap, and abundant, and there was a calming continuity in seeing the waitresses wearing the same dark green, overtight polyester pants suits that they had sported for the last thirty-five years. A willingness to wear azure eye shadow with thick eyeliner, not to mention a Marie Antoinette-inspired shellacked coiffure, seemed mandatory for employment there. And somehow the waitresses always knew which customers required a menu in Spanish and which needed one printed in English.

The restaurant had been renovated a few years before, but I thought they had dulled the place's tacky charm rather than improved it. I had loved the etched-mirror walls running around the main dining room, and the glass chandeliers, and the plastic tables and chairs. The old Versailles was a restaurant in a time warp—the eatery that time forgot.

The new Versailles was a modern, upgraded version of the same.

Rodrigo ordered a platter of fried plantains as an appetizer, and arroz con pollo—chicken and yellow rice, the national dish of Cuba—as his main course. I usually order arroz con pollo, but I didn't want to eat the same food as he did. Instead I ordered *ropa vieja*—"old clothes," the second national dish of Cuba.

We waited together in silence, fiddling with everything on the table that wasn't bolted down—our iced teas, the bread, the plantains with their delicious garlic sauce. I tried not to react when I saw a tow truck outside the window, its driver emerging from the cab to quickly hook up Rodrigo's Lexus. Within minutes it was gone. If nothing else, this lunch would cost him plenty when he tried to recover his car.

"Lupe, I hope I can speak honestly to you," Rodrigo finally said, breaking my splendid reverie.

I nodded my assent. I didn't want to make this easy for him. He called me to meet, so as far as I was concerned, he could do the talking.

"I know this is a delicate question," he continued, fixing his eyes on me. "But did Margarita say anything to you about her having a baby?"

I nodded again and dipped another plantain. Technically, I wasn't lying to him. Margarita, after all, had mentioned that Rodrigo wanted to have a child. She also said they hadn't slept together in six months, but there was no reason for me to admit I knew that.

"Oh," he said brightly, his manner easing. "So then you knew she was pregnant?"

I nodded, just a little, avoiding his eyes. This was tricky territory. I was spared from saying anything right away when the waitress arrived with our main courses. Rodrigo must have been distracted by the heady fumes coming off his chicken, or maybe he didn't want to press me for an answer, because he plunged right ahead.

"I spoke with a lawyer," he said. "He told me I can sue the county for money. That exit ramp Margarita crashed on had a problem—it was too steep, and it gets really slick in the rain. There have been five other serious accidents there in the last seven years, so he said I have a good case.''

I looked at him for a moment to see if he was serious. Of course he was. It took a lot of self-control not to spit out my mouthful of *ropa vieja*. ''You're thinking of suing?'' I asked.

''Of course,'' Rodrigo said. He leaned back with a triumphant smirk. ''Margarita had a clean driving record, and she wasn't drinking or on drugs. And, of course, she was pregnant at the time of her death. I would say the county owes me something.''

I felt as though I had just stepped in something sticky and warm. I could barely look at him. But I had to stay. I had to find out precisely what this greedy, heartless loser had in mind.

''Who is this lawyer you talked to?'' I asked. I wasn't particularly interested, but I wanted to keep him talking.

He was happy to oblige. ''Fernando Godoy,'' he said. ''He has an office right next to our Red Road shoe store. After Margarita's death he came over to talk to me. I don't even have to pay him anything, just thirty percent of the money I win from the county.''

''How much money is that?'' I asked, afraid to hear.

''Millions.'' Rodrigo's eyes glinted with barely concealed glee. ''It was millions when Margarita died alone, but since she was pregnant, Fernando says, we can get a lot more. A baby helps the case a lot, especially in a jury trial.''

He looked right into my eyes and said, ''So, did Margarita ever discuss the baby much with you?'' I could see he was watching me closely.

I played around with my food, and when I looked up at him, my eyes were watering. ''I mean, whether it was a boy or a girl, things like that,'' he added hastily. I could see he was scared I might start crying.

My silence apparently satisfied Rodrigo; he shoveled some more arroz con pollo into his mouth and looked away. I knew then why he had asked to meet me. He wanted to find out if Margarita had told me anything about their marital problems. I wondered if he told Godoy the ambulance chaser that he hadn't slept with his wife in six months, and that she was three months pregnant when she died. This little fact certainly would put a kink into their big-money plans.

My food might as well have been a plate of gravel, for all the appetite I had left. I don't know why I felt so surprised. Rodrigo had lived off Margarita while she was alive, and now he would make her his meal ticket after her death as well.

He was as pleased as could be, already close to finishing his food. "Excuse me for a minute," I said, picking up my purse.

Rodrigo nodded distractedly and took a swig of iced tea. He had obviously met with me out of fear that I would jeopardize his lawsuit. My evasions had satisfied him, and I hadn't confronted him with any new information. Now that he thought he was safe, I could tell he had no use for me.

I walked straight out to the parking lot. They would fine the hell out of Rodrigo for parking in a handicapped spot, I thought, but if he got his way he could afford to park wherever he wanted.

Not if I had anything to do with it.

I RETURNED TO Solano Investigations for the first time since Margarita's death. Leonardo was so startled that he dropped the telephone receiver he was holding when I walked through the front door. He rose from his desk and enveloped me in hugs and kisses, telling me how good it was to have me back. Thankfully, he refrained from shoving all my messages and mail at me. And when he was secure in the fact that I was glad to see him too, he let me go into my office alone and shut the door behind me.

It seemed as though it had been a year instead of a week since I had been to work. I sat quietly at my desk looking out the window, pleased to see that the parrots had built a new nest in the upper branches of the avocado tree in the yard. Life goes on.

I noted with approval that Leonardo hadn't touched anything on my desk, as per my standing orders. I had a look at the steno pad I had doodled on while waiting for Margarita to arrive from Palm Beach.

I had written the name Arango next to Margarita's name. This puzzled me for a moment, until I remembered her last words to me on the phone. She had wanted to talk after hearing I was hired by the Arangos, and it sounded like it was important to her. And she specifically responded to the name Alonso Arango, I recalled when I ran through all the details of the conversation. I couldn't imagine their connection; she had never mentioned the name Arango to me before, of that I was certain.

I picked up the phone and called Leonora at MMV Interiors. It was a long shot that she might be there now that her boss was dead, but it was worth a try. I shouldn't have worried. She answered on the first ring.

"Leonora," I said. "It's Lupe Solano. How are you?"

"Oh, not very well," she said in a wavering voice. "And you?"

"I take it a day at a time," I said, pulling out my stock answer. If anything, I was trying to forget how I felt. "I wasn't sure you'd be at the office, but I thought I'd try anyway."

"Oh, I'm here. I have nowhere else to go." She sounded positively pitiful. "Besides, the lawyers told me Rodrigo is going to sell the business. I have to close out all the accounts and send out final bills. I'm taking my time, because my job is gone when I finish. The job market isn't very good right now, you know. And at my age . . ."

Leonora trailed off. That bastard. It was just one more reason for me to despise him.

"Can I ask you one question?" I asked. "Does the name Alonso Arango mean anything to you?"

"Sure," Leonora said immediately. I should not have been surprised at the swift reply. My friend had told me that in spite of her failings, Leonora had the memory of an elephant for clients and jobs. "Margarita did his house in Coral Gables, for him and his wife. What was her name— Isabel? It was last year or the year before. Why do you ask?"

"It's nothing, really," I said. "Their name came up in a conversation, and I remembered Margarita saying something to me about them. Do you remember her mentioning anything about them?"

"I don't know," Leonora said. "She had so many jobs, you know. She worked hard, all the time."

For once, Leonora didn't volunteer any personal information to me, which meant she didn't know anything. "Listen, Leonora," I said. "If you need anything, anything at all, you call me."

This seemed to open the floodgates. Leonora sobbed. "Oh, Lupe, I miss her so much! I worked for Margarita for six years, you know."

"I know," I said.

"She kept me on, even though she could have hired someone younger with better skills. I tried to take a computer course at Miami-Dade, but I couldn't follow it. Margarita said don't worry, that it didn't make a difference. Oh, she had such a heart."

"I know," I said.

Leonora talked some more, and sobbed a lot more, and finally hung up after a halfhearted goodbye. I truly felt for her. I didn't want to think what might happen to her now that she no longer had Margarita to shield her from the real world.

I sat in my quiet office and pondered everything I'd learned about my friend in the last ten days. Her marriage to Rodrigo wasn't going well, big surprise. But I had never thought that she might be having an affair—and yet there was no other way to account for her pregnancy. I immediately discounted as too improbable the notion that she might have used a sperm bank. I would have said the same about her cheating on Rodrigo, but the sperm bank scenario would only confuse my thinking.

Why had she kept her pregnancy a complete secret? The blood tests said she was three months along, which meant she wouldn't be able to hide the physical signs for much longer. She had only succeeded in hiding it to date by wearing clothes that camouflaged her condition.

And what was her business with the Arangos? This disturbed me the most. What in the world did she know about them? What could be so important that she drove to her death to tell me? I owed it to her to find out, so I picked up the phone.

"Tommy, this is Lupe. Do you still want me to work the Arango case for you?"

ELEVEN

I ARRIVED AT Optima Jewelers promptly at noon, and told the young salesman busy arranging a display of pearl necklaces at the front counter that I had come to meet with Mrs. Arango. Remembering my interview with Alonso at the Stockade, I knew I had to be speaking with George Mortimer, the only Anglo employed there. He looked up from his work and motioned for me to follow him the length of the store, through the door in back, and into the office.

Isabel Arango awaited me there. She was a beautiful, dignified woman of about fifty, though she looked almost a decade younger. When I introduced myself, I felt a warm rush of amusement. She didn't know how to treat me—as an employee or as an equal.

I knew plenty of women like Isabel. Her eyes roved all over me as she determined that my Armani suit—black label, not Le Col-lezioni—was real, and that the Cartier tank watch—croc strap—on my wrist was authentic. I only had time to count to twelve before she rose from the desk, arms outstretched, and squeezed both my hands in hers. I was pleased at her decision to approach me as a social equal, though I could have lived without the pinch of her diamond rings.

"Lupe—may I call you Lupe?" She waited for my assent. "Oh, good. I'm so happy to meet you. I just know, with you and Mr. McDonald helping us, that Alonso will soon be free. It has been such a nightmare for my husband and me."

Isabel shuddered for emphasis and closed the door for privacy. We were side by side for an instant, and I saw the fine lines that crossed her face, artfully concealed behind exquisite makeup. I could also discern faint scarring at her hairline—the only remaining clues of a face-lift, no doubt. Her chin-length chestnut hair flattered her, its golden strands casually lending the illusion that she had just run a comb carelessly through it. In reality, I knew, that style took hours at the hairdresser to achieve. I also recognized her light green linen Escada suit from my latest Saks catalogue. Isabel Arango didn't scrimp at all in putting together her look.

She moved past me to return to her seat behind the desk, and a whiff of her perfume reached me. Chanel No. 5. I felt as though I had been struck, because that had been my mother's scent of choice—the only perfume she ever wore.

I settled into the delicate gilt faux French Provincial chair across from Isabel, opened my black lizard-skin envelope briefcase, and took out the files inside. Isabel kept her eyes on my every move.

"This must be a stressful time for you and your family," I said, offering her a sympathetic smile. "Hopefully we'll resolve everything soon, and your husband will be able to go home."

Her chair also was gilt faux French Provincial. She sat straight up in it and made the sign of the cross. "Please God and the Virgin that you are right," she said. "And that Alonso will be free soon."

This display of enthusiastic piety took me by surprise, and I had to remind myself not to judge someone too quickly based on appearances. Of course, I also knew that she may have intended just that effect, and may have wanted me to think of her in a certain way. Whichever was the case,

I knew already that there were many layers to Alonso's wife.

I didn't acknowledge her spontaneous prayer. "I asked your husband if I could have a look at your personnel records," I said. "Did he mention that to you?"

Isabel opened the top drawer of the delicate faux French Provincial desk and took out a notebook. "You can keep this," she said. "I made you a copy. Our current employees are the only people ever to work at Optima Jewelers, so these records are complete and accurate."

At least she was making things easy for me. Without looking at the notebook, I thanked her and put it in my briefcase. "I understand you weren't here when the shooting happened."

"No, I was at home." Her cool gray eyes met mine. "I hardly ever come to the store anymore. Alonso really doesn't need me here. And you know, Lupe, I worked here so much when the store was starting out that I prefer not to."

Isabel had the ability to smile with only her mouth, while her eyes remained unchanged and still focused on me. It made me anxious. And she seemed detached and perfectly composed—not exactly what I had expected in a woman whose husband was in the Stockade for pumping six bullets into a stranger.

"Then you don't know anything about what happened here, except what you were told afterwards," I said. "Is that accurate?"

"Yes, that's right. Alonso called me right after the shooting and told me what happened."

"He called you before he called the police?"

Her eyes narrowed almost imperceptibly. "I suppose so. I hadn't really thought about it until you mentioned it just now."

I didn't want to break the flow of the interview by taking notes, so I concentrated hard on everything Isabel said. I also knew that she would speak more freely if she felt she was involved in a conversation rather than in an investigative interview. I worked for her, and I was on her side, but

I also needed to extract information from her without being perceived as threatening.

So I said, as casually as possible, "What exactly did your husband tell you?"

"I was in the shower when the maid knocked on the door to tell me my husband was on the phone, and that it was urgent," Isabel said. "I remember that I wrapped myself in a towel and hurried to the phone on our bedside table. Alonso was very upset, and I had trouble understanding him, but he said a man with a knife had tried to rob the jewelry store and that he had shot him. I asked if he was all right, and he said yes. He said I should come to the store right away, and then he hung up."

Isabel and I stared at one another for a moment. A faint hint of defensiveness had crept into her tone.

"What happened after that?"

"I called each of our three sons," Isabel said. She began to run her fingers through her hair slowly, starting at the scalp and working her way down to the ends. "I told them about their father."

"Were you able to reach all three of them immediately?"

By now Isabel had fairly well wrecked her expensive hairdo. From what I thought I knew about her, this was a desperate act. "Actually, no," she said. "I reached Ernesto on his car phone. He was on his way to his office. I reached Alonso junior at home. Mariano, the youngest one—I had to leave a message for him."

"Then you went straight to the store?"

"Well, I dressed first." Again, the smile. "But yes, I went straight to the jewelry store."

"What happened when you got there?"

"There were quite a few police cars," Isabel said. "I had to drive around a bit and park a block over, because the police had closed off the street. An ambulance had just arrived when I walked into the store. The police let me in when I told them who I was."

Mercifully, Isabel stopped fiddling with her hair. It had started to drive me crazy.

"I went back behind the counter, and the place was full

of people. Some were in uniform, some were in regular clothes.'' Isabel was expressionless. ''Alonso was in Silvia's office, sitting in a chair. He looked simply terrible. I was worried about him, because he has very high blood pressure, you know, and his doctor has told him not to get upset. I asked him how he was, and he didn't answer. After a moment he told me to call our neighbor, Carlos Gutierrez, and tell him to have his lawyer—his criminal lawyer—come over right away.''

''Did that surprise you?'' I asked.

''It certainly did.'' Isabel's bottom lip twitched twice in succession. ''I couldn't understand why Alonso would need a criminal attorney. He had shot and killed a man, but that man had tried to rob him with a knife. I thought you could kill someone to defend your own life.''

''Did you call your neighbor, Mr. Gutierrez?''

''No, Alonso junior did. He arrived at the store right after me. I wanted to stay with my husband. I didn't like the way he looked.'' Isabel's features flashed a second of dismay, because, I knew, she wondered why I needed all this detail. But she pressed on. ''After Alonso junior called the lawyer, the detectives took my husband away to the jail and told us we had to leave. I heard later that they stayed here in the store for four hours.''

''Did you know the dead man, Gustavo Gaston?''

A split-second hesitation, her eyelids flickering. ''No. I never saw him before. Never in my life.''

Now not even her mouth was smiling. In my experience, people who deny something three times make a denial too many. Once was natural. Two denials, well, okay. But after three emphatic denials my antenna was up and humming.

But I had had enough from Isabel Arango for the day. After all, this was only an initial interview. I began gathering my papers to indicate that we were finished.

Isabel gave me a confused look. ''That's all? No more questions?''

''Not for now,'' I said. ''But I'll have other things to talk to you about as I get deeper into the investigation. I have quite a bit to do before then, though.'' I stood up. ''Could

I look around a bit before I go?'' I asked. ''Maybe you could point out a couple of things to me.''

''Certainly.'' Isabel stepped delicately from behind her desk, every bit the refined hostess showing her preferred guest around.

''I know you weren't present when the shooting occurred,'' I said. ''So I guess there's no point in asking about that.''

''No, that's not true,'' Isabel said eagerly. ''I do know about that. I was here when Alonso gave his statement to the police. I saw and heard everything that went on.''

I couldn't account for her overemphatic tone of voice. ''Well, then, let's start with the spot where Alonso was standing when Gaston came in.''

Isabel walked behind the counter. ''Here. Alonso said he was standing right here when he first saw him.''

She stepped aside when I came over to check out the spot. From my vantage point I had an unobstructed view of the store, all the way to the double glass doors leading out to the street—that is, if the door to the back of the store was open at the time. If the door was closed, or just ajar, Alonso wouldn't have seen Gaston until he was almost upon him.

''Did your husband say if this door was open or closed that morning?'' I asked.

''Oh, that door is always kept closed,'' Isabel said. ''We don't like the customers to be able to see into the back.''

I pointed to a closed door across from the counter where Alonso had been immersed in repairing the watch. ''Is this Silvia Romero's office?'' I asked.

Isabel said it was and, since it was currently empty, I was welcome to have a look. It was superficially like the office she had first received me in, though apparently Silvia didn't rate rococo gilt furniture. This office looked like a clearance sale at Office Depot, and I noticed right away that there were no photos or personal mementos to be seen. That was strange, because according to Alonso, Silvia had been with Optima Jewelers for a total of four years, the last year full-time. This office offered no clue whatsoever about the nature of the woman who worked there.

"Silvia isn't here because she leaves every day at noon to pick up her daughter, Alejandra, at play school," Isabel said, following me inside. Her voice turned cold. "She takes her to her mother's to stay until she is done with work. It's a bit of a complicated arrangement, but it works out well most of the time. And it's the only way she can work for us full-time."

I led the way out of the office. There wasn't much to look at. I gave Isabel my card, as well as the standard speech about doing everything in my power to investigate the case and help Tommy free Alonso.

Driving away from Optima Jewelers, I couldn't account for my sense of relief to be out of there and no longer dealing with Isabel. And I could think of nothing in what I saw or heard that related to Margarita, or what she might have wanted to tell me before she died. There was nothing to prevent me from casually asking Isabel about Margarita, but that would have been tipping my hand.

And to gain what? A reaction, and nothing more. The Arangos had hired Margarita as a decorator, and that was certainly no scandal.

I also knew intuitively that Isabel was sharp, and that she would tell me only what she wanted me to know—for good or for ill. I didn't know what I was looking for as far as Margarita was concerned—and when I thought about it, I didn't have a concrete agenda for the Murder Two, either. But I had worked murders before. Losing a close friend who took important information to her grave was a new one for me.

I SPED UP to make the light at the intersection of U.S. 1 and Douglas Avenue, heading back to the office. Tommy was due to meet me there, and he was usually on time.

I had debated whether to tell Tommy about Margarita's cryptic message before she was killed, and had finally decided against it. I didn't want him watching my every move, trying to determine if my loyalties were divided between

Margarita and his client. I told him I was taking the case to stay busy and to keep my mind off Margarita's death, which was a partial truth.

His reaction surprised me. At first he was delighted, but then he asked me if I was sure I was up for it. It had been only a week since she died, he said, and maybe I needed more time off. This new, touchy-feely Tommy was a revelation.

Of course, he had also called me before I left to meet Isabel, picking my brain for ideas and insisting we meet after the interview. The honeymoon was already over. He was in full Tommy mode, and would deluge me with calls and questions until the case was finished.

When I pulled into the lot, I saw that Tommy had parked his Rolls in my spot. It sat there like a gleaming chrome insult. It was common knowledge that I considered anyone's mooching my spot a mortal sin. So I stormed into the office, ready to give him hell, only to find him with Leonardo in the kitchen, concocting some sort of drink.

They made quite a sight. Tommy was dressed in a tailored navy-blue pin-striped suit. Leonardo was in tight black biker shorts and a Popeye T-shirt. They were staring into the juicer as though they were Marie and Pierre Curie peering into a microscope. They were so engrossed in their study that they didn't even notice my dramatic entrance. I cleared my throat to announce my presence. Pure futility. Tommy bent over the plastic jug even farther, his eyes wide.

"Excuse me!" I shouted. "I hope I'm not interrupting anything important!"

When Leonardo looked up, his eyes were crossed from staring so long. "Oh, hi, Lupe," he said sheepishly. "Sorry, I didn't hear you come in."

Curiosity got the better of me. "What are you guys up to?"

Tommy straightened to his full imposing height, put his arm around my shoulder, and whispered conspiratorially in my ear, "Lupe honey, Leonardo is telling me all about this drink he's working on. A drink that can change the world.

He wants me in on the ground floor, to invest in the production end.''

I shot daggers at Leonardo, who pretended not to notice. One of our rules was that he wasn't supposed to hit on the clients to back any of his projects. But I was willing to go along for the ride. Tommy seemed genuinely excited, and he led me to the kitchen table.

"Here it is!" he said, pointing to the juicer. "The drink that will change the world."

I stuck my finger into the thick, pinkish liquid and looked at it closely. Just as I raised it to my mouth both of them grabbed my arm, shouting for me to stop.

"What the hell's the matter with you two lunatics?" I asked, startled. "It's a drink, right? Doesn't that mean you're supposed to *drink* it?"

"It's not for women," Leonardo explained somberly. "It's only for guys."

"Oh, I get it," I said. "So it'll only change half the world. What does it do, make you better endowed?"

"God no, nothing as crude as that." Tommy looked at me with disgust. "Men who drink it improve dramatically in every way."

I looked at them with new eyes. They weren't lunatics at all—they were idiots.

"We're serious, Lupe," Leonardo said, the hurt puppy.

"You really believe that?" I asked in disbelief. "How do guys who drink this stuff improve?"

"In all ways," Tommy said mysteriously. "Physically and emotionally. It's like magic."

"Well, forgive me if I don't rush out to buy stock," I said.

"You don't understand, Lupe—this is for real," Leonardo insisted. "I've had a chemist here in the Grove working on this for more than a month."

"Not the Hare Krishna guy!" I bellowed. From the guilty look on my cousin's face, I knew I had guessed right. "I can't believe you, Leonardo. That guy's a total junkie."

"What are you saying?" Tommy asked. He took a step away from the juicer.

"He manufactures designer drugs," I told him. "He's been busted so often he exchanges Christmas cards with corrections officers."

Tommy covered his mouth with his hand and looked at Leonardo as though my cousin had just sprouted a second head.

Leonardo stared at the floor. "He said it was all legal," he said.

I hated to burst their bubble like that. No, really I loved it. Tommy probably thought Leonardo's chemist was an MIT Ph.D., not a religious nut with a taste for better living through chemistry. No wonder the drink was "magic."

By now Tommy had his fingers on his carotid, checking his own pulse. "Come on, you big sissy," I said. "A minute ago you said it was going to be a miracle."

I walked to the juicer, poured myself a small glass, and downed it in a single gulp. Tommy, probably scared of dying with only Leonardo to keep him company, looked relieved.

"Now let's get to work," I said. "Before we start hallucinating fire coming out of our noses."

"Oh, Lupe," Leonardo whined.

"Any messages?" I asked him.

"On your desk," he said, taking apart the juicer with an air of utter defeat.

Once in my office, I had Tommy close the door behind us. "I can't believe it," he said, wiping his forehead with a handkerchief. "I was really ready to invest. Still, you were hard on him."

"I have to be," I said. "Or else he'd be even worse."

Tommy seemed to see the wisdom in this and nodded sagely. He took off his jacket and made himself comfortable on my couch. I was a little tired, so I lay down at the other end, stretching out my legs on his lap. Tommy started rubbing my feet while I brought him up-to-date on the Alonso Arango case.

"Isabel is a real piece of work," I began. "Butter wouldn't melt in her mouth. Speaking of her mouth, I think she's using it to lie to me."

"Is this just an impression," Tommy asked. "Or do you know anything for sure?"

"It's an impression, *querido*. But remember, she and I have the same chromosome count." I closed my eyes. Tommy's foot-rubbing skills were exquisite. "She's lying, just like her husband—it must be a family trait. I just don't know yet what they're lying about. You'd better straighten them out. Give them that speech about never lying to your doctor or your lawyer."

"Lupe, you know how much faith I have in you." Tommy moved up the couch and started working on my neck and shoulders. He had great hands. "But I need something more solid than 'Mr. and Mrs. Arango are lying' before I slap their knuckles with a ruler."

"I first started to suspect Isabel when I asked her if she knew the dead man. Her eyes flickered away from mine. Just for a second, but it was enough for me to notice."

"Maybe she had a twitch. How would Isabel Arango, wealthy jeweler's wife, know a rafter?" I reached up and loosened his tie. "It's not like they met on the tennis courts at the Riviera Country Club."

"It wasn't a twitch. She knew him, Tommy, or knew of him. Also, I can tell she hates Silvia Romero. When she talked about her, she might have been describing an embarrassing smell." Tommy's hands started to explore a bit more. "And you should have seen the way they furnished her office. You wouldn't understand, Tommy, but women pick up on these kinds of things."

"Let's see, then. We have a twitch. We have ugly furniture." Off came his jacket. Mine was already on the floor. "We have a strange tone of voice. All this adds up to one conclusion: Isabel Arango is a liar. Great, Lupe, that'll stand up in court. I might as well go to trial right away. The case is solved."

Tommy stood up to lock the door. He knew the drill.

TWELVE

ELSA AND OLIVIA Ramirez were already waiting for me at Solano Investigations when I arrived just after nine the next morning. Elsa sat primly on the love seat in our reception area, the perfect lady. Her hands were folded in her lap, her feet crossed at the ankles. Olivia, however, was in the kitchen boisterously demonstrating to Leonardo how to make the perfect cup of coffee. For most Cubans, the search for coffee perfection is like the search for the Holy Grail—never-ending, all-consuming, and in the end, probably futile.

Though Elsa and Olivia were first cousins, the resemblance between them was so striking they could have been twins. And they were obviously as dissimilar in character as they were physically alike in eye color, skin tone, and bone structure. I invited them into my office, tearing Olivia away from Leonardo, and motioned for them to sit.

I had to marvel at the Ramirez family gene pool. Elsa had shoulder-length dark brown hair showing strands of gray, porcelain skin, and luminous cornflower-blue eyes. I knew from her personnel file that she was forty-one, but she somehow seemed older, in the gravity of her expression and

the prim precision of her movements. She wore a long flowered skirt and cream-colored blouse, light stockings, and
white low-heeled plain pumps. So help me God, the woman
smelled of rosewater. I almost expected her to get the vapors, like a delicate flower wilting in my office.

Olivia was three years younger than her cousin. It must
have been a hell of a three years for Elsa, if she had ever
been anything like her younger cousin. Olivia wore tight
black bolero pants with a matching vest, and expertly ma-
neuvered into my office in red stiletto heels, apparently
ready for Ladies' Night at Chippendale's. Her ringleted plat-
inum hair cascaded down her back and was held in place
by combs—not just any combs, but glittery combs that
matched the diamond earrings dangling from her generous
lobes. Olivia had beautiful sky-blue eyes framed by striking
false eyelashes. My first impression was that she wanted to
be Little Havana's answer to Dolly Parton. If that was the
case, she was doing a pretty creditable job.

"Wow, so this is a private investigator's office," Olivia
enthused. She leaned forward, her ample chest squashing the
purse she cradled in her lap. "Do you have a gun? Hey,
have you ever shot anyone?"

"Yes, I do have a gun." I had to laugh. "And no, I've
never had to shoot anybody with it."

Elsa was mortified. "Miss Solano, please, I apologize for
my cousin. She acts so silly." She looked as though the
vapors were becoming a possibility. I wondered if we had
any smelling salts.

"No, it's all right," I said. "I don't mind, really. People
ask me questions like that all the time."

Elsa grimaced and looked down, while Olivia beamed at
me like a hyper puppy. Though it was a bit scary, seeing
yin and yang—total opposites—personified like that, it was
time to plunge in.

"You both know why I asked you to come, right?" I
asked. "Did Mrs. Arango explain to you who I am, and
what my role is?"

"She told us you work with the lawyer who is repre-
senting Alonso," Elsa said quickly. "She said to cooperate

with you, and to tell you everything we know.''

"That's right," I said. "I work with Thomas McDonald, Alonso's attorney. We want to get Mr. Arango out of jail as soon as possible.''

This set Olivia's chest in motion again. "Oh, we'll do anything to help,'' she said breathily. "Anything.''

"Usually I interview witnesses separately, one at a time. So, if it's all right with you, I'd like to speak with one of you while the other waits outside." I stood up and held the door open. "It doesn't matter who goes first. You decide.''

Elsa and Olivia looked at each other, then Olivia stood. I could see that between the two of them, Elsa took care of the serious matters. I waited for Olivia to sashay out of my office and closed the door behind her. I ignored Leonardo's look of torture—or ecstatic anticipation, I couldn't be sure— as Olivia approached his desk.

Elsa sat and awkwardly adjusted her skirt. I gave her some time—there was a lot of skirt there to get right.

I smiled, trying to put her at ease. "Maybe you could start by giving me some background, before we discuss the events in the store." I could not help but compare Elsa to Miss Manners. Even in a private investigator's office she looked as if compelled to behave in a socially correct way— proper posture, her outfit just so. I watched her with amusement. It was a few moments before she seemed satisfied with the adjustments to her person and was prepared to answer my question.

"Well, I've been with Alonso, one way or the other, for about fifteen years." She suddenly blushed crimson, realizing the couple of ways in which her remark could be interpreted. "I don't mean—I, I mean just that I've known Alonso for that long.''

This was fascinating. The woman was straight out of Jane Austen. Her face and neck sprouted red patches of embarrassment, and I thought—maybe a little callously—that they went well with the demure flowers on her skirt.

Elsa decided to just keep talking, a wise move. "Alonso and I worked together in another jewelry shop on Miracle Mile for four years before he left to open Optima Jewelers,'' she said. "I knew his ambition always was to open his own store. He had stores in Cuba before the revolution, you know. So when the time was right, he asked me if I was interested in leaving my job and coming with him."

I could have raised an eyebrow then and completely driven Elsa out of her mind, but it would have been too cruel. "I knew Alonso was going to be successful," she continued. "He's hardworking, and he knows the business. So I agreed to work for him. I've been very happy at Optima." She beamed at me like a schoolgirl who has just answered a question correctly.

"What about the other employees at Optima?" I asked. "What can you tell me about them?"

"You met Olivia," she said. "And there's George. We're the three salespeople. There's Reina, the cleaning lady. Then there's Silvia Romero, the bookkeeper. She's Puerto Rican, you know."

Elsa wrinkled her nose. It's no secret that Cubans and Puerto Ricans basically don't like each other. Each feels the other gives Hispanics a bad name.

"What about Isabel Arango?" I asked, as innocently as I could.

Elsa fidgeted with her pearl necklace. Up until that moment her hands had stayed in her lap. "What about her?"

"Try telling me about her," I said. "How often does she come to the store? Is she usually involved in the day-to-day business operations?"

She thought about it for a moment and decided to hedge. "I don't think I'm a good person to ask about Isabel," she said quietly. "Alonso can tell you much more than I can. She's his wife."

From Elsa's reaction I basically got what I wanted about Isabel, so I let it go and changed the subject. "Now can you tell me about the Saturday of the shooting?"

Elsa was visibly relieved that I had moved the subject away from Isabel. She told me what she had seen, or rather not seen, and she didn't have much that helped me. She had been tidying up the drawers under the counters when Alonso shot Gaston, so she wasn't in a position to see the store.

Sitting on the floor tidying the drawers was her Saturday ritual, something she did early so she wouldn't be interrupted by customers.

"I was untangling some gold chains when I heard the shots," she said in a monotone. "I knew that horrible noise—I'd heard it often enough in Havana during the revolution. Still, I was concentrating so hard on the chains that the noise disoriented me. George ran to the back and yelled out that someone had attacked Alonso, and that Alonso had shot the man. The next thing I knew, the store was full of Coral Gables policemen."

"You didn't see anyone come in or leave the store just before the shots were fired?" I asked, watching her closely.

"No, I'm very sorry. I was on the floor. I didn't see or hear anything before the shots."

"Did you know the dead man, Gustavo Gaston?" I asked.

"No," she said. She shuddered as though chilled, but my office was perfectly warm. "The police showed me a picture of him later, so I had a good look at him. But I never saw him before."

"Did the police say anything about him?"

"No, not much," Elsa replied, looking at me curiously. "They said he came to the States on a raft from Cuba a few years ago."

"When did they show you his picture?"

"They came the Monday after the shooting," she said. "They spoke to everyone in the store. I never saw him, you know. He was on the floor in the back, and I didn't want to go in there."

Elsa looked at me with her wide-open blue eyes. Either she was telling the truth or she deserved an award for best actress in a detective series. It was still early in the investigation, and I had no reason not to believe her.

"Thank you," I said politely. "I want you to know that I might have to talk to you again, if anything develops." She gave me a pinched smile, as though in acknowledgment of a distasteful fact of life, and called for her cousin to come in.

Elsa left and Olivia breezed into the office, plopping down where her cousin had sat. "Is he married?" she asked when the door was shut, motioning with her head to the outer office—where Leonardo no doubt sat prostrate, recovering from her.

"No," I answered.

"Girlfriend?"

That was a tricky one. "Well, not that I know of." Leonardo hung out with women, but I don't know if anything ever came of it. Actually, I had long ago ceased to speculate on Leonardo's sexual preferences. Our family had covered that particular line of speculation well enough, without my added contributions.

Olivia got that centuries-old female predatory look in her eyes as she arranged her voluptuous body in the chair. It was quite an operation; she apparently needed to sit just so in order to keep everything properly in its place.

"I need to ask you a few questions about that Saturday morning at the store. All right?" I began.

"Yes, yes, absolutely," she gushed like an open spigot. "Like I said, I'd do anything to get Alonso out of jail. The man is a saint, let me tell you! He has already earned his place in heaven. He gave me a job when I really needed it, you know. He is one of the kindest men I have ever met in my life."

She barely stopped to breathe amid this declaration of undying loyalty, and I found myself warming to her. It was hard not to. Unfortunately, despite her good intentions she couldn't help me much.

"I'm so sorry," she said. "If I knew that horrible man was going to attack Alonso, I would have run to the back of the store to stop him! But I was on the phone with my mother, and my back was to the store because I was sort of hiding."

"Sort of hiding?" I asked. "What does that mean?"

"Alonso doesn't like us making personal calls at the store during working hours," she said. "Except for emergencies, and this wasn't an emergency. But don't get me wrong—Alonso is very fair to us."

Olivia certainly was quick to defend her boss. "My mother was giving me a new flan recipe that she'd tried at my aunt's house," she said. "I was writing it down. People think it's easy, making flan, but it's not true."

I couldn't think of a response, and Olivia seemed to realize she was drifting. "Anyway," she said, "flan is tricky. Timing is everything when you make it, so that's why I was concentrating so hard writing down the recipe. I didn't want anyone to hear my conversation, so I was really quiet with my back to the store. There weren't any customers that early, so I really wasn't doing anything wrong. But *ay!* I kick myself. I should have seen what happened. I might have done something to help Alonso."

Olivia's eyes started watering. In an instant teardrops ran freely down her face and onto her generous neck, and ultimately cascaded into her cleavage. From there they vanished from sight.

"It's all right," I said. "There's nothing you could have done."

I should have given her a tissue, but I was riveted by this impromptu display. Olivia produced a lavender lace handkerchief from the depths of her purse. She honked into it.

"And the recipe wasn't even that good!" she wailed. "The flan didn't even turn out."

The injustice of it all set her off crying again; but this time, she was prepared with the handkerchief. I was a little disappointed. It was strangely enthralling to watch the tortuous road south her tears took, from her wide eyes to her spectacular bosom.

But this was going nowhere, and fast. I took out a photo from my desk and slid it across to her. "Do you recognize this man?"

Olivia shook her head.

"This is Gustavo Gaston, the dead man, the man Alonso shot. Are you positive you don't recognize him?"

She started to shake her head again, but instead she picked up the photo and examined it. "Oh, this looks like the picture the police showed us when they came to the store," she said. "Who is he? Why would he attack Alonso?"

It was my turn to shake my head. "That's what I'm trying to find out. Can you think of anything that might help me?"

Olivia took another sad honk into her hankie, and told me no. That was that. I stood up and walked her to the outer office, where Elsa patiently waited.

I gave them both my card. "Don't you have a card?" Olivia asked Leonardo, flashing her lashes.

Leonardo buried his head in a pile of mail. "No, I'm the assistant here. I don't need a business card."

"Well, *Leonardo*," Olivia said, pouting now. "I guess I can always reach you here, if I have to."

By then Elsa had a firm grip on Olivia's vest. The older cousin trailed apologies the entire way as she dragged Olivia out.

When they were gone I sat in a visitor's chair and stared at Leonardo. He finally looked up and saw me smiling.

"What?" he yelled.

"She's some piece of work, isn't she?" I asked.

Leonardo shifted uncomfortably and pretended to be fascinated with a junk mail fax. "Which one?" he finally asked.

I burst out laughing.

He did his own Jane Austen blush. "You know, Lupe," he said. "Whatever you pay me, sometimes it isn't enough."

THIRTEEN

GEORGE MORTIMER ARRIVED punctually at two o'clock for his interview. My heart sank when I quickly found that his story was much the same as the Ramirez sisters'—he didn't see or hear anything until the shooting had occurred. At least he had a good excuse: George had spent a considerable amount of time in the bathroom that Saturday morning, paying for eating a particularly vicious hot burrito from Montezuma's, a local Mexican place, the night before.

"How long were you in the bathroom?" I asked.

"I can't tell you for sure, but it seemed forever," George said. "I swear, I think the cook at Montezuma's is still bitter about losing Texas or something. I'll tell you, they picked the right name for that restaurant. Someone definitely got revenge on me."

"Tell me about your job at Optima Jewelers," I said.

He was as glad as I was to change the subject. "I'm the newest salesperson there," he said. "Five years this March. I never planned to work in a jewelry store, you know—it was just a job until something better came along. But I liked working there so much I ended up staying. Everyone there is really nice, and when things get slow Alonso lets me read. I love to read, practically anything.''

"That's great,'' I said. "But why don't you start at the beginning.'' I gave him an encouraging smile. I had the strong feeling that if I didn't steer this conversation, it would never get anywhere.

"Sorry,'' he said sheepishly. "I graduated from F.I.U. four years ago, with a degree in medieval history. It was interesting but not too practical, as I'm sure you can imagine. I sent my résumé to about a million places. I networked like crazy, answered want ads, bugged my relatives—the whole bit. But I got nothing in the way of offers. And I mean *nada*.''

I knew about George's general background from Isabel Arango's personnel files, but I wanted to hear his version. It was hard for me to believe he was as old as twenty-six, only a couple of years younger than me. With greasy hair and a few more pimples he could have passed for sixteen, though he was good-looking in his adolescent way. His wavy blond hair could have stood a cut, and his pale, dead-looking skin could have stood a professional cleaning. Though he was dressed traditionally—in khaki pants, navy-blue blazer, white pressed shirt, and a mild floral tie—there was a bit of a wild man's mischievous glint in his eye. His clear light brown eyes looked directly into mine as he spoke, and every minute or so he would edge closer to me in his seat. I had the impression that he wasn't taking this interview as seriously as he might have, considering that his boss was in jail for murder.

"So it must have been quite a switch from the Middle Ages to the Miracle Mile,'' I offered.

"It sure was!'' George flashed a winning smile—well, it must have won someone, at some point in time. "So, after six months of looking for work, I decided it was time to knock on some doors. I started with the stores at the top of Miracle Mile and worked down. I was in the middle of the second block when I walked into Optima.''

"You went door-to-door looking for work?'' I asked. I

didn't know the market was so bad, even for a young-looking medievalist.

"Hey, whatever works," he said shyly. "And my timing couldn't have been better. Optima was full of customers. Alonso was working the counter, Olivia was wrapping a huge order in the back, and Elsa was out sick. Alonso was swamped and desperate, and he offered me a job on the spot. It was only supposed to be until Elsa came back, but I ended up staying on. It's a great place to work."

"I see. What can you tell me about Isabel Arango?" I asked, trying to catch him off guard while he was in a chatty mood.

Instead of answering right away, George squirmed uncomfortably in his chair, shifting his eyes away from me. "I don't really know her too well," he said. "I mean, she really doesn't come into the store very much. I hardly ever have to deal with her."

I decided to let it go. Still, I knew Alonso's wife was worth the extra attention; I just had to figure out why. "You're sure there's nothing else you can tell me about the morning of the shooting?" I asked.

George shook his head, visibly relieved that I no longer wanted to talk about Isabel. I opened my desk drawer and pulled out the same photo of Gustavo Gaston that I had shown the Ramirez cousins. "Do you recognize this man?" I asked.

George took the picture and studied it closely. A shock of his blond hair tumbled onto his forehead. "Should I?" he asked.

"He's the dead man," I said. "The one Alonso shot."

"Oh, right, now I see. The cops showed me a picture of this guy. It was a lot like this one."

George dropped the picture onto my desk as though it had suddenly burned his fingers. "I'll tell you what I told them," he began. "That I never saw him before. Well, that's not technically true—I saw him on the floor when he was dead. He didn't look like this, though, he was all crumpled up and bloody. I looked away too, but I had a couple of dreams about him already."

He had a talent for babbling, it seemed, that had flowered with this traumatic memory. "He was the first dead person I ever saw," he said. "I mean, I've never even been to a funeral."

"That's fine, George. I didn't really expect you to know him or recognize him. It was just a long shot." I returned the photo to my desk, hoping he would calm down. "I saw from the police report that you were one of the first people on the scene."

George nodded. "I was just coming out of the bathroom when I heard banging sounds. I didn't know what they were, but I could tell they came from the back room." He spoke in a monotone. "Before I went into the bathroom I knew that Elsa was near the front door arranging some drawers, and that Olivia was on the phone. I looked over at them first to see if they were all right, and they were just standing there with these stunned looks on their faces. I knew Alonso was in the back repairing a watch, so I went to check on him."

"How long did you wait before going back there?" I asked.

George shrugged. "Not long, not even a minute. Just long enough for me to see that Olivia and Elsa weren't hurt, and then the time it took me to walk across the store."

"What did you see when you got to the back room?"

"First I was relieved when I saw Alonso standing there. At the time I didn't know that what I heard were shots, but I remembered feeling glad that he was okay." George shut his eyes, visualizing. "Then I also saw Silvia there. She and Alonso were both looking down at something on the floor, but from where I was standing I couldn't tell what it was. I had to walk around the work counter to see the body on the floor. Then I saw the gun in Alonso's hand."

I stared at him. "What were Alonso and Silvia doing?"

"Nothing. They were just standing there like statues." George laughed nervously. "It was like something on TV, you know, *Murder, She Wrote*, or something. I asked them what happened."

"What did they say to you?" I asked.

"Nothing. They didn't say a thing. They just stood there, not moving, not saying a word." George shifted and crossed his legs. "It was kind of weird. I told them we had to call the police. My voice sounded really loud, like I was shouting at them."

"Did either Alonso or Silvia explain what happened?"

"They didn't say anything at all," George replied. "They were in shock. I found out that the dead man had tried to rob the store when I heard Alonso tell Isabel what had happened."

I jotted a quick note. "Did you call the police?" I asked.

"Not right away. Alonso said he would. He went into his office and called Isabel first, and I could hear what he said because he didn't close the door all the way. Then he called the police, and they were there before we knew it."

I tapped my pencil on my desk, giving George what I hoped was a reassuring smile. "Did you think it was strange that Alonso called his wife before he called the police?" I asked.

"Yeah, actually, later I did think it was a little unusual. But at the time, everything was so confusing I barely noticed," George said. "They're really close, Alonso and Isabel, so maybe I thought that explained why he called her. Really, you know, how is someone supposed to act just after they kill someone?"

He had a good point. "What was Silvia doing during all this?"

"At first she was just standing there. But she started pacing around when Alonso went into his office to use the phone. She looked like she was really nervous and upset."

I took a long sip of Leonardo's juice; it was warm, having sat on my desk for more than an hour. George was willing to talk, but he had to be prompted every step of the way. I felt like a talk-show host with a slightly dim guest. "What about the rest of the staff?" I asked. "What were they doing?"

"Elsa and Olivia came running toward the back of the store pretty soon after I got there," George said. "I stopped them in the doorway and told them what happened. When they heard there was a dead man back there, they waited for the police in the front of the store. Reina came in soon after. She must have come in through the rear door, because I didn't see her come through the store. I guess that accounts for everyone.''

George gave his wristwatch a pointed, regretful look, so I knew I had to wrap up the interview or lose his focus. Though he hadn't told me much, he had helped me fill in some important gaps.

I stood up to indicate we were finished, and he rewarded me with another smile. ''George, thanks so much for coming in,'' I said. ''You've been very helpful.''

He tilted his chin jauntily and batted his long eyelashes—definitely flirting. ''Lupe, you've been asking me all the questions. It's my turn now. How about you coming with me to Espuma Night at Amnesia on South Beach?''

Oh, brother.

I WAS IN the reception area, still shaking my head at the wonder of George's invitation to a ''foam'' night at a trendy club when Leonardo took a call and put it on hold.

''It's Silvia Romero,'' he said.

When I picked up the phone in my office, I was greeted by a soft, whispery voice. ''This is Silvia, the bookkeeper at Optima Jewelers,'' she said. ''I know you've been trying to reach me to make an appointment, and I want to apologize for not returning your calls. My little girl has been sick, and I haven't had much free time.''

''That's okay,'' I said. ''I'm glad to finally get in touch with you.''

''Could I come to see you this afternoon?'' she asked. ''That is, if it would be convenient.''

It sure would be. I had left messages for her, both at the store and at home, without a response. I couldn't imagine why she would avoid me, but I felt a suspicion that she had. As the first person to see Gustavo Gaston dead after Alonso shot him, she was a key component to my case. We agreed to meet at my office within the hour.

She arrived in a half hour. Silvia Romero was a small,

slight, soft-spoken woman who appeared to be around thirty. Though she had striking jet hair and dark eyes, she wasn't exactly pretty. I'd call her delicate-looking rather than attractive. She looked as though she would bruise if someone held her too tight.

I almost had to grab her right hand from her side to shake it when I greeted her. Some might find her sort of shyness and delicacy appealing, but I considered it merely wimpy.

"Miss Romero," I said, after I closed the door behind us. "Would you please tell me what happened that Saturday morning at Optima Jewelers?"

"Well, I don't know too much about what happened. I went out to buy stamps at the post office." A vein throbbed in her slender throat as she spoke. "They close at noon on Saturdays, you know, and I needed to mail a few things. I walked to the Coral Gables post office, which is only a few blocks away. I left my usual way—out the back door, which leads to an alley."

She seemed almost to be afraid of me, but I had the feeling that she acted this way around everyone. "And what happened when you returned from the post office?" I asked.

"I came back the same way, through the back door," she said. "I saw Alonso standing over a man laid out on the floor. The man was bleeding, that's what I remember most—blood. Alonso was holding a gun in his hand. I don't remember much after that. The police asked me a lot of questions, and I answered them all, but I don't really know much about what happened except what I was told later."

I remembered what George Mortimer had told me only an hour before, that Silvia had seemed calm if a little dazed. From my experience, this was consistent with how people often act when they come upon a shocking or grisly scene. They don't appear nervous or upset—they go into a zombielike state for a while. Silvia, for all her petiteness, suddenly struck me as a strong, smart woman. I decided to take another approach.

"Let's start from the beginning," I said. "Tell me a little about yourself."

Silvia fidgeted, tucking her shirt tightly into her plain

skirt. She was so tiny it was hard to believe she had given birth to a child.

"There's not too much to tell, really." She seemed embarrassed. "I'm thirty years old and an only child. I'm Puerto Rican, born in Miami. I live in Westchester, behind my parents' house. I studied accounting at Miami-Dade and started working as a bookkeeper eight years ago."

I let her go on without interrupting. Her manner grew increasingly prim and reserved. "I used to work part-time at different businesses around Coral Gables, mostly on Miracle Mile, but now I work mainly for Alonso. I like working in one place much better. I still do some work on the side for other businesses, but Optima Jewelers is my main place of employment."

Most of this was known to me from her personnel file, but it's always useful to hear people describe themselves. It was interesting, for instance, that she said nothing about her marital status or about her daughter. Silvia wasn't wearing a wedding ring, and in my background searches on her I couldn't find any husband listed. She didn't seem likely to volunteer anything in this area, though, and it would have been counterproductive to ask her.

"Let's go back to that Saturday morning," I said calmly. "Is there anything you know that might help Alonso Arango with his defense?"

For the first time I saw evidence of the spirit I suspected lurked within Silvia. Her cheeks flushed and her tiny hands balled into fists on her lap. "I don't understand why he's in jail," she said. "The man came at him with a knife. That makes it self-defense, doesn't it?"

"The knife was never found," I pointed out. "And Alonso fired six bullets. The police and the judge think that's too many for a man only trying to defend himself. If the knife were found we would have a different story. Our greatest problem is that we have no witness to corroborate Alonso's claim."

"I guess I'm the closest thing to a witness you're going to find," Silvia said, with a surprising steely edge to her

voice. "I was there right after it happened. What can I do
to help?"

Everyone was saying they wanted to help, and no one
could. I shrugged. "Find me a witness, or find me the
knife," I said. "Either one will do very nicely."

Silvia's eyes locked into mine. "Tell me, please, what
do you think is going to happen to Alonso?"

The little alarms were silently going off in my brain. I
hadn't thought it important to look into Silvia Romero very
thoroughly, but now I wasn't so sure. I was witnessing a
subtle transformation in her, from mousy accountant to a
passionate woman trying to help her boss. It wasn't exactly
inappropriate, but people don't shift personas so rapidly
without a good reason.

"It's very hard for me to say," I offered. "A lot depends
on my investigation, and then what kind of deal Alonso's
lawyer can cut with the judge."

"When you say 'judge,' you make it sound frightening,"
Silvia observed.

"Don't ask," I said. "Alonso's lawyer, Mr. McDonald,
is trying to get Alonso bonded out of jail. He's trying to get
the prosecutor and the judge to see that Alonso has a clear
record and close ties to the community. He wants to convince them that Alonso is unlikely to flee the country while
awaiting his trial."

"Alonso would never run away from his trouble," Silvia
said. Her tiny hands shook. "I know that for sure."

That was it. I was convinced it would be worthwhile to
look deeper into Silvia's past. "Those are all the questions
I have for you right now," I said. I stood and handed her
one of my cards.

Almost as an afterthought I held Gustavo Gaston's photograph up to her. "One more thing—I almost forgot, forgive me." Silvia looked up questioningly at me. "Do you
know who this is?"

Her head shook almost imperceptibly. She lowered her
eyes, clearly uncomfortable.

"It's Gustavo Gaston, the dead man," I informed her.

Silvia jumped up as if I had pinched her butt. Her relief

was utterly transparent as I led her out of the office, holding the door for her. I watched her drive away in her white Toyota.

Leonardo came up behind me. He bent over to adjust the weights he kept strapped to his calves. "Penny for your thoughts," he grunted, still bent over.

"Something isn't kosher here," I said, still looking out at the street. "I smell lies."

"Well, I smell happy hour at Café Tu Tu Tango," he said. "Let's go have some margaritas. You can eat the fried stuff and I'll load up on vegetables."

Within five minutes we had all the lights off, the doors locked, and the alarm system activated. Leonardo donned formal wear—a shimmery silver track suit—and we were off.

It was time to clear my head before moving forward. I had suspicions, intuitions, and vague hints. Leonardo didn't want to hear any of it. We headed out for Cocowalk, and he pulled my arm to make me walk faster. It would be criminal to show up after our local hangout ran out of food.

FOURTEEN

———————◆———————

THE NEXT MORNING I awoke at my apartment, showered, dressed, and headed out to the office early. I was intent on putting in a few hours of work before the daily distractions began. But I didn't arrive early enough. There were two cars waiting in the driveway next to the cottage when I pulled into my spot.

As soon as I walked into the office I heard a familiar sound: Leonardo's grunts from the exercise room. Someone could have been torturing him in there, and I would never have suspected that anything was the matter. I heard a clatter of metal followed by a chilling shriek, like a buffalo giving birth. Shuddering, I walked past his closed door and into my office.

"Lupe, *querida*," said a voice from my sofa. "Here are the reports on Gustavo Gaston. My bill is on the table. Wake me if you have any questions. Otherwise, let me sleep."

Nestor Gomez, my favorite contract investigator, had his eyes closed and his hands folded beatifically on his chest as he nestled deeper into the sofa's padding. I looked at his lined face. He was thirty years old, but he easily could have passed for fifty.

Originally from Puerto Plata in the Dominican Republic, Nestor had only one goal in life—to bring his twelve brothers and sisters to Miami as soon as possible. Nestor did nothing but work; as far as I knew, he rarely ate or slept, and I supposed sex and romance were out of the question.

The last time I had dared to ask him how he was doing, he said that he was "halfway there"—meaning that half his family now lived with him in Miami. I was happy for him, but I secretly and selfishly dreaded the day the entire Gomez family possessed Miami mailing addresses. Nestor was a beast, capable of carrying out back-to-back twenty-four-hour surveillances at a moment's notice. And in the seven years I had known him, he had never screwed up. He was expensive, but I never complained. He was worth every peso.

"Anything interesting?" I asked. I put my purse in my desk and opened his report.

"Come on, Lupe," Nestor moaned. "Read the damned thing and let me close my eyes for a few minutes. I've had a domestic three days running, and I'm beat. I've been doing your stuff during the day, and following this wife at night."

I wanted to keep him talking, so he wouldn't slip into a coma and be rendered incapable of answering questions about the Gustavo Gaston report. "Three days?" I asked. "What was that about?"

"The husband thought his wife was fooling around on him, so he told her he was going to Vegas for a three-day medical convention, just to see what she would do. Turns out he was right. The wife dropped him off at the airport, gave him a real juicy French kiss, and stopped off at her boyfriend's apartment for an afternoon delight. I got some great pictures of her and the guy—he rents Jet Skis in Key Biscayne. It's going to be hard, living on lover boy's rental money, compared to what she's used to. The soon-to-be-ex-husband's a cardiologist. You buy your ticket and take your chances."

Nestor told me this entire story in a subdued monotone, never once opening his eyes. At least he stayed awake, giv-

ing me a chance to scan through his report on Gaston. While
I read, something nagged at me. Even worse, I couldn't tell
precisely what it was, just something trying to get my attention from the back of my mind.

According to Nestor's report, Gustavo Gaston was forty
years old when he died. He had come to America from Cuba
on a raft six years before, picked up by the Coast Guard
just south of Key West. After spending a few days at the
transit center there, he was processed out and had moved to
Miami. He remained there, and his address was listed as an
apartment building in southern Little Havana.

Gustavo was born in Miramar, a Havana suburb, and he
had studied architecture at the University of Havana. Amazingly, he had won a series of prizes for designing houses
for the masses in communist Cuba. He was very educated
and accomplished for a would-be petty thief. I wasn't really
surprised to see that he had no prior offenses on his record.

A Social Security search revealed that Gustavo had
worked a series of jobs in Miami. Some were full-time,
some part-time, but all had one thing in common—they
were menial and low-paying. In a man with such an accomplished background it was surprising to see so little evidence
of ambition. I saw that upon his arrival in Miami, Gustavo
had worked briefly in some warehouses near the airport. For
the past six years he had worked almost exclusively in the
Coral Gables area. His last three jobs were as a deliveryman
for a pretty diverse group of businesses: a bridal store, a
fish shop, and a framing store. The bridal shop was on Miracle Mile, only two blocks from Optima Jewelers.

I was jolted back to reality by an earsplitting snore from
the prostrate form on my sofa. Nestor had covered his face
with his hat and was breathing so heavily that it seemed to
rise and hover above his head. Nestor was snoring! Though
I was disappointed, still it was gratifying to see solid evidence that he was human.

I threw a balled-up sheet of paper at him. "Nestor, wake
up!"

Sleeping Beauty didn't budge. Even a pathetic shriek
from Leonardo in the weights room didn't wake him. I

started in on the paper clips and pencil erasers, aiming between his legs. When his slacks started to look like a deranged Slinky disaster, he finally moved.

"*Mierda*, Lupe," he rasped. "What do you want? I was dreaming I was in bed with Gloria Estefan."

I ignored his complaint. From what I knew, he was always shacked up with Gloria Estefan in his dreams. The only variable seemed to be the position in which they consummated their lust.

"What else do you know about Gaston?" I demanded.

"Not much," Nestor mumbled. "I wanted you to see the background before I did anything else. What kind of budget do we have on this case, anyway?"

I had to lean over my desk to hear him, because his hat still covered his face. "The client is in jail, on a Murder Two and without bail," I said. "We have pretty much of a free hand, but don't go overboard."

This perked him up a bit. He gave a little stretch, his hand holding the hat in place. "Well, let's bring in Marisol, then," he said. "She's good, and she's quick."

"Good idea," I said in a loud voice, to keep him from drifting away again. "She'd be perfect for this."

Marisol Velez was one of the best investigators I knew, and certainly the best with video. She was from Asuncion, Paraguay, and had lived in Miami the last ten years or so. She was tall, blond, and voluptuous. She oozed sex from every pore, and she wasn't shy about using it to her advantage; she'd learned early in her career to capitalize on her attributes. I knew of a few instances in which Marisol had succeeded in gathering information from a source—male, of course—when other, more experienced investigators had failed. I never asked how she did it. I was just grateful for the results.

Apparently Nestor finally figured out I wasn't going to let him rest. He heaved himself up from the sofa with a hearty grunt and walked over to the small round mirror on my wall. It took him a minute to arrange the bags under his eyes into a position he could live with. He made a desultory attempt to tuck in his shirt and headed for the door.

"I'll get right on this," he said. "You'll hear from me as soon as I have something to report."

I shook my head and shot him a nasty look—which he, of course, didn't notice. Nestor's methods always annoyed me. I prefer my investigators to check in with me on a regular schedule, instead of deciding for themselves when they have something that warrants my attention. But I was resigned to waiting. Nestor was very good at what he did, and it was too late to teach him new tricks.

Nestor stopped in the open doorway, then turned to me with a concerned look on his face. "You know I don't interfere with anyone's personal life, Lupe," he said. "But have you got yourself involved in anything weird lately?"

I was ready for a gag, but I saw Nestor was serious. "What in the world are you talking about?"

"It may be nothing," he said. "But I recognized Tom Slattery watching this place."

"You need some sleep," I said. "Who the hell is Tom Slattery?"

"You know who he is. He's that investigator who used to work for the State Attorney's Office—until he got fired over a breaking and entering." I must have looked blank, because Nestor gave me a frustrated sigh. "You remember— big guy, tall, greasy black hair, beady eyes, green buck teeth that stuck out like a beaver."

Nestor's description, accented with narrowed eyes and a screwed-up mouth, was full of so much derision that I knew there was no love lost between him and this Slattery.

Suddenly I did remember him; Nestor's description jogged my memory, and I made a gagging sound. "How could I forget? He was so gross, he used to bump into me on the elevator at the courthouse and try to feel me up."

"Well, *querida*, he's watching your office from outside." Nestor opened the door. "I just thought I'd let you know. You'd better watch your back."

I stayed at my desk when he left, trying to digest this information. Why would someone be watching me? It might have to do with the Arango case, or it could have been one of the hundreds of cases I'd worked in the past. Whatever it was, this wasn't good news. Slattery was slimy and nasty. I didn't need him in my life.

Suddenly Nestor poked his head back in my door. "If you need help with this guy, you call me," he said. "I can get rid of this problem if you want. Just let me know."

Nestor made me agree to consider his offer before he left. In a way, I really didn't want to think about what he meant.

I heard a wail from the next room, and the sound of weights hitting the floor and bouncing. Leonardo muttered to himself, breathing heavily. Who would dare mess with me? I thought. It was perfectly obvious to anyone within earshot that I had a man locked in my cottage and was torturing him within an inch of his life.

FIFTEEN

AT TEN O'CLOCK I was home in my apartment, but I was still technically on the job, waiting for Marisol Velez to report back to me on what she had accomplished that day. I used the time to review my notes on the Arango case. I had done a lot of work, and had amassed reports, but a clear picture still refused to emerge. And I was no closer to tying Margarita to the Arangos than when I began. She had decorated their house in Coral Gables. Gaston the rafter was once a distinguished architect. The knife Alonso claimed he had defended himself against was still missing. It all went deeper, I knew, and led somewhere.

Frustrated, I took care of some chores I'd neglected. Between my nights coming home late and nights spent at Coplum, I had let my plants dry up, the dishes stagnate in the sink, and my laundry pile up on my bedroom dresser. Oh, well. Domesticity was never something I'd put on my computer-dating profile, on the off chance I ever got desperate. I settled for opening the doors on my patio and letting the cool night air circulate through the apartment. And I took mercy on the plants, giving each one some water and a spritz on its leaves. I was looking for the plant food when the phone rang. I was edgy, and I jumped in the air. When I landed, I answered on the second ring.

"He works for who?" I screamed into the phone. I could not hear clearly what was being said, I was so distracted and full of anxiety.

Marisol repeated the name again patiently: "Fernando Godoy. It wasn't hard to find out. The guy made a beeline for Godoy's office three times today."

"I know that name, I just can't think of who it is." I hit my head, as though that would make me remember.

"He's a scumbag lawyer," Marisol said with venom. "He works out of a second-floor walk-up on Red Road in South Miami. I'd never work a case for *him*, that's for sure."

"Mierda!" I shouted. "Now I know who that *hijo de puta* is." He was the lawyer Rodrigo had retained for his suit against Dade County, the one who would make him rich over the dead body of Margarita.

"Listen, *chica*, do you need me anymore? I'm beat. I need to go home." Marisol did sound exhausted. I had been working her long hours for a few days now, without any breaks.

"You did a good job. Go home," I said. "And thanks. Just tell me what your bill is on this one, and don't write it down. I'll pay you cash." This tab was mine.

"Cash is king. I'll talk to you tomorrow." She hung up.

After Nestor had told me that Tom Slattery was watching Solano Investigations, I took his advice and hired Marisol—but instead of using her for the Arango case, I contracted her to find out who had hired Slattery. Marisol first produced videos of Slattery watching me, this big ugly goon peering through binoculars at the cottage from his car. Then she caught him following me to a Cuban deli, where I had lunch alone.

It might have been funny, until I learned about Godoy. This was no coincidence. Rodrigo had to be behind it, but why? What was so important to him about my comings and goings?

Before I went to bed I had a glass of Gevrey-Chambertin, then another. It's impossible to stop with one glass of such good wine. I sipped it on the terrace while I thumbed through the yellow pages under the shoes section. I ripped out the page and left it beside the phone.

AT EIGHT THIRTY the next morning I called Rodrigo's shoe shop. I almost suspected he wouldn't be there, since he was counting on becoming a millionaire soon. But he was there, and to my surprise, it was he who answered.

I heard all kinds of noises on the phone as he fumbled with it after hearing my voice. Then he cleared his throat and got himself together. "Lupe! How nice to hear from you again!" His voice rose in midsentence from bass to a nice soprano. He reminded me so much of an adolescent caught smoking in the bathroom that I almost expected to hear peach fuzz growing on his chin. "I was just thinking of calling you."

"Great," I said. "I was just calling to see how you were getting on, as the time passes."

I had no plan in mind, but I knew Rodrigo would help. "Oh, I'm getting along," he said. "And how about you?"

I could visualize his Adam's apple bobbing up and down. "Same here. I just wanted to touch base." It was hard to keep my voice pleasant and neutral, knowing the son of a bitch had a tail on me—and not a very good one. The least he could do was respect me and hire a real professional. But Rodrigo always was cheap.

"That's so nice," he said, stuttering a little.

"Hey, I wonder if you'd like to get together," I said sweetly. "The last time we met, I was so upset I ran out on you. I hope you weren't offended. I certainly didn't mean anything, I was just a little out of my mind." I was rambling, but I knew that would appeal to him. He was a sexist and would grab onto any evidence that he was in control while I wasn't. Stupid man.

"That would be just great," he gushed. "But I'm a little busy this week. How about next week sometime?"

Coward.

"Next week would be fine—I'm caught up in a lot of things myself. It's good to hear the shoe store is keeping you busy. I always say, there's nothing like hard work to keep your mind off your problems during a difficult time." I felt like a complete jerk talking this way, but I was hoping he would get chatty and give me something I could use.

"It's not just the shoe store. It's MMV Interiors as well." Rodrigo actually sniffed into the phone. At least he respected me enough to try some acting. "I have to help Leonora close things up, but I keep putting it off. I don't want to go through Margarita's things, it's so painful. But I guess I have to."

"You have to be strong, Rodrigo." I hoped Margarita was having a good laugh in heaven, watching me butter up her husband like this.

We hung up after agreeing that we would get together in a week. I wondered if Slattery would tail me on that particular excursion.

Our conversation convinced me that if Rodrigo was planning to clean the place out, I could no longer procrastinate about visiting Margarita's office to search for clues about her private life. I called Leonora to make sure she would have the place open and set off for MMV Interiors.

The trip from my apartment to MMV Interiors took only a half hour, even with the circuitous route I took in case I was tailed that early in the day. I kept checking the mirror for Slattery's battered Chevy, but I never saw it. I didn't even know whether Slattery was still on the case; another investigator might have taken his place.

There was also another slight possibility. Godoy might have hired Slattery with the knowledge that he would be burned. Rodrigo and his lawyer would count on my becoming complacent about Slattery and assign a second investigator to tail me, someone so good I might not detect them. This practice was smart, and not all that uncommon, but I didn't think it was the case here. Rodrigo was too cheap. Just in case, I drove fast, pushed through yellow lights, and doubled back a couple of times—until I was relatively satisfied that no one had followed from behind.

Leonora was waiting for me at the reception desk. The poor woman looked as though she had aged a decade since I last saw her—and she hadn't looked great then. When I walked in she came out from behind her desk to greet me. Before I could protest she hugged and kissed me, breaking into tears.

I almost had to use jujitsu to pull free. "I'm glad to see you, too, Leonora," I said sternly. I didn't need her histrionics to rekindle the grief I had just about managed to put at bay. "Would it be all right if I looked around Margarita's office? There are a few things of hers I would like to take with me. Just keepsakes, nothing valuable."

"Anything you want, dear," Leonora said, more in control of herself. She sat on her desk and motioned toward Margarita's open office door. "Rodrigo called right after you did. He said he would be coming by today to look over her things before the sale."

"Sale?" I asked. "What sale?"

"He's not only selling the business, but he's selling everything else along with it." Leonora folded her arms and bit her lip, obviously appalled. "All of it. I knew he would sell off the client list, but he's selling her personal things, too—her paintings, the furniture she picked out, even the rugs."

I couldn't stand to hear this. "Well, I won't take long," I said.

I went into Margarita's office and nudged the door so it was barely ajar. Leonora hadn't packed the majority of Margarita's personal things yet, so I could poke around without missing much. I had no idea what I was looking for. I started with the in tray on the left side of the desk and worked my way to the out tray. I opened the top drawers, but nothing jumped out at me. It was already starting to look hopeless.

The office phone—with a speaker and speed dial—was at my right hand, but when I swiveled around I saw a private phone on the credenza behind me. There was an answering machine attached.

It felt like a violation of Margarita's privacy, but I played back the ten messages on the machine. Two were from me.

Five were hang-ups. Three were from a man who identified himself as ''me.'' He wanted her to call him as soon as she returned from Palm Beach. His first two messages were in a normal tone of voice, but the third contained some anxiety. The man's voice definitely wasn't Rodrigo's.

I removed the tape and shoved it in my purse, then noticed a black electrical cord running from the phone over the credenza to a stack of files. I followed the cord, moved some papers, and saw it led to a caller ID gadget.

I pressed the button and the last ten numbers appeared on the screen. From the order of the calls, I could see that the five hang-ups had come either from long distance or from a cellular phone—because lines instead of numbers appeared on the screen. My number appeared twice, and the man's number showed up three times. I wrote down his number, unplugged the machine, and put it in my purse as well. I had no idea why Margarita kept so many telephone machines in her office, but I had a strong feeling they had something important to tell me.

On my way out I thanked Leonora profusely and patted her shoulder. We talked for a while, and I showed her a picture of Margarita and me that I kept in my wallet. Leonora was a churning cauldron of emotion and sentimentality. It took a great deal of self-control to get out of there without breaking down myself.

There was no point in telling Leonora about the answering machine and the caller ID device. I trusted Leonora, and knew she was sincere, but I couldn't count on her not to blab. She was the sort of person who would reveal secrets without thinking, just to continue talking to someone. For the first time I realized that she was profoundly lonely and that the loss of Margarita meant much more to her than losing her livelihood and a dear friend. I suspected it also meant losing much of her contact with the outside world.

I drove to Solano Investigations with one eye glued to my rearview mirror. It was turning into a habit.

SIXTEEN

I SHIFTED IN my chair uncomfortably, made ill at ease by the intense scrutiny of three sets of nearly identical dark eyes. The outcome of the Arango gene pool—Alonso junior, Ernesto, and Mariano—faced me in a claustrophobic semi-circle. None of them had spoken a word since our introductions.

I had called this meeting, which they asked to have at their parents' house in Coral Gables rather than at my office. This was fine with me, because it gave me the chance to check out the place. Isabel and Alonso lived in a handsome old Spanish house near the University of Miami. It was almost invisible from the street behind lush native trees. Coral Gables zoning regulations required that homes be set back a certain number of yards from the street, in order to ensure the uniformity city planners considered so essential to the residents' happiness—not to mention to real estate values. The Arangos had tripled the mandated distance and had aggressively planted the land with foliage. Water sprouted high in the air from a stone fountain in front of the portico. Apparently it was there for drama, and it worked.

The house itself wasn't as sprawling as it might have been, but it made up in charm what it lacked in size. Flower-laden balconies jutted from every window, blending with the trees and shrubs to lend an air of tropical perfume. The abundant flowers and plants that greeted me when I entered the house made the place a splash of color. I have nothing against plants—though mine might say otherwise—but all the pollen in the air was making my eyes water.

A uniformed maid escorted me into the living room, where the brothers were waiting. Their mother must have briefed them about me, because they seemed unsurprised by my appearance and greeted me as a social equal. I was offered Cuban coffee and accepted.

The room's furnishings demonstrated one thing—that the mistress of the house didn't restrict her fondness for gilt French Provincial furniture to the office. I fixated on the idea that Margarita had decorated the place. She had indulged her professional taste for simplicity as well as she could have, given Isabel's apparent penchant for predominately feminine, gold-colored decor. The compromise exuded an air of quiet sophistication and highlighted the owners' Cuban art collection. I had immediately spotted a Wilfredo Lam nicely displayed in an alcove within the entrance walkway. And as I turned the corner into the sunken living room, my eye had caught on a pair of Emilio Sanchez oils hanging side by side.

Margarita had always encouraged her Cuban clients to buy art from their countrymen, and I wondered how much of this collection was here before she'd been hired. If that hadn't been cause enough for conflict, there must have been plenty of others. I knew how Margarita loathed French Provincial style, and gilt would have sent her over the edge. Margarita hated anything delicate. She thought houses were for living in, not for show. It seemed to me a little odd that she had been hired to decorate the Arangos' place, given the obvious opposition in their tastes. I realized that I didn't know who had made the referral.

My coffee finally came, and only then did the brothers

break their collective staring. "Thanks for the coffee," I said. "Delicious."

Alonso junior muttered something incomprehensible. The maid retired, leaving us alone to our delightful social interaction. I set my cup down, recognizing the pattern on it— Herend birds. Business at Optima Jewelers must have been spectacular, because Hungarian porcelain stuff was prohibitively pricey.

"I'll start," I said, alternating my focus among the three as I spoke. "I know from the police report, as well as from employees at Optima, that none of you were at the store when the incident took place. I requested this meeting in order to find out if there is anything you might add to my investigation."

I gave them an encouraging smile. I really didn't have much hope that they would be of help, but it never hurts to make your client's family feel you're doing everything possible in the investigation. After all, you're not only earning your money, you're also spending theirs.

Alonso junior cleared his throat. As the oldest, he obviously carried responsibility for the three. "What are our father's chances if this case goes to trial?" he asked soberly. "We've discussed this among ourselves, and we don't want to speculate about a jury trial here in Miami. But supposing the worst, what do you think will happen?"

Alonso junior was about six feet tall, well built, with thick curly dark brown hair and penetrating eyes. Even with a deep tan his skin had an olive tinge, which contrasted nicely with his hair. He wore casual khakis, an open-necked button-down shirt, and well-worn moccasins without socks. The background on him told me he was twenty-eight, and that he had owned his own business—AAA Lines, a yacht brokerage in Coconut Grove—for the last five years.

"Let me be honest," I said to him. "I'm not trying to put you off here, but I'm not the person who can answer that sort of question. You need to speak to Mr. McDonald for a realistic, informed opinion. My job is to gather information for your father's case. Right now, my only goal is to get him out of jail entirely."

"Of course," Alonso junior said. "You can understand that we're very anxious."

He turned to the middle brother, Ernesto, and exchanged a look. Ernesto was a banker in the bond department at Barnett Bank in downtown Miami. He wore a formal, impeccably cut gray pin-stripe suit, with black wing tips shined to mirrored perfection. He was only a year younger than Alonso junior, but he could have passed for a man well into his thirties—his demeanor was as grave as his suit. His skin was much lighter than his brothers'; it looked as though he never saw the sun, a difficult feat to accomplish in Miami, where you can get a tan going out to the mailbox. He was also the tallest, and considerably thinner than the others. His hands were manicured, with short, buffed nails, and apart from a slim gold watch he wore no jewelry. He seemed to be a man who valued control.

I flipped my notebook to the section containing my interview with Isabel. "You all know that I spoke with your mother last week, right?" I asked.

All three shifted in their chairs in unison. Their interaction with the furniture had been strained and careful to begin with, and now the chairs groaned with their every movement. I wondered what kind of woman would choose delicate French furnishings when her immediately family was composed of four large men.

"She told me in detail what happened that Saturday morning," I said.

Instead of fidgeting—all three seemed to have realized that their best chance was to stay still and hope the chair legs didn't collapse beneath them—I received three half-hearted nods as a reply. At this point I realized that Mariano, the youngest brother at twenty-three, was making an extra effort to be friendly. His smiles and eye contact had officially gone beyond Miss Manners-recommended host behavior.

From my file on him I knew he was co-owner of Best Plants, a landscaping company in southwest Miami. Like his oldest brother, Mariano was casually dressed, in blue jeans and a pink polo shirt. His looks, especially in profile, were strikingly similar to his mother's. As he leaned forward, his sleeve slid up on muscular biceps, revealing a tattoo. I couldn't make out the design. He saw me looking at his tanned arm and gave it a flex.

"Alonso," I said. "Your mother told me she reached you at home."

"Yes, I was at home," the younger Alonso said. "It was on the weekend. I have to get up so early during the week that on the weekends I stay in bed until about noon. Besides, I had company."

Alonso blushed crimson, and Mariano gave an appreciative chuckle. I kept myself from smiling. It was sort of cute that Alonso—a twenty-eight-year-old man—would be embarrassed to mention his romantic life to a lady.

I decided to let him off the hook. "And you, Ernesto. Your mother said she reached you on the way to the office. You went to work on a Saturday?"

"Yes, but not because I wanted to," Ernesto said in a flat, modulated voice. "I'd been out of town since Tuesday, in New York, and I wanted to check my mail and messages so I wouldn't be overwhelmed on Monday. I only planned to be there a couple of hours."

Definitely a Type A personality, I thought as he discreetly checked his watch, the kind who goes through secretaries like bathwater.

Mariano piped up without being asked anything. "My mother couldn't reach me right away because I was in my car, going out to a job," he said. "I have a car phone, but my car had just been broken into, and I hadn't replaced it yet. My mother beeped my pager, and I had to find a gas station with a phone before I could call her back. I was pretty scared, Miss Solano, to tell you the truth. In the four years I've had a pager, this was the first time my mother had ever used it. I knew something serious had happened."

Ernesto forced out a quiet cough, as though to silence his talkative younger brother. "In any case," he said, "all three of us showed up at the store within minutes of each other. Our mother was already there."

"It was terrible, as you can imagine," said Alonso.

"There were police everywhere. The dead man was still on the ground—we could see him. And the press was starting to arrive. We stayed there until they took our father off to jail."

This part wasn't hard to visualize. I knew how chaotic, and draining, crime scenes generally were. I cleared all expression from my face and asked, "Did any of you know the dead man, Gustavo Gaston?"

They all shook their heads. "The first time we saw him was in the back office, lying on the ground in his own blood," Alonso said. His eyes creased at either side, and I could see that the recollection genuinely disturbed him.

"And you don't know anything else about what happened?" I asked. Before they could say no, I plunged on. "Think carefully, please. Maybe there's something you didn't remember right away. Something insignificant. Anything."

I was pleading for help, even though I knew it was hopeless. I looked from one brother to the next, and all three seemed to be sincere, scouring their memories for facts. Of course nothing came.

There was no point in grilling them, and Ernesto's glances at his watch had become showy displays of impatience.

"Thank you," I said. "I'll keep you informed about the investigation. You all have my card, so don't hesitate to call me if anything occurs to you."

Gentlemen to the end, they escorted me out to the Mercedes. Alonso helped me with the door, screening me from Mariano like an oldest brother protecting a young female guest from the overactive hormones of his youngest sibling. Which, I guess, was a fairly accurate description of what was going on. Ernesto was in his Saab before Alonso had closed my door with a grim smile and a weak wave.

I still had no useful connection between the Arangos and Margarita.

SEVENTEEN

I DROVE TO Tommy's office early the next morning so we could update each other on the Arango case. Tommy said he had some documents he wanted me to examine and suggested we go to the Stockade for another interview with Alonso. I was against the latter idea; I didn't have a clear enough picture of what I might want from a second conversation with Alonso, and I didn't want to use him up as a resource without a definite plan. I knew from the past that Tommy liked to meet with his clients as often as possible for a variety of reasons—including his wish to make sure his clients felt he was earning the obscene sums that would appear on their bill.

Alonso had a hearing coming up in a week, and Tommy felt pressured. Which meant he passed that pressure down to me. I still hadn't told him about Margarita's elusive connection to the Arangos, and I didn't intend to. And I said nothing to him about being followed by investigators hired by Rodrigo's lawyer. It didn't help my nerves to think someone might be watching me, but enough time had passed that I knew their work was restricted to surveillance. My meeting with Rodrigo would clear up why they were hired in the first place. I hoped.

I drove north on U.S. 1, one eye plastered to the rearview. Unless I had a tail who had trained at the same spy academy as James Bond, there was nothing to make me suspicious. There was the usual microcosm of the American social stratum—BMWs next to old Chevys, a Lexus pulling around a four-cylinder compact—but no single car caught my attention.

It's hard to express the difficulty of conducting a proper moving surveillance. Hadrian Wells, the investigator who first introduced me to the field eight years before, had told me the general guidelines. He had what I considered the equivalent of a doctorate in surveillance, having worked as a federal field agent before retiring into private practice. According to Hadrian—who typically delivered his lectures with one arm around my chair and creeping closer to my shoulder—three cars were required for a proper surveillance. The first was the "eye car," which kept the subject in view at all times. This car would alternate with the other two cars, taking turns as eye car, so the subject wouldn't become suspicious and burn them. And, he added, there should always be two autos between the eye car and the subject.

Hadrian would then cough cigar smoke into my face and complain bitterly about the half-assed surveillances he had to conduct since he left the Feds. The three-car system was costly, in terms of money and manpower. Most of the time, only the government could afford to hire three drivers to tail a subject.

I was lucky that my first surveillance was one of these rare three-man jobs. I was still an intern at White and Blanco, and I was assigned to work an insurance fraud case with possible criminal ramifications. The subject was a fifty-year-old teacher whose third wife had just passed away under questionable circumstances—that is, she drowned in the tub while reading the latest Danielle Steele novel. The insurance company was on the hook to pay a million dollars on the policy, unless it could prove foul play. The company was determined as hell not to pay, because they had already shelled out two million dollars to this teacher for the accidental deaths of wives one and two. White and Blanco was hired, with a blank check for expenses, to find out what happened to wife number three.

The surveillance was typical—it was irritatingly difficult. The teacher's house was in the middle of a short treeless block, with no camouflage whatsoever. We had to position ourselves two streets over, parallel to the teacher's, with lousy sight lines. I sat in my car for hours in the blistering sun, my bladder about to burst. I remember that in the depths of my boredom, I became obsessed with the chips in my nail polish. Like a medieval theologian, I pondered the implications of touching them up myself or holding out for my next appointment with the manicurist.

Then the call came through on my radio: "Suspect going north. Car two—he's yours!" White and Blanco didn't believe in spending lots of money on top-rate equipment, so I wasn't sure I'd heard correctly. The message was repeated again, louder and laced with obscenities. I was car 2—no one ever used real names on the radio—and the teacher was heading my way.

I started the car and, adrenaline pumping, pressed the accelerator. I was all set to burst through the intersection when I screeched to a stop. "Car one," I said in a panic. "This is car two. One thing. Is north left or right?"

"Left," he snarled. "Fucking broad."

Luckily I pulled it off, so I could continue to show my face at the disgusting pit where we worked. The teacher was caught visiting a woman who was waiting in the wings to become wife number four. Understandably, she lost her enthusiasm when she was told about her fiancé's history with women. And the teacher, though he never confessed to any wrongdoing, had a run-in with the County Prosecutor's Office and pled out to lesser charges. He only did a few years in jail, but at least he never got his third million. Of course, his first two were nowhere to be found, probably in a bank in Switzerland or South America somewhere. But as cases go, this could be considered a success.

Later that day I went to a hardware store and bought a compass for my car dashboard. I had learned my lesson.

IT WAS ALMOST nine now, and incredibly, I would be on time to see Tommy. His firm took up the top two floors of the tallest building downtown. He practiced with only three other lawyers, but their client list was so large that they employed more than fifty people in various jobs—assistants, paralegals, secretaries, clerks, interns. The operation was so successful that the office manager had her own staff. The place reeked of money. I loved going there, not only for the prosperous feel of the place but also because they served outstanding coffee.

I wandered back through the halls to Tommy's office. As usual he looked as though he had stepped out of a man's fashion magazine, in a faint blue pin-striped suit and a crisp white shirt. He sat behind his massive desk before a picture window that stretched wall to wall behind him and lent a postcard view of Biscayne Bay. He waved and blew me a kiss when he saw me come in.

He was on the phone, something else I could always count on. I walked to the window and watched the birds flying in graceful arcs in the hazy morning sky. Tommy's office was so high in the air that I was actually level with the birds. I often told him he should install a feeder.

I didn't want to eavesdrop on Tommy's conversation, but it was impossible not to. He was practically screaming, and the speaker phone was on, so I could also hear the hapless client.

"I told you not to screw around with drugs!" Tommy said, like a high school principal. "There's nothing I can do for you now. Nothing! The cops were just waiting for you to fuck up—just like I said. You're on your own now, *chico.*"

He leaned back in his chair and put his feet on the desk. We both admired his spit-shined Peels. He winked at me, covered the phone with his hand, and whispered, "I'm just jacking up my fee. I'll let him sweat it out in the Stockade a couple of days, then I'll get him out. He'll be begging me to let him pay my fee. Serves him right. He's been acting like an asshole.''

I hated this part of the business, and I didn't much care for this side of Tommy. I could hear the client sobbing into the phone. ''Listen, I'll see what I can do for you.'' Tommy sighed. ''Hang in there.''

Tommy unceremoniously clicked the phone off. He had a taste for melodrama, but even he had his limits.

''Stupid!'' Tommy muttered. ''Guy has a sheet as long as my arm. I've gotten him out of trouble so many times, I should consider him my annuity for when I retire. I should list him as an asset if I ever have to draw up a financial statement.''

He turned to me, coming out of his rant and addressing me in the somber tones of a professor speaking to one of the duller members of his class. ''Don't forget, though,'' he said. ''It's clients like that who pay the rent and keep everything going.''

''Tommy,'' I said. ''What's going on in the Alonso Arango case?''

Tommy looked surprised that I had cut off his fount of wisdom. ''Not much, actually,'' he said. ''I asked for bail again, and Sparky denied me. We entered a plea of not guilty, and the case was set for trial. I have a motion being heard next week, but I can pretty well predict the outcome.''

''That bad?''

''That bad.'' Tommy took out his leather-bound calendar and flipped through the pages. ''Let's see, today is Wednesday, March twentieth. Trial starts bright and early Monday, June tenth. Less than three months from now.''

''That's probably too soon,'' I said. ''Are you going to ask for a continuance?'' I found the silver tray set on the credenza and poured myself a cup of steaming coffee. It smelled like the beans had been picked and roasted that morning.

''Depends on what you have to tell me before then.'' Tommy took his feet off the desk, sat up, and straightened his tie. Transformed into a stern lawyer, he pulled out a thick file and started reading the jacket—the front page, which shows everything official that has occurred in the case to date.

"Who's the ASA on it?" I asked.

Tommy looked up at me and tittered. "We got lucky," he said. "The assistant state attorney is none other than Ms. Aurora Santangelo. Your personal favorite, and mine."

"That bitch," I said. When would I get some good news? "How did we rate getting her?"

"I knew it would make your day," Tommy said, his nose buried in the file.

Aurora Santangelo was a tough prosecutor; she hated losing a case, any case, and would do anything to win. She had hated me since we had a run-in a few years before, when she accused me of witness tampering.

I had been hired by a Miami defense attorney—not Tommy—to get a victim's statement in a felonious assault, after the victim had stopped cooperating with the prosecution. Aurora was the prosecutor, and without the female victim's statement, she had no case because there were no other witnesses. My job was to obtain a statement from the victim saying, in effect, that she had reconsidered and didn't want the case to proceed. The victim herself had contacted the defense attorney, and then personally told the prosecutor she didn't want to pursue the charges. I got the statement, had it notarized, and handed it to the defense attorney, who presented it to Aurora.

Aurora treated the victim like something she had scraped off her shoe, losing her temper and accusing her of being a coward. The victim simply didn't want to testify and expose what happened to her one night, when she had too much to drink and did a couple of stupid things. My heart ached for this woman—she was a quiet, modest middle-aged lady, a churchgoing mother who let her drinking at a party get her into a shitload of trouble. In a sense I couldn't blame her for not wanting to expose her behavior to the world.

Aurora couldn't get the woman to change her mind, so she came after me instead. I actually had to take the witness stand and defend my actions. It was sickening. Even though the charges against me were trumped up and wouldn't stick, I went into a spiral of anxiety and lost four pounds in a week. The judge dismissed all charges against me, and then reprimanded Aurora for wasting the court's time with a personal vendetta. She had been gunning for me ever since.

Tommy pressed the buzzer on his desk, still smiling at me. I knew he sympathized; he had plenty of enemies in town.

His secretary appeared a moment later. "Sonia," he said. "Make a copy of this file for Lupe, would you please?"

Of course she would. Sonia was twenty, pretty, and knew a good thing when she saw it. Tommy pretended not to notice.

I took a seat on the other side of his desk, opened my notebook, and told him about the series of interviews I had conducted. Tommy took his listening pose—with his chin in his hand and his eyes half shut.

Before I could finish telling him about the Arango sons, my beeper went off. I dialed my office from Tommy's phone.

"Lupe, I know you're in a meeting, and I'm sorry to disturb you," Leonardo said. There was music in the background, and it seemed that Leonardo was having one of his Lupe's-not-here parties, but he sounded serious and spoke fast. "The number on Margarita's caller ID came back, just a second ago."

I had made Leonardo call up our contacts at the cellular phone company to trace the number for us. It cost a small fortune.

"Yeah?" I said, pulling out a pen. "Who is it?"

"Are you sitting down?"

"Leonardo, don't play games," I said. Tommy looked up from his file. "Who is it?"

"Alonso Arango, Jr."

I wouldn't need a pen. I could remember that name. I hung up and turned to Tommy. "Something just came up. I'll call you later."

I raced out of his office, leaving him with an unvoiced

question on his lips. I stopped only long enough to take a handoff from Sonia—the just-copied file.

Mierda. No wonder Margarita had wanted to speak with me about Alonso Arango. She had had information for me, all right—probably more than I could have imagined.

EIGHTEEN

WAITING FOR THE elevator outside Tommy's office, I hunted through the Arango file for Alonso junior's phone number. I found it by the time the doors opened on the ground floor, and in the lobby I found a pay phone—Leonardo had lectured me recently on the astronomical charges I routinely ran up on my cellular phone. I balanced the files on my hip and searched through my purse for a quarter. I called Alonso junior's work number, praying he would be there.

He was—he answered himself, on the third ring. "Mr. Arango, this is Lupe Solano speaking," I began. "There are some additional questions I'd like to ask you. Would it be convenient if I came by your office this morning?"

"This morning?" he asked. He sounded startled, more than he should have been. "I'm afraid I can't. I have some clients coming by to look at a yacht this morning, and I planned to take them out on the water all day. Can I call you later to set up a time?"

He was avoiding me. "Sure," I answered sweetly. "You have my number, right?"

"Yes, I do," he said stiffly. "I'll call you."

The hair on the back of my neck was standing up, which meant he was lying. I couldn't think of a good reason for Alonso junior to avoid me, but I was sure one existed.

Within minutes I hit the freeway, heading to the Coconut Grove boatyard I had listed for Alonso's office address. I broke a few laws and was there within twenty minutes.

I spotted a fire engine-red Camaro parked next to an orange cone right in front of the office. From my file I knew it was Alonso's. The office itself was a single-story, utilitarian building looking out on Dinner Key Marina, adjacent to a large boatyard at the north end of the Grove.

I parked in a no-waiting zone across the street while I tried to decide what to do. I took my binoculars from the glove compartment and focused on the bronze nameplate beside the front door. Two tenants were listed for the building: AAA Lines, Yacht Brokers; and Miami Marine Underwriters. That made my job easier. There would be less traffic in and out of the building.

I circled the parking lot in one lazy circle, trying to determine where to park. I pulled under a massive oak in the western part of the lot—my dashboard compass still served me well—and made myself comfortable. I wasn't too worried about being spotted. A lone woman in a Mercedes wouldn't set off anyone's alarms. From my vantage point, I could see both the office building and Alonso's Camaro.

I checked my watch. Ten o'clock. I cursed when I realized the only reading material in the car was yesterday's *Herald*, but I hadn't had a chance to read it yet—which meant that whatever was in there was news to me. Technically, investigators shouldn't read during a surveillance, but the *Herald* was never known as a particularly engrossing paper. I figured it wouldn't interfere too much with my job.

Fifteen minutes later I was done with the paper—no surprises, it was mostly ads. I folded it up neatly and settled in to wait. No one had entered or left the building. I regretted the double espresso I had for breakfast, and the coffee I had at Tommy's office, because I knew it wouldn't be long before the bill was due. Just to torture myself a little more, I conjured a mental picture of the cool, spacious marble bathroom in Tommy's building—the one I neglected to use before setting out.

The oak tree lent plenty of shade, but the day was already getting hot. I took off my suit jacket and laid it carefully across the back seat, then peeled off my panty hose, being careful not to snag the delicate fibers with my long nails. I put my hair into a French twist, then found a tortoiseshell comb in the glove compartment to hold it in place.

After staring at the yacht brokerage door for a few more minutes, I decided to really use my time constructively. I pulled my purse onto my lap and started rummaging around inside it. With a sigh of satisfaction, I found what I was looking for, under the Beretta. I pulled down the driver's-side visor and started plucking my eyebrows with the tweezers I keep on hand for such special occasions.

I was admiring the line I created on my right eyebrow when the office door opened and Alonso came barreling out. He jumped into the Camaro, fired the engine, and roared off heading south. I threw the tweezers over my shoulder and followed, breaking every rule in the book to keep up with him.

Alonso drove so fast I was almost certain I would lose him. Racing down U.S. 1, I consoled myself by thinking that even that wouldn't be such a disaster. I knew he had lied to me about his all-day clients, and that he wanted to avoid me. He might have been a son who wanted to see his father let out of jail, but he had other items on his agenda.

It took racetrack driving to stay on Alonso's tail without getting burned as we sped along the highway. My main fear—apart from crashing at seventy miles per hour—was that I would get caught for speeding. I didn't need another ticket, and I needed to be spotted by Alonso even less. I prayed we would get to where we were going—together—before my luck ran out.

A few miles later Alonso turned on his blinker, signaling a right onto 144th Street. I slowed down and let some distance fall between us before turning after him. I was in no hurry now, because I had figured out where Alonso was headed. I drove into the parking lot of Mariano Arango's nursery about a full minute after he entered, and parked out of sight.

Alonso spent about an hour in his younger brother's office before he came out, hopped into the Camaro, and drove north. This time, to my infinite relief, he took the trip at a normal speed. My bladder had issued a red alert by then, but I followed him back to Dinner Key, where he parked his car in the same spot and went into the building. Fifteen minutes later a young boy on a bicycle pulled up, gingerly carrying a horizontal paper sack stapled at one end.

So, Alonso was brown-bagging it. So much for lunch with his clients.

I looked at my watch. One o'clock, time for my lunch as well. It would be a cold day in hell when I skipped a meal for no good reason.

NINETEEN

I RETURNED TO my office, and had just finished half of the pita hummus sandwich I picked up at The Last Carrot on the way back from the Alonso Arango, Jr., surveillance when Leonardo walked in with a stack of papers in his hand.

"Very good." He nodded approvingly at the mess of bean sprouts and organic goo oozing onto the napkins on my desk. He peered into my plastic to-go cup. "But what are you drinking with that?"

"Carrot juice," I answered. Just so he wouldn't be too pleased with his influence on my dietary habits, I wrinkled my nose in distaste. "I need the vitamin A for my eyes. I was just out on a surveillance and I felt like I couldn't see as well as I used to."

"It might have been my imagination, though," I hastily added when I saw him about to say something—probably a recommendation to start doing push-ups with my eyes. I took another bite of my sandwich.

While I chewed, Leonardo sat in the chair opposite my desk and arranged his fanny pack so it lay just right in his lap. Then he pulled down the legs of his fuchsia bicycle shorts so they were evenly lined up on his lower thighs.

I had another bite and kept watching; I knew the ritual wasn't over yet. Sure enough, he messed with the neck of his tank top until he was satisfactorily comfortable. Sometimes I worried about him. Not only were his adjustments a little disconcerting, it seemed that his outfit selections had grown more and more deliberate. The hue of his tank top was the perfect complement to his spandex pants. I realized for the first time that he had several fanny packs. Today's was a shimmering black, truly a nice choice to offset his marine theme.

I was about to comment on the practical ramifications of the term "casual wear," when he sighed and handed over his stack of papers.

"The Social Security background information came in this morning," he said. Leonardo had taken the time to type up the employment records of Optima Jewelers' five workers. I thought it would be useful to cross-check the government records against those supplied to me by Isabel Arango.

I put the files side by side and scanned through them meticulously. Elsa and Olivia Ramirez checked out fine, and so did George Mortimer. The cleaning lady, Reina Sotolongo, had omitted some of her places of employment in her dealings with the government, but that was no great surprise. She was almost surely paid in cash, and had held back on information for tax reasons.

The real surprise was the bookkeeper, Silvia Romero. She had failed to tell Optima that she had once worked at a bridal shop on Miracle Mile. This triggered something in my memory, so I pulled out Gustavo Gaston's file and started reading. Bingo. Nestor included in his file all the places where the dead man had worked, and there it was. Five years before, Gustavo had been employed at the very same Miracle Mile bridal shop, and at the very same time as Silvia Romero.

I sat for a few minutes just staring at the files. Leonardo was still there, but he knew better than to interrupt me when I was concentrating. He used the time constructively, I saw out of the corner of my eye—he unzipped his fanny pouch, took out a few plastic vials, and popped a few pills into his mouth. Despite the fact that our cottage measured no more than two thousand square feet, he obviously couldn't take a chance by not keeping his health pills on his body.

If I hadn't just found a solid lead, I would have chastised him. But what the hell, it was a harmless form of insanity.

Instead I stood up and grabbed my purse. "I'll be back in an hour, with any luck," I said. I left before he asked me to explain.

I got in the Mercedes and headed toward northwest Miami. I was acting on a hunch, but it made sense. And if I was wrong, I had wasted a couple of hours. Anyway, it was almost time for Leonardo's second workout of the day—and he was due to work on his glutes. A futile chase was more rewarding than listening to my cousin endure agony while trying to tone his ass.

The parking lot behind the Bureau of Vital Statistics was full, as usual, so I slipped the attendant five bucks to let me park in the employees-only area. I hopped out of the Mercedes and turned on the alarm, looking at the car as though it might be the last time I ever saw it. Vital Statistics is just behind the Dade County Jail, in a part of town where cars disappear in a minute. With one final pat to the hood, I left and went into the spectacularly ugly building.

I blithely bypassed the regular request window and tapped on the frosted glass that read, "Funeral Directors and Officers of the Court." I groaned when the window opened. It was one of the assistant supervisors, a Class A bitch with seemingly chronic PMS.

"Good afternoon," I said, my voice full of saccharine, hoping she wouldn't recognize me from past visits when we clashed.

"Identification?" she snarled, her face contorted into its usual grimace. Her gaze passed behind me, as though there was a rotten smell in the waiting area that she couldn't quite identify. Though I never learned her name—she never volunteered it—I could spot her face in any crowd. Stringy brown hair, dishwater eyes, pasty skin, crooked teeth—so she had been shortchanged in the looks department. I guess she'd never heard of compensating by cultivating a good personality.

I rummaged in my purse, peering past her trying to spot my friend Mario Solis in the cavernous inner office. Finally I took out my wallet and showed her my investigator's ID.

"You don't belong at this window," she said wearily. Well, this wasn't big news to either of us. Still, I didn't think she'd recognized me—if she had, she would have been even nastier.

I apologized profusely in a loud voice, hoping Mario was back there and that he would hear me. Over the supervisor's shoulder I saw someone waving. Squinting—I never finished that carrot juice—I saw that it was Mario. I nodded slightly in acknowledgment and apologized again to the supervisor. Mario had told me that she suspected him of giving out information to unauthorized parties—like me—in the past, and I didn't want to get him in trouble. She looked away and closed the window in my face.

Five minutes later Mario came out a side door and joined me in the hall. I kissed his cheek with a little more heat than I should have, but I was about to ask a huge favor. I had known Mario for years, ever since my White and Blanco days, and he had helped me out a lot in the past.

"Oh, you look great, Mario," I lied, shamelessly.

He puffed out his chest and sucked in his belly—I hoped he wouldn't pass out—pleased as he could be at my compliment. Mario was a decent family man, but I always suspected that one encouraging word from me would be enough to make him leave his wife and five children in a heartbeat. I was fond of him, but truthfully, it was difficult to draw the line between Mario the person and Mario the county employee who had access to information I couldn't get otherwise.

"Lupe, I've missed you!" Mario gushed, looking deeply into my eyes. "What have you been up to?"

"Working, you know. The usual."

"Tell me the truth, now. Did you come just to visit me, or do you need some information?"

The man actually held his breath in anticipation while he

waited for an answer. It made me feel like a genuine shit.

"Both," I said. The relief in his eyes made me feel a little better. "I always like seeing you. You know that, Mario, but I also do need to find out something."

"Okay." He shrugged. I suppose this was better than nothing. "What can I do for you?"

"I need a birth certificate."

Mario rocked on his heels, his chest deflating. "Lupe, we've been through this before," he said. "You know perfectly well I can't give you a birth certificate without a court order."

"I know that, Mario," I said. "But please, just this once."

I could see the war ensue within Mario's mind. On one side was pleasing me. On the other was the punishment he might get from my friend at the window.

"I could lose my job over this, you know," he said.

That's what he always said. "No one would have to know, Mario. I have the mother's name right here, and the probable date of the baby's birth." I reached out and straightened the knot of his tie. "Please, Mario. I really need this. It will only take you a minute to look up."

Mario shoved his hands into his pockets and muttered under his breath. "All right," he finally said. "But this is the last time I help you. I swear it's the last time."

I handed him a piece of paper, which contained all the information he would need.

"Wait for me by the rest rooms," he said, looking up and down the empty hall. "This could take me a while."

"No problem," I said. "I'll be there."

When he spun on his heels and went back to his office, I could see that Mario had already begun to enjoy himself. He always complained that I was using him—and I was, mercilessly—but I knew he was too smart to let himself get caught looking up unauthorized records. My appearance in his life gave him a thrill, and let him imagine he was involved in cloak-and-dagger shenanigans.

Two hours passed before Mario appeared again. I was on

a bench in the hall leading to the rest rooms, and followed a few steps behind him.

He went into the men's room and emerged a few minutes later, conspicuously acting as though he didn't see me. Instead of going back to his office he walked over to the water fountain. I followed, and got in line behind him. When he finished his drink he turned, bumped into me, and pressed a folded paper into my hand. He apologized for his clumsiness and headed back toward his office.

The man was incredibly paranoid. There was no one around, and he was acting as though he was being watched. I was starting to worry about him—maybe he had spent too much time reading microfiche.

Watching him skulk away, it was all I could do not to laugh. His usual waddle turned to a suave swagger for a few steps. Mario was definitely charged up. I doubted Mrs. Solis knew what she was in store for that evening, when James Bond returned from his latest mission.

I headed back to the parking lot and fired up the air-conditioning of the Mercedes. It was only then that I unfolded the paper Mario pressed into my hand.

I might have guessed. In my hand I held a photocopy of Silvia Romero's daughter's birth certificate. In the space for the father, Gustavo Gaston was listed. As clear as could be.

TWENTY

"LOURDES?"

"Mmmmm. What?"

"Why are you worried about getting a tan line? After all, you're a nun. I mean, who's going to know?"

"God and I will know, little sister," she mumbled, her face buried in a towel. "God and I will know."

This always made me curious. "Is that the same logic behind your bikini waxes every few months?"

"You got it." She turned over to sun her front.

Lourdes and I were sunbathing topless at the Cocoplum house, on a ledge overlooking the Granada Canal, but obscured from view. When Papi was drawing up plans for expanding the dock years ago, my sisters and I talked him into devising an area where we could get some sun without being seen by the neighbors. Papi always encouraged modesty, so he agreed. I don't know if he'd have been so compliant if he knew that the ledge would also be used by his frisky adolescent daughters for other activities. Those chaise longues saw a lot of action over the years.

I squinted into the sun. "*Chica*, remember when you

were rounding up Cuban-American volunteers to help process the rafters arriving at Key West?'' I asked.

"Sure, that was a few years ago. Why do you ask? It's a little late to volunteer now." Lourdes grimaced. "After all, Clinton is sending them all back to Cuba."

"I don't want to volunteer," I said. "It's about a case I'm working. A man who was killed came to the States on a raft from Cuba, and was processed through the transit center at Key West. I want to follow up on an idea I have about the client's wife and this rafter."

That got Lourdes's attention. She turned her head to look at me, all the while still extending her face to the sun. "Go on," she said.

"My contract investigator, Nestor, did some background on her. It turns out she's volunteered with several Cuban causes, including helping the rafters. I want to find out if she ever worked at the transit center."

The idea that Isabel was connected to Gaston was stuck in my mind, and I had to find a connection. Just then the sun hid behind a menacing cloud, so I could open my eyes.

It was just after noon; with my neck craned I could see the boats heading out the Gables Waterway to the bay. I put on my bikini top and stood up for a better look. The sun sparkled on the water like tinsel. With great care, I climbed up on a rock jutting out over the water, knowing that now I could be seen. It wouldn't be long before men started waving at me from passing boats.

I could have set my watch by it. Sure enough, the horns started sounding. I got a couple of shouted offers for an afternoon cruise. Never fails. I climbed down off the rock.

"Got tired of your admirers so soon?" Lourdes laughed when I returned to her.

"I've had all the fun I can take for one day," I said. I poured myself some fresh iced tea from a pitcher Aida had prepared for us. "Want some?" I asked my sister.

"Sure, thanks," she said, wiping off her forehead. She looked up at the cloud still covering the sun as though she was willing it to go away. "What do you need to know about the volunteers at the transit center?"

"I need a list of female volunteers from Miami who worked there." I handed her a glass. "From January through March 1990."

Gustavo Gaston was picked up on the Florida Straits by a sports fisherman's boat on New Year's Day, 1990, so I figured he must have arrived at the transit center very soon after. I had no idea precisely when he left Key West for Miami, but I figured that two months gave me a reasonable cushion.

This part of my investigation involved working the numbers backwards. I knew from Social Security background checks that Gustavo Gaston started working his first real job in Miami—at the bridal shop on Miracle Mile—in June of 1990. He was employed there as a deliveryman/man Friday for the next eighteen months. Allowing a few months to find his first work as a new immigrant, I guessed he left Key West within eight or ten weeks of his arrival. None of the rafters stayed there long, and who could blame them. They all wanted to reach Miami as soon as they could.

Lourdes processed my request for a few minutes, tracking the cloud's progress against the sky. "You know that what you're asking is almost impossible," she finally said. "Some of the volunteers worked as little as a day. Some gave only first names. Some came as part of an organization, and in that case we sometimes only got the group's name."

"I understand," I said. This wasn't what I wanted to hear.

"The whole thing isn't that strictly organized," she said. "I want you to know that."

"Just do your best," I said.

She turned to look at me. "Because you have a hunch."

"Because I have a hunch," I repeated.

She shook her head slightly, then looked up. The cloud was gone. She settled back, her eyes closed. "Well, from the sound of your voice," she said, "I'm willing to guess you're onto something."

TWENTY-ONE

ON THE TELEPHONE was a man's voice, hesitant. "Miss Solano?" he asked.

"Lupe," I automatically corrected him. Leonardo had just told me Alonso Arango, Jr., was on the line. Two days had passed now since I'd called him to request a meeting. I had wondered how long it would take him to gather the courage to get back to me.

"Lupe, then," he said with a quiet, uncomfortable chuckle. "Would it be convenient for you to meet with me today?"

"Sure," I said. "Where, and when?"

We agreed to meet at his office at noon. It was close to eleven already, so I had to rush to finish some reports before I set out for Dinner Key Marina.

I had spent the entire morning working on Gustavo Gaston's background. I found so many contradictions that it felt at times as if I were investigating two separate people. There was Gaston, the educated, sophisticated, successful Cuban architect. Then there was the man who took menial jobs and lived in an efficiency apartment in a run-down part of Little

Havana. I had no conception of the real Gustavo, and both versions clashed with that of the man who allegedly came at Alonso with a knife almost a month before.

I spent a long time staring at the photo of Gaston, looking into his intelligent dark eyes, trying to determine what might have gone on in his mind. I could see that he was the sort of man women would find attractive; I had his driver's-license photo, and he even looked good under the glare and blurry focus of a Division of Motor Vehicles photographer. In real life, he must have been something.

Silvia Romero listed him as the father of her child on the birth certificate. It didn't take a detective to conclude that she had lied to me when she said she never knew the dead man. Because of this, I had assigned Marisol Velez to tail her.

Lourdes had accomplished the near impossible for me, obtaining a list of volunteers at the Key West transit center. Isabel Arango had indeed been there during the time Gustavo passed through. I didn't think Lourdes could do it, but I suppose being a nun and having God on your side makes it easier. Isabel had been part of a group of Cuban-American society ladies from Miami who volunteered to work two days a week taking food and clothes to recent arrivals from Cuba.

I had visited the transit center on several of my trips to Key West. The refugee center was a small, one-story building on Stock Island, just north of Key West. It was a place full of emotion: the hope of the rafters who had survived the terrifying sea crossing, and despair because of all the others who had died or been lost at sea attempting the same escape.

The transit center layout was such that two people there at the same time couldn't possibly avoid seeing each other. I had firmly placed Isabel and Gustavo at the same place, at the same time, and I had established an opportunity for them to meet. At this point nothing could sway me from my conviction that Isabel had known the dead man.

My next step was to check out Gustavo's Little Havana apartment, to see what more I could learn about him. I knew the police had just taken the crime scene designation from the place, so I could probably get in without too much hassle. Until Alonso junior called, I had planned to go there that afternoon. Now I had to wait.

At a quarter to twelve I started packing up my files. Before leaving, I beeped Marisol to see if she had anything to report on Silvia Romero. In addition to following the bookkeeper, Marisol had conducted a canvass of the neighborhood where Silvia and her daughter lived. Their home was a garage apartment behind her parents' home in Westchester, a predominantly Cuban part of western Miami.

Marisol didn't call right away, but that didn't really worry me. She would call me when she had something to report, I knew, and probably not before. For a moment I wished she and Nestor were on my regular payroll—I could send them a memo forcing them to change their ways and check in regularly. But I learned long ago about investigators—they did things their way.

When I arrived at AAA Lines, Yacht Brokers, Alonso junior was waiting for me inside the front door.

"It's good to see you," he said cordially. "Thank you for your patience with me. Please, have a seat."

He pointed to a chair by a window. Alonso was dressed as I'd seen him before, in khakis, open-necked blue cotton shirt, and Top-Siders over sockless feet. I envisioned him as the sort of man who bought each item of clothing in multiples, lining them up in his dresser and closet so he wouldn't have to concern himself in the morning with what to wear that day.

From what I could see, the company was strictly a nofrills operation. The office was utterly utilitarian, from the battered metal desks and chairs arranged haphazardly in the open common office to the calendars on the wall, which were giveaways from banks and gas companies. There seemed to be no secretary, no administrative assistant, no receptionist, no gofer. As far as I could see, Alonso junior *was* AAA Lines.

He sat on the edge of a desk. "You wanted to speak with me." It was a statement, not a question.

I decided not to mention his lies to me. "Yes, not only about your father's case, but about a personal matter."

Like I said, I planned to play it straight. But the words just slipped out, and there was no way to take them back.

His brown eyes darted away from me, just a fraction. "Well, then. What do you want to speak about first—my father's case, or this personal matter of yours?"

This conversation had a life of its own. I took a deep breath. "You knew Margarita Vidal, didn't you?"

Alonso straightened his slacks and stared at a picture on the wall of a boat cresting a wave. "Yes, I did," he said. "She decorated my parents' house in Coral Gables."

"I have telephone records which prove that you called her direct personal line at her office several times on the day she died," I said.

Alonso pursed his lips and nodded his agreement. "Let's go outside and take a walk," he said. "I need some fresh air."

We left the office, which was starting to depress me, and walked together to the seawall behind the building. For a few minutes we stood in silence, watching the delicate waves break against the dock. Then Alonso walked toward the jetty, with me following. There was a stone bench there, and we sat.

"I knew Margarita, and not just because she decorated my parents' house," Alonso said. He narrowed his eyes, not only because of the breeze, I could tell. "I met her several years before that, when she was the decorator for a yacht some Brazilian clients bought from me. I recommended her to my father and mother when they wanted to hire professional help for their house."

"She was my best friend," I said.

"I know. She spoke of you to me." Alonso shook his head, as though angry with himself. "When I found out you were working on my father's case, I didn't know what to do. It was such a coincidence. She died before I had a chance to tell her."

"She knew," I said. "At the very end. You're the father, aren't you?"

I could see that Alonso was a man who had a hard time dealing with his emotions. He looked out at the water with no expression. "She went to Palm Beach to think about what she was going to do," he said. "She knew she couldn't hide things much longer. Soon it would be obvious she was carrying a child."

Alonso stood up and leaned against the jetty railing; waves broke against the rocks below and splashed up on him. It wasn't long before his shirt was stained dark blue. He didn't seem to notice.

"She wanted to tell you," he said. "She wanted to tell you very much, but she couldn't. Not until she had decided for sure to leave Rodrigo."

"I had no idea," I said miserably. "She did a good job of hiding everything from me."

"She knew that you, and practically everyone, opposed her marriage to Rodrigo. They were married for only a few months when she knew it was all wrong. But she was too stubborn and proud to admit the truth, so she suffered in silence."

I listened, stunned, to this. Alonso's voice was suffused with such intimacy, such caring, and I realized that Margarita had shared parts of herself with her lover that she never revealed to anyone else. It made me sad and, at the same time, jealous.

Alonso's emotions finally overwhelmed him. He let out an enraged, inarticulate sob, then pounded the railing so hard I feared he would split his hand open.

"She was with you when your mother called that Saturday morning," I guessed, "to tell you that your father shot Gustavo Gaston?"

Alonso looked surprised for a second, then nodded. "She was with me in my apartment. She had found out two weeks before that she was pregnant, but she had waited to tell me."

"Why?" I asked, though I could have guessed.

"She said she wanted to think for a while, by herself. God, you can imagine what it was like—within five minutes, I heard about the baby, then about my father!" Alonso raked wet hair from his forehead. "I had to leave her right away. With everything surrounding my father, I wasn't able to meet with her for days.''

I didn't even want to imagine how Margarita felt during that time. It was no wonder she was so distracted and wan-looking when we met for lunch at South Beach. Guilt washed over me yet again—I hadn't done anything to help her. I knew she had hidden everything from me for good, logical reasons: she had a serious secret to keep, and she had to look deep within herself to decide what to do. I didn't know where to start; could I forgive myself, her, even Alonso? The part that stung hardest was that it didn't really matter what I thought about her difficult situation. Her prob-lems had nothing to do with me. Until now.

''Do you know that Rodrigo plans to sue Dade County for her death?'' I asked.

Alonso's face dropped. ''What?'' he asked. ''That son of a bitch is going to do what?''

I explained the whole business to him, including the part about the baby—his baby—as the centerpiece of the lawsuit that would really bring in the cash for Rodrigo. There was no point keeping anything from Alonso; he would read about it in the papers when the suit was filed. And I had no doubt that Rodrigo and Fernando Godoy—two heartless bloodsuckers—would waste no time in doing precisely that.

Alonso could only laugh bitterly. Not only had he lost his lover, Margarita, whom he had to mourn in secret, but he had to stand by and watch as the estranged husband prof-ited from the death of his own child.

''Whose child does Rodrigo think it is?'' he asked, al-most as an afterthought. ''Does he have any idea?''

''He called me to dig for information, so I don't think he knows anything,'' I said. ''I suppose he's counting on the father to stay silent and not sully Margarita's memory by naming her as an adulteress.''

It took a long time for Alonso to respond to what I said. He stared at me, his arms at his sides. ''In other words, Rodrigo is taking a calculated gamble,'' he said.

I shrugged. ''That's my guess.''

We stayed on the jetty in silence, Alonso at the railing,

me on the cool stone bench. I felt myself relax, watching the water and feeling the soft wind. I could see now why Margarita was drawn to the younger Alonso Arango. He was solid, and decent.

"You also wanted to talk to me about my father, didn't you?" Alonso asked after a while.

"Another time," I said. I knew he had little to help me in my investigation, and I had opened enough wounds for the time being. I wanted to know if his mother had met Gustavo Gaston in Key West, but there were better ways of finding out.

TWENTY-TWO

MY HEART STUTTERED in my chest when I pulled into the parking lot back at the office. Parked in the visitor's slot was Marisol's car—an incongruously nondescript four-door black Buick. I hurried in, because if Marisol had come to Solano Investigations she must have found information about Silvia Romero.

Leonardo wasn't at his desk when I came in, but I knew where to find him by following my nose to the kitchen. I should have known he and Marisol would be in there cooking up a storm; Marisol was Leonardo's favorite investigator, not just because she was pretty and charming but because she shared his passion for health food.

Of course, they achieved dramatically different results from their mutual fixation. They both adhered to a no-frills, no-fat, no-preservatives, no-sugar diet. As a result, Leonardo had evolved into a muscular, streamlined specimen, with a rippled belly. Marisol had become, if anything, more curvaceous, well rounded, and sensually voluptuous. Which led me to wonder how strictly she kept to her regimen. I knew for a fact that Leonardo often strayed. Most men, however, would surely not care what Marisol did to look that way—as long as she kept doing it.

I walked into the kitchen just as they finished decorating a carrot cake with cream cheese frosting. It didn't look like health food to me.

"Hey kids," I said. "Save me some of that frosting."

"Hi, Lupe," Marisol said through a mouthful of raw batter. She and Leonardo had nearly finished scraping the bowl. "I didn't hear you come in."

"Well, when you're finished, could you tear yourself away long enough to give me a report on Silvia Romero?" I asked.

"The report's on your desk. I'll give you a few minutes to read it while we finish the cake."

"Low-sugar," Leonardo mumbled, icing on his chin.

"This is the best cake we ever made," Marisol said. "I'll bring you a piece when we're done."

I didn't mind; I love carrot cake. I had a seat at Leonardo's desk and started reading. Marisol had done a good job, and I was pleased to see that my instincts had been correct—I hadn't lost my touch. The shy, mousy, mild-mannered bookkeeper was more than she seemed. She had been having an affair with Alonso Arango, Sr., for years.

Marisol had conducted a thorough neighborhood canvass, finding that an older Cuban gentleman had been visiting the garage apartment for years—so long and so often that Silvia's little girl called him "Papa." One neighbor in particular, an old widow across the street, provided a complete description of the man, down to the car he arrived in. It was a Cadillac Seville, navy blue. Alonso's.

The gossipy old ladies on the block said the older man didn't live with Silvia and their daughter because of Silvia's devotion to her parents, and her insistence on living close to them. "Papa" didn't fit in the apartment, so he lived in his house, which he used to share with his wife, who unfortunately had died years before. Another story around the neighborhood was that Silvia was the young second wife, and that perhaps "Papa" hadn't wanted the child and had expressed his displeasure by living alone. Some people will believe anything.

I took the report into my office and read it over a second time. Marisol soon walked in bearing an enormous slice of cake on a paper plate. It looked and smelled incredible, so I shoved the report aside.

Between mouthfuls I said, "Tell me about Silvia."

Marisol opened the window and elegantly perched on the sill with one leg in and one leg out of my office. I was so used to her ways that I barely noticed. Her report was more important than her antics.

"It's all there on paper, *chica*," she said casually. "The bookkeeper was getting it on with her boss. It's an old story—older married guy, younger single woman. What else do you want to know?"

"How did you get the neighbors to talk to you?" I asked. Marisol was a master at making people open up to her or, as she once said, "allowing" them to do so. She operated on the premise that most people walk around with stories they're dying to tell, and that they're merely waiting for an appropriate ear. As theories go, this one was hard to refute.

"Really, it wasn't hard," she said. "On my first swing down the street I saw a bunch of old ladies talking on a porch. I knew they would be a home run. I parked the Buick on a side street and walked up to them. That gave them time to check me out. They knew I wasn't going to rob them or anything."

Marisol gazed out at the trees. "By the time I arrived at the porch they were so curious they would have paid to talk to me," she said. "I just pretended I really liked the neighborhood, and said I was a college student looking to rent a room or an apartment. I asked them if they knew a family who wanted to rent to a nice, quiet girl."

I could just picture it. Marisol would be in her element with a gaggle of chatty old ladies.

"I asked about a bunch of houses on the street, so by the time I got to Silvia Romero's, they didn't suspect anything." She beamed at me, basking in her own brilliance. "Then I asked them how safe cars were on the street. That's how I found out about Mr. Arango's Cadillac.''

"Good one," I said.

She swung her leg back inside and sprang off the windowsill, dusting off her shorts. "Anything else you want me to do today?" she asked.

"Not for now," I said. "But I'll call you. I'm sure I'll need you again soon."

"Of course you will," Marisol said. With a wink, she left my office. I heard her and Leonardo engage in a mild tiff over how to divide their cake. Leonardo claimed the lion's share because he had provided the ingredients. He had a point.

As for me, I was happy that I could still tell when someone was hiding something. And Silvia Romero certainly had plenty to hide.

TWENTY-THREE

WHEN I WAS done with my cake I left for Little Havana to check out Gustavo Gaston's efficiency apartment. My beeper went off along the way, and I absentmindedly dug for it in my purse while I kept my other hand on the wheel. My mind was still on Marisol's report. I had to tell Tommy, but I wanted time to digest it all.

The child's birth certificate listed Gaston as the father—but that didn't mean he was. A woman can name practically anyone on that document. But Silvia lying about Alejandra's paternity seemed too much of a stretch, considering that she and Gaston had worked in the same bridal shop at the same time—a time that coincided with the child's approximate date of conception. Then there was Silvia's subsequent affair with her boss. And Isabel Arango's connection to Gaston. I imagined triangles and squares in my mind.

I still couldn't say what Margarita had wanted to speak with me about the day she died. It may have been simply about her relationship with Alonso junior. Did she know me well enough to understand that I would find out sooner or later, now that I was on a case involving the family? Maybe she wanted to tell me, rather than have me find out. But my instincts told me there was more than that.

I was still groping around for my beeper when it whined a second time. I finally found it and read its display. I gasped when I saw my own office number, followed by a 911 code. I quickly pulled over, found a place to park, connected the cellular, and phoned in.

Leonardo answered on the first ring. "Lupe, Marisol just called," he said, agitated and nearly breathless. "You have a guy on your tail again!"

"What are you talking about?"

"Marisol. She came back to the office." He tried to calm himself. "She walked out and forgot to take her part of the cake. She said she saw you leave, then she saw another car pull out behind you. She didn't like how it looked, so she followed. The guy has been behind you ever since you left the office. Marisol tried to call your car phone, but you had it turned off. She called me instead."

"Did she get the tags?" I asked, knowing that she did. Marisol was too good not to.

"I'm running them right now," Leonardo said. "Be careful."

"Where's Marisol now?"

"I don't know," Leonardo replied. "I had her stay on the line, but she hit the Black Hole of Calcutta, and I lost her."

"*Mierda!*" The Black Hole of Calcutta was a bad stretch of Twenty-seventh Avenue, where cellular phones inevitably lost their connections. "Tell her to call me," I said. "I have the phone turned on now."

I hung up. Less than thirty seconds later, my phone rang. "*Oye, chica*," Marisol said. "You're very popular. First that asshole Slattery, now this one. I lost him a few minutes ago. What have you been up to in your spare time?"

I wasn't in a joking mood. "What did the car look like?" I asked.

"Like mine, one of those American jobs, nondescript," she said. "Dark blue, no markings. I gave Leonardo the tag."

"What about the driver?" I asked, checking my mirrors. I didn't see anyone. "What did he look like?"

"I didn't get a real good look at him," Marisol said. "In his twenties, maybe thirties. Baseball cap, Ray Bans. Sorry, I couldn't see much more than that."

"You're sure it wasn't Slattery?"

"Definitely not," Marisol said. "This was a new guy."

"I owe you one. Thanks."

I hung up and tried not to let anxiety cloud my thinking. Was Godoy behind this again, or someone else? Were they after me personally, was it the Arango case, or was it a case I worked in the past?

I looked up and realized for the first time that I was in a gas station parking lot. I stared at a big tanker loading gas into the station's underground holding tanks, trying to compose myself to head back into Miami's murderous traffic. Then the phone rang again.

I answered it before the first ring was finished. "It's no good, Lupe." Leonardo's voice crackled through the wire. "The car's a rental."

I bit my lip. "What company?"

"I never heard of it before," Leonardo said. "From the address, I think it's one of those fly-by-night companies by the airport. Primerissimo Rent-A-Car. Can't they think of a better name than that?"

"I guess not," I said absently.

"Is that guy still on you?"

"I don't know," I said. "I just talked to Marisol, and she said she lost him. I'm going to call back and tell her where I am. I'll have her check the area to see if he's still around."

I called Marisol and did just that. She mentioned what I had already thought of: that I could be the object of a big-budget operation, with more than one tail. I didn't even want to think about it.

We stayed on the line, and Marisol was soon close to my location. "I don't see him yet," she said. "I think he's gone. He knows he got burned. But be careful."

She hung up. Marisol was good, and if she couldn't see

anyone, there was probably no one to see. Still, there was no point leaving anything to chance. I pulled out of the lot and did every double-back, yellow light-running maneuver that I knew. After fifteen minutes of that nonsense, I headed toward Gustavo Gaston's apartment, right off Tenth Street in Little Havana.

Gustavo had lived on the second floor of a two-story building, one of many shabby abodes built for low-income refugees. I parked on a sad, dry patch of grass in front and took the stairs—the elevator looked like a death trap. Within a minute I was at Gaston's apartment.

The door was open. I knocked softly and went in, pausing in the entranceway to have a look. The room where Gaston had spent the last year of his life was bland and cheerless, furnished in various depressing shades of brown. There was an unmade twin bed in the corner, next to a corroded metal night table. Not far away a brown Formica dining table with two chairs composed the dining area. There was a single standing lamp next to a coffee-colored armchair set in front of the apartment's only window.

A tiny, wrinkled, dark brown man of at least eighty emerged from the closet that passed itself off as a bathroom.

"Can I help you?" he asked, swinging a toilet-scrubbing brush. He sent a spray of water to his feet, and I moved toward his free hand in case he got emotional and started gesticulating with the brush.

"I heard there was an efficiency apartment available for rent in this building," I said. "Is this it?"

"This is it," he said. My instincts were right again; he swung the brush in an arc toward me, sending water flying. "You want to rent it?" he asked suspiciously.

There was no way he would believe I wanted to move into that depressing place. The furniture alone predated Fidel Castro. "No, not for me." I laughed. "It's for a man who works for my father. He just came from Cuba."

"Oh," he said, apparently satisfied. "Three hundred a month, including utilities. Two months' deposit. He can move in as soon as I've cleaned. You can look around, if you want."

The old man turned to go back to the toilet. Gaston's personal effects, if he had many, seemed to be almost entirely gone. I didn't even know what I might have been looking for.

"It looks like the last tenant left in a hurry," I said to the man's back.

He turned and cupped his hand behind his ear. "What?"

"Well, the bed's not made," I said.

"You're right. He left in a hurry."

"I see he even left some of his clothes behind." I moved to the open closet door, which hadn't been cleaned out. I looked inside, as though I were measuring the area. There were three pairs of shoes on the floor, two sets of sneakers and a pair of brown dress shoes.

"Don't worry about it," the old man groused. "It'll all be gone by this afternoon." Apparently deciding he'd done enough on the toilet, he started cleaning the single counter that served as an entire kitchen. On it was a hot plate, a coffeepot, and a toaster oven. Not exactly accommodations for a gourmand.

There wasn't much else to see, and I didn't want to arouse the old man's curiosity—providing he had any. "Thank you for your help," I said. "I'll tell Ricardo— that's the man who works for my father—about this place."

I opened the door to leave. "Don't wait too long," the old man called after me. "I have several other parties interested in the room."

Yeah, sure. I sauntered down the corridor, hoping to meet some neighbors. I hit pay dirt two doors down; there was an older lady in a rocking chair in front of her open doorway. She hadn't been there when I arrived, and was obviously curious. She pretended to be engrossed in crocheting doilies, and she was obviously a permanent fixture in the place. It was perfect.

When I reached her door I felt a breeze from her big electric fan inside. "Beautiful," I said, indicating her work. The needle was moving in and out, creating a delicate web of lace out of creamy white yarn. Her hands were moving so fast they blurred before me.

"Thank you," she said, clearly pleased. "I'm making these for my granddaughter's wedding. I have six done, six more to go."

She opened a plastic bag in her lap and showed me the doilies she had already finished. I cooed appreciatively; they really were individual works of art.

Finally her curiosity took over. "Are you visiting someone in the building?" she asked.

"Actually, I came to see the efficiency apartment for rent," I answered brightly. "The one that just became vacant."

"Oh, that one." The needle clicked away, its sound against her nails somehow ominous now. "I know that one."

"My father has an employee, a rafter, who just came over from Cuba and needs a place to live," I volunteered. "Have you lived here long?"

"Long enough." Click, click. "Seventeen years."

"Then you must think this is a good building, right?"

She stopped working and looked up at me. "Do you know why that apartment is for rent?" she asked.

"The last tenant left." I gave her a nervous laugh. "At least, that's what the manager said. Is there something I should know?"

"He's a liar!" she said proudly. "The last tenant who was there, he was a rafter, too. But he was killed. That's why the place is empty."

"Killed!" I covered my mouth in shock. "Here?"

The needle started flying again. "No, he was killed robbing a jewelry store. The police came here a few times and looked over the apartment."

"Oh, my," I said.

"They had the place sealed off with yellow tape," she said. "And they just let the manager back in. That's why he's ready to rent the place out again."

She was as pleased as she could be to tell me about this. I was probably the first person all day she was able to tell who didn't already know. She was almost done with her doily.

"It's sad," she added. "Because he has a daughter, a little girl." The needle went into overdrive on this one.

I held my breath. This was much better than I'd hoped. "How sad," I said. "I didn't see anything in the apartment that looked like it belonged to a little girl. Did she live with him?"

My new friend clucked and shook her head. "No, she lived with her mother. It was so sad. The day before he was killed, the mother, a tiny little woman, was here. They had a terrible fight. So sad, that they fought just before he died. Even if he was killed trying to do something bad."

The old lady stopped her work long enough to cross herself. I was sorely tempted to try to pry more out of her, but I didn't want to press my luck. She had told me enough. I would have loved to know what Silvia Romero and Gustavo were fighting about, but it wasn't a question that a prospective renter might ask. The old lady was a gossip, but she also seemed to have a sharp mind. I didn't need to become the subject of a future story.

"Thank you for talking to me," I said sincerely. "I have to tell my father's employee about the dead man. I don't know if that will affect how he feels about the apartment."

I walked out, thanking God for the observational powers of elderly Cuban widows. Marisol would have been proud of me.

Before I hit the stairs I looked back. The manager had closed Gustavo's door. There were two green plastic garbage bags in the hall, neatly assembled with twist ties holding together what remained of the unlucky Gustavo's life. It wasn't much of a memorial.

TWENTY-FOUR

"CHARLIE? IT'S ME."

"Lupe, hey, what's up? How are you? I miss you."

I was on the phone with an old friend—Charlie Miliken, Assistant State Attorney. I was relieved to hear genuine happiness in his voice when he knew it was me. Honestly, I hadn't behaved very honorably the last time I saw him.

"I'm keeping busy," I said. "And how about you? Are you going to take over Janet Reno's old job anytime soon?"

"Nope, I like what I do just fine." His tone of voice had changed. "So why are you calling me out of the blue like this? You never call because you miss me, only because you want something from me. It hurts my feelings."

I sidestepped that one. "Hey, do you want to have dinner soon?" I asked. "My treat, of course."

"How about tonight?" His voice softened. "The curiosity is killing me. I can't wait to find out what you want from me."

That's what I liked about Charlie: his absolute lack of pretense. Five years before we were talking about marriage, but I pulled the plug. Instead of being furious with me and never speaking to me again, he continued our relationship—only as a friend and not a lover. Which didn't preclude picking up where we left off from time to time.

"Great. Where do you want to go?" I couldn't believe he was available on such short notice. Charlie was popular with women.

"You pick," he said. "I have no real preference."

"Let's go to Caffè Abbracci. I feel like Italian food."

"Sounds great," he said. "It's a good thing I wore a suit to work today. Hey, Solano Investigations must be doing pretty well, if you can pick up a tab at Abbracci's."

"What can I say, we're the best. Is eight o'clock all right?"

I would have preferred a reservation for nine or later, but Charlie was an American and he liked to eat early. Since I planned to use him mercilessly, I figured it was only right to accommodate him. This was also why I chose Caffè Abbracci. Besides liking the place, I knew everyone there smoked. Charlie the chain-smoker would feel comfortable lighting up. This evening took some planning.

After work I went home to my Brickell apartment. At a quarter of eight I hopped in the Mercedes and headed to south Coral Gables. I didn't know what to expect from the evening, but I dressed to have a good time. I wore my drop-dead black tube dress, which allowed a hint of lace from my brassiere to show, and stiletto shoes. My outfit was carefully chosen because I knew Charlie responded to visuals. He also liked good perfume, so I applied a lot—it would have to get through the cloud of cigarette smoke in which he lived.

I kept one eye on the rearview mirror along the way to see if anyone was following me, but I didn't really expect to spot anything at night—unless my tail was a complete amateur. Though I didn't know why anyone would follow me, I calculated that was all they wanted—to watch me, and where I went. Whether they were there or not, I would go about my business. Eventually I'd find out who was so interested in me.

I drove south on U.S. 1 and turned west on LeJeune;

against my usual nature, I was at the restaurant on time. I noticed Charlie's blue Chevette parked across the street. Unlike me, Charlie didn't believe in valet parking. Frankly, I think his choice had less to do with money and more to do with pride—no self-respecting valet would touch his car. The mess inside was so terminal that a passenger would be smart to check her inoculations before jumping in. All sorts of foreign bacteria were in there, I was convinced, living in the wrappers and old cups. And there was another hazard: the glove compartment latch never closed quite securely, so it would inevitably crash down on the passenger's knees. I adored Charlie, but riding in his car was too stiff a test.

When I went inside, I spotted Charlie at the bar, deep in conversation with the bartender. I counted three cigarettes in his ashtray, but that didn't mean he'd been there long. Charlie could puff through an entire tobacco plantation in an hour, I was sure. A more reliable indicator of his wait was the fresh glass of Jack Daniel's that the bartender had just served him.

Charlie sprang from his stool when he saw me, all kisses and hugs. I shuddered when my nose met his neck. It was a familiar scent, and it still had an effect on me. I was momentarily tempted to cancel dinner and conduct my interrogation in a horizontal position, but the maitre d' showed up to take us to our table.

The place was half empty. No surprise there, Abbracci's catered overwhelmingly to Latin Americans and Europeans. On Friday and Saturday nights, the most difficult reservations to secure were those after eleven o'clock.

Charlie and I had a corner table, in a quiet part of the main dining room. Since I was treating, I looked over the wine list and ordered a very good Barolo. Our waiter was back in a blink, and after I approved the wine he launched into the specials. We listened patiently, then both ordered the veal. Abbracci's chef could do magic with veal.

I let the Jack Daniel's and Barolo do their work before bringing up any business. We chatted about mutual friends, and when the food arrived we did more eating than talking. This gave me a chance to just look at him. I admit I have a weakness for tall, fair-haired, blue-eyed American men, but Charlie was exceptional.

Charlie gave me a blissful grin over a glass of wine. I asked, as casually as I could, "Are you familiar with the Alonso Arango case?"

His eyes narrowed. "Don't tell me. You're working that one."

I stayed quiet, hoping I'd misinterpreted the hint of scorn in his voice. "You are, aren't you?" he demanded. I hadn't misinterpreted a thing. "That's a dog of a case. Your client is going away for a long time."

I ignored his snide expression. "Well, now that you mention it, I *have* been working on it."

"I didn't mention it, you did," Charlie said. "You know who the assistant state attorney is on that one, don't you? Your old nemesis, Aurora Santangelo."

"I know."

Charlie shook his head, apparently at my stupidity in getting involved in such a mess. "And I also know that Sparky Markey is the judge on the case! Lupe, how could you?"

Thankfully, the waiter had exquisite timing. He arrived, cleared our empty appetizer plates, and poured more wine.

Then we were alone again. "So," I began sheepishly, "you know all about it?"

"Aurora's office is two doors down from mine." Charlie devoured another forkful of veal piccata. "I'm surprised she hasn't said anything to me about you being the defense investigator. It's not like her to refrain from gloating about how she's going to get you."

"What's the office gossip about the case?" I asked, bracing for impact. I knew Charlie would spare me nothing.

"Let's just say the case looks like a touchdown for the State, and a two-point conversion. The guy pumps six bullets into a burglar, claiming the other guy came at him with a knife. Then no knife was found. Doesn't look good for your guy."

Charlie finished his glass of wine and reached over for the bottle, but it was empty. He raised his eyebrows and looked at me questioningly. I shrugged, and Charlie took it as a resounding yes. He signaled the waiter for another.

"Hey, wait a second," Charlie said, as though his mind was really whirring now. "Isn't Tommy McDonald defending Arango? Of *course*, that's how you got involved. It was McDonald!"

I smiled and nodded, but I was miserable. The news was worse than I thought. The State Attorney's Office was crowing to itself already. They weren't usually so confident, unless they thought a conviction was a given. Alonso was truly screwed.

"Do you think Aurora's going to agree to bail him out?" I asked.

I shouldn't have. Charlie nearly leapt out of his shirt. "You have to be kidding! Lupe, you worry me. You used to be realistic. What happened to you?" He took off his glasses and rubbed them with his tie. "Aurora needs a big win these days, and she knows she can get it with Arango. Her cases have been going nowhere lately, and she wants to make division chief this year. I hate to tell you this, but nailing Arango is her ticket to success."

"Thanks. I appreciate your sharing that with me," I said caustically. "Look, Charlie, I've been working this case for weeks, and everything I've uncovered points to Arango telling the truth."

It was a nice try, but Charlie completely ignored me. The waiter arrived, and Charlie initiated a lengthy discussion on dessert choices. He knew my last comment was bullshit; it was how the game was played. I knew some chocolate would make me feel better, so I skipped the list and asked for the most chocolate-laden dessert they could make. In an Italian restaurant, that's a lot of chocolate.

After our espressos Charlie and I sat, no longer talking about work, exchanging expectant looks. I gave the waiter my American Express card, not even daring to look at the total. I had heard enough bad news for one evening. I vastly overtipped, as usual, and we stepped out into the warm night together.

I turned and looked at Charlie, and I saw from his expression that he had reached the same conclusion as I had:

it wasn't the kind of evening that had made either of us eager to rekindle an old flame. We kissed for a while in front of the restaurant, until the valet brought my car.

"See you," Charlie said. "Thanks again."

"You're welcome, Charlie. Let's talk soon." He bent down and kissed me goodnight through my open car window. I remembered the smell of his aftershave the entire way home, in between glances at the rearview mirror.

TWENTY-FIVE

I WAS AT work early the next morning and barely into my first cup of coffee when Leonardo came on the intercom: "Lupe, George Mortimer from Optima is on line two for you. He says it's urgent."

I hoped George's definition of urgency wasn't another invitation to a cross-dressing night party at a South Beach club. I still couldn't believe his brazen invitation to Espuma Night.

"Hi," I said. "This is Lupe."

"They found Reina. Reina Sotolongo, our cleaning lady," he said, speaking so fast I could barely understand him. "They found her in the Dumpster in back of the store this morning!"

"George, slow down. Take a deep breath," I instructed. "Start at the beginning. Who found Reina? What was she doing?"

George ignored my exhortations and continued speaking in a weird, clipped overdrive. "The Coral Gables garbage people," he said. "They found her. When they tipped the Dumpster into their truck to empty it out. She's dead. It looks like she was stabbed. The police are all over the place now.''

"Hold on for just a second, George.'' I put him on hold and pressed the intercom button. "Leonardo, call Marisol and tell her to get over to Optima right away. Tell her to park in the garage across the alley, and to take pictures of the crime scene there. I want her to focus on the weapon—if they find one, it'll be a knife.''

Leonardo agreed; I clicked George back onto the line. "Sorry about that,'' I said. "Tell me what you know.''

"I came to work this morning a little before nine o'clock, and I saw a bunch of police cars turning into the alley behind the shop. I parked in our reserved space in the municipal lot, as usual, and then went over to see what all the commotion was about.''

George spoke slower now, his voice tinged with a sadness I wouldn't have expected. He didn't strike me as the sentimental kind, and I didn't think he had ever had much contact with the cleaning lady. "Olivia and Elsa were already there.'' He sniffed. "They told me about Reina.''

"So what's happening right now?''

"Nothing, really,'' he said. "The police are asking questions, to see if anyone knows anything. Reina's body is still in the Dumpster, I think. I'm not sure. I haven't been back there, so maybe they took it out already.''

"That's fine, George,'' I said. "It's fine either way.''

"Do you think this has anything to do with Alonso and the other killing?'' he said. "This is the second body here in a month. Do you think there's a connection?''

George had gone from ruefulness to unbound anxiety in about a minute. I thought he had read too many Agatha Christie novels in which the protagonists were picked off one by one. But then, to me it was as possible as not that there was a connection between the two deaths. And I hadn't read much of anything at all lately.

"I don't know, George—don't think about it,'' I said firmly. "I'll be right over. Don't worry about a thing.''

I gently replaced the receiver in its cradle. Why in the world would anyone kill the cleaning lady? I asked myself.

There was a simple explanation: she worked in a jewelry store. She might have interrupted a break-in, or someone might have attacked her to get into the store. Hopefully, the police had established a time and place of death. I had to get over there right away, but first I had to call Tommy.

"What's up, *querida*?" Tommy's voice boomed over his speaker phone. I could never stand his chipper attitude in the morning.

"Another body, honey," I said. "In the Dumpster behind Optima."

"Anyone we know?" Tommy asked, not missing a beat. I should have known it would take more than a dead body to rattle him.

"Reina Sotolongo, the cleaning lady."

"Did anyone we know do it?" Tommy actually chuckled. "Well, we know it wasn't Alonso. He's locked up nice and tight in the Stockade."

"Very funny," I said. "The information I have so far is sketchy. She was found about an hour ago, and it appears she was stabbed. I'm on my way over now. I just thought you should know."

"Thanks," he said brightly. "Listen, you want to have dinner tonight? Just you and me?"

"Sure, we still have to eat. I'll call you when I get back from Optima." I hung up, gathered my things, and hit the door.

I raced to Miracle Mile, beating my previous personal best time of eleven minutes by a full sixty seconds. If it weren't for school zones along the way, I might have made it into the single digits. I may break nearly every driving law, but I never speed through school zones.

I turned into the public parking lot on the far side of the alley behind the store. I had to circle the three-story lot twice before I spotted Marisol's Buick, illegally parked next to a stone column by the elevator on the top floor. One of Coral Gables' diligent meter maids had already issued her a ticket. I groaned, because I knew Solano Investigations would end up paying it. I parked right next to her—legally—got out, and started looking. After fifteen minutes I gave up and called her on the cellular phone.

"Where the hell are you, Marisol?" I groused. "I've been walking around looking for you for a quarter of an hour. It's getting hot."

"Obviously, you didn't try the roof," she said, ignoring my complaints. "Come on up."

I found the stairwell that led to the roof and climbed the steps, holding my nose when the scent of dried urine hit me. When I reached the top I heard Marisol's voice call my name, from somewhere that seemed far away.

The sun was in full beam, and I was blinded when I emerged from the stairwell. I squinted and looked over the roof, which stretched before me for more than half a block. "When was the last time you had your contacts checked?" Marisol called out in a mocking voice.

I finally saw her; she was flat on her stomach on the farthest corner of the roof, a video camera pressed hard to her face. She was extended out, with her elbows resting heavily on the structure's gutter. It didn't look particularly safe.

Walking low, I joined her, then stretched out beside her so I wouldn't be spotted from the ground. "Got anything yet?" I asked, holding my breath and looking down. I'm scared of heights. Lying out three stories high, with no rail to keep me from falling, wasn't how I wanted to spend the late morning.

Marisol, of course, shifted around as though she were sunning herself on a comfortable lawn. "They found the murder weapon," she said. "A knife, in the Dumpster. I took a close-up with the zoom."

The camera muffled her diction, so I had to think for a minute to realize what she said to me. "What about the body?" I didn't see anything down there that looked like a corpse.

"The coroner came and took it away a few minutes before you showed up," Marisol said. "The crime scene guys were only here for a little while—they left already, along with most of the cops. I get the feeling this isn't a high-priority case for them."

"Did you see Reina Sotolongo before they took her away?"

Marisol grimaced. "It was not a pretty sight," she said. "The woman was covered all over with blood on the front of her body. It looks like they got her in the chest. You'll see. I got plenty of pictures."

I peered over the ledge, praying the structure was sound, and that the contractors had built the place to code. Once a contractor's daughter, always a contractor's daughter. I had sat through far too many dinners listening to Papi rail about substandard materials used on newer buildings to trust a building to be up to specs.

There were only two police cars down there that I could see. "Well, I guess it's basically over," I said.

Marisol had apparently decided she had filmed enough. She rolled onto her back, scooted down the ledge to a place where she couldn't be seen from below, and sat up. "I saw two guys in suits, homicide cops for sure," she said. "They knocked on the back doors of all the stores along the alley."

I joined her, carefully imitating her technique, and started helping her put away her equipment. "I'll have the pix for you in a couple of hours," she said. "I'll develop them myself."

With a wave, she stood up and started to walk away. While she was still in earshot, she turned and said, "I also filmed the cars parked up and down the alley. I'll run the tags just for the hell of it. And to jack up my bill, of course."

She blew me a kiss and soon was gone. I waited a few minutes, then walked down the stairs slowly. By now I believed it was too much of a coincidence that Reina was murdered at the same site as Gustavo Gaston—and like I said, I'm not much of a mystery reader. The two deaths had to be connected, somehow.

When I reached the ground floor, I walked around to the front of Optima Jewelers. Two detectives were there, questioning Olivia Ramirez. I spotted George and Elsa in the

back of the place. Silvia Romero was nowhere to be seen.
Neither was Isabel, but that was no surprise. I imagined the
detectives would go to her house later to question her.

George spotted me walking by and started to greet me,
but I shook my head sternly and kept walking. There was
no point going in; the cops would want to talk to me, and
have me explain who I was. I could talk to the Optima
employees later, asking them what the detectives revealed
through their questions, and I knew from experience that the
police might be antagonized if I showed up and interrupted
their interviews.

I didn't know the two detectives, so they must have been
new. The relationship between cops and private investigators has always been prickly at best—that's the one thing
the TV detective shows tend to get right.

There wasn't much to keep me there. I walked back to
the Mercedes and headed to the office. There was a lot to
sort out, not the least of which was my choice for dinner
with Tommy that night. In Miami the possibilities are end-
less.

TWENTY-SIX

I WAS AT my desk not much later, catching up on reports for the Arango case, when Marisol came in without knocking. "I think you might be very interested in this," she said. Instead of heading to the window ledge, or sprawling on the floor in the corner, she sat down in my client's chair. I knew this was going to be a good one; she'd never have opted for such a conventional seating arrangement.

She tossed me two manila envelopes. The larger one was labeled "Fragile Pictures." The second bore no marks. I started to open the former, and Marisol impatiently said, "No, no, not that one. Open the smaller one."

I frowned at her, irritated, but did as I was told. Inside was a printout of license plate numbers. "Halfway down," Marisol said. "Remember when I told you I took pictures of the cars in the alley behind the store? I ran the tags when I got to my office. Take a look."

In the middle of the page was a tag that corresponded to a white 1993 Toyota. Its owner was "Primerissimo Rent-A-Car." *Mierda.*

I opened the second envelope and examined Marisol's

blowups of the bloody knife found in the Dumpster along with Reina Sotolongo. To my eye, it looked like a bloody steak knife. Nothing was particularly exceptional about it, and it would be hell trying to find out where it came from. Of course, it had yet to be established that this was the knife used to kill the cleaning lady, but it was a damned good bet. No doubt the cops were checking it for prints right now—and I knew they wouldn't find any. That would be too easy. Nothing in this case was easy.

My plan for the moment was to show Alonso senior the knife pictures, to see if the knife was similar to the one he claimed Gustavo Gaston attacked him with. He said in his police statement that the weapon looked like a common kitchen utensil to him. At the moment, it was hard to concentrate on cutlery. Primerissimo Rent-A-Car weighed heavily on my mind.

I thanked Marisol, accepted her long, itemized bill, and herded her out of my office. I pulled out the Miami yellow pages, and found thirteen pages listing car rental agencies. Miami was a tourist town, with plenty of rentals on the road, but spotting two rentals from an obscure agency in one week was far too much of a coincidence. I jotted down the address and made to leave. On my way out I heard Marisol and Leonardo deep in a health food discussion, about the nutritional benefits of birdseed or something. I shook my head at them and told my cousin I would be gone for a couple of hours.

Once I was near the airport, it took me a while to spot Primerissimo. Their ad said they were on the airport road, but this wasn't exactly right. They were a half-block down a side street, hidden from the main road. I guessed they could claim they were on the airport road on a technicality, because their lot was on a narrow alley leading out to the greater street. I pitied the tourist just arriving in town for the first time who tried to find the place.

When I pulled into the parking lot, I knew Hertz and Avis needn't lose any sleep over Primerissimo. There were only six cars in the lot, two of which had familiar tags—a dark blue Ford Tempo, the one that had followed me on my way to Gustavo Gaston's apartment, and the white Toyota spotted that morning behind Optima Jewelers. I jotted down the tag numbers on the other four, just in case.

The office was in a double trailer at the far end of the patchy lot. Through the large windows in front I saw there was only one person staffing the place. Walking closer, I saw it was a young man, smoking a cigarette and leafing through *Motor Trend* magazine. The place was not a beehive of activity.

I said a silent prayer and walked in. In these kinds of situations, there are no second chances. My best hope was that the young kid wouldn't listen too closely, or think too hard, about my story.

"How are you doing?" I said, smiling at the kid and sidling up to the counter.

"Hi yourself," he said. Bingo. He met my smile with an even broader one, showing some rather yellow nicotine-stained teeth. Mr. Charming. "What can I do for you?"

I put an elbow on the counter and looked into his eyes. "I am a good Samaritan, you know that?" I said.

"Really?" *Motor Trend* dropped to the floor.

"See these?" I dangled a set of keys on a heavy brass ring before his eyes. His head bobbed at them as though I was hypnotizing him.

"Sure, I see them." He looked away, his gaze finding my chest. Sometimes I hate my job. "What about them?"

"I found them in a parking lot in Coral Gables a week ago Thursday." I gave him my own shit-eating grin and giggled. It was humiliating. "They fell out of a guy's jacket pocket getting into that white Toyota you have out on your lot. I ran after him, but he drove away."

The attendant scratched his head and asked in a puzzled voice, "I don't get it. How did you know it was one of our cars?"

Now there was a legitimate question. By law, rental cars in Florida cannot be marked as such. The entire country knows why—too many criminals have taken advantage of tourists' disorientation on the way out of the airport. The killers would wait outside rental agencies until the visitors got into their cars and drove off; then they would assault and rob them. This had a wretched effect on tourism, so the law got smart. They could not prevent criminals from waiting for their victims outside the car rental agencies, but they could make sure there were no stickers or medallions, and the telltale "Z" marking on license plates was abolished.

"Well," I said, leaning closer and giving him a conspiratorial look. "I have a girlfriend who goes out with a policeman. I knew he could trace the owner of the car from the license plate. I saw it on TV."

The kid smiled at my cleverness. "Wow," he said.

I positively beamed at him. "I memorized the number. I have a good memory for numbers. And here I am!"

The attendant nodded with approval. "Thank you," he said, his voice sinking a notch deeper than before. "You're right—you're a real good Samaritan. I'll check the records and see that the owner gets his keys."

Here was the part I had feared. I knew rental companies wouldn't give out the names of their clients. Most outfits were strict in adhering to this policy, but I figured a mom-and-pop place like Primerissimo might bend the rules.

"Oh, I was hoping I could give the keys to him myself." I pouted. "They look pretty important, like house keys, car keys, office keys."

I kept several key rings in my office desk for situations such as this. Most people realize the value of keys, and are willing to take unusual steps to get them back to someone. They know it's a pain to replace them, and as long as an item has no monetary value, people become trusting and willing to help.

"We're not supposed to give out that kind of information, you know," he said, as though he was dying to. "I'd lose my job for sure if my boss found out I told you anything."

I went into a world-class pout. "But I went to all this trouble! I traced the license plate, I came all the way out here, and now you won't let me return the keys to their owner?" I gazed into his eyes so deeply I must have made him nervous, because he looked away. "And that poor man.

He must be going crazy wondering where he lost them."

"Well, let me just see who had the car out that Thursday," he said. "It might be someone from out of town, and then I'll have to mail the keys to him."

The kid was weakening, I could feel it. I smiled sweetly and waited while he looked through his computer records. A few minutes passed. It seemed impossible that it would take so long to find a record—after all, Primerissimo couldn't have had more than a dozen cars, from the size of their lot. Then it dawned on me: my new friend had indeed found out who the renter was, and he was stalling until he could decide whether or not to give me the information.

"You found out who it was?" I asked, trying to keep my eagerness in check.

When I leaned forward to try to look at his computer screen, he tilted the screen slightly away. I couldn't see a thing.

"You're pretty cute," he said. "You got a boyfriend?"

"Not at the moment," I said through clenched teeth. Just a couple more inches, and I could have seen the screen.

Finally he got to the point. "So, um, do you want to go out sometime?" I'd wondered when he'd get around to it.

"I'd love to!" I nearly squealed. "You like to go to clubs on South Beach?" I was halfway there—another inch or so, and I could read the renter's name.

"South Beach! Yeah!" His eyes glittered. "Tomorrow night?"

"Terrific! I can't wait." I inched forward; the record was just beyond my field of vision.

God must have been listening at that precise moment. My new boyfriend bumped the screen toward me in a burst of nervous agitation, just the fraction of an inch I needed.

I almost yelled aloud when I saw the renter's last name: Arango. Then the Fates deserted me. The door opened behind me, and the attendant turned the screen away from me again. I could have wept with frustration.

"Señor Pascual! How are you?" he greeted the newcomer with an employee's effusiveness. "Miss, this is my boss, Señor Pascual."

I smiled wanly, my chance gone to see exactly who rented the two cars. I had the name Arango, but nothing made sense to me, and my mind was a complete jumble. Hanging around at the front counter of a fourth-rate car rental agency, with a young kid panting over me, was no way to get answers.

"This lady is interested in a weekly rental of one of our cars," the attendant weakly explained to the plainly suspicious Señor Pascual. It was obvious that the kid had been hitting on me.

I didn't blame him for trying to cover his ass. I could have cost him his job—and finding jobs at which you get paid for reading *Motor Trend* is a tough task. But I had all I would get, and it was time to leave. I thanked the kid effusively and told him I would call about the rental, all the while ignoring the paper he thrust in front of me for my phone number.

I called Marisol as soon as I was back at the office and asked her to stake out the Primerissimo front entrance for the next few days. I told her I wanted photographs of everyone who went in and out of the place.

There was no doubt that the attendant would call an Arango—which, I didn't know—to tell him that a woman dropped off the keys he had lost. There were only three suspects, the brothers, since Alonso senior was safely locked away at the Stockade. I ruled out Isabel, because Marisol had been clear that it was a man who had followed me. Whoever it was, he would know the keys weren't his, and I was confident his curiosity would compel him to pick them up personally. I put myself in a vulnerable position by offering the keys as bait, because whoever came for the keys would undoubtedly get a complete description of me.

Which would make us even. It could be hours, or a day, but soon I would know who had followed me. And they would know I knew, as soon as Primerissimo called them to report that I had returned the keys to the rental agency.

The afternoon sun slanted through my office blinds. I

closed my eyes and breathed in the flowers outside, listening to the clucking and complaining of the birds. I still had no definite idea what Margarita had wanted to tell me the day she died.

TWENTY-SEVEN

IN BETWEEN BITES of exquisitely prepared filet mignon, I announced, "Tommy, this case is completely screwed up."

We were seated in the back dining room at Christy's, the venerable old steak house in Coral Gables. We were only blocks away from Optima Jewelers, now the site of two murders.

I had already polished off a burgeoning Caesar salad, half a loaf of homemade bread slathered with butter, and a basket of potato skins. I was on my third glass of Merlot, and working hard on my filet mignon. In other words, for the moment I was at peace with the world.

Tommy claimed he loved taking me out to dinner, though I'm certainly not a cheap date. He said I was a refreshing change from the skin-and-bones model types he was used to, the kind of women who ordered a lettuce leaf, with vinegar on the side, as their main course. What could I say? God blessed me with a healthy metabolism.

"Tell me exactly what's going on," Tommy said, pouring more wine. "I have your reports, but I want to hear it again from you."

I gave him a summary on the Arango case. First was Silvia Romero, who lied about knowing Gustavo Gaston, and had in truth given birth to his child. I moved on to Isabel Arango, and the gray-area possibility—though I saw it now in stark black-and-white—that she had met Gaston at the Key West transit center. Then I told the lurid, embarrassing story of my visit to Primerissimo Rent-A-Car.

It was quite a story. I could have written it up and pitched it as a movie of the week. It also had more loose ends than a centipede has legs. Tommy became fixated on Silvia Romero's presence in Gaston's efficiency apartment the day before the first murder, and their argument. He seemed in a pensive mood, so I told him about Margarita's involvement with Alonso junior.

Tommy didn't comment. That was fine with me—I didn't want to talk about it. By then dessert had arrived, and I was attacking a three-inch-tall slice of carrot cake when I told him more about Reina Sotolongo's unfortunate end.

Tommy heard me out, staring at his wineglass and saying nothing. We had worked together for years, and I knew he respected my techniques; in fact, he always gave me free rein on cases. He trusted me, and based his court strategies almost wholly on my investigations.

This time, though, all I seemed to be doing was uncovering more and more ambiguous information. Instead of tying everything up neatly for him, I just seemed to be creating more confusion. I didn't expect Tommy to be angry, or professionally disappointed, at my overall report. But there was an important fact that I knew he didn't forget for a second—while I was out investigating, his client remained in jail.

"I don't like this business about people following you," he finally said. "It makes me worried."

"I'm a grown-up," I said. "It's taken care of."

"According to your sources," Tommy asked, speaking slowly, "do the cops suspect that Reina's murder had anything to do with Gaston's?"

"My guy at the Coral Gables Police Department told me that as of this moment, they're treating the two killings as unrelated," I said. "Remember, they know they have Gaston's killer in jail. If they assumed the two killings were related, they'd have to reopen the Gaston case."

"Makes sense," Tommy said, and groaned a little.

"Unless they find out anything else, they're assuming it was an unfortunate coincidence," I continued. "Reina was cleaning the store, and a burglar came in and surprised her. The alarm was off, as it always was when she cleaned. According to the police, it was just bad luck."

"What do you think?"

"I don't buy it," I said. "I think Reina was killed because she knew something."

Tommy had left a couple of bites of his chocolate mousse, and I reached over and scooped some of it onto my spoon. He watched me with an amused smile.

"Where the hell do you put it, Lupe?" he asked, taking a sip of his espresso. "Your capacity for food never ceases to amaze me."

I shrugged. "It takes lots of fuel to run a high-energy machine."

"But what about Margarita?" Tommy asked, as though he hadn't heard me. "From what you told me, she didn't sound like the type to fool around. I guess if I was married to a jerk like her husband, I'd take a lover too. Alonso junior. Go figure."

My expression must have turned pained, because Tommy quickly changed the subject. "Tell me about her connection to the Arangos," he said. "I don't remember what you said about that."

Tommy knew now about Margarita's call to me the day she died—I made it a part of my case summary—but he hadn't mentioned it. "I've tied her to the Arangos twice," I said. "Obviously, through her affair with junior. And then when she decorated Isabel and Alonso senior's house. I have to assume all the Arangos had contact with her."

"Some more than others," Tommy said. I had to smile. "Just keep the billing separate, all right?" he added. "Margarita is on your tab—unless you can establish a real connection between her and the two murders.''

"Of course," I said. "Margarita is on me. But I tell you, Tommy, I'm starting to dream about this case at night. There's so much going on, and I'm finding more connections than real answers.''

Tommy kissed my cheek. "I have faith in you," he said. "You'll figure it out. Not just for me—for Margarita.''

Tommy really knew how to push my buttons.

"Anyway, you've never let me down," he added with a wink. "And besides being the best investigator in town, you're beautiful.''

He was incorrigible. But I was glad to hear he still had faith in me, because I felt as though I was groping through a maze in the dark. Tommy had one trait that always kept me on an even keel—nothing shocked him. I could tell him his client was a cannibalistic serial killer, and he'd start hammering away at search-and-seizure technicalities. There were plenty of people who didn't like him, but they still kept his number in their Rolodexes, in case they ever found themselves in trouble.

We finished off our dinner, soaking in Courvoisiers and the atmosphere. Christy's had dark red walls, comfortable leather chairs, small individual lamps on each table, and aged prints on the walls. It felt like a men's club that had just been forced to admit women. I loved it.

"I have another question," Tommy said, stroking his chin. "In your opinion, is there anyone in Miami who hasn't had some contact with Gustavo Gaston?''

"As far as I can tell, no," I answered, smiling.

"Tell me more about Margarita," he asked, with new concern in his eyes.

"I can't stand it," I said. "I pry secrets out of people for a living, and I don't know it when my best friend is having an affair. The Division of Licensing should revoke my private investigator's license.''

"Don't beat yourself up about it," Tommy said. "What I'm more worried about is Fernando Godoy having anything to do with you. He's probably racked up more complaints to the Florida bar than any other lawyer in town. He's a complete embarrassment to his profession.''

I had a sip of water, because it would have been mean to laugh in Tommy's face. Talk about the pot calling the kettle black. Tommy wasn't exactly a pillar of the community, and if he felt this way about Godoy the guy must truly have been scum.

''I can't figure out why Godoy would have me followed, unless Rodrigo told him to,'' I said. ''I never worked a case against him. I never even heard of him until Rodrigo mentioned him at Versailles, when he told me about his wrongful death suit. He mentioned the baby then, but I was pretty sure he believed that I thought he was the father.''

Tommy looked at his watch and signaled the waiter for the bill. ''Are you coming home with me tonight?'' he asked casually.

''Shit, Tommy,'' I said. ''Do you think Rodrigo had me followed because I might lead him to the real father of Margarita's baby?''

Tommy was busy signing the American Express chit. ''What did you say?'' he asked.

''That's it!'' I almost screamed. ''Rodrigo stands to break the bank over this suit, because of Margarita's pregnancy. He knew the baby wasn't his, but I assumed he would stay quiet and hope for the best.''

I grabbed Tommy's arm. ''But what if he came clean to Godoy? They would still try to get the money. I should never have told him I knew about the baby! How could I be so stupid?'' I pounded the side of my head in disgust.

''Under Florida state law, a child conceived while two parties are married is presumed to be the husband's child.'' Tommy focused his full attention on me now, speaking slowly as he caught up with what I'd just told him. ''I'm not too strong on family law, but I know that much.''

''I'm not sure how long I've been followed,'' I said. ''I think Alonso junior is safe for now. Even if I was seen with him, I certainly could have been there to talk about his father's case. But if they find out, Alonso's life could be in danger. Godoy and Rodrigo are looking at millions, Tommy.

That's the kind of money that can make people willing to kill anyone in their way. If Alonso decides to challenge Rodrigo's paternity, and can prove it, then Rodrigo's case is blown. A jury probably wouldn't be as sympathetic to an adulterous woman pregnant by another man. Goodbye millions.''

We walked out together. I had been tempted to go home with Tommy, but now I was too distracted. This was getting dangerous, and I had been merrily cruising along, never seeing the obvious.

I hugged Tommy. "Will you give me a rain check?"

"Anytime," he said. "You know you have my heart." But he wasn't going to let me off that easy; he kissed me long, and deep, and I could tell he was trying to make me change my mind.

"Listen," I whispered in his ear. "I just decided something. I'm going to break into Optima Jewelers tomorrow night. I know there are answers in there, if I could just have a look around."

He pulled away, just a little. "Don't tell me about it," he said. "I don't want to know. Just be careful, for God's sake."

We crossed Ponce de Leon Boulevard and started walking toward my car. I had parked almost two blocks away.

I wasn't surprised by Tommy's reaction to my sudden decision—as a lawyer, he would have to distance himself completely from any kind of illicit investigational tactics.

Everything revolved around that store. From what I gleaned from the police and from the Optima employees, it looked as though Reina Sotolongo was knocked out in the store, dragged outside, stabbed there, and thrown in the Dumpster. There were no bloodstains in the store, and Reina had a blunt instrument injury to her head, so this was the most viable theory for what had happened. I could have asked Isabel Arango for permission to search the place more thoroughly, but I couldn't trust her. I was sure she had lied about knowing Gaston. I didn't particularly relish the thought of getting busted for breaking and entering, and though there were investigators who wouldn't think twice about breaking the law to get information, I wasn't one of them. But I was convinced, completely, that my choices had narrowed to a point of desperation.

Tommy was silent as we walked; I know he was walking his own internal ethical tightrope. I squeezed his hand. "You'll bail me out if I get busted, won't you?" I asked.

"Sure, I'll stop at an ATM tonight and get some cash just in case, but remember—my track record lately for getting clients out of jail hasn't been the best. Alonso's still in there, along with a couple of my drug dealer clients." Tommy laughed bitterly. "Of course, I meant to ask you to come with me to see Alonso this week. It'll be a lot easier if you're already in the Stockade."

"Very funny. Just be prepared, like the Boy Scouts." I kissed him again.

He responded passionately; no great surprise. "What the hell," I said. "Let's go to your place. If I end up in jail, I want something good to remember."

I wasn't sure what had gotten into me, but I suspected it had something to do with dinner at Christy's. Red meat always makes things happen.

TWENTY-EIGHT

THE NEXT MORNING I sat at my desk drawing a spider-web flowchart on a piece of legal paper. The three Arango brothers had their own special section, one that led back with a dotted line to Primerissimo Rent-A-Car. Marisol was still watching the little rental agency, but I needed to act. I called Alonso junior, and asked if we could meet again. I wanted to eliminate him from the very short list of suspects.

He sounded confused when I called, but agreed to meet right away. I made another call, one that I knew could land me in trouble, and left. Alonso met me on the familiar jetty behind AAA Lines.

"How many people knew about your relationship with Margarita?" I asked him, sipping from a paper cup of coffee I'd bought along the way.

If Alonso was surprised by my question, he didn't show it. "No one that I know of for sure." He paused for a moment. "The closest anyone came to discovering us was my brother Mariano. He came by my apartment one time without calling, to bring me some plants from his nursery. When he was walking up the drive he saw Margarita leaving, and he knew her from her work for my parents.''

"What did he say?" I asked.

"He called out to her, and said hello," Alonso said. "She told him she was showing me some carpet samples for a client's boat.''

"Do you think he believed her?"

"Of course. Well, I'm as sure as I can be." Alonso's brow furrowed. "Why are you asking me about this?"

I hated to worry the poor man. I instinctively trusted him, though, and he deserved to know what was going on. For my part, I also felt I owed it to Margarita to see that her lover continued to live.

"Someone has been spotted following me on two occasions," I said. "Remember when we spoke last, when I told you about the case Rodrigo plans to file against the county?"

Alonso flinched. "Of course I remember. It's disgusting."

"One of the people following me was an investigator who works for Rodrigo's lawyer, Fernando Godoy." Alonso didn't react. "I didn't think of it at the time, but it's obvious to me now that Rodrigo and Godoy hired this investigator hoping that I would lead them to Margarita's lover and the real father of her baby."

We walked in silence to the cool stone bench where I had sat just the other day, at the end of the jetty. Aside from a rising wind, it was a perfect South Florida day, the kind the Chamber of Commerce prays for. The humidity was low, and the sun filled the sky above lazy wispy clouds. We watched a sailboat float across the water in the distance.

"Margarita was very impressed with your abilities as an investigator," Alonso said. "So I take what you say seriously. Do you think I'm in some sort of danger?"

"Possibly," I replied. "I don't want to alarm you, but you're the only person who can stand in the way of Rodrigo's money and Godoy's percentage. I don't know what either of them is capable of.''

Alonso stared out at the water. If he was frightened, it didn't show. "Our speaking today, as well as before, is legitimate," I said. "I'm working your father's case and need to interview you. But Godoy might have other information. Are you sure Mariano is the only person who might suspect your involvement with Margarita?"

His big brown eyes met mine. "We were very careful," he said.

I almost told him about the Arango rental at Primerissimo, but I stopped short. There was a line in my mind—and on my desk back at the office—connecting Slattery, the blue Tempo that tailed me to Gaston's apartment, and the white Toyota parked in the alley where Reina Sotolongo was found. I hadn't drawn this line in ink, and I didn't want to tip my hand—even to Alonso.

"Maybe I'm just being paranoid," I said, and put my hand on his arm. "Just be careful, all right?"

I had an impulse to hug him then, but it didn't seem appropriate. Instead I left him at the jetty, alone with his thoughts and his memories. His loss was the kind that couldn't be consoled. He mourned in secret, and now he knew his secret could cost him his life.

Besides, I couldn't stick around. I had laws to break.

TWENTY-NINE

"*MIERDA*!" I SWORE under my breath. "Shit! Damn it!"

I was sweating so hard from the evening heat—or maybe it was sheer terror, though I didn't want to admit it to myself—that I dropped my flashlight. Needless to say, it landed on my foot, almost hard enough to crack bone. I hoped my sneakers would protect my feet, because I'd had a pedicure that afternoon after meeting with Alonso junior. If I went to jail, it would be with freshly done nails.

Almost an hour and a half had passed since Bridget O'Leary and I broke into Optima Jewelers. First we picked the lock and neutralized the alarm—two of Bridget's specialties—and then we searched every inch of the store's back area. I told her we were looking for anything strange, any irregularity that might tell me what my witnesses couldn't, or wouldn't.

Bridget was my partner-in-crime for the evening, and hers was a number I didn't have cause to call very often. She was prohibitively expensive, and worth every cent. Bridget was a rogue agent of the ATF—the Federal Bureau of Alcohol, Tobacco, and Firearms. She had worked with them for six years, specializing in undercover work as well as semilegal projects—the kind the government denies it's engaged in. Finally she burned out and quit. In the beginning she tried to hold down straight jobs—as an office manager for an oral surgeon, selling cosmetics at a department store, then as a mortgage broker. She hated them all.

Now, at age thirty, after two years of trying to go straight, she had given in and advertised her services and expertise—discreetly, of course, and to the very same criminal defense attorneys whose clients she had helped put in jail. I didn't know her personally, or understand much about her, but I always suspected she did her current work for the thrills. She was listed in my Rolodex only by her initials.

She had come to Optima earlier that day, just after my call to her, to familiarize herself with the place. She claimed to be shopping for an anniversary present for her husband, and even sweet-talked her way into the bathroom to look in the back. She came to a quick conclusion: that the alarm system at Optima was so antiquated that security companies no longer sold them. Her old ATF equipment got us into the place within minutes. Even the dead bolt was no problem for her.

"Over here," Bridget called out to me.

Bridget had searched Alonso's office while I did Silvia Romero's. So far, nothing, and pretty soon we would have to get out. There were only three areas left to search: the large, open area where Gaston was shot, the bathroom, and the supply closet where Reina's things were kept.

Bridget whispered to me again, and I swung my flashlight around, illuminating her face. Her bright red hair shone in the light, her green eyes looking as though they were caught in high beams.

"Will you please point that fucking light down at the floor and not at me!" she hissed angrily.

I rubbed my aching toe and joined her by the utility closet. I had to push aside a half dozen mops and brooms to get to where she crouched.

"Here," she said. "Feel this."

Bridget took my hand and ran it along a barely discernible seam in the closet wall, facing the back area of the store.

I shone my flashlight along the line. It ran from the floor to about three feet high, and was about two inches wide. Bridget roughly pulled me into the closet, shut the door behind us, and turned on the light.

"There has to be an opening in here somewhere." She started to feel around. "Here, under the carpet. This is it."

To my amazement Bridget started pulling at a large panel until it swung out into the closet. She stepped aside, allowing me to maneuver in front of her and squeeze into the narrow, confined area she had exposed. Bridget was a tall woman, hovering around the six-foot mark. It took no discussion to find the best candidate for entering a tiny crawl space.

Though I didn't want Bridget to know it, this was my first real B&E. I had gone into places I shouldn't have, sure, but I had never gone this far. I had spent the day alternating between Pepto-Bismol and Kaopectate in anticipation. I would probably be constipated for a month—but if I ended up in jail, that might be a blessing.

I couldn't have Bridget thinking I was scared of crawling into the dark; it was a matter of professional pride. I went farther in and shone my flashlight on the walls. Once I was well inside I could stand up to about three quarters of my full height—not comfortable, but bearable. As I groped my way along the wall, I expected to find another wall in front of me. There wasn't any. I realized that the space ran parallel to the entire length of the back wall.

I pointed the flashlight beam ahead of me, and still couldn't see the end of the passageway. However much I wanted to learn more—quite a bit, in spite of a warning rumble from my stomach—I didn't want to take a chance of being caught.

I turned around, slowly and quietly, and came back out. Bridget was waiting, so calm she seemed bored. "Well?" she whispered. "Find what you're looking for?"

"I think so," I said. I felt a bead of sweat move down my neck and past the collar of my shirt. "Come on, let's get out of here."

We made a quick search to ensure that the Optima employees would have no reason to suspect they'd had uninvited guests during the night. When Bridget and I parted in a parking lot a block away half an hour later, the night sky was beginning to grow lighter at the eastern horizon.

"I'll come by tomorrow to submit my bill," she said, tossing her things in the trunk of her car—a Lincoln Continental, an arms dealer's confiscated former prize possession. "I'll expect cash, of course."

"Of course," I said, shaking her hand.

When I got into the Mercedes, just before I closed the door I noticed an odd dust on the soles of my sneakers. It was strange, so I took them off and put them on the passenger seat next to me. I wanted to look at them, but even more I wanted to get home before a night patrolman asked me what I was doing.

Driving home in my socks, I thought that Alonso should know that he needed a new security system. If I had been lobotomized, I would have told him. Instead I made a mental note to tell Tommy, who was a master of slipping unattributed facts into a conversation.

I pulled into the garage of my apartment as dawn began to spread across the sky. When I got in the elevator, I finally had a better look at my shoes. They were canvas, and navy blue, and the fine gray powder was easy to distinguish.

THIRTY

————————————◆————————————

MY OFFICE FELL into afternoon shadows, and I lay on the sofa wondering what the hell to do next. Every time I followed a loose end, three more seemed to pop up. It was like trying to cut off a Hydra's head. I thought I was on one case, two if you counted my search for the truth about Margarita. Now it seemed I was on so many cases at once that I couldn't keep track of them all.

Not to mention my professional dilemma—I had intermingled the two cases, morally and financially. It was difficult, but I was trying to keep separate billing records; it was the only way I could continue and still feel ethical. The Arango case was twisting around like a snake, worse than any case I could remember. I decided to keep working, and to confront my ethics when I had all the answers.

That morning I had tried to justify the continued expenditure of keeping Marisol on the Primerissimo Rent-A-Car surveillance, and I couldn't. A few days had passed, and no one even remotely resembling an Arango brother had shown up at the agency.

There was a folder on my desk containing the reels of

pictures Marisol had taken. Next to it was the magnifying glass I used to pore over the photographs. Next to that was the bottle of aspirin for the headache this futile task gave me. After beeping her, I remembered that she had a date that night and probably wouldn't respond to a page. I left a message on her machine instead, ordering her off the surveillance. If anything, I thought she would be grateful. She craved action, and she wasn't seeing any waiting on a dusty airport road.

I was burning through Alonso senior's money at an alarming rate, without much to show for it but a bunch of questions about peripheral players. Somehow I knew the key was the women—Silvia and Isabel—but I wasn't sure how to approach them. If anything, I had let my investigation of Silvia hang for the moment. One possibility was that Alonso, Silvia's lover, killed Gustavo, the father of her child, out of jealousy. I was looking for the truth, but I was also working for Tommy. I had to try everything else before seeking out avenues that might prove his client's guilt.

I sat up, my head spinning a little. In the outer office I heard Leonardo's blender whirring away happily.

I wasn't going to solve anything by just sitting there. I opened up the case file and made two quick calls. If neither of the two younger Arango brothers was going to show up at Primerissimo, then I would go to them.

MARIANO'S NURSERY, BEST Plants on Southwest 144th Street, was very familiar to me—it was where I had followed and staked out Alonso junior less than two weeks before. It was on a long, narrow lot, a twisting labyrinth of canvas covers and two separate greenhouses.

Mariano had sounded pleased to hear from me when I called him. When I walked into the office, which doubled as a seed and implement shop, a young woman in coveralls, a bright smile, and a long ponytail greeted me.

"You must be Lupe," she said. She wiped her hands clean on a rag and offered one to me. A loop of her long black hair came out of its barrette when we shook. "Mariano told me you were coming. I'm Maria Miranda, Mariano's partner.''

"You have a nice place here," I said. They were having a special on daisies.

"Oh, thanks," Maria said, blushing with pleasure. She couldn't have been older than twenty-two or -three, and she acted even younger.

"Lupe Solano!" Mariano emerged from the back office; he dropped a file onto the front desk and came to me with a big smile. There were smiles everywhere in there. Mariano, though, like his mother, was capable of smiling only with his mouth. "Welcome to our little business," he said, a little patronizingly. "Did you have trouble finding us?"

"Not at all, thanks."

He ushered me into a big sunny office off the reception area, thanking Maria—for what, I didn't know. He seemed to be going out of his way to act generally agreeable. "Can I get you something to drink?" he asked. "Coffee, tea, maybe a sparkling water?"

The bottom part of his tattoo strained to peek out from the sleeve of his shirt, just as it did during our first meeting. I still couldn't tell what it depicted. "No thanks, I'm fine," I said.

Mariano motioned to a comfortable chair in front of a desk covered with papers and even a couple of bags of potting soil. "You'll have to excuse the mess," he said, sitting behind the desk. "Maria and I share this office. We're always arguing about who's the bigger slob."

"It's fine," I said. "I appreciate your meeting me on such short notice."

Mariano nodded, as though he agreed that he had done me quite a significant favor. "So how is your investigation going?" he asked. "It's been almost six weeks now that my father's been in the Stockade."

A low blow, but not entirely out of line. "I have a lot of leads," I said, truthfully. "You've heard about Reina Sotolongo, I'm sure."

"Yes. I hardly knew her, but it's very sad." His mouth

formed a grim taut line. "Do the police know who killed her?"

"It's being treated like a robbery, from what I've heard," I said. "I don't think the police have much to go on."

"Can I ask you a question?" Mariano asked, shifting forward and fixing his eyes on mine. "Why have you asked to talk to me today? I don't mean to be rude, but when we spoke last I told you everything I knew."

"I know that," I said, a bit more defensively than I would have liked. "But I've learned in this business that sometimes a person who thinks they've told everything they know is actually wrong."

Mariano shook his head dismissively. "I don't follow you."

"All right, let me tell you what I mean," I said, crossing my legs because his gaze had drifted to my thighs. For someone who acted so cooperative, Mariano was doing a good job of giving me a hard time.

"I talked to a lady a few years ago who was assaulted in her own apartment," I said. This got his attention. "She lived on the top floor of a three-story building. The masked assailant came up from behind her, raped her, knocked her unconscious, and locked her in a closet while he robbed the place. She eventually got free and called the police, and when they interviewed her, she said she was working on a report for work at her dining room table all night, and that she hadn't gotten up once. From what she said, no one could figure out how her attacker could have gotten into the place and surprised her without her hearing anything."

Mariano looked at me warily. "What happened?"

"She said she only got up once," I said. "At the beginning of the evening, to make herself a pot of tea. The detective saw the pot on the table, saw that it was empty, and also saw that it held five or six cups of tea. When he brought this up to the victim, she realized that she had gotten up once more to go to the bathroom. That's when the attacker came in through the window, and the sound of him coming in was drowned out by the flushing toilet. This narrowed down the time when the guy broke in. It turned out that

someone saw a man on the fire escape right around that
time. The rapist was someone who lived in the same building—and the police never would have caught him if they
hadn't been able to ask the right questions.''

"And they wouldn't have known what to ask if they
hadn't kept talking to this woman?'' Mariano offered.

"Exactly. It's true of everyone—sometimes we know
more than we give ourselves credit for.''

Mariano laughed softly. "That's a good story,'' he said.
His condescension was beginning to truly irk me. "But I'm
afraid I'm not like this woman. I wasn't at the store when
my father killed that rafter in self-defense. I don't know
anything about what happened.''

"So the first time you knew of, or saw Gustavo Gaston,''
I asked, "was after his death?''

"That's right,'' he said.

"And as far as you can say, did anyone else in your
family know him?''

Mariano narrowed his eyes. "Why do you ask me that?
Why should we know him?''

"No particular reason,'' I lied. "I'm just curious about
why this man would resort to robbery. He was an architect
in Cuba. He won prizes and awards before coming to the
States. He had no criminal record, not even traffic viola-
tions.'' I stared at Mariano. "Maybe you can help. Why
would a man like this rob a jewelry store with a knife?''

While I explored this line of speculation, Mariano started
rocking in his chair, tipping it back on two legs. He looked
bored. And he didn't seem to want to talk much more.

After waiting in vain for a response, I said, "So no one
in your family knew the dead man? How about the Optima
employees?''

"I can't see why.''

"Do you have any idea why Reina Sotolongo was
killed?'' I asked.

His eyes widened in innocence—but damn it, I couldn't
tell whether or not it was forced. "The police say it was a
robbery,'' he said. "I don't see why I should argue. She
was in the store alone, which shouldn't have happened, but

it obviously gave someone a chance to break in.''

''Does your father have any enemies?''

Mariano's chair rocking increased; he grabbed the edge of the desk to keep his balance. ''My father is well liked and respected by everyone,'' he said flatly.

He got up, walked around the desk, and perched on it. His face was close enough to mine that I could smell toothpaste. ''Look, I don't know what you're getting at,'' he said. ''This guy wanted to make an easy haul on a jewelry store, and he picked the wrong one. And that's the entire story.''

It was obvious I was hauling my load up a steep hill. Mariano still seemed cordial, but he flashed anger the longer we talked. I didn't know how much to read into that—I would be angry too if my father was thrown in jail.

Mariano leaned back, away from me. ''Have I helped you at all?'' he asked. ''I'm sorry this didn't turn out like the lady you told me about.''

He smiled insincerely, as though he wanted me to know he was mocking me now. He stood up; this was over, as far as he was concerned. We walked out together through the front room, where Maria was selling a batch of seeds to a pinched older woman.

Mariano stayed in the doorway as I walked out to the parking lot. ''If you need anything else, please don't hesitate to call,'' he said in an entirely unconvincing manner. With a wave of his hand, he went inside. I realized as I unlocked the Mercedes that I had failed to get a better look at his tattoo.

I called Ernesto from the car phone as soon as I pulled out onto the street—Leonardo had left me a memo that morning asking me to cut back on expensive cellular calls, which I balled up and tossed in the trash. Ernesto sounded harried, and irritated by my second call of the day. But he agreed to meet with me.

I drove fast on U.S. 1, filled with a strange feeling from my conversation with Mariano. The first time we met, he seemed to come on to me. I suspected his older brothers had told him it wouldn't be constructive to play footsie with the woman charged with getting their father out of a murder charge. Now he was polite, but seemed to regard me as an irritant. This could have meant anything; maybe he was the Arango on the Primerissimo computer screen, or maybe he was just a misogynist who didn't care to be particularly friendly to women he wasn't trying to get into bed.

Ernesto had given me directions to the parking garage beneath his downtown office building, and left my name with the guard in the lobby. Within minutes he stepped out of the elevator, greeting me with a mild nod. He was dressed in the same three-piece suit he wore when I first met him— or one so similar I couldn't see why he had bothered to change.

He didn't offer to shake my hand. "Instead of talking in my office, I thought we could grab a quick lunch at a coffee shop across the street." He didn't wait for an answer; he put a hand behind my back and propelled me out of the building.

Without speaking a word, Ernesto led me into the street. We jaywalked across four lanes of deadly traffic, sprinting across the final lane and barely avoiding an oncoming van. I hoped this coffee shop was worth risking my life.

Ernesto chose an oversized window booth. I slid into it, across a seat covering that stuck to the backs of my bare legs. I pushed and pulled myself against several feet of pink plastic, hoping no one would misinterpret the sucking sounds coming from my bottom. By the time I regained my dignity Ernesto had shoved his face into a laminated menu.

Having a look around, I had to conclude that the place wasn't worth losing my life over. It was the place that time forgot—down to the pinup calendar on the wall, opened to July 1984. The lunch counter had twelve stools, but two lacked seats. The whole place seemed to have been dipped in pink vinyl and plastic—which kept it looking new, in a way, though the most recent remodeling had probably taken place about a decade before they last changed the calendar.

The half-dozen other diners had a distinctly homeless look; most sat nursing coffee, surrounded by plastic bags and metal carts. Somehow I couldn't see Ernesto as a regular there—which was probably the point. He had probably brought me to this dive to ensure that he wouldn't be seen with me by anyone he knew. The question was why this might be important to him.

I found myself engrossed by my paper place mat, which featured a child's-drawing-quality map of Cuba. "Order anything you want, it's on me," Ernesto said. "Everything is good here."

He signaled for the waitress, and I tried to decipher the dog-eared menu. Five minutes later, Ernesto was still waving. I looked over my shoulder; the elderly waitress sitting alone with a cigarette at the far end of the place showed no signs of noticing us.

Finally she looked up. *"Sí, sí,"* she said in a tremulous voice. She rose with a groan and slowly worked her way over to us. The closer she got, the older she looked. With great difficulty she extracted an order pad from the hidden depths of her pink uniform. When no pencil appeared I decided to speed things along, and offered her one of my own.

"I'll have a tuna fish sandwich, and an iced tea," I said. It seemed a safe enough choice, as long as they refrigerated the mayo.

"Make that two," Ernesto said. I saw with alarm that our waitress wrote only the number "2" on her pad, and nothing more. She shuffled back to the kitchen, talking softly to herself and taking my pencil with her.

"So, what can I help you with?" Ernesto said. I felt as though I had slipped into another dimension, because the coffee shop and the quality of service didn't seem to faze him. It seemed strange for a conservative banker to risk his stomach eating in a place like this.

"I've spoken with your brothers individually about your father's case," I said. I smiled and looked into his eyes, as though I could tell from his reaction whether he had rented the car at Primerissimo. I couldn't.

"I'd like to help you, but I really can't," Ernesto replied. "I only know what I told you before. I'd do anything to help my father, but there's nothing else for me to say."

Iced teas had arrived at our table, and Ernesto sipped his. I debated telling Ernesto the story I'd shared with Mariano earlier, but decided not to. I didn't want them comparing notes and making fun of me. Besides, it didn't seem to impress the younger Arango, though it had worked in the past.

"You didn't know the dead man in any way?" I asked.

Ernesto shook extra sugar into his tea. "The first time I saw him was at the store," he said. "When he was lying dead on the ground."

"Can you imagine why someone would try to rob your father at knifepoint, on a Saturday morning, with the place full of employees?"

Ernesto shook his head slowly. His white shirt was so clean it reflected the sunlight that shone through the window. "No, I can't," he said. "It was a stupid thing to do. And this Gaston paid with his life."

"Do you know if anyone in your family knew Gustavo Gaston?"

"No, why would they?" Ernesto seemed mildly offended. "He was just a *balsero* who did odd jobs. He was not the kind of person we would know."

"Well, that's not such a given," I said politely. "Gaston was an accomplished architect in Cuba. He won several prestigious prizes."

Ernesto laughed harshly. "That means nothing to me. Communist prizes!" He lowered his voice, but his sudden bitterness still shocked me. "Those prizes mean nothing in a free country. Everyone knows they're given out for political reasons that have nothing to do with talent. The best party member wins."

Mercifully, the waitress shuffled over to our table and broke up our conversation. She held a tray with one hand, barely, and the two white plates atop it knocked against each other. Ernesto and I both reached out and grabbed a plate, before they ended up on the floor. When I lowered the plate to the table, I was absolutely shocked.

"I consider myself a connoisseur of sandwiches," Ernesto announced imperiously. "But the sandwiches here are among the best."

I could go him one better—I considered myself a connoisseur of tuna fish sandwiches. And the one before me was undoubtedly the most appetizingly presented, aromatic, and enticing I had ever seen. Chunks of white, fragrant tuna spilled over perfectly toasted wheat bread. Under this was a bed of Bibb lettuce fanned out like exquisite seashells. A small mound of grated carrot perched on a leaf of purple cabbage. I admonished myself for judging the place by its appearance—then decided to let myself off the hook. Who could have known?

It tasted as good as it looked. If I took nothing else away from my second meeting with Ernesto, I had found the tuna sandwich of my dreams. Ernesto apparently agreed, because he dug into his sandwich as though he had been digging ditches all day instead of crunching numbers.

Our plates were empty within minutes. As we finished—at the same time—we exchanged looks of mutual ecstasy. We sat back, contented. For once, I didn't mind having tuna breath. I finished off my iced tea, thinking the ice was broken for good between us. I was wrong.

Ernesto wiped his mouth with his napkin. "Is there anything else I can help you with?" he said. "I must say, I don't think it was necessary for us to meet face-to-face. I don't presume to tell you how to do your job, but you probably should be following other leads rather than interviewing my family over and over again."

He gave me a thin-lipped smile, which didn't do much for his looks. There wasn't a lot I could say, because he was basically right. Unless he was the brother who had rented the cars.

Without waiting for the check, Ernesto dropped a twenty on the table. He stood up and glared at me. With as much dignity as I could muster, I also stood. I was glad I didn't make too many gross sounds on the plastic seat cover.

"Thanks for lunch. That was easily the best tuna sandwich I ever had," I said truthfully.

"You're welcome," Ernesto said, now a bit more friendly, but not much. We repeated our daredevil run across the street, and he left me standing in front of his building.

Before he disappeared inside, he turned and called out to me. "You should try their ham and cheese." Ernesto put his fingers to his mouth and kissed them loudly. "Perfection!"

Who was I to criticize the small passions of a banker? It was a damned good sandwich.

I found my car in the underground lot and warmed it up, letting the air-conditioning stream into my face. I had met with the two younger Arango brothers, stared into their eyes, and come away with nothing. So much for my legendary intuition. I couldn't tell who was lying.

THIRTY-ONE

I DROVE SLOWLY around the Coral Gables City Hall, looking for a parking space. Nothing, damn it. I made an illegal U-turn and started back, hoping that by some miracle a spot might have opened up in the minute since I last passed by. I knew this wasn't very smart of me: the streets there were usually crawling with cops during the day. But I couldn't face the failure of parking in the municipal lot and walking back a block. No one walks in Miami—unless their car's been stolen, or else they're tourists and simply don't know better.

Ignoring the sound of tires squealing behind me, I crossed over four lanes of traffic when I spied a portly guy with an armful of envelopes getting into an official city car. Bingo. I stationed the Mercedes inches from his rear bumper, to prevent anyone from poaching the spot. I felt a twinge of compassion for the bureaucrat as I watched him struggle back and forth, trying to get out without hitting me. As soon as he was gone, I zipped in, checked my makeup in the rearview mirror—I never knew who I might run into at City Hall—and stepped out of the car.

I put coins into the meter. The Coral Gables City Hall was on Biltmore Way on the southern end of Miracle Mile, where four streets intersect. I could see the facade of Optima Jewelers in the distance, two blocks away.

City Hall itself was majestic, even though it was only three stories high. It was made of coral rock, in Spanish colonial style, with high ceilings, arches, and courtyards that evoked an elegant and less frantic era. I used to go there with Papi as a young girl, when he would pull contractors' permits.

Instead of taking the elevator, I walked up the wide stone staircase. On the second-floor landing was a mural by Denman Fink, depicting an underwater scene in blue and green, with languid tropical fish and seaweed. It was soothing, especially to me; when I was a little girl I would imagine myself swimming in the deep with fish friends.

I also saw the array of photographs depicting all the mayors of Coral Gables—starting in 1925 and ending in 1993. Maybe I'm too sensitive, but I couldn't help flinching when I saw again that of the twenty-one mayors there, all were white and only one was a woman. Given the city's diversity, I thought we might do better than that. There was now a Cuban mayor, and none too soon, but his picture hadn't made the main wall yet. It was on the side, not immediately apparent. I hoped it was simply an oversight, and not a sign of something more sinister. That's the problem with working as a private investigator—I'm always looking for hidden motives behind innocent situations.

I sprinted up the last flight of stairs to the third floor and the Department of Building and Planning. I stopped on this landing too, to check out another mural. This scene depicted an idealized Coral Gables, by a John St. John. It evoked images of a place called "The City Beautiful," and the "Miami Riviera." I suppose no one asked Gustavo Gaston or Reina Sotolongo for their contributions.

Inside the office I presented my power of attorney from Alonso Arango, and requested copies of the building plan for Optima Jewelers. My authorization gave me legal right to request the documents, but the clerk pored over every micrometer of the paper as though looking for a reason not to turn over the plans.

It took half an hour for them to find the plans and make copies, time I spent looking out the window at the steady stream of business on Miracle Mile. When I saw I had the right plans, I paid the fee and took the stairs down again.

Curiosity overcame me. Instead of waiting until I was back at the office, I unrolled the papers as I was walking to my car. I thanked the Fates again that Papi was a contractor, and that he had taught my sisters and me to read building plans when we were girls. I suspected he would have considered our education incomplete unless we knew how to build a house from scratch—which any of us could.

I leaned against my car's closed door, completely engrossed in the plans. When I switched off the car alarm I put the plans on the roof with my free hand.

This was when I saw the set of keys on the roof. I felt my knees shaking. It was the same set I had left with the kid at Primerissimo.

I tried hard not to hyperventilate. I searched in my purse for my own keys, my hands betraying me by shaking. Someone was following me, I thought—all right. I knew that already. But now they wanted me to know it.

Whoever put the keys there was probably watching me, I knew. I snatched them off the roof, opened the door, hopped in, and gunned the engine. It seemed like seconds before I was back at Coconut Grove and walking quickly into my office.

"What's up, Lupe?" Leonardo asked as I walked past him into my office. I waved him away. The last thing I wanted was to explain to anyone, even my cousin, what had just happened. I hadn't composed myself enough yet. With my purse still on my shoulder and the keys in my hand, I placed a "911" page to Marisol. I just stood there, tapping my toe on the floor while I waited for her to respond. She called back within a minute.

"Lupe, what's the matter?" Marisol sounded worried; a "911" page could do that to a person. "Are you all right?"

"I'm fine for now," I said. "Listen, the surveillance at Primerissimo—you're still on that, right?"

"No, I'm off that one, as of yesterday," she said, sounding irritated. "You left a message on my machine, remember? I just started another case this morning, a domestic."

"Damn." In my panic, I forgot that I'd taken Marisol off the case. Naturally—the one time I was cost-effective, I screwed myself.

"Lupe, you told me to quit," Marisol said, more annoyed now. "Your message was very clear, and that's why I took this other job. I need to make a living, remember?"

"I wasn't swearing at you," I explained. "I'm just mad at myself." The last thing I wanted was to make Marisol peeved at me; at times she could be extraordinarily thin-skinned.

"So what's the matter?" she asked, more kindly. "Why did you page me?"

I told Marisol about the keys on my car roof. There was a long silence on the other end of the line.

"*Mierda*, no wonder you're upset," she finally said. "And to think—I spent three days in that car watching the place, sweating like a pig, with my bladder about to burst. And the guy never showed up."

"I know," I said. "He must have picked up the keys just after I called you off the job."

"Listen, Lupe," Marisol said. "This is a terrible thought, but do you think he burned me? Maybe he saw me, and waited until I didn't show up to pick up the keys."

It wasn't as though the thought hadn't occurred to me. "I don't know, Marisol," I whispered. "I don't know what to think anymore."

I knew that if Marisol had been spotted, it was because her prey had been very, very smart. Marisol was the best. I could feel a nasty headache coming on, starting at my temples.

"How could he have spotted me?" Marisol blurted. "I swear to you—there's no way that guy could have burned me!"

"Marisol, I'm not questioning your work," I said wearily. "You have to believe that. It could all be a coincidence."

"No, I don't believe that." Marisol was capable of contradicting herself in a single breath. "I think he burned me."

At this point, I thought so too. But I wasn't about to let one of my top investigators get paranoid on me. I'd seen it before—an investigator loses confidence in their work, and they're never the same.

"What about the last batch of photos?" I asked, just to change the subject. "Do you have them ready?"

"*Sí*, I'll come by within the hour. I'm about done with my domestic, anyway. It's a bitch: Coral Gables."

Marisol hung up; no further explanation was necessary. Coral Gables was the most frustrating place in Miami to conduct a surveillance, as I knew from experience. There was little concealment, noisy neighbors, guard dogs, big mosquitoes from the canals, and trees on residential property to obscure the investigator's view.

After hanging up with Marisol I walked out to the reception area. Leonardo was waiting there with a plastic cup containing a strange yellow substance.

"Here," he said. "I thought you might need this. It's a mango vitamin mixture—protein, carbos, even jelly for your nails."

"Ay, Leonardo," I whined, taking the cup. "The shit has hit the fan on this one." I told him about the latest developments on the Primerissimo fiasco.

Leonardo listened patiently, though he indulged in a few neck rolls while I was talking. "What are you going to do?" he asked when I was done. "The client's going to be pissed as hell if you show him a big bill, with no results."

It hurt to have him point out my recent futility, but it was nice to hear him thinking about our finances. "I don't know," I said. "We might have to swallow it."

I took a big mouthful of mango shake, shuddering at the thickness of the weird liquid. But it didn't taste bad. I imagined I could feel my nails growing stronger.

"Don't tell me that." Leonardo shook his head sadly, his

expression that of a kid who has just been told that Santa Claus is a Madison Avenue invention.

I was instantly suspicious. "What's the matter?" I asked. In the past we had swallowed our mistakes without too much pain. This was why Solano Investigations had such a good reputation—we didn't charge the client when we screwed up.

"There's a new piece of equipment I wanted to buy," he said. "I read about it in a magazine. It works the ass really good. I, um . . . I was budgeting part of the Arango fee to buy it."

Leonardo walked over to the mirror and pirouetted around, examining his rear end from all angles. He had a great ass, I had to admit, especially in black spandex. I never would admit it, though—he was my cousin, after all.

"Leonardo, cut that out," I barked. "You can work your ass on the equipment you have. Anyway, be realistic. We're Cuban. We all have big asses. It's our birthright. It's stamped on our passports. It's one of the few things Castro couldn't take away from us."

The mango shake wasn't working its magic; my headache was growing worse. I didn't want to talk about asses anymore. I went back to my office and closed the door behind me.

I had been so shocked to find the key ring that I hadn't closely examined the plans from City Hall. When I sat down and had a closer look, it was just as I thought. The hidden passageway in the cleaning closet ran all along the block, behind all the stores in the long building where Optima was located. There were three old doors, now in disuse, which provided access to the passageway from the alley.

There were notes on the plans. Apparently, when the building was constructed in 1927, the contractor needed the passageway for access to the false ceiling he installed to hide all the necessary electrical wiring. Ventilation had been a problem then, and there were all sorts of notations on the plans detailing the installation of ceiling fans. It was only with the addition of central air-conditioning decades later that the passage was enlarged to conform to the new code, which demanded that access to the ceiling be high and wide enough for a worker to fit through without too much difficulty. From extra notes made by some nameless bureaucrat dozens of years ago, I saw that closing off the passage was a code requirement when the building was remodeled.

As far as I was concerned, I finally had an answer as to how Reina's murderer could have gained access to Optima without being seen, and with no sign of entry. He or she could have entered through one of the closed-off doors in the alley, then come in through the cleaning closet. I would have bet money that if I examined one of the old doors in the alley, I would find one had been opened recently.

At least now I had a solid piece of information to work with, and to take to Tommy. Hopefully, this would be the start of a trend.

By the time I finished writing preliminary notes, Leonardo's voice came on the intercom. True to her word, Marisol had arrived within the hour. Still aglow with what I found, I was in a marginally better mood when I received her.

"Here are the last pictures," she said, and handed me an envelope from Eckerd's. She looked terrible, her face blotchy and her eyes ringed in raccoon black. She was starting to look like Nestor.

"Hi yourself," I said. I quickly flipped through the pictures. For the past three days I had become an expert on Primerissimo Rent-A-Car's clientele. They never had more than a dozen customers in a day—which led me to believe car rental wasn't their primary line of profit. They must have been a front for something, and if I had time and the resources I might have looked into it. But I had neither.

"Nothing," I said to Marisol. "No Arangos here."

"Mostly tourists." Marisol stifled a yawn. I had never seen her this wiped out before. "You know, it's a miracle they still come to Miami—considering it's open season on them."

She flopped down on my sofa, in a classic Nestor pose, with one arm over her eyes. "What now, Lupe?" she half groaned.

Good question—I was wondering about that one myself. I had a suspected murderer out there following me around.

"I'll let you know," I said. "Get some rest, will you? You look like you could use it."

I stood up and walked around my desk to escort her out. She looked so bedraggled that I suddenly felt overwhelmingly concerned for her. On impulse, I hugged her.

She stared at me in astonishment. "Lupe, are you all right?" she asked. "I think Leonardo is getting to you. You've never been touchy-feely before."

No, I hadn't. Maybe fear had made me soft. "I'm fine," I said, backing away. "Listen, I'll call you."

"That's what all the boys say!" she shouted as she walked out. Now *that* was more like the old Marisol.

She left the door cracked, and I could hear her and Leonardo talking in the reception room. I hoped she wouldn't tell him that I'd hugged her. I wasn't in the mood to have Leonardo barge in and congratulate me for finally getting in touch with my feelings.

I sat back down and had three aspirins, washed down with the lukewarm mango shake. Marisol had asked a good question: What now?

THIRTY-TWO

I WANTED TO talk things over with Tommy, but I also needed to work out my problems on my own. I felt my independence was at stake, as well as my professional integrity. The keys, the Arango name on the Primerissimo computer monitor—neither of these had a specific connection to Alonso senior, Tommy's client.

His secretary put me through to his office. "Tommy?" I asked. "Do you have any time to talk today?"

"I always have time for you," he smooth-talked. "But not during working hours today. How about over dinner?"

"Maybe," I said. "But it would be strictly business."

"I'll book a table at Christy's." Tommy chuckled.

"Absolutely not." I felt my face go as red as filet mignon. "We'll go somewhere else—maybe for fish."

"You can order fish at Christy's," he said. "Or chicken. Whatever you want. Do you want me to pick you up, or should we meet there?"

"I'm not sure," I said. "Let me call you. I want to see how a few things pan out."

A moment's silence. Then: "Lupe, is there something

you need to tell me? Is it the Arango case?"

"Not specifically," I said weakly.

"What's going on?" Tommy asked. "Is someone bothering you? Has someone been following you around again?"

"I'll tell you later."

"All right," he sighed. Tommy knew better than to dig at me for information. Nothing would make me shut down quicker. "Call me when you've decided. Don't wait too long. And cheer up—you sound really down."

Of course I was down. Who wouldn't be? I felt this case closing in on me—figuratively and literally. I had begun to take it all personally, I knew, which broke my cardinal rule.

I looked at the digital clock on my desk and saw that it was almost three o'clock. With any luck Leonora would be at MMV Interiors, if the company still existed. I dialed the number and let the phone ring at least twenty times before hanging up. Well, at least it wasn't disconnected.

I buzzed Leonardo. "Do me a favor," I said. "In our office phone directory I wrote down Margarita's assistant's home number. At least I think I did. Her name is Leonora. Could you look it up?"

A few minutes later Leonardo poked his head into my office and handed me a piece of paper. "Here it is," he said. "I found it."

I thanked him, took the paper, picked up the phone, and noticed that Leonardo hadn't left yet. Even worse, he had his serious, earnest expression—the one that meant things weren't going to turn out well for me.

He sat down in the client's chair. "Lupe, we have to talk about something that's troubling me. I don't want to bring you down, or put you in a bad emotional space, but—"

"Spit it out, Leonardo," I said. He looked hurt, so I added, "Come on. You know you can talk to me about anything." How bad could it be? I thought. An investment in harmonic-crystal mining? Starting an alternative religion under our occupational license?

Leonardo looked relieved; he adjusted his heart monitor. "You know, Lupe, the Arango case is the only one you've worked for the past few weeks. I know you've had me refer some other work to other PIs, but the Arango case is currently our only billable case."

I *really* didn't like the sound of this. "What are you trying to say?"

"We're losing money." Leonardo folded his hands on his lap and talked slowly, like a little boy in the principal's office. "We need something else to keep us going. As of today, I'm going to have to pay next month's bills out of our emergency account."

I suddenly felt cold; this was worse than I thought. "What about receivables?" I asked. "Don't we have a lot of cases I've already finished that we haven't been paid for?"

I started chewing on a pencil. I didn't want to start on my nails. If what Leonardo was telling me was correct, I might have to forgo manicures and pedicures for the foreseeable future. I shuddered at the thought. It was far too horrible to contemplate.

"That's the problem," Leonardo said. "We sent out bills just thirty days ago, and not too many checks have come back."

Leonardo sank miserably into the chair, as though our world was coming to an end. As a matter of fact, we were closer to ruin than I ever thought we'd be. Though Papi had given me money to start the agency, I had long since paid back every dime, and I had never asked for more—I couldn't ask for more, it was a point of honor. Poor Leonardo looked as though his heart was broken. I simply couldn't be cruel enough to ask him how we had paid for the more recent additions to his office gym.

"Do you want to look at the numbers?" he asked sheepishly.

"No, I believe you. It's just weird—this has never happened to us before."

Leonardo squirmed some more; it was too painful to watch him.

"Why don't we hire a collection agency to make sure we get paid?" I asked.

"I already called two of them," Leonardo said. "They told me we'd have to wait until the bills are more than thirty days due before bringing them in. Besides, a lot of these people are repeat business, and we don't want to piss them off by sending a bill collector after them."

"You're right," I admitted. This was a disaster, but it was nice to see Leonardo developing a little business savvy.

"I just wanted you to know," Leonardo moaned, as though this conversation had drained his reservoir of will. "The money is my department, I know, but I have a responsibility to let you know what's going on out there."

"Leonardo, come on," I said. "We're going to be fine. Don't torture yourself like this. Please." *Mierda.*

He seemed not to hear me, talking on in the same broken, wrenching voice. "I wasn't going to say anything, at least not yet," he said. "But I had no choice after you said we had to swallow that three-day surveillance by Marisol at that car rental company."

"I know, I know." I shook my head. "That was my mistake."

"Well, there's the number for Leonora." Standing up, Leonardo put his hands on mine. "I know you're still upset about Margarita, even if you don't talk about it anymore. I know how much you loved her, and how much you miss her. I hope you know that if you ever want to talk about it to me, you can."

My cousin Leonardo. With the body of a male stripper and a heart as good as they come. I squeezed his hand. "Thanks," I said. "I appreciate it. I really do."

Leonardo got up to leave. I looked down at the piece of paper, on which was written a number and the name: Leonora Muñoz. Strange. I had known her for years, and had never known her last name.

Leonardo was about to close my office door. He looked relieved to have unburdened himself; I wished my conscience worked like that. "Hey," I called out to him, "if things get really bad, I can always hire myself out to one of the escort services around here. You too!"

"Lupe, don't even joke that way," Leonardo said crossly.

"I was only kidding. Don't take it all so seriously. This case will be over soon, and then we'll go back to being a moneymaking machine. You'll see."

But by then I was alone in the office. My reassurances sounded forced and hollow even to my own ears. I was glad I hadn't picked on Leonardo about his workout equipment; hell, I considered that part of our office expenses, along with the staples and legal pads. The real problem was that I had let my obsession with my friend's death take over. I was working two cases at once, with Margarita's expenses coming out of my pocket, solving neither, and bringing in zero money. It was a perfect recipe for running an investigative agency right into bankruptcy.

Leonora answered on the sixth ring. She didn't sound too awake—in fact, she had trouble placing who I was. Her words were slurred, and I was pretty sure she was drinking.

"Leonora, this is Lupe. Margarita's friend," I repeated. I spoke slowly, enunciating every word.

"I know!" she said, her voice coming alive with recognition. "How are you doing?"

"Fine. Listen, can I come see you sometime soon? I'd like to speak to you about Margarita."

"Oh, Margarita." Leonora's voice shifted to a sad murmur. "Sure, that would be nice. How about right now?"

I didn't exactly relish having a serious talk with someone who had been drowning a run of bad luck in alcohol, but this was the best response I'd had to an interview request in weeks. In my business, people tend to change their mind about talking to you rather quickly.

"Great," I said. "I'll be over there in a little while."

"Don't you want to know where I live?" she asked.

Well, maybe she wasn't as far gone as I feared. I didn't tell her that I already knew where she lived, because I didn't want her to think I had checked up on her, though I had looked up her address in the Bresser's directory, which cross-references phone numbers and addresses.

"Of course," I said. "Please give it to me." The address

Leonora gave me was the same one I found in Bresser's— on Thirty-seventh Avenue and Fourteenth Street in Little Havana.

I drove over there right away, fighting the growing rush hour and unsure even what I expected from talking to Margarita's assistant. It was a feeling to which I was growing accustomed.

Leonora's place was easy to find. She lived in a modest, nondescript one-story beige stucco house. She was leaning on the front porch railing, waiting for me, when I pulled up.

While I parked the Mercedes I kept one eye on her, trying to gauge her level of sobriety. She at least was keeping her balance, and the look on her face was reasonable, if a little depressed. I got out and walked up the paved drive leading to her house. Leonora watched me without saying a word.

"Hola!" I cried out.

When I drew nearer, I was shocked by her appearance. Leonora looked stooped and tired, and seemed as though she had aged years in the brief time since I last saw her. I knew she had to be in her late forties, at least, but she had always looked and acted much younger. Whatever had kept her going had obviously left her.

She was dressed in a shapeless faded pink housedress, her feet in pink plastic flip-flops decorated with yellow daisies. I realized this was the first time since I had known her that I ever saw her in casual clothes. Her office attire was always meticulously neat—sharp dresses, stockings, high heels. However I imagined her dressing in her off hours, it wasn't like this.

"Come in, Lupe. It's nice to see you." She opened her front door and motioned for me to enter. "I don't have too many visitors, you know."

I could believe it. The place was dark and dank, with a stagnant air of decay and lack of use. It was a place of cobwebs in the corners and dust balls around the furniture. The feeling of abandonment must have predated Margarita's death, which made the place seem even more melancholy. Truthfully, I didn't know Leonora well at all—I saw her at MMV, and I knew what Margarita told me about her. But

I would have imagined Leonora to be the kind of person who would take pride in her home. I suddenly felt privy to a sad, shameful secret.

The bulk of the house seemed to be taken up with a main, large room—which, I could see, served as a living room, a dining room, and a home office. The cream-colored plastic shades were drawn all the way down, blocking out the late-afternoon light; still, some light shone through, casting the place in dim sepia tones.

I was surprised that dust didn't rise from the dark red velveteen sofa when I sat down. Leonora settled heavily in a straight-backed cane chair across from me. She didn't seem inclined to light any of the lamps placed haphazardly about the room. I didn't much care to conduct this interview in a ghostly penumbra.

"Would you like anything to drink?" Leonora asked, and started to get up. When she leaned over, I got a strong scent of liquor mixed with mouthwash. My heart sank. It was one thing to be an afternoon drinker; it was something more pathetic to feel the need to hide it.

"No, no, that's all right," I said. Leonora seemed vaguely disappointed. "How have you been?" I asked. "I haven't spoken to you since I visited MMV Interiors."

This was a gentle push, but apparently it was enough: Leonora's composure completely gave way. She began sobbing, with deep gasps and messy exhalations. Ashamed, she wouldn't look at me. Now the smell of booze and mouthwash permeated the air.

When the storm had passed for the moment, I spoke. "Leonora, I want to be honest with you. Margarita wanted to tell me something important just before she died. She never got to say it."

"Something important? Like what?" Leonora pulled her chair nearer to me. I thought I might suffocate from her warm breath so close to me.

"I'm not sure," I said. "But it had to do with the Arango family."

"The Arango family?" I could almost see the wheels

turning. "Her clients in Coral Gables? The jewelry store owners?"

"That's who I mean," I said gently. "Do you have any idea what she might have wanted to say to me?"

Leonora sat back in her chair. Her eyes narrowed, and she clasped her hands before her. I wasn't about to hurry her. As far as I was concerned, I had all the time in the world.

Finally, she opened her mouth to speak. I leaned over expectantly, but then she closed it again. Leonora and her house made me feel as though time had lost its meaning. I might sit there forever, the shades drawn, breathing gin and Scope. In a strange way it was almost comforting.

Leonora glanced at me, then focused her gaze on a mess of laundry in the corner. In a quiet voice, she said, "I have her papers, you know, Lupe. Would that help you?"

"Margarita's files?" I asked, stupidly.

"She began giving me her personal papers for safekeeping years ago." Leonora talked faster, and with more clarity. I could literally see her shoulders rise as she unburdened herself. "She suspected that Rodrigo might come snooping around one day."

I had trouble believing what I was hearing. Maybe, I thought, I was getting drunk on secondhand gin. "Where are these files?"

Leonora pointed over my shoulder, to a closed door. "In there," she said with a slight smile. "In her room."

"Her room?"

Leonora nodded soberly. "Yes, her room. The room I keep ready, in case she ever needs a place to live."

"Ah, of course," I stammered. "Margarita's room. Well, can I see it?" I stood up, not giving her a chance to change her mind about the files.

I walked around the sofa to the closed door; Leonora seemed to understand that I was going in there, no matter what she said, so she had no choice but to follow. I put my hand on the doorknob, my heart skidding. It was becoming very clear that Leonora wasn't well. At all.

"Excuse me." With alarming speed, she nudged me

aside and positioned herself between me and the door. "I loved her, you know," she said. "I really, really loved her. She was the daughter I never had."

With that, Leonora pushed open the door. I tried not to gasp, or do anything that might make Leonora edgy. The little room was a shrine to my dead friend. I saw a photograph of Margarita—one I knew well, because I had a framed five-by-seven copy of it on my dresser. But this one was blown up to near poster size, and was in the absolute middle of the back wall. In front of it was a table, complete with lit votive candles.

There was a little display on the table of personal items that had belonged to Margarita: a silver brush-and-comb set I remembered seeing in her parents' house, a portfolio of her work, a picture of her in her first Communion dress. In the corner I saw three cardboard boxes. Those had to be the files.

The room was impeccable: bright, clean, and well lit. I was speechless. I knew Leonora was fond of Margarita to the point of doting, but this was . . . obsessive. I tried to clear everything out of my mind, especially the implications of what lay before me, concentrating entirely on the boxes.

"Are these the files you kept for Margarita?" I asked, in as normal a tone as I could manage.

Leonora brushed past me; I almost jumped. "I've never even looked in them," she said. She seemed proud. "I've had them for years, and I never violated her privacy."

"You were a very dear friend to her, Leonora," I said. "She often spoke of you to me."

This seemed to please her. "I'm sure she wouldn't mind if I let you look through them," she said. "You were her close friend. I was only protecting them from Rodrigo."

Leonora bent over one of the boxes and picked it up. I stood there, frozen like a statue. "Do you want to look through them here," she asked calmly, "or do you want to take them with you?"

I couldn't believe it. She was actually willing to let the files out of her sight. It was then that I understood I had nothing to fear from Leonora. She might have been a little cracked, but we were on the same side—we both wanted what was best for Margarita, which now meant taking care of her affairs the way she would have wished us to.

"I think it's better if I take them back with me," I said. "I would hate to impose on you by staying here to look through them."

Leonora nodded sadly, as though she knew that was what I would say. I didn't want to give her a chance to change her mind, so I quickly picked up one of the bigger boxes and walked out to my car. When I came back for the second box, Leonora was on the sofa. She made no move to help me. I felt as though I was taking something important from her, a treasured part of Margarita.

When I had all three boxes in my trunk, I walked back to the house and met Leonora on the porch. On impulse, I hugged her. Twice in one day had to be some kind of record for me. I turned away when I saw her eyes glisten with tears. It wasn't comforting to imagine what she might do in that mausoleum after I was gone.

"Call me if you need anything," I said. Leonora looked away, but she squeezed my shoulder, hard. "It'll get better, Leonora, a little every day. Don't forget that."

When I pulled away from the curb and made a U-turn to head back to the Grove, I kept an eye on the rearview mirror. I knew these files could well be dynamite in my possession, and that I might be in danger as long as I had them. Even if the boxes gave me nothing on the Arango family, there had to be important information in there for Margarita to want to hide them. Her faith in Leonora wasn't misplaced. I suspected Leonora would have died rather than let the files fall into the wrong hands.

On the drive back to my office I took deep breaths and tried to shake the feeling of weirdness that had come over me. The boxes had been standing in the room, the only things that seemed out of place there. I suspected that Leonora had pulled them out of her closet or attic when I called, knowing the time had come to turn them over.

I didn't bother taking a roundabout path to my office. If anyone was following me, they would easily be able to guess where I was headed. When I pulled into my spot, though, I was crestfallen to see that Leonardo had left for the day.

"Of course," I muttered to myself as I hauled in the first box. "It's his yoga day. How could I forget?"

Then I recalled that he had another meeting after yoga—with a new society formed with the goal of toppling Castro from power using nonviolent means. By meditating him away, or some such nonsense. When I had all the boxes in, I did something unusual: I turned on the office alarm. I was usually leery of messing with it, because I was terrified of setting it off and having my brains explode with the piercing noise.

I didn't want anyone to look in the front door and see me with the boxes, so I took them into the spare room and lined them up behind Leonardo's free-weight rack. For once I was happy there was so much equipment in there—it provided a good temporary hiding place.

I sat on the Soloflex and looked at the boxes. I wished they would just spill their secrets voluntarily, and that I wouldn't have to rummage through Margarita's life like an intruder. Then I suddenly remembered my promise to get back to Tommy about dinner at Christy's. It was after six-thirty, and in Leonardo's floor-to-ceiling mirror I saw myself: I looked tired and stressed out, I wasn't wearing any makeup, and I was in the same short khaki skirt and tight black T-shirt I had worn all day.

That clinched it. I couldn't imagine sitting in Christy's anyway, trying to concentrate on my food while knowing that the boxes waited in my office. I called Tommy and told him something had come up, and I hung up before he could pry any answers out of me.

In the kitchen I found only health food drinks and bean sprouts, and was about to resign myself to going hungry when I found a bottle of champagne hidden in the refrigerator's crisper drawer. I grabbed a tulip glass and headed back to the weights room.

There I drank a toast to Margarita, asking her to forgive me for what I was about to do.

THIRTY-THREE

BY THE TIME I found what I was looking for, it was almost midnight. An empty champagne bottle and a pot of what had been strong Cuban coffee sat empty on one of Leonardo's torture machines, and the office was enveloped in silence.

The boxes' contents were a revelation. When I first opened them I was hesitant, trying to shake off the uneasy feeling that looking through Margarita's things gave me. I kept repeating to myself that I had no choice. As time passed, I worked more quickly, and my interest grew more intense.

I had always known that Margarita was a hopeless romantic, but I never imagined that she had kept every love letter, card, and note sent to her from her every lover and suitor. Going through her carefully stored mementos, I was surprised at some of the names that appeared. Of course we moved through the same social circles, and I had dated some of the same guys, but I never knew the true scope of her appeal. The more I delved into her keepsakes, the more I wondered why, with all these lovers and admirers, she chose

Rodrigo. Several of the letters alluded to marriage proposals that she hadn't accepted. I tried not to read any of them too closely; as soon as I saw they had nothing to do with the Arangos, I would move on.

No wonder Margarita didn't want Rodrigo to get his hands on any of this stuff. He would have had enough ammunition to make her life miserable well into the next century. It wasn't that Margarita had done anything wrong with any of these men—since they all predated Rodrigo—but I knew he would have tortured her with jealous allusions and petty references designed to keep her on the defensive. A man who would sue to recover damages for pain and suffering over the life of his wife and her unborn child—who wasn't his—was obviously into playing dirty. No wonder she had taken a lover. My only surprise by then was that she had waited so long before doing so.

The second box's contents were similar to the first's, in terms of personal mementos, but there were other items: tax returns, receipts, insurance forms, the mortgage on her condominium, car papers, expense ledgers. There was nothing very interesting, until I came across an envelope stamped with a photo developer's insignia. It was Fotografía Universal, with an address in Westchester.

The envelope gave me a tingling feeling—I knew it was important. I unsealed it and looked at the pictures inside. For a second I thought the champagne, the coffee, and the late hour had worked together to make me hallucinate. But it was real.

I held in my hand five photographs of Mariano Arango and Gustavo Gaston, standing together next to a car in a parking lot behind a sand-colored building. That was it. There were no other pictures inside. Whoever had taken the shots did so at a distance and without a telephoto lens, because the two men looked far away. But there was no mistaking their identities.

There were no names or dates, or anything, on the backs of the pictures. And the people at Fotografía Universal apparently didn't believe in dating the pictures they printed. There were only some numbers, which I took to be a coded receipt of a claim-check number, on the envelope's upper corner.

I took the pictures into my office and found the magnifying glass in my desk. My back felt as though it was on fire. Almost six hours hunched on the floor looking through papers had made me a wreck.

"What the hell was Margarita doing with these pictures?" I asked the empty office. Did she take the shots, and have them developed, or did someone else? The walls mocked me with their silence. I turned on my desk lamp and laid the pictures out side by side.

Two photos were virtually identical, showing Mariano and Gustavo standing close together and apparently arguing. They were looking into each other's faces, and pointing at each other simultaneously.

The third and fourth pictures were shot from an angle that allowed me to see the building in the background. Looking closer, I saw something on the corner window on the second floor. I held the picture so close to my face that my breath slightly fogged it. I could barely make out a sign of some sort, red in color.

I stared at the sign for a long time, but it remained a blur. I moved on to picture four and did the same. My eyes started to burn. Finally the shape, the color, everything, came together. "Of course," I almost shouted. It was a red cut-out sign wishing the world a Happy Valentine's Day.

I did some quick calculations. Gustavo Gaston was killed in early March, on the second. If the sign on the window had been placed there this year, to commemorate February 14, then the two men were meeting less than three weeks before the murder.

At the very least, Mariano had lied to me when he said he didn't know the dead man. And the photographer—whoever it was—knew that the two men were familiar to one another. I was back to having more questions than answers.

I told myself to relax and examined the pictures anew, slowly passing the magnifying glass over every corner. In picture five I saw a navy-blue station wagon with a sign on its side that read: "Or——Travel Agency." I couldn't make out the rest of the name, because the letters were blocked by a parked motorcycle. I hoped I had enough.

Three quarters of the way into the yellow pages section for travel agencies I found it: Orestes Travel Agency, with an address in Westchester not far from Fotografía Universal. This gave me an adrenaline rush so powerful I started sweating through my shirt.

I took out my case file and looked up Silvia Romero's home address. Then I found a map in my file drawer, spread it out on the floor, and marked the three Westchester addresses with colored pins. Silvia's apartment, Orestes Travel Agency, and Fotografía Universal were all within a couple miles of each other.

I finally had something. I closed up Margarita's boxes, checked the locks on the front door, and settled into the sofa to sleep for a few hours. I wanted to be rested for my drive to Westchester the next morning.

AFTER I STOPPED off at my apartment for a quick shower and fresh clothes, it took me thirty minutes to get to Westchester. Between past cases and my map study the night before, it felt like a home away from home. I found Orestes Travel Agency within minutes. It was in an off-white, unadorned five-story stucco building, which I hadn't been able to see in the pictures. It was virtually indistinguishable from the dozen others on the block, but to me it looked as beautiful as the Taj Mahal.

The possibility of finally unraveling this case made me feel like a teenager on a date. I pulled around to the back of the building and found the visitors' parking lot. There things looked more familiar—this was definitely the building in the photos. I parked and walked around the lot until I found the spot from which the photographer had taken the shots. I stood behind a wide, ancient olive tree, looking out on the parking lot, and had a strong sense of déjà vu.

And there it was—the travel agency's station wagon with the logo on the side, parked in its reserved spot. I looked up at the second-floor window, praying the Valentine's Day sign would be gone. It was. That meant whoever put it there wasn't the sort of hopeless romantic who might keep it up all year to promote love and romance.

I walked to the spot where Mariano and Gustavo had been photographed. There was nothing remarkable there, but I wondered why they had met at that particular spot. And why they hadn't been considerate enough to leave me any clues—say, a signed and dated confession taped to the olive tree. It never hurts to dream.

Inside the building, I took the creaky elevator to the second floor. At the end of the corridor was the office whose window I saw in the pictures. A carefully stenciled sign on the door's frosted glass read, "Menendez Packets." To my surprise, it was a firm that exported eyeglasses to Cuba.

Only sepulchral silence came from inside, so I opened the door and went in. I gave a cheery hello to a middle-aged, overweight, and undergirdled woman sitting at a typewriter.

She stood up with shock, clutching her ample chest. She looked at me like I was Fidel Castro himself, and had come in smoking a cigar and dressed in green fatigues. I assumed Menendez Packets didn't have much walk-in business.

The receptionist pulled a handkerchief from her dress and started fanning herself, ignoring me. Soon the small office smelled of violet water. I peeked over the desk to see what she had been working on, and I couldn't believe what I saw. Menendez Packets hadn't exactly hit high gear on the information superhighway. The poor woman was working on an actual manual typewriter—and using carbon paper.

"Hi there," I repeated.

My new friend finally realized I wasn't about to go away and leave her in peace. "Can I help you?" she asked in a husky voice.

"I hope so," I said brightly. "I have something very strange to ask you."

The receptionist wore a gold necklace that spelled out her name—Eloisa. "You mean you don't want to send eyeglasses to Cuba?" she asked, puzzled.

"No, I'd like to ask you a question." No reaction. "Please."

Eloisa didn't exactly trust me, but she relented a bit. "We have a price list," she said. "It tells you how much it costs to send glasses. It costs more to send them to Pinar del Río. Are you sending them to Havana or Pinar del Río?"

"This doesn't have anything to do with glasses," I said. "This is a personal question."

"How can you ask me a personal question?" Eloisa's chest heaved in about four different directions at once—which was quite a sight. "I don't even know you!"

"Do you remember a sign on your window," I asked, smiling. "A Valentine's Day heart?"

"Oh, those signs!" Eloisa said, relieved I hadn't asked her anything stranger. "I know what you're asking about. Betty puts them up. She has dozens of them!"

Eloisa and I shook our heads together at the wonder of it all. "Betty?" I asked.

"She's the other secretary that works here," Eloisa said. "But she's not in right now."

"Oh, I wanted to know where she got that sign." I leaned over the desk. "You see, that sign brought me luck."

Eloisa seemed truly perplexed, but I had her interest. This was obviously better than shipping eyewear. "How did it bring you luck?"

"My fiancé and I were in your parking lot in February," I said, doing my I'm-in-love face. "We've been going together three years, and he never said anything about getting married before. At mass every Sunday I always prayed he would ask me."

Eloisa made a weird cooing noise, and I knew I had her. This was better than glasses and *telenovelas* put together.

"Well, we were in the parking lot and when he looked up, he saw the sign in your window and said it was a message from God telling him to marry me! So it was the sign that did it!" I bounced up and down on my heels with rapture. "I want to get one just like it—no, I *have* to—so I came here to find out where you got it."

I hoped Eloisa would assume I had a single-digit IQ, and not think that I was crazy. She fanned herself some more. "Betty could tell you where she got it, but she's not here," she said. "She loves her decorations. She puts them up the week before the holiday, and leaves them up for a week after."

Eloisa looked around the drab office a bit mournfully. Steel file cabinets lined the walls, and overflowing cardboard boxes were stacked everywhere. Someone must have been fond of mustard yellow, or else they were color-blind, because the walls and the industrial carpet shared the same nauseating tint. It made me feel as if I were standing inside the intestines of a bug I had just squashed. I wouldn't have stopped at decorating the window—I would have opened it and jumped out.

"This isn't a very cheerful place," she said, revealing herself as a master of understatement. "And Betty likes to make things prettier. But she's home because her son is sick with chicken pox. You'll have to come back later in the week to ask her."

Eloisa still wanted to talk, even if I seemed like an escaped mental patient. "Betty, she's crazy," she said. "She celebrates all kinds of holidays—she just got done with that one where they drink green beer. And you don't want to see what she does for Easter, all those rabbits and pink-and-yellow eggs. You're lucky your fiancé didn't see those signs and decide to propose—you would be having a baby a year until you died!"

She laughed hard, sending her chest into startling motion. "I'll come back and talk to Betty," I said, shaking her hand. "Thank you for your time." I slinked out the door, leaving Eloisa to her triplicate carbons.

Bingo. I had an approximate date—but not the year, though my instincts told me it was this one. Now it was time to nail the photographer. I drove the short distance to Fotografía Universal, trying to come up with a better story than the one about the boyfriend who saw cardboard decorations as signs from God.

Fotografía Universal was in the middle of a block-long shopping center, just a few minutes from Menendez Packets. I was the only customer in the store, and there were two people behind the counter—a man and a woman. By the looks of them—their faces shared the same half-frown—I assumed they were a married couple.

I poked around aimlessly and waited for them to look up from their work. The husband was engrossed in cutting strips of negatives, and the wife was filling up a white leather album with wedding pictures. The front of the place was full of photographic supplies for sale, while the back was work space and a storage area. The business looked as though it was in a downward spiral; everything looked old, and the shelves were stocked with a spotty selection of film and camera straps.

Neither of them seemed ready to look up from their work, so I cleared my throat loudly. They raised their eyes, sharing the same half-annoyed expression, and I threw the five photographs down on the counter as though I were pissed off. That got a reaction. The wife put down the wedding album and joined me at the counter.

"Can I help you?" she asked apprehensively.

"I hope so." I tried to seem aggravated. After the past month, it wasn't hard to pull it off.

The husband, sensing there was a problem, carefully put his negatives down on his worktable and walked over. "Yes?" he asked.

"These pictures," I spat. "There are only five in the envelope."

I counted off the pictures in front of them. It never hurts to back up a story with visual aids. The three of us stood there, staring at the five photos of Mariano and Gustavo.

"So where are the rest of my pictures?" I demanded.

The man picked up the envelope and saw his shop's insignia. He glanced at his wife. "The rest of the pictures?"

"Yes," I said indignantly. "Surely you don't think I would buy a roll of thirty-six exposures and only use five?"

"Just a minute," the wife said; she took the envelope and pictures to some milk crates near her worktable. The husband straightened a pile of flyers while she rummaged through a box of receipts. She pulled her glasses closer to her face, carefully comparing the numbers stamped on the receipts and on my envelope.

I knew then that I was right—the number was a claim check. Now I had to pray they kept customers' names and dates on their receipts. While I watched the wife move deeper into her stack I prayed to the Virgin, promising that if this worked I would start going to mass every Sunday and not just when the spirit moved me—such as when I felt guilty about something.

Then the woman looked up. "Silvia Romero?" she asked.

I was careful to neither confirm nor deny that I was Silvia. "Did you find the rest of my pictures?" I asked.

"You must be mistaken about the rest of the roll," the wife said, as if expecting me to challenge her. "There were only five pictures developed because there were only five on the roll."

"I can't believe that." I shook my head. "I would never take only five pictures from an entire roll of film."

The wife let out a sharp breath, and I sensed her husband flinch. She was obviously the tough one. But she was also from the old school of customer relations—meaning that I was always right. And from the looks of the place, they couldn't afford to send anyone away mad.

"Look, here it is," she said, and marched over to me with the receipt.

My eyes almost crossed trying to read the scrawl on the faded paper receipt. Silvia Romero's name was the first thing I made out. Under that was the due date: 2/15/96. And under that, in caps, "FIVE EXPOSURES ONLY." I vaguely wondered what price the Virgin planned to extract for this windfall. Maybe the Virgin thought I deserved a break and—a frightening thought—she intended to take me up on my promise.

These people were trying to earn an honest living, and there was no point prolonging their agony. "You're right, I'm sorry," I groveled. "Please forgive me."

I could afford a little humiliation. I had gotten what I came for, and more. To make it up to the couple I bought three rolls of film. This improved the wife's attitude considerably.

I got into the Mercedes and started the engine; the couple watched me through the glass windows with puzzled expressions. I knew what they were thinking: if I was able to afford a luxury car, what was I doing arguing about a stupid roll of film?

I had my own puzzle. Silvia had shot the pictures and had taken them in to be developed in the middle of February, within three weeks of Gustavo's death. But how in the world did they end up with Margarita's things?

THIRTY-FOUR

A FEW MINUTES after six I spotted Silvia Romero's car turning onto her street in Westchester. I sat a half-block away in my Mercedes, watching her perform what looked like a nightly routine. She parked and put a bright orange Club on her steering wheel, testing it to make sure it was properly locked. Then she gathered her purse and a few things from the passenger seat and got out of the car. She tried the driver's-side handle to make sure she had locked it, then headed toward her apartment.

I had read about Silvia's obsessive caution in Marisol's reports, and now I saw it in person. She was certainly a creature of habit.

When she approached her parents' house to pick up her daughter, I hopped out of my car and sprinted after her. I was almost immediately short of breath—too many late nights, too much food and drink. I vowed to let Leonardo whip me into shape when this was all over.

Silvia either had excellent hearing, or I was breathing harder and louder than I thought. I didn't have to call her name to get her attention. She turned, and, when she saw me, her face filled with a bemused expression.

"Lupe, hello," she said.

"*Hola*," I panted. "Can I speak with you?"

Silvia was a small woman to begin with, but she seemed even more fragile now than when I met her in my office. She wore a dark blue cotton suit, plain to the point of severity. Her only jewelry was a Timex watch with a too-thick black plastic band which hung from her wrist. Her chin-length black hair was held back from her face by a black headband. She looked as though a stiff wind would pick her up and carry her away.

"Is this going to take long?" she asked, still pleasant. "My parents expect me to pick up my daughter at a certain time every day. If I'm even a few minutes late, they start to worry."

"You'd better let them know you'll be delayed for a while," I said.

She didn't seem surprised. She walked up to the house, let herself in with a key, and called out to someone inside.

Silvia motioned for me to come up the steps. "We'll go up to my place," she said. I followed her up a set of wooden stairs alongside the garage. She opened the door, switched off an alarm, turned on the lights, and invited me in.

The garage apartment Silvia shared with her daughter was nothing like her sterile, impersonal office at Optima Jewelers. It was warm and inviting, a place that gave me a good feeling. The front room doubled as a dining room, with a small dining set not far from two red-checkered sofas arranged opposite one another. In the corner was a comfortable-looking armchair placed in front of a television. Silvia had lots of photos arranged on every table—apparently of her family. There was no sign of Gustavo Gaston or any member of the Arango family.

Silvia invited me to sit on a sofa. I waited while she finished her routine—turning on more lights, lowering the shades, going through her mail. My throat felt hot and dry, and I was a little annoyed that she hadn't offered me anything to drink.

Finally able to relax now that she had done her daily

rituals, Silvia took the couch across from me and looked up expectantly. I felt suddenly irritated—as though all the bullshit and lies over this case had finally caught up with me.

"As I told you before," I said, "I was brought into this case to conduct an investigation into what happened Saturday, March second. My job was to find anything I could to substantiate Alonso Arango's version of what happened."

Silvia gave me a thin, patient smile. The only hint that I might be getting to her was a slight narrowing of her eyes. It was the kind of wince you make involuntarily when you are preparing for a blow but don't want your adversary to know you're frightened. She did not appear to be as fragile as her slight size and build would suggest.

"Since I began this investigation I've found out that almost everyone involved has lied to me, in one way or another," I continued.

"What does that have to do with me?" Silvia asked.

"Have you ever heard the expression 'Don't lie to your doctor or your lawyer,' Silvia?" I asked. She shook her head. "Those are people who can help you—but only if they know what's really going on."

Silvia shrugged, just slightly. "As part of my investigation, I've had to delve into the personal lives of everyone who works at Optima," I said. I saw a vein pulse on Silvia's neck. Finally. "I was surprised at what I discovered about you, especially since you seemed so honest and straightforward when we spoke at my office."

The vein jumped again. I didn't want to feel vindictive about this, but I was tired. Tired of this case, and tired of being lied to.

Silvia crossed her legs clumsily and folded her arms across her chest in a self-protective posture. She knew the body blow was coming, and she wanted to be ready. Her eyes never left mine.

"I know about your relationship with Alonso Arango." Silvia shifted her weight and crossed her legs the other way. "Does he know Gustavo Gaston is the father of your little girl?"

The question hung unanswered between us. As far as I was concerned, I had all night. I just wished I had a glass of water.

"Is that important to anyone?" Silvia asked.

"It's very important," I said slowly.

"Why?"

"It gives Alonso a motive for killing Gustavo. Or vice versa." Silvia looked at me as though through a fog. I could see I had to walk her through this. "Jealousy. You were having an affair with your married boss, and Gustavo found out. Maybe he tried to blackmail Alonso, to threaten to tell Isabel. Does this sound familiar?"

By then I was fishing, but Silvia bit. "How did you find out that Gustavo is Alejandra's father?" she asked. Her voice turned brassy. "No one knows that."

I decided the best approach with Silvia was to barter information. "I saw her birth certificate," I said.

Silvia looked at me as though I had just stepped out of a spaceship. I saw that the fight in her was gone.

I reached into my purse and produced the pictures I found in Margarita's box. "Tell me about these."

Silvia bit her lip. "Where did you get those?"

I tossed aside my plan to exchange information. "You tell me," I said.

"I took them before Gustavo was killed," she said.

I refrained from pointing out that this was obviously true.

"I followed him one day and took the pictures when he met with Mariano."

That told me nothing. "Why did you follow him?"

"I wanted to have proof that he met with Mariano," Silvia explained, as though I were now the dense one.

"Silvia, you have to start at the beginning," I said. She looked skeptical, and I realized that her willful streak ran deep. "It's the only way to help Alonso."

Again the stony stare. She got up from the sofa and said, a bit too cheerily, "Would you like something to drink?"

"Yes," I said. It was as though she had finally read my mind. My mouth was so parched I was licking my lips. "Anything cold would be fine."

Silvia went into the kitchen; I could see her from my sofa, and I made sure she went in there solely for refreshments. She opened the refrigerator and took out a can of juice. "Pineapple all right?"

I said that was fine, and watched her pour the juice into rather pretty crystal glasses. She opened a drawer, and I stiffened—but she was just looking for the right napkins.

She came in with a tiny silver tray bearing the napkins and glasses arranged in perfect symmetry. We took sips and smiled approvingly at each other. Miss Manners would have been proud of us.

A change seemed to have taken place within Silvia; she seemed more relaxed. "Tell me one thing," she said. "Where did you find those pictures? I've been looking for them for a while."

What the hell. "I found them among the personal belongings of Margarita Vidal."

"Margarita Vidal?" Silvia frowned with perplexity.

"The decorator," I said. "She did the Arangos' house."

"That's right!" Silvia seemed too pleased to have put this little mystery in order. "I paid her bills. MMV Interiors, right?"

"She was a friend of mine."

"Was?" Silvia asked. She read my expression. "Oh, I'm sorry. But still, how did she get my pictures?"

"I have no idea," I said truthfully. "I hoped you could tell me." Investigator's code decreed that information should never be given out, except to receive information in exchange. I was following that one really well—because I had so little to tell.

Silvia sighed. "I said to Alonso that we should have told the truth from the very beginning," she said. "But he didn't want to, and he forbade me to say anything to you."

This was a surprise. "Alonso told you to hide information from me?"

"Yes."

Great.

I smiled reassuringly, and felt the first sharp stab of a tension headache. "Well, now you can make up for that."

"You know about Gustavo, then? How he came here on a raft, and about his accomplishments in Cuba?" I said that I did; Silvia seemed proud. "He tried to become an architect here, but he found out that his license was worth nothing. He had to take courses and pass tests—he said it was complicated. When he took a job as a driver on Miracle Mile, it was just supposed to be for a little while. But as time went on, he lost his ambition to become an architect again."

Silvia took a delicate sip of her juice. I had drained mine already. "I met him when we worked at the same store," she continued. "I was there part-time, he was the driver. At the time, he promised he would become a professional man again. I believed him."

I heard betrayal in her voice. "You can guess what happened," she said. "I fell in love with him and got pregnant. He didn't offer to marry me. An abortion was out of the question. So I had Alejandra and named Gustavo on the birth certificate simply because I couldn't bear to leave the space blank. I knew by then that he wouldn't help me with her."

"I'm sorry to hear that," I said. Silvia seemed all right for a moment, then a tear rolled from her eye. She grabbed a box of tissue and took out a handful. For such a small woman, her nose blowing was enough to hurt my ears. It sounded like a foghorn I heard once in San Francisco.

Silvia sealed the tears inside her; I sensed she was ashamed to break down in front of me. "My parents have been wonderful, helping me with Alejandra," she said. "And when Alonso offered to take me on full-time at Optima I was so happy. I could support us, you see, and not have to worry all the time."

"But when did—" I began.

"I worked there two years before anything happened between us," she interrupted.

"And does Alonso know who Alejandra's father is?"

"No one does," she said. "He thinks it was someone I met at a bar one night when I had too much to drink. A simple mistake."

I had guessed that Silvia led a complicated life, but this

was even more than I had imagined. "What about Gustavo and Mariano?"

"Sometimes I went over to Gustavo's apartment to visit," she said. She gave a little laugh. "He was a bastard about Alejandra, but he could be nice. And it was important to me that he never tell anyone he was her father. One time, I went there and from the hall I heard him talking on the phone. He was shouting at someone named Mariano. The only Mariano I knew was Mariano Arango, so I eavesdropped for a minute."

I briefly considered asking Silvia if she ever thought about getting into investigations. She wasn't half bad. "I heard Isabel Arango's name a couple of times," she said. Then Gustavo agreed on a time and place to meet. I had no idea why. I went there, and for some reason I took a camera. I guess I wanted proof if anything bad happened. Gustavo sounded very angry on the phone."

I couldn't fault her methods. "What kind of bad thing did you think might happen?"

"I don't know," she said. "It worried me when they mentioned Isabel's name."

"So you followed them there," I said, imagining her surveillance work. "I assume they didn't see you." I almost said "burn you."

"No. But I couldn't get close enough to hear everything they said." Silvia took a deep breath. "But I did hear that Gustavo knew Isabel—and he said he was having an affair with her. Mariano was shouting at Gustavo, calling him a liar, saying his mother would never take up with scum like him."

I remembered Mariano's distaste when I mentioned Gustavo. "I was scared Gustavo would tell Mariano he was Alejandra's father," Silvia said. "I don't know what Gustavo wanted, maybe money to keep quiet. They weren't there for long, and Mariano was furious."

"What did you do with the pictures you took?" I asked.

Silvia answered quickly. "I took them back to my office at Optima and taped them underneath my desk drawer. I saw that on TV."

Poor Silvia. She didn't realize that that was the first place to look for hidden papers. But I still couldn't understand how Margarita had gotten them. "When did you know they were missing?" I asked.

"The day of the murder. When Gustavo was killed, I knew those pictures were going to be important—I didn't know exactly why, but I was sure of it." Silvia's expression was grave. "I figured the police would search my things at the store, and that they might find them."

The girl had watched too much television, where police departments are depicted as flush with resources and bright-eyed detectives. But then something occurred to me. "Has anything changed in your office in the past few months?" I asked. "The furniture, the rugs, anything at all?"

Silvia thought for a while. "The rugs," she said. "We had area rugs, but then Isabel ordered wall-to-wall carpeting for the entire store. She said it made the place look bigger."

"You pay the bills," I said. "Who ordered the rugs?"

Silvia caught my train of thought. "MMV Interiors."

"Were you there when the carpets were put in?"

"No. Yes." She frowned, upset with herself for not remembering right away. "Wait. I was there for a while, but all the furniture had to be taken out of my office to lay the carpet. I couldn't get any work done, because my desk was taken out."

"Did they take out the drawers to move it?" I asked.

"Yes." She was with me now. "I guess the photos could have come unstuck. Alonso junior came to help move the furniture. Alonso senior asked all the boys to help, but only Alonso junior came."

Touchdown. I could see it now. Alonso junior saw the envelope and opened it. He saw pictures of his youngest brother in a parking lot talking to a strange man, and probably gave them to Margarita for safekeeping until he could figure out what was going on—and why they were taped to his father's bookkeeper's desk.

And maybe this was what Margarita wanted to tell me about before she died—that she saw those pictures, and that Alonso might have been worried about them. When she heard that a murder had occurred, she might have known that the pictures could have played a part. She obviously knew the pictures were important, or she wouldn't have stored them with her private things.

There were a lot of maybes in this hypothesis, but it was the only thing that made sense. What surprised me was that Alonso junior hadn't said anything about this—I thought we had developed a good rapport. Maybe he was protecting his brother. Maybe he had forgotten what Gustavo looked like in the pictures, and had failed to make the connection between him and the man his father murdered.

Silvia watched me expectantly, as though she thought I might start spitting pearls of wisdom at her. But we weren't finished, I was sure of it. "What really happened that Saturday morning?" I asked. "I can't help Alonso unless I know."

She sat up ramrod-straight and flashed me a surprising angry look. "Are you accusing me of lying?"

I could have laughed; instead, my headache grew nastier. Silvia had lied to me about knowing Gustavo, lied to Alonso about the father of her child, and she had told me that Alonso had ordered her not to tell me the truth. There was no need for me to accuse her of anything.

"Let's start with the knife," I said. "There was no knife found at the scene. Two weeks later a similar knife was found in Reina Sotolongo's chest. And why did Alonso empty the gun into Gustavo? One or two shots from that cannon would have stopped a buffalo in its tracks."

Silvia looked away from me with a coquettish turn of her chin. "It looks like a crime of passion, Silvia," I said. "I'm not alone in thinking that. And Alonso's case is going to be heard by a judge known for sending people to the electric chair."

I vaguely wondered what Silvia's parents might be thinking; we had been talking a long time. I was about to hammer away with tales of Sparky Markey when Silvia turned to me, her face red.

"I killed Gustavo," she blurted out. "I came in from the post office earlier than I said, and I was in my office when

Gustavo came in. I had the knife because I was cutting open a supply box that was sealed with thick tape. There *was* a knife. But I had it, not Gustavo.''

I must have looked ridiculous. I tried not to react—after all, Silvia had just confessed to murder—but I felt the corners of my mouth twitching. I had stayed away from Silvia, stumbling down blind paths. And the answer was with her all along.

"I heard voices in the back room," she said in an eerily calm voice. "I recognized them as Gustavo and Alonso. I thought my heart would stop, but he wasn't saying anything about me. He . . . I knew that he was going to tell Alonso that he and Isabel had been having an affair. But he never got a chance. It would have destroyed Alonso.''

"Why?" I asked. "Alonso was having an affair with you.'' But I knew what she was getting at. There's a double standard in Cuban marriages—the husband is allowed to fool around, but the wife has to stay pure. I had seen it countless times.

"It was because of the arrangement," Silvia said.

"What arrangement?"

Silvia leaned forward and spoke more quietly. "Years ago Isabel stopped complying with her marital duties. She wanted to stay married but end their physical relationship. Alonso was very disappointed, because he loved his wife dearly.''

I couldn't believe this. Silvia, narrow-boned, delicate Silvia, spoke as easily as if we were at a picnic. "He made a proposal to her," she said. "They would stay married. He would pay all her expenses, including supporting her good-for-nothing relatives—but in exchange, she would take no lovers. And that's the way it was until Gustavo came along.''

I felt a throb of pain creep into my temples. But this wasn't the time to ask for an aspirin. "Knowing Isabel broke her promise would have killed Alonso," Silvia continued. "I don't think much about killing Gustavo. I saved Alonso's life.''

In my life I have heard plenty of rationalizations, and

come up with a few myself, but this was one of the best. Unfortunately, Sparky Markey wouldn't give a damn.

"I didn't plan to use the knife," Silvia said. I wondered if she was already preparing her story for the police. "I just wanted to scare him, but he wasn't scared, and he kept coming at me. That's when Alonso reached for the gun under the counter."

"To protect you?" I asked.

"Yes, to protect me," she said. She was breathing faster now, reliving the moment. "But I got there first. I threw the knife down and grabbed the gun. Gustavo didn't seem frightened even then. It was very strange. Then he started talking again. I don't know what he said, I couldn't hear anything, but that was when I shot him. To shut him up. I shot him again and again."

Silvia looked at me defiantly. This wasn't going to play well in court. And I felt terrible. Silvia didn't realize it, but when she admitted to shooting Gustavo I was no longer on her side—that is, if I ever was. Silvia's confession to me was Alonso's ticket out of jail, and the end of my investigation for Tommy.

"Why did Alonso take responsibility for the shooting?" I asked.

"We had a moment before the others came rushing in to see what happened," Silvia said. "Alonso made up the story on the spot, and I went along. Alonso wiped off the gun barrel and put his fingerprints there. He even rubbed the gun barrel on his hand, so he would have powder there. He kept telling me not to worry, that he would go free because he would say he was defending himself."

"And didn't he ask you why you shot Gustavo?"

Silvia shook her head and stared into her empty glass. "I don't think he wanted to know," she said. "He must have suspicions, but he doesn't want to know. He thinks I panicked; at least, that's what he told me."

"And what happened to the knife?" I was fairly convinced it ended up in Reina Sotolongo's chest—but I didn't know how it got there.

"I don't know," Silvia said. She looked out the window.

"The last time I saw the knife was when I threw it. It was toward the back of the office, near the cleaning closet."

The cleaning closet. My antennae began to throb.

"Oh, Lupe," Silvia said. She began to cry again, not bothering to control it this time. "This is such a mess. What's going to happen now? Are you going to tell the police?"

She genuinely seemed not to have considered this in advance. "No, I won't," I said. "Under Florida law, our conversation is confidential. But I have to tell Thomas McDonald, Alonso's attorney."

What I told her was the truth. She was in the deepest trouble, and we both knew it. And I knew that Silvia's confession would clear Alonso as a murder suspect, but that he still could be charged as an accessory.

It was almost eight o'clock, and the neighborhood outside was calm in the early night. "Your parents must be wondering what happened to you," I said, trying to smile.

Silvia held her head in her hands, and didn't seem to have heard me. I sat and waited for her sobs to pass.

It was ironic. As Alonso's investigator, I had uncovered the very facts that he was trying to hide—and these facts would get him out of jail for the time being.

I stood up, put a hand on Silvia's shoulder, and told her that I was going to leave. She was still in her own world. I couldn't judge Silvia, and I couldn't pretend to understand everything she had gone through. All that was really left for me was to do my job. In the morning I would dump all these problems in Tommy's lap.

But there was still a glaring problem. Who killed Reina Sotolongo, and why?

I let myself out. In Silvia's parents' window I saw a little girl watch me climb into my car. She looked a lot like Silvia.

THIRTY-FIVE

I WOKE TOMMY early the next morning with a phone call; I told him I'd be in his office in a few hours, and that it was extremely important. I didn't say that kind of thing often, and even though he was half asleep I could hear his curiosity in his voice.

I didn't want to be alone after talking to Silvia, so instead of sleeping in my apartment I spent the night in the Coco-plum house. I had a lousy sleep; there was a late-night storm, and my dreams came complete with a nightmare of what could happen to Silvia in a women's penitentiary. After that one, I gave up all pretense of trying to sleep and went outside to the terrace. I jumped into the pool in the predawn chill and swam laps until my arms felt as though they would fall off.

I was in the kitchen making myself a double cup of Cuban espresso with steamed milk—whole, not skim—when Aida came in. She almost passed out from shock at seeing me awake and about before she was—and in a wet bathing suit. I hadn't been up so early in the house since college, and then only because I'd stayed up all night, usually with

Margarita. I was never known as an early bird.

"Don't make any noise, I don't want you to wake Papi," Aida warned, a finger over her lips. "He went to one of those Cuban Liberation meetings last night. He drank too much rum and fell asleep listening to the Cuban national anthem, over and over. Osvaldo had to carry him to bed."

I thought of frail old Osvaldo. "I'm amazed Osvaldo could carry Papi," I said.

"It almost killed him!" Aida cried. "Your father's not light, you know."

Aida kept chattering as she began her morning kitchen routine. I only half listened to her, as usual. I sipped my espresso and looked at yesterday's newspaper. In no time at all, the smell of freshly baked Cuban bread wafted around the room. As soon as Aida took it out of the oven I broke off a huge slice, slathered it with a thick coat of butter, and popped the whole thing into my mouth. The next bite I dipped in a fresh mug of Cuban café con leche Aida made for me. I ate the whole dripping mess and watched the grease float on the surface of my coffee. It might seem repulsive to some Americans, but that's the only way to attack a Cuban breakfast—with gusto. It's definitely not for the weak of heart, or stomach.

Breakfast made me feel infinitely better. I kissed Aida on the cheek, thanked her, and went upstairs for a shower. I always felt vaguely guilty that I didn't spend more time with Aida and Osvaldo; after Mami died, they held the family together by taking care of everyday life, even though they loved and missed Mami almost as much as we did.

I wanted to dress to fit in at Tommy's office, so I chose a demure two-piece cotton khaki suit with a sleeveless tight brown T-shirt underneath. Black open-toed leather sandals set everything off. Now, that was power dressing.

I had one stop to make before going to talk to Tommy. I wanted to ask Alonso junior about the pictures I found in Margarita's private things. Mainly I wanted to verify my theory about how they got there—and find out why Alonso had never done anything about them, or mentioned them to me.

I called him at home but there was no answer. I left a message on his machine, figuring I would find him at Dinner Key, already at AAA Lines. He seemed like the kind of man who went to work early. I called his office, but he wasn't there, either. But I reckoned he could always be on one of his boats, or en route to work.

I blasted over to Dinner Key, and was relieved to see Alonso's red Camaro parked in his usual spot under a poinciana tree. I pulled into the visitor's space next to it. When I got out I noticed that his car was covered with quite a few leaves and flowers, as if it had been there for a while. That didn't seem right. I would have guessed that Alonso kept his car spotless, and when I saw it before, it had been.

Walking up to his office, I remembered the storm the night before. There had been lots of rain and wind. It was then that my heart started to beat faster. It seemed that Alonso's car had been sitting there all night.

I banged on the door of AAA Lines. No response. I quit pounding, afraid that I might set off the alarm. I walked around and looked in the windows, which was hard because they were taller than I am. There was nothing for me to grab hold of to climb up, so I was reduced to jumping up and down to see inside. It was then that a car pulled into the parking lot and a young girl stepped out.

She looked alarmed when she got out of her car. "Is there anything I can help you with?" she asked. She couldn't have been older than eighteen. And I was sure I looked crazy to her, and maybe a little scary. I mean, I don't look like your typical burglar, but as the tourist ads said a few years back, "Miami, the rules are different here."

I tried to look harmless. "Yes. I'm looking for the gentleman who owns AAA Lines."

"You mean Alonso? He's around somewhere. That's his car." She pointed to the red Camaro.

"Yes, yes, I know." I tried to stay calm. Maybe she had a key to his office. "Do you work here?"

"I work next door, at Miami Marine Underwriters." She walked past me to the entrance. "I've been temping there for three months. I don't have a key, but Bill, my boss, does." She must have noticed how worried I was. "You can come in and ask him if you want."

I didn't need to be asked twice. I followed her, noticing that she was pretty sexy in her micro stretch black skirt and cropped top. I hoped she wouldn't drop anything, because she would start a riot if she bent over. Whoever Bill was, he was sure to miss her when she was through temping— that is, if he had a heartbeat.

She told me her name—Melissa—and introduced me to Bill. Bill was about forty, with a pink face, sandy hair, and the beginning of a paunch beneath his sea-green polo shirt. He did indeed have a heartbeat; I saw his eyes waging war with themselves trying to decide whether to look at my legs or Melissa's ass. I told Bill I was looking for Alonso, then told him about the Camaro and the unanswered calls.

I could tell Bill thought I was making a big deal out of nothing, but he came out into the hall and opened Alonso's office. He even knew the codes to disconnect the alarm system.

There was no one in AAA Lines, and it didn't look as though anyone had been there that day at all. The air was stagnant and stale, the windows all closed. But everything seemed in its place, and there was no sign of forced entry or theft.

Then I saw Alonso's briefcase leaning against a chair behind his desk. Now it was time to panic. Something was very wrong.

Some of my worry seemed to rub off on Bill, and he started walking around as though looking for clues. "Alonso always takes his briefcase with him when he leaves," he said. "But his car's outside. He must be somewhere, don't you think?"

"Let's look outside," I said. Bill followed me, then Melissa. I went out the back door, to the docks, where the boats were stacked up side by side on dry docks and three jetties.

The wind whipped around and stirred up the morning silence, but there was no one around. Bill shrugged, apparently happy to give up and go back to his warm, dry office.

He started to do just that, and noticed Melissa standing in his way.

"We can't just give up, Bill," she said. "The man's obviously missing! We have to look for him."

I could have kissed her. I definitely had to get the name of her temp agency, in case Leonardo took off on some Iron Man retreat to get in touch with his inner child.

I wanted someone with me, and I knew Bill wouldn't want to lose face with Melissa. I could see him thinking: he might even score points with her if he was the one who found Alonso.

"Of course not," he said. "I was just looking around to check out the parking lot."

We couldn't see the parking lot from where we stood, but I wasn't complaining. We split up; Bill took the northern jetty, Melissa the middle, and I the southern section. There must have been twenty boats stored there on dry docks, none bigger than about thirty feet. I was about to look inside a Mako when I heard a chilling scream from the middle jetty. Melissa came running out, pointing back to where she had been.

"He's there!" she yelled. "He's bleeding!"

Bill and I both arrived at the boat at the same time. It was a Cigarette, a sleek speedboat. I climbed in and saw Alonso huddled on the floor. Blood was matted on his head and dried on his cheek.

"Is he dead?" Melissa screamed in my ear. "Is he alive?"

I flinched in pain; the volume of her voice almost made me lose my balance. "Call nine-one-one," I said. "He's still alive. Do it now!"

Melissa ran toward the offices, and Bill hovered over me, unsure what to do. "He has a pulse," I told him. "Not much of one, but I feel something."

Alonso looked much too pale. "Alonso, can you hear me?" I said. "It's Lupe. You're going to be all right." No response. I shook him gently. "Alonso, can you hear me?"

His eyelids fluttered a bit. I brushed some of the blood-matted hair away from his eyes. "It's okay," I said. "An ambulance is on the way."

While we waited I saw that all the blood came from a wound high on his forehead. It didn't look like a bullet wound, and my guess was that he was hit with something heavy. I glanced around the boat for obvious weapons, but there was nothing. I knew the cops would declare the boat a crime scene when they got there, and make it off limits to civilians, so this was my only chance to check things out. But I knew I shouldn't let go of Alonso. Bill wasn't much help. His urge to play hero seemed to have disappeared with Melissa.

Soon I heard the sirens. A few moments later three paramedics came round the side of the building, following Melissa. When they got to us, they took over.

They checked Alonso's vital signs, lifted him onto a stretcher, and took him away. On the way out of the lot they crossed paths with the police, who arrived in force. I gave a brief statement to the officer in charge.

There was nothing much to tell him: I came looking for Alonso, became suspicious when I saw his car in the lot, and started looking around. I didn't go into anything about his father's case—I was sure the cop didn't need a confusion headache so early in the day. Melissa and Bill told him the same. We were free to go after giving our names and addresses. Our story was too familiar in Miami.

I reached the Mercedes just as the police started to cordon off the area. I called Isabel on my portable phone and spoke to the maid, informing her of Alonso junior's situation and telling her he was at Mercy Hospital.

It took me a few minutes to pull myself together. What happened to Alonso wasn't an ordinary Coconut Grove mugging. It had to do with the case or, God forbid, Margarita. I hated the notion that I might somehow be responsible.

I drove slowly north toward downtown, too shaken to deal with a speeding ticket. Tommy was waiting for me when I walked into his office. I felt as though I was in a dream.

"Lupe, Jesus, what's the matter?" Tommy asked, getting up. "You look like hell."

"I'm not surprised," I said, flopping wearily on his sofa. "You have no idea what I've been through the past couple of days."

Tommy sat down next to me and held my hand. "Tell me."

I went through most of it: the keys on the roof of my car, last night's interview with Silvia, finding Alonso in the boat. Tommy heard me out, nodding and listening. I lay back on the sofa; I don't know what took more out of me, the experiences themselves or having to tell about them.

"This changes everything," Tommy said pensively. He went to the humidor on his desk and took out a cigar. Soon the sweet smell of a Montecristo Number One filled the room. The embargo had no effect on Tommy.

"What are you going to do?" I asked.

"Obviously, the first step in our new strategy is to get Alonso out of jail as soon as possible." Tommy blew a huge smoke ring. "I have to tell him what you uncovered. If he agrees to it, I'm going to write Sparky Markey an emergency motion for dismissal. Or at the very least, a reduction of charges."

"He might not want to go along with you," I said flatly. "According to Silvia, he thought up this whole lie to protect her."

"Almost sixty days in the Stockade might have changed his feelings," Tommy said. "That, and the fact that his son is in the hospital."

Leave it to Tommy to take the pragmatic approach. But I wasn't so sure. I knew Alonso senior was a Cuban man of the old school. Women and children first, always. He might not want to turn Silvia over out of honor, even though we had tripped him up.

"What do you think happened to the son?" Tommy asked, shifting gears.

"It wasn't a street mugging," I said. "It either had to do with his father's case, or with Margarita Vidal."

Tommy puffed so strenuously on the Montecristo that a

cloud formed over our heads. It didn't help my feelings of dread that it looked like a mushroom cloud.

"Tell me why you think it had to do with Margarita," he said.

I had been riding a fine line with Tommy, not wanting him to know how my loyalties might be divided over the case. Now I went through the whole thing, from Margarita's last words to Rodrigo's lawsuit and the surveillance I had found myself under. Tommy nodded for me to talk faster through the parts he already knew, and listened closely to the parts he didn't. He scowled at the mention of Fernando Godoy, and finally said, "It's weird. I wouldn't think someone could follow you, or get close enough to do this thing with the keys."

"Everyone screws up sometimes." I shrugged. "But I'm afraid I might have led Godoy right to Alonso junior. Rodrigo must have thought Margarita would confide everything in me—including the name of her child's father. Only she didn't. I was just hoping that if I was seen with Alonso, they would think it only had to do with the case."

"Well, is there any way to connect Alonso junior with Margarita?" Tommy asked logically.

"The only person who might have a clue is Mariano Arango." I sighed. "He saw Alonso and Margarita together one time, at his apartment. Alonso said he explained it away, but he didn't know if his brother believed him."

"So you don't know for sure." Tommy took a volcanic drag on the Montecristo.

"No," I admitted. "I was going to talk to him about that, in connection with the photos I found, when—well, you know."

"There's no point beating yourself up about this." Tommy sat down beside me again and hugged me tight. I must have looked like I needed reassurance, and I did—even though I had to pull back a little to ensure that the cigar didn't set my hair on fire.

I thanked Tommy; he could be quite human, when he was pushed far enough. "But don't forget Reina Sotolongo," I said.

Tommy gave me a sly smile; it was problem-solving time. "Any theories?" he asked.

"One."

"Are you going to do the cops' work for them?"

"No way," I said. "It's a loose end, but this case has driven me crazy. Everyone lies. I'd rather have an all-day root canal."

Tommy held up his hands in mock surrender. "If you want me to, I'll take you off the case," he said. "No problem, I'll just give it to someone else. It's almost over, anyway—you did all the dirty work. You can go take that vacation in Key West with that dropout lover of yours."

Tommy laughed out loud. He knew me too well. It would take a crowbar and a team of horses to get me off this case. He also knew that I simply had to complain from time to time, just to make sure he appreciated me. It was a CAP—Cuban-American Princess—thing.

"Why is it that I don't feel any better now?" I wondered aloud. "I got a confession to help the client. And I feel like shit."

"Jesus, Lupe, for such a smart woman you can sound dumb sometimes," Tommy said. The tip of the Montecristo looked like Vesuvius about to destroy Pompeii. "You feel like shit because you broke the first commandment: you got personally involved."

He was right, and I hated it. I got up and smoothed out my skirt. I wanted to make a stop on the way back to my office, and I didn't want Tommy to know about it.

Tommy could see I was leaving and he stood, towering over me. I cursed my sandals with their dainty little one-inch heels.

"Go home and get some rest," Tommy said. "Don't hate me for saying it again, but you look lousy."

He bent over and gave me a chaste kiss on the cheek. I could smell his cologne. "Tell Aida to fix you a nice lunch," he said. "And eat it in bed. Then call me tonight. Promise?"

I promised. But only to the part about calling him that night. I had no intention of heading home for a quiet lunch in bed.

THIRTY-SIX

"I DON'T KNOW why the hell I'm meeting with you like this. I hope no one from my office sees me with you. It's not like my job is so secure that I can afford to jeopardize it! I know you don't think much of what I do, Lupe—but hey, it pays the rent."

Charlie Miliken was grousing, even more than usual, in the passenger seat of my Mercedes. I ignored him and pulled away from the curb as quickly as I could. I hoped he hadn't noticed that my nemesis, Aurora Santangelo, had chosen just that moment to step out of the Justice Building. Her timing always was exquisite.

"Hey, Charlie, you're looking great!" I tried to sound as carefree and casual as I could. My cheeks still hurt from pinching them on the drive over from Tommy's office. I read years ago in a magazine that in times past only women of ill repute wore makeup, and well-bred ladies would pinch their cheeks to have good coloring without resorting to artifice. I didn't know if it worked, but after being told twice that I looked bad, I was willing to give it a shot.

"Cut out the ass-kissing," Charlie growled. "What do you want?"

"Why are you in such a bad mood?" I asked. Charlie could be a champion grouch, but this was excessive.

"Some genius took it on himself to declare the area two blocks around the Justice Building a smoke-free zone." Charlie took out a cigarette and lit it. "Two blocks! I might as well have to go to Fort Lauderdale for a smoke! What fucking jerks!"

It didn't take much perception to see this wasn't a good time to pump Charlie for information. I'd have to put him in a better mood. "Do you want to go somewhere for a drink?" I asked.

"Lupe, I don't have time for this." He took such a long drag that he almost smoked half the cigarette in one puff. "I'm overworked and underpaid. I have stacks of files on my desk taller than I am. You know I love to see you under any circumstances, but I don't have time for games today."

Charlie was ready for a second smoke; he lit it off the first. I realized that there was no way for me to avoid smelling like an ashtray that day. "So what do you want?" he said, staring straight ahead.

"Information." There was no point in being coy.

"I see. And on what case?" We had stopped at a red light, and Charlie turned to look at me. I wished he hadn't done that. I had a weakness for his eyes, even when they were narrowed with grumpiness.

"Well, actually, it's about two cases."

"Oh, fine. Make my day. Let me take a wild guess: Alonso Arango, Senior, right?" I nodded. "And the other?"

"Reina Sotolongo."

"You lost me on that one," Charlie said. "Refresh my memory. Who is Reina Sotolongo?"

"The cleaning lady found stabbed in the Dumpster behind Optima Jewelers the week before last," I answered helpfully.

"The cleaning lady. Right." Charlie smoked some more. Driving aimlessly around the Justice Building isn't as easy as it sounds. Between the cutthroat traffic and the smoke, I felt that I might pass out.

"Let's go have lunch," I said. "You gotta eat."

This time I didn't give him a chance to object. I drove straight to Calle Ocho, to Versailles, where I had last eaten with Rodrigo. Charlie bitched about being short on time, so we parked and ordered from the walk-up window. We asked for two *medianoches*—ham and cheese on sweet Cuban bread, along with mango milk shakes. It was a far cry from eating Aida's delicious food in bed.

A minute or two later the waitress yelled out that our order was ready. I paid, and we gobbled our food in the car in the parking lot. I left my window open, because Charlie smoked through the meal. I guessed he was trying to get ahead on his nicotine count, since he was staring down a smoke-free afternoon.

I waited until we were halfway through before asking about Reina again. "Lupe, you know I could be fired for talking to you about that case," Charlie said. "Or about any case."

It was hard to take him seriously with mango shake on his cheek, but what he said was true. He put his career in danger every time he discussed a case with me. But he had done it before, and I knew he would do it again.

"I know, Charlie," I said. "I'm just grateful for anything you can tell me. And you know I'd never betray your confidence."

"That's the only reason I'm talking to you now," Charlie said, with his mouth full. "Aurora Santangelo would burn my ass if she knew we were having this conversation. She wants to get you any way she can—and this Arango case is a perfect chance. Completely unprofessional, but bad blood never goes away."

Curiosity got the better of me. "What did she say about me?"

"You want the whole, dirty story," he asked, "or the edited version?"

"The unabridged edition."

Charlie ate some more, and took another drag. His hands

were moving fast from shake to food to cigarette, and back. "She said you've slept with every attorney in town," he said. "And that's how you get so many cases."

"That's not true," I protested. "I didn't sleep with all of them—only the men."

"Well, tell me first if you decide to pursue an alternative lifestyle. I'd be interested to see what you'd do with that."

I ignored him. "Reina Sotolongo."

"God damn, Lupe, you're like a bloodhound," Charlie said. "All right, let me think. I remember there's something funny about that one. It was going to be filed as a B and E the cleaning lady got in the way of, but I think it's being treated differently because of the Arango killing. Aurora doesn't believe in coincidence."

"What about prints on the knife? Has the time of death been determined yet?"

"Lupe, for Christ's sake, give me a break!" Charlie finished his sandwich and wiped off his face. "It's not my case. I just know what I hear around the office. And if I leaked anything, Aurora would toast my ass. She's just waiting for me to fuck up. She hates me strictly because of my association with you. She'd be ecstatic if I went down in flames."

Again I thought about Aurora walking out of the building just as Charlie got in my car. If she saw us, he'd find out soon enough.

"Do you think there's any chance you'll find out the results of the investigation anytime soon?" I asked.

Charlie sighed; smoke came out of his nose. "Lupe, I don't think you're listening. I'm already under a cloud of suspicion—all because of you."

"Please," I said. "I need to know."

"Oh God, don't look at me that way," Charlie cried. "You don't play fair."

I gathered up the remains of my lunch and walked over to the trash can on the corner. I walked slowly, letting Charlie watch me walk. I knew the effect it had on him.

He was right. I did play dirty.

THIRTY-SEVEN

———◆———

I DROPPED OFF long-suffering Charlie and drove to Mercy Hospital to find out Alonso junior's condition. The front-desk volunteer told me he was on the fourth floor, in intensive care. At least he was still alive. When I stepped off the elevator I found Isabel and Ernesto Arango waiting outside the double doors leading to the ICU.

They were engrossed in a grave conversation on a sofa in the lounge, and didn't notice me. I decided to stop off at the ladies' room before I talked to them. I went to the nurses' station, asked for directions, and headed down the hall. As I rounded a corner, I heard a voice I thought I recognized.

"Why the fuck did you hurt him?"

I stopped dead. That voice belonged to Mariano Arango. Moving back behind the corner, I looked up and saw a sign with bathroom and telephone symbols, and an arrow pointing toward where I had been headed. I stood very still and listened.

"You almost killed him, you asshole. How dare you touch my brother!" Mariano's voice had sunk to a loud, angry whisper. "I'm in the hospital right now."

I couldn't decide what to do—go back, and pretend I had just arrived, or stay and risk getting caught to find out who Mariano was talking with.

"Look, I don't want to hear your explanations," Mariano said. "My brother is in intensive care. If anything happens to him, I'm going to kill you. You'd better pray he makes it."

With this, Mariano slammed down the receiver.

It was too late to find a good place to hide. I heard Mariano's footsteps approach from around the corner. The corridor where I stood was deserted, save for two sofas on either side of the wall. I threw myself on the ground behind the nearest one. For once in my life I blessed the fact that I was vertically challenged. I was able to squeeze myself between the couch and the wall—squashed breasts, my nose full of dust balls, and all. I saw a pair of men's dark brown loafers topped by jeans pass by.

As soon as the footsteps were gone I sprang from my hiding place. By then a young, pretty black woman in a nurse's-aide uniform was passing by. She did a classic double take, and we stood there looking at each other.

"Contact lens," I said lamely.

She walked up to me and looked into my eyes. "Are you sure?" she asked. "It looks like it's in there."

"Oh." I rolled my eyeballs around like a maniac, as if testing her theory. The last thing I needed was hospital security asking me why I was lurking behind the furniture. I tried to look sheepish, which wasn't a challenge. "You're right. Thanks."

I watched the woman walk away, checking over her shoulder every few steps to see what I was up to. I turned the corner and pushed the ladies' room door so hard it banged loudly into the wall.

Inside, I tried to make myself look presentable. After working all the dust balls out of my hair I retied my braid and put on some lipstick. My cheeks hurt from my earlier pinching, so this time I painted them.

I was fairly confident that Mariano didn't know I was

there, but I didn't want to take chances. I peeked into the intensive-care waiting room and saw him with his mother and brother, then took the elevator down to the ground floor. There I stationed myself by an enormous planter near the elevators—hidden from sight, but with a clear view of anyone coming in or out. I prayed that Mariano would come down soon, so I wouldn't have to spend the rest of my day with an underwatered palm tree.

Three o'clock. I watched the Mercy Hospital day shift go off duty, and the afternoon shift come on. I hoped I wouldn't be around for the night shift as well. But I had a feeling Mariano wasn't the type who would hang around a hospital, especially if he had unfinished business.

I went outside for a while and came back in. When it was close to six I called Leonardo and told him to phone Mercy Hospital to find out Alonso's condition. I could have gone back to the front desk, but then one of the Arangos might have come downstairs and seen me.

Leonardo called back five minutes later to say that Alonso was in critical condition but he was improving. He was expected to be moved out of the ICU in a few hours, when his condition would be changed to guarded. It wasn't the best news I'd ever heard, but it came close. When I held Alonso in that boat, it had seemed entirely possible that he would die from his injuries.

About twenty minutes later a security guard came around the planter. He was young, with deep-set eyes, and he looked serious.

"Is there anything wrong?" I asked. I tried to summon up a look of vacant shock. Sympathy was my only hope.

"Well, I didn't know anyone was back here," the guard said. "Then I heard you talking on that portable phone."

"I'm so sorry. I wasn't trying to hide," I lied. I shot out my lower lip. "It's just that . . . well, my husband—"

"I'm sorry to hear that," the guard said. My ploy worked; I could tell that the last thing he wanted to hear was whatever god-awful story I seemed ready to tell him. "It's just that, well, I don't have an outside line in my security booth, and I was supposed to tell my girlfriend if I had to work late.''

He eyed my purse, where I had just put my phone; I took it out and handed it to him. I hoped Leonardo would forgive me for yet another expensive cellular call.

The security guard punched in a local number; I sighed with relief. ''Janie?'' he said after waiting a few seconds. ''It's me. I just wanted to tell you I'm working a few hours late. I know, I know . . .''

At least he had joined me behind the planter. If Mariano came out then, he wouldn't see us. I tapped my foot on the floor, wishing this kid would get off my phone. ''I know we were supposed to have dinner with Ken and Nina. It's not like I *want* to work late.''

He was lying, I could tell; this Ken and Nina must have been a barrel of laughs. I kept an eye on the elevator doors while he talked. Naturally, they parted and Mariano stepped through.

''I *do* like your friends,'' the guard whined. Mariano was walking fast, as though he was angry. He passed the front desk and headed for the doors.

''We'll have them over for pizza later,'' the guard said. I grabbed the phone out of his hand. Mariano stepped outside. ''Janie, he'll call you later,'' I said into the phone.

I threw the phone into my purse and made for the doors before the guard could react to what I had just done.

In the parking lot I saw Mariano just as he climbed into his Explorer. My Mercedes, luckily, was parked in another row, so I was able to move low and head toward it without him seeing me. When I got closer I heard him gun his engine and pull out of his spot.

I jumped into the car as he raced through the lot toward the parking attendant's booth. By the time I had it started he was one car away from the front of the line. I found my ticket on the dashboard and snatched a five out of my purse.

The wood gate rose for Mariano and he drove through. I gunned my engine and made for the booth, cutting off a Honda. With horns blaring behind me, I gave the attendant the ticket and my five, and told him to keep the change. The gate opened instantly.

Mariano was just pulling into traffic when I got to the street. He changed lanes and sped off. It looked as though he was one of those speed demons who break every law in the book in order to reach their destination a few seconds earlier. I was very familiar with this type of inconsiderate driver, being one myself. They're a bitch to tail.

Thankfully, there was a lot of traffic, and Mariano wasn't able to drive very fast. Our stretch of the road turned single-lane in our direction, so I was able to relax and keep him in sight.

I shouldn't have relaxed. Mariano suddenly turned right onto Twenty-seventh Avenue and hit the accelerator. Soon he was weaving in and out of the slower cars. I cursed, because I realized that he was heading for U.S. 1. The only factor in my favor at that point was that night had begun to fall. It would make it harder for him to spot me.

Mariano was only a marginally better driver than his older brother Alonso. I worried about getting pulled over, because to keep up with him I had to pull all sorts of idiot maneuvers. I gave up on keeping two cars between us and settled for one—and sometimes not even that. If I drove cautiously, I would lose him.

I hoped he was so angry and intent on his driving that he wouldn't notice that the same set of headlights had been in his mirror for the last five miles. But I knew from experience that people don't tend to worry about having an expensive car behind them—it's the old, battered junkers that give them pause.

This was all too much for me; my jaw hurt from gnashing my teeth. We zoomed south, past Coconut Grove. Coral Gables went by in a blur. We had just entered South Miami when I saw that Mariano was signaling for a left turn onto Red Road.

I couldn't afford to pull up right behind him at the light, so I turned left one street before him. I drove one short block and made a sharp right, arriving at the corner of Red Road just in time to see him speeding by. Perfect. Two blocks later, Mariano pulled over to park the Explorer.

I was in no real hurry to follow him. I knew exactly where he was headed. I made a wide U-turn and parked in the lot across the street.

I sat in the Mercedes for a while, just watching the activity on the street. This was early-evening traffic—couples going to movies at the multiplex on the corner, a few shopkeepers closing for the day, Rollerbladers and joggers, a few patrons heading for the bookstore across the street.

I waited until Mariano disappeared up the staircase of the building before I crossed Red Road. In the lobby I checked the registry of tenants, running my finger down the column until I found the name I was looking for.

Fernando Godoy. Suite 212. I laughed out loud. This place was such a low-rent operation that "suite" sounded ridiculously grand.

The outer door wasn't locked. From across the street I had seen quite a few lights still burning on the second and third floors, so I knew the office building stayed open late. The doors probably weren't locked until eight or nine.

I went upstairs and tiptoed down the hall until I was standing in front of door 212. I couldn't hear anything inside—which wasn't surprising, since the door was made of heavy wood. I put my ear to it and heard only my heart, beating fast. Soon I heard another sound—footsteps behind me. I turned in time to see Rodrigo Vidal heading my way.

"Lupe! What are you doing here?" Rodrigo shouted to me, his voice echoing in the carpetless hall.

"Rodrigo, nice to see you. How are you? You're looking great." Who was I going to fool? I was crouching outside Fernando Godoy's office at seven o'clock at night.

"What are you doing?" Rodrigo repeated.

The contact lens story wasn't going to fly here, and none of the windows were decorated. I smiled stupidly, wishing I could disappear without having to answer.

At that moment Godoy's office door swung open and Mariano Arango appeared. He was followed by Tom Slattery, with a third man bringing up the rear—Fernando Godoy, Esq., I presumed. I hadn't seen Slattery in years, and unlike fine wine, he didn't improve with age. He was bigger, fatter, greasier, and meaner-looking than ever.

"Well, well," Godoy exclaimed in a deep voice. "If it isn't our own little Cuban Nancy Drew!"

I hated him on sight, and I didn't even dignify him by replying. I turned to leave.

"Actually, I've been meaning to speak with you," Godoy said. "Won't you come in?"

Without waiting for an answer, he nodded to Slattery, who grabbed my arm and pulled me into the office. I barely had time to look over the reception area before I was unceremoniously shoved into an inner office. Godoy indicated that I was to be seated in the chair across from his desk, and whispered something to Slattery.

The big oaf left the room. Mariano and Rodrigo positioned themselves in chairs on either side of mine. I was the ham in their sandwich.

I stayed quiet for the moment. I heard the office door open behind me, and heard Slattery's heavy footsteps. I didn't think much of them until a sweaty hand reached around from behind me and shoved a handkerchief into my face.

The fabric smelled sweet and sticky. My last thought was that I knew this odor—from dental work a few years past. I prayed that what happened to me next wouldn't be as painful.

THIRTY-EIGHT

I HAD NO idea how much time had passed before I woke up. I was on my side on a cold concrete floor, and I felt a bit bruised, but I was basically unhurt. This is not to say that I was comfortable. I had a foul taste in my mouth, as well as a smelly cloth, and my hands and feet were tied behind my back with some kind of rope. And I couldn't see a thing. There was a handkerchief tied around my eyes. I held my breath and listened for sounds. I was alone, and too miserable to be scared.

I lay there quietly and tried to remember what had happened to me. My last memory was of having a cloth pressed over my nose in Godoy's office. Now I had the mother of all headaches. Thinking too hard about anything only caused me more pain.

The ropes denied me much movement, and when I tried to move they cut hard into my skin. I was able to wiggle my fingers, so I did, to keep the blood circulating to my hands.

This was beyond deep shit. No one knew where I was, except of course for the fine gentlemen who had put me there—Mariano Arango, Fernando Godoy, Rodrigo Vidal, and Tom Slattery. I saw their faces in my mind like a twisted Mount Rushmore.

I had walked into the hallway just minutes after Mariano, I remembered. He had been angry going over there, mad about the beating someone had given Alonso. But he didn't look very angry when I saw him. Of course, I wasn't seeing a lot of detail then. I was preoccupied with saving myself.

Which I didn't do, seeing as I was tied up and blindfolded and at their mercy. There was no point in cursing my own stupidity for being so foolhardy as to have exposed myself to such risk, so I allowed myself to feel sorry for myself for a while instead. I couldn't do it for long, though. I realized that I had to free myself, wherever I was.

First I had to remove the handkerchief from my eyes, so that I could at least look around. I rubbed my head backward and forward on the concrete a few times, which didn't accomplish much besides removing a few layers of skin, causing extreme pain. I could feel that the handkerchief was knotted at the back of my head, so I concentrated on trying to move it in a circle to dislodge it.

As I worked, I had to bite down hard on the gag in my mouth to stifle my sobs of pain—my hair was caught in the knot, and it was being pulled from my scalp. I quickly established a routine: circle left to right five times, then take a break.

After a half-dozen tries I felt the knot slip a bit. Encouraged, I worked harder. Slowly, painfully, I was able to move the handkerchief down on my face enough to peer over it. After a few more tugs it was completely off my face and hanging down my neck. It took me a few moments before I could open my eyes completely; they had been sealed shut for so long—but I didn't mind. Any progress at all gave me hope that I might live through the day. Or night, whichever was the case.

My eyes gradually adjusted, and there wasn't much to see. The only light source was a little sliver of illumination under what I took to be a door. After a few minutes I could see a little better.

I was in a small room, and there was something familiar about it. I rolled over and over on the concrete until I had touched three walls. The room was about five feet wide, and long. I lay on my back and looked down at my black T-shirt. In the dim light, I saw that it was covered in light-colored dust.

When I realized what this meant I inhaled sharply, which sent the gag farther down my throat. I quickly decided that the gag was next to go, so—even though I knew this would hurt—I repeated the circular, grinding motion I had used to remove my blindfold. Tears of pain ran down my face, and I knew I was rubbing my skin completely raw. But in time the gag came off.

I blew the disgusting rag out of my mouth. Even though my hands and feet were still tied, I felt as though I was home free—especially because I now knew where I was being held. The light dust on my shirt was the same substance I had seen on my shoes the night Bridget O'Leary and I had paid a nocturnal visit to Optima Jewelers.

Now I had to remember precisely where I would find the passageway out. With my hands tied I couldn't feel the wall to tell where I was, so I would have to guess. I closed my eyes and tried to visualize the architectural plans I had pulled from Building and Planning. I couldn't afford to screw up. As far as I knew, the men could return for me at any time.

I was as ready as I would ever be, so I positioned myself on the floor in what I thought would be the right spot. I flipped over all the way onto my back, pulled my legs to my chest as far as they would go, and kicked out as hard as I could.

The impact ran a shock all the way to my aching head, and I cried out in pain. I opened my eyes to see what had happened. Not much. The wood was barely dented. It would probably take another dozen or so kicks before it would give way. I didn't get discouraged or give in to the pain—because I guessed I was in for worse than this if I didn't get out. After countless kicks the wooden board splintered. I was gasping so hard, and kicking so blindly, that I barely noticed when it happened.

I lay quietly to see if anyone had heard and was coming to get me. I heard nothing, so I rolled over on my side and looked around on the floor. I pinpointed the sharpest, most jagged piece of wood I could find, and nudged it in front of my feet. I kicked off my sandals and picked up the wood with my toes.

"Deep breaths," I whispered. The air was still and hot, and I had to keep from hyperventilating. I arched my back as far as it would go, until my hands and feet were touching, and started sawing through the rope with the wood.

I thought what I had done before had hurt, but I was wrong. It was nothing compared to this. Every now and then I missed, and cut my hands instead of the rope. They felt sopping wet, and I prayed the moisture was sweat and not blood. It was almost a blessing that the closet was so dark. I knew I would have freaked out if I saw the condition of my hands.

It became harder to breathe. The wood kept slipping from my toes—because it was so wet, it was almost impossible to keep hold of it. I wished I could have used my hands to help, but the angle at which I needed to hold the wood so that it would be effective made it impossible. I tried not to let frustration overcome me. My clothes were completely soaked through with sweat. I prayed to the Virgin to keep me going.

I was running on automatic when the rope finally started to give, but it was too dark for me to see how deeply I had cut into it. Biting my lip to keep from screaming, I finally cut through it. The final strands slipped away, lubricated by my wet hands.

I bent over to untie the ropes on my feet and fumbled through stiff fingers and the wetness. I stood up for the first time in hours, for once in my life thankful that I barely cleared five feet in height, groaning loudly as my muscles protested. I stretched as best I could, because I knew by then that I would probably have to crawl to get out. I didn't dare open the door into Optima. For all I knew, the men were inside the jewelry store at that very moment.

I made the sign of the cross, thanked the Virgin, and got down on my hands and knees. I was weaker than I thought. I simply couldn't remember how far I had to go before I reached the farthest entrance out of the passageway. It was so dark and smelly that I was tempted to take the nearest way out, but I suspected I would set off alarms if I entered any of the other stores. I sure as hell didn't need the ever-vigilant Coral Gables police questioning me on a possible B&E charge. Besides, the more distance I put between me and Optima, I figured, the better were my chances of staying alive.

I tried to move a little faster, but there was so little air in the passageway that I started to feel dangerously dizzy. My bones ached, my skin was raw, and I was perspiring so hard the sweat blurred my eyes. I could have crouched and walked semierect instead of crawling, but staying low to the floor seemed safest in my condition. I worried about falling and hitting my head on the concrete.

By the time I reached the far end of the passageway, I was hallucinating stars and colors. I felt for the door, pushed it open with my last bit of strength, and emerged gasping for air in the cool, bright moonlit night.

My first attempt to stand was a dismal failure. When I finally made it to an upright position, I leaned against the wall of the building, shaking, my teeth chattering. I walked blindly until I spotted a phone booth across the street, and staggered over to it, trying to look around to see if anyone had noticed me. I saw the clock on the Coral Gables City Hall tower: 3:20 in the morning. No wonder no one was on the street.

I closed myself in the telephone booth, thinking irrationally that this would help me if Slattery or Godoy found me. I picked up the receiver and pressed ''O'' for the operator.

I saw myself reflected in the mirror of the store window right outside the booth. My legs gave way when I saw what I looked like. As I slid to the floor I told the operator I wanted to make a collect call.

''Tommy?''

"Lupe? Is that you?"

"Can you come get me?"

Tommy told me later that he'd found me curled up on the phone booth floor, passed out, smelling like an open sewer, half naked, barefoot, covered in blood, with the receiver dangling over my head.

THIRTY-NINE

"LUPE, YOU HAVE to go to the police with this," Tommy said. "Don't be stubborn."

He tried to force another spoonful of chicken soup on me, but I resisted. I was capable of feeding myself. I didn't feel like an invalid, I just needed some time to recuperate.

"Kidnapping and attempted murder," he went on. "You can put them away for years. All of them."

I knew Tommy was angry with himself for letting me talk him into taking me to his condominium the night before, instead of to the hospital. I didn't remember much, but he told me that I had almost gone into hysterics when he mentioned the emergency room. Finally he took me to his place and hauled me into the elevator at four in the morning, thanking his luck that there was no one around to ask questions.

I had been in such bad shape that he marched me straight to the shower, peeled off what was left of my clothes, and held me under the water. He said my skin was so raw he was afraid to use soap. When he offered me water I drank four glasses in succession. He finally let me collapse in his guest bedroom, and when he was sure I was resting and out of possible danger, he went to his office. I had assured him that all I needed was rest—and a lot of it. I had slept straight into late afternoon.

"Tell me the truth," I said as Tommy took the soup away from the table. "How do I look?" Twelve hours of sleep, followed by a long soak in a hot bubble bath, had done wonders for me.

"You look like a different person, that's for sure. It's those Cuban genes. I'm the one who looks like shit. I think you scared five years off my life last night."

"Thanks for getting my car out of the parking lot," I said. "I'm lucky no one broke into it and stole my purse from the glove compartment."

"It's a miracle the car was there at all," Tommy said.

He gave me my handbag; I pulled out my emergency cosmetics and a mirror. Not too bad, nothing some concealer couldn't handle. I didn't want to worry Tommy by asking him if he had checked under the passenger seat for my Beretta.

"On my way to work this morning I called Leonardo to tell him you wouldn't be in today," Tommy said. "I told him we were spending the day together. I didn't want him sending a search party after you."

"Oh, Tommy, what would I do without you?" I found myself gushing, and I reached out to hug him. Just stretching my arms that much hurt like hell.

"Seriously, Lupe, you have to go to the cops," Tommy said. "These are big-time felonies we're talking about."

I started to say something but Tommy put a finger over my lips. "Listen, these guys know by now that you got away. They're going to come after you. If you don't talk to the cops, I will. I mean it."

"No, no, not yet," I begged. "Tommy, I'm so close to finishing this case. There are just a couple of things left to do. I need a little time, and it's all over."

"What the hell else is there to do?" Tommy asked. "You got a confession from Silvia Romero. You know that

Mariano is up to his ass in all this. Let the cops sort it out. Your involvement in this case is finished.''

Tommy sat heavily on the bed. Arguing with me always was too much for him. "This case is nuts," he moaned. "You work to save the client, and you do—by finding information he was hiding from us."

"I know," I said. "Am I still going to get paid?"

"Good question," Tommy said, very seriously. "You'll get paid. I'll make sure of it. You're too damned good, Lupe. You don't give up—that's what makes you the best in town."

"Thanks for the compliment," I said. "You can mail the check directly to my office."

Tommy didn't even notice that I was kidding around. He never joked about money. "Lupe, this goes against my better judgment." He sighed. "But how much time do you need to wrap all this up?"

What a prince. I knew I would wear him down. "Thirty-six hours," I said. Actually, I only needed a day, but I knew what his answer would be.

"Twenty-four," he replied. "And that's final. And I'm through compromising. I could get in serious trouble with the bar over this."

This didn't make much of an impression on me. Tommy was always in trouble with the Florida bar. "Listen, I hate to ask this," I said, "but do you have any clothes I can wear out of here? You saw what shape mine are in."

"I put them in a bag, in case we need them for evidence later," he said. "I'll let you borrow something—if you promise not to make any snide comments."

Tommy and I walked over to his big guest closet and opened the double doors. I was stunned at what I saw. The entire rack was full of women's dresses, skirts, and pants, in a variety of colors and sizes. A promise was a promise, so I kept silent as I looked through them. I knew that Tommy was no monk, but this was ridiculous. I chose a dark green shirtwaist dress. I made a mental note to ask him after the case if I could keep it.

"Listen, Lupe, I'm willing to grant you an extension before going to the police," Tommy said, closing the closet. "But I have to insist you spend the night here. You're still in no shape to drive."

"Fair enough," I agreed. I was relieved. I felt a little better, but I was still tired and sore. And my apartment might not have been safe.

Tommy went to his own room, and returned with an oversized T-shirt for me to sleep in. "You're a classy guy, Tommy," I said, and kissed him on the cheek. Tommy reminded me where the food was, if I wanted a snack, then left me alone. I crawled into the bed, relishing the feel of cool clean sheets against my skin.

I had one more thing to do, however, before I drifted off. When I heard Tommy head down the hall, I picked up the phone and called my home number. I punched in the code that let me hear my messages.

I had nine messages on the machine. Two were from my sisters, wondering why I hadn't checked in with them over the last twenty-four hours—Cuban family stuff. One was from Leonardo, who sounded annoyed because he had paged me and I hadn't answered. Five were from telemarketers, including a really good deal on a prepaid cemetery plot; the salesman must have been new or desperate, because they never leave messages, only say that they wish to speak with Ms. Solano and they'll call back—never giving their names or numbers for me to return their call. They all have the same technique. I finally got to the last one; it was from Charlie Miliken.

"Lupe, I have some information on that matter we discussed," he said. "Give me a call at home."

I hung up and immediately punched in Charlie's home number. It was a little hard to remember it, since I had kept him on speed-dial for so long.

"Charlie?"

"Lupe, where the hell have you been?" Charlie growled. "I beeped you about a dozen times!"

"So sorry," I said. I would tell him later that I hadn't exactly been waiting by my pager all day. "You left a message for me?"

"This could cost me a great deal, both personally and professionally, you know," he began pompously. I hated it when he got that way. "But I got some information on your cleaning lady—Reina Sotolongo."

"What did you get?" I asked eagerly.

"Aurora is definitely going to tie it in with the Gustavo Gaston murder," he said.

"The breaking-and-entering theory is officially off?" I knew it would be.

"Apparently the lab came back with some information that made Aurora reconsider," he said. "Turned out that traces of a white powder were found in Sotolongo's lungs. She wants to look into it further."

Mierda. That meant I had the same junk in my own lungs. I'd certainly spent enough time in that same closet. "What else?" I asked.

"That's all you can say?" Charlie asked bitterly. "I put my ass on the line for you, and this is the thanks I get?"

I thanked him profusely for a while. It must have worked, because he kept talking. "Aurora's after everyone on this," he said. "She has the whole crew working overtime—the investigating officers, the crime scene guys, the lab guys, the prints guys. She's really making an ass of herself, because she's convinced there's a conspiracy going on involving all the Arangos. And she's after your blood on this one, Lupe. I don't know how your investigation's going, but don't fuck up. She wants to get you for obstructing her investigation."

"I know," I sighed. "Damn, it's been years since I made her look like a jerk, and she still wants to make me pay. She has a long memory, that one."

Charlie laughed. Some part of him loved it when people were at each other's throats. It didn't matter who they were. "Here's some good gossip," he said, his mood vastly improved. "Rumor has it that she carried around the beeper number for the sign painter at the Justice Building. She wants to reach him at a moment's notice so she can change the sign on her door to read 'Division Chief.' "

"She's a classic," I agreed. "Thanks again, Charlie. You

know how much I appreciate you.'' I blew a kiss into the phone and hung up.

Before I went to sleep—or more accurately, passed out— I called up Mercy Hospital. After being transferred around for a while I reached the information desk, where I found out that Alonso junior had been moved to a private room, and that his condition was steadily improving. I was happy to hear that. I had lots of questions to ask him.

It gave me something nice to think about while I drifted off. And I had the relief of knowing that tomorrow would be my last day on the Arango case—one way or another.

FORTY

———◆———

I SLIPPED OUT of Tommy's apartment just as the sun was coming up. It had been a long time since I'd gone to work at that hour, but I wanted to take advantage of every moment that Tommy had granted me. I was very clear in my understanding of what I had to do.

The Mercedes was parked in Tommy's guest spot, next to his Rolls-Royce, in the underground garage. I hopped in and ran my hand under the passenger seat. The cold steel of the Beretta felt like an old friend. I had never used it, and didn't intend to, but it gave me security.

I adjusted my seat belt for minimum wrinkling of the green shirtwaist and set off. Traffic was light into the Grove. My first stop was at the office, for coffee. Tommy had only American coffee at his place, and I couldn't start an important day with that watered-down stuff.

For once I was happy that Leonardo never set foot in Solano Investigations before the civilized hour of nine-thirty, because I wouldn't have to waste time answering his questions. I parked the Mercedes in my spot and walked into the office. No one was around. Every familiar step calmed my jangled nerves.

I stopped briefly at Leonardo's desk to check the mail before heading for the kitchen, ignoring the blinking light on the answering machine. In the kitchen I pulled out the espresso machine with the eight-cup capacity, and filled it to the brim. Leonardo is not a gourmand and neither am I, but when we renovated the cottage we insisted on a good kitchen—me because I love to eat, and Leonardo so he could refuel after his workouts. I took some whole milk from the refrigerator—making Cuban coffee with any other milk is a sin—and poured some into a saucepan and set it to simmer.

I walked into my office, settled into my chair, and looked out the window. I tipped the chair back as far as it would go and looked at the avocado tree branches, trying to spot the parrot family's nest. The parrots tended to be most active in the early morning. I couldn't see anything, so I got out my binoculars.

Success! I counted at least a dozen bright, jewel-green birds in the upper branches. It was reassuring that they hadn't abandoned the place. I figured that they hadn't gotten a good look at Tom Slattery lurking outside a couple of weeks ago. His face was enough to scare away anything.

I pulled out the Arango file and rummaged through it, because I needed to make some calls before I set out. I found what I was looking for, reached for the phone, and punched a few numbers.

Five minutes later a delicious coffee aroma drifted into my office, and I sprinted into the kitchen just in time to see the thick, dark liquid bubbling out of the espresso machine. I poured a hefty serving into my white china mug, topped it with frothy milk, and stirred in three spoonfuls of sugar.

It was so good I didn't even mind my burned tongue. I took the cup into my office, where I opened the wall safe and found the spare nine-millimeter clips for the Beretta. I checked to make sure there were enough bullets, and put it in my purse with the loaded gun. It never hurts to be prepared.

After coffee, I decided to pass on the hard Cuban bread in the kitchen and get started with my day. I stopped only to leave a cryptic note for Leonardo, saying that I wasn't returning until I was finished with the Arango case. I had no idea what he would make of that. Hell, I wasn't positive what I meant myself. I reset the alarm and walked to the Mercedes, one hand in my purse in case anyone was waiting for me in the parking lot.

I drove south, and made it to Best Plants, Mariano's nursery, in twenty minutes. It was eight now, but the heavy traffic was moving north. I circled the place, hoping to spot Mariano's car in the parking lot. I had called the nursery from my office and Mariano had answered. I had immediately hung up.

Mariano's black Explorer wasn't around, but on my second pass of the property I saw a dark blue Chevy parked in the northern corner of the parking lot, next to a tall mound of black dirt. I slowed down, trying to remember where I had seen the car before. I stopped and closed my eyes for a few seconds and tried to visualize it in another context—a mind trick I learned from a veteran investigator at White and Blanco.

Then I remembered. I grabbed the Arango file from the passenger seat and flipped through it to the section containing Marisol's notes. There it was. It was Tom Slattery's car, the one Nestor had spotted outside Solano Investigations weeks ago.

I kept on driving, to be as inconspicuous as possible, all the while looking around the lot for movement. Satisfied that I was alone on the property, I pulled the Mercedes next to a big oak tree with a thick trunk. It wasn't perfect camouflage, but it was the best around.

I heard my heart pounding in my ears when I turned off the car, reached into my purse, and pulled out the Beretta. This time I wouldn't be caught unprepared. Remembering what these men did to me filled me with such rage that I realized I was willing to pull the trigger. Before I stepped out I touched the religious medals that Lourdes had pinned to my brassiere and insisted I always wear, my eyes turned heavenward to catch the Virgin's attention—I knew I had her working overtime. I got out of my car and walked toward the Chevy, slowly, looking all around me. There was no one in sight.

The car was unlocked. I saw now that the pile of black dirt beside it was labeled "Dangerous Chemicals," complete with a skull and crossbones. I put my hand on the car hood, which was cool to the touch. The Chevy had been parked there for at least a couple of hours.

The smell from the dirt pile was incredibly nauseating, like rotten eggs, with something even worse mixed in. The wind shifted over the abandoned car, and I had a very strange feeling.

I opened the Chevy's driver's-side door and looked in, hoping to find some kind of clue—not that I wanted to meet Tom Slattery face-to-face again, but it was unimaginable for an investigator to leave his car unlocked in an open area like this. The car was completely clean, which was weird. Most private investigators spend so much time in their cars that their vehicles look like second offices. I sat in the car and sniffed the air. It smelled nastier toward the back of the car.

I got out of the car and walked around it. No doubt about it—the stench in the back was almost unbearable. I had to fight the urge to vomit, at the same time as I felt a knot in my guts. I knew I had to open the trunk, and I didn't want to.

I jogged back to the Mercedes, opened the glove compartment, took out my tool kit, and found the slim tool designed for breaking into cars. Back at Slattery's Chevy I walked right up to the trunk, not allowing myself time to lose my nerve.

When I popped it I was hit by an overpowering smell that made me jump back a couple of feet. At first all I could see was dirt in the trunk, the same dirt mounded next to the car. When I looked closer, I saw there were also two people in there.

I looked around for something to brush off the toxic soil, so I could identify the bodies without touching anything.

The dirt must have contained an acid, or some strong corrosive element, because the bodies were already in poor shape. I ran to the oak tree, grabbed a lower branch, and swung on it until it gave way. This made my arms hurt like hell, but it worked.

Standing before the mess in the trunk, I held my breath and used the branch to clear away some of the dirt. It was Tom Slattery and Fernando Godoy. I couldn't tell what had killed them, because of the chemical eating away at them. But they were certainly dead. Now that I knew who they were I felt horrified; they had acted like animals toward me, but this wasn't the sort of ending anyone deserved.

Walking slowly, I got back in the Mercedes and drove away. When I put a few blocks between myself and Best Plants I spotted a pay phone, pulled over, and called the police. Without identifying myself, I told them about the bodies. I figured that if my prints were found on Slattery's car I could explain it away somehow. And Tommy surely could get me out of any mess—after all, I had done my civic duty and reported the crime.

Two down, one to go, I thought. I dialed Isabel Arango at home, and hung up when she answered. It was just a few minutes before nine, and I drove north now, toward Coral Gables. The coffee I had drunk earlier made a valiant attempt to come back up my throat. I was glad I hadn't eaten that half-stale bread as well.

The trip to Isabel's house took longer than I would have liked, because I had to fight commuter traffic. I was almost glad for the distraction—otherwise, I would have to think about what I had seen in the Chevy. When I neared the Arango house I parked a block away. There was no need to announce my arrival.

I walked fast toward the house, ducking behind bushes, and approached the place from the side. I looked for Mariano's black Explorer, but saw only Isabel's burgundy Jaguar. I stood there trying to decide what to do next. I intended to confront Mariano—my anger was propelling me forward, with the Beretta in my purse giving me courage. I was tired of being jerked around. I wanted this over. Then I heard footsteps behind me. I cursed myself for letting the same thing happen twice.

"Lupe? What in the world are you doing here?" Isabel Arango said. She was still in her bathrobe, clutching a batch of pink roses in one hand and gardening shears in the other. I almost fainted with relief. At least it wasn't Mariano.

"Come inside the house," she said. "I'll get dressed."

"I came to see Mariano actually," I said as we walked toward the house. "I figured he might be here with you."

"He's not here," Isabel said. "I haven't seen him since yesterday, when we were at the hospital. I want to thank you for finding my son and getting him medical attention."

We walked into the house together, and she told me to wait in the living room. From the way she acted, it was as though this was just another average day in the Arango household. But I already knew never to take Isabel at face value. She was a world-class liar.

I sat in the rickety gilt chair I had occupied while interviewing her sons at the beginning of the case. I wished the maid would show up and offer me a glass of water—I tasted bile in the back of my throat—but there wasn't anyone around.

Isabel finally emerged in yet another beautiful Escada suit, a light pink two-piece with white buttons. I was impressed with her ability to pull together such a good look in just a few minutes. She sat in the rickety chair across from mine.

"Now, tell me, Lupe," she said, her eyes friendly. "Why were you looking for Mariano?"

I took a deep breath, trying to keep in mind that this woman had lied to me, and that I had no idea what she might have really been up to. "Because I think he's responsible for three deaths and two attempted murders," I said, all my senses alert. The situation was unpredictable; I knew how horrible this accusation was.

"What are you talking about?" Either she was sincere, or it was Oscar time. Isabel's expression went from serenity to anger. She shifted her weight to the edge of her chair, ready to pounce at a moment's notice. I cautioned myself that I was dealing with a mother defending her child. I had to be very, very careful.

"Let's start with Reina Sotolongo." I held up my index finger and started counting from there. "Then the lawyer Fernando Godoy, then a private investigator named Tom Slattery. Then the attempted murders: myself, and Alonso junior—your son and his brother."

I focused all my attention on Isabel's eyes. I wanted to be able to anticipate her attack, if there was going to be one.

"You're out of your mind!" Isabel stood up with a lightning crack of fury. "I won't listen to this! I don't know why that lawyer McDonald hired you in the first place, but I'm firing you as of this instant!"

I hadn't moved. "Let's talk about Reina Sotolongo. He killed her because of what she knew about—"

"Shut up!" a man's voice called out loudly behind me, sending a chill down my body. I turned to see Mariano walk into the room, a big .357 Magnum cannon pointed at me. I had been so focused on Isabel that I hadn't heard a thing.

"Mariano, no!" Isabel's eyes grew wide. She stood up, tall and ramrod-straight, and held out her hand. "Give me that gun. This is no way to resolve this."

I kept my eyes on Mariano. He was going to shoot me, and soon. I prayed that his mother had enough influence over him to make him stop. The gun's safety was off, and his finger trembled on the trigger. It was as though the world was switched over to slow motion. Suddenly a telephone started ringing. I recognized it as my portable, buried somewhere deep in the Chanel bag at my feet.

"That's my phone," I announced, trying to keep my voice steady. "I have to answer it, or they'll know something is wrong at my office. I said I was coming here. I have to answer it. I always answer it."

I was babbling, but it was my only hope. Mariano moved closer to me, waving his mother back. The phone kept ringing. The tension was unbearable; I felt my blood, poker-hot, pounding in my ears.

"Answer it," he said. "But don't say anything suspicious. Just answer it and then hang up."

Mariano was a few paces away; there was no way he would miss me if he shot. I pulled the purse to my lap and looked inside, as though I was searching for the phone. I grabbed the Beretta instead, aimed, and fired it straight through my bag. The recoil knocked me flat on the floor, but the bullet struck Mariano in the chest. He dropped the gun and looked at me with almost pitiful surprise.

Mariano hit the floor hard. I took the phone out of my purse and answered it, just to make it stop ringing.

"Lupe, how are you?" It was Leonardo. "I just got to the office and read your note."

I picked myself up off the floor and pulled myself back in the chair, the Beretta dangling in my hand. Sobbing, Isabel ran to her son. "Lupe, Lupe?" Leonardo said. "Are you all right?" He was screaming into the phone.

"Call Tommy," I said. "Tell him to come to Coral Gables, to the Arango house. Tell him that I shot Mariano Arango. And call nine-one-one. Get rescue over here, even though I think it's too late. Oh, and get the cops here too." My voice was quavering; I looked at Mariano's body on the floor, unable to comprehend that I had really shot him.

I switched off the power, leaving Leonardo in midsputter. Isabel knelt over her son, who lay on his side with his eyes open. An ever-widening pool of blood stained the carpet.

"He's gone. You killed him," she said, looking up at me with hate flashing in her eyes. "He's dead. And it's my fault. I'm responsible for it all."

She was icy calm, which sent fear through me. Mariano's gun was uncomfortably close to her on the floor.

Shooting during target practice in a shooting range hadn't prepared me for this. When I pulled the trigger on Mariano, it felt as though it was the first time I ever held a gun in my hand. The smell of gunpowder still hung in the air.

"You wanted to know about Reina Sotolongo," she said, stroking her son's hair as she might have when he was a baby. "Mariano did kill her. He did it to protect his father and me. He was not a killer, or a bad person. He just loved us."

The room was silent for a moment, and surreal. Isabel

looked up at me. "Reina was a snooping little bitch," she hissed. "She used to spy on all of us at the store. That's what she was doing that Saturday morning—spying on Alonso and Silvia. Damn it, I've known for years that my husband is having an affair. It doesn't bother me." She continued to stroke her son's hair with great tenderness.

"But Mariano didn't know, did he?" I asked.

"Mariano thinks his parents are perfect," Isabel moaned, looking into his vacant face. It was chilling. "He thinks we have an ideal marriage. All his life he's told us how happy it makes him that his parents get along and have stayed together."

I heard the first sirens; time was running out. I had to get information from Isabel. "What happened?" I asked.

Isabel contemplated her answer as if she had all the time in the world. "I might as well answer your question. You probably know most of this anyway." She took a deep breath and continued. "Reina saw what happened that Saturday morning. She told Mariano she had been there, hiding in the closet, and had witnessed everything that happened. She used to do that, you know—hide and spy on people. She told Mariano she saw the knife, and she took it during the confusion. A few days after Gustavo's death she called Mariano to blackmail him. She told him Alonso and Silvia were lovers, she told him about Gustavo and me. She wanted money to go away. And . . . and Mariano killed her to shut her up. He didn't want to believe his parents didn't have a perfect marriage. He wanted to protect us, but we already knew about each other's lovers!"

"You both knew?" I asked, my voice thick. I saw red and blue lights flash on the walls through the front windows. "Alonso knows about your affair with Gustavo Gaston?"

"Alonso's not stupid," she said. She kept stroking Mariano's hair, and I had to look away. "We had an arrangement. It was fine for the first few years, but it began to bother me that Alonso had a lover and I didn't. After he took up with Silvia, what was I going to do? But when I became close to Gustavo, Alonso could tell right away. It was about the same time he figured out that Gustavo was the father of Silvia's child, Alejandra.''

I sat there on the floor, my mind reeling. Isabel talked faster, as though she wanted to get it all out before anyone else came. I realized in that instant that she trusted me, or respected me, or something. It seemed important that she tell this to me first.

"I've known Gustavo all my life," she said, looking out the window. "His family and mine were neighbors in Havana. I was friends with his sister, Alicia, and he was the baby. I was so surprised again when I saw him at Key West. I couldn't believe he made it here. For a while we saw each other, just as friends. But then . . . you know."

The cops and the rescue squad arrived at the same time. I watched as the paramedics tried to resuscitate Mariano, but he was beyond help. As they lifted him from the floor on a stretcher I had a chance to see the tattoo on his left biceps. It was a heart with Isabel's name written in calligraphy in the middle. I watched them cover him with a sheet, and looked into his eyes one last time. He looked young, and innocent, and still surprised. My vision blurred with tears.

I told the cops that my lawyer was on the way, and that I would give them a statement when he was with me. They didn't trouble me too much after Isabel patiently explained that her son had pointed a gun—which still lay on the floor—at me and seemed ready to shoot. I showed my permit for the Beretta, and my investigator's license. Isabel acted as though nothing much was the matter, and calmly, repeatedly told the police that I was only defending myself.

Through the window I saw Tommy's Rolls pull up. He ran up to the house with his hair flying wild, pulling on his suit jacket as he leapt over a flower bed. He rang the bell, and by the time the door was opened he had rearranged himself, looking calm and composed.

Sure enough, he had me out of there within the hour. Isabel left for some other part of the house, looking back at me with a strange mixture of shame and relief. I knew from my experience with Margarita that it would take time for

her shock to wear off, before she really felt her loss. I tried
to convey in that brief glance that I was sorry I had shot
her son. I knew my own shock had yet to wear off.

Tommy guided me out the front door after I handed over
my Beretta; I watched the cops put it into a plastic bag and
seal it away for evidence. I told Tommy I was too shaken
up to drive. All I could think about was the fact that shooting a man was so different from shooting a target at a firing
range.

Driving away in the Rolls, we passed the Mercedes
parked a block away. "I'll send someone over later to pick
up your car for you," he said. I thanked him—it seemed he
was taking care of me a lot lately.

"So what the hell happened in there?" he asked.

"Tommy, it was just like I told the police."

"No, I'm not talking about that." He pulled out into
traffic, suddenly looking irritated. "I'm talking about the
case. I'm asking you both as your employer and your lawyer."

"The bottom line, Tommy, is that there was so much
deception in that family that it got their son killed, another
in the hospital, and the father in jail," I said. "And it was
all over appearances."

Tommy frowned. "You lost me. Explain."

"Silvia Romero killed Gustavo Gaston, the father of her
child, to spare Alonso senior from learning that Gustavo was
having an affair with Isabel." I paused. "Fine. But Silvia
didn't realize that Alonso already knew about the affair.
Mariano Arango killed Reina Sotolongo to protect his
mother from learning about Alonso's affair with Silvia. It
was all so pointless. His mother knew about it all along.
And he was ready to kill me to protect his mother from
finding out."

"And this business with Godoy and Slattery." Tommy
shuddered. "Godoy was a sleaze, but he didn't deserve
that."

I had told the police at Isabel's about the dead attorney
and investigator, saving them a lot of work. "It must have
all gone bad," I said. "Mariano was infuriated that his

brother Alonso had been beaten. It took him a day, but he got his revenge."

"What a soap opera," Tommy said. We stopped at a red light, and he shook his head. "I meet a lot of wackos in my line of work, but being willing to kill to protect someone from uncomfortable information—what, is this some kind of Cuban thing?"

I had no real answer for that one. I looked at my watch; not even noon yet. "Tommy, according to our deal, I still have six hours left to wrap all this up," I said.

"You're still holding me to that?" Tommy asked. "Haven't you done enough for one day?"

"I have some loose ends to tie up," I said, tossing in my most winning smile. "Can you drop me off at my office?"

Silence.

"Please?" Still no reply. My charms weren't working—oh well, there was a first time for everything. Just as I was about to give up I got an answer, not very gracefully volunteered.

"Sure, why not," Tommy growled, making an illegal U-turn to head back toward the Grove. "At this rate, you'll be paying me a retainer."

Tommy dropped me off in the driveway. Before he had pulled around the block Leonardo sprinted out of the office. He hugged me so tight I worried my ribs would crack.

"Are you all right? Are you hurt?" He showered my cheeks with kisses. "Can I do anything for you?"

"I'm fine, I'm fine. Don't worry." I led him into the cottage and sat down at his desk. "Look, don't be offended, but we can talk later. I have to make some calls right away."

"You should go home, Lupe," Leonardo said. "You've been through a terrible experience. Go home, rest, let Aida take care of you."

"Later, later," I said. I went into my office and looked up the number for Rodrigo's shoe shop. I ended up talking to one of the clerks, who said he was unavailable. "Find him," I said, "and tell him that Lupe Solano wants to meet

him within the hour at MMV Interiors. And that he'd
damned well better be there.''

I hung up and lay down on my sofa, closing my eyes.
My body still ached, so I got up and took some aspirins.
And I loaded the spare Beretta I kept in the safe, slipping
it into the Chanel bag that I had ruined with a gunshot hole.
Only in Miami, I thought, could I go through two guns in
one day.

I badgered Leonardo into loaning me his Jeep—and into
cutting out his demands that I go home—and drove north
to the design district. My hands were steady as I drove.
Rodrigo's Lexus was parked in front of his wife's office
building when I arrived. There's nothing like guilt to make
a man punctual.

Once out of the car, I dispensed with the formalities.
''Listen, you slime, you son of a bitch,'' I began.

Rodrigo threw his arms in the air. ''Lupe, it wasn't my
idea, I swear to you. I just went along with them because
they threatened me. Ask them, they'll tell you.''

''I would if I could,'' I said. ''But you're the only one
left alive. You're really fearless, you know, kidnapping a
five-foot-tall woman.''

Rodrigo's eyes widened with fear. It was the best I felt
all day. ''What do you mean, the only one alive?'' he asked.

''Your buddy, Mariano, killed Fernando and Slattery.''

''Godoy dead?'' Rodrigo said. ''And Slattery?''

''And Mariano.'' I wanted to hit him with it all at once;
his jaw dropped, and I went for the jugular. ''I shot him
about an hour ago.''

Rodrigo started backing away from me. Excellent. ''I
know how you got teamed up with Godoy, and Slattery,''
I said. ''But how did you get involved with Mariano?''

''I—It was very strange.'' I backed Rodrigo up to the
wall of MMV Interiors. He talked fast. ''After Margarita
died, a few days after the funeral—it was after I had lunch
with you at Versailles, I remember that, because my car got
towed to Homestead—I got a call from Mariano. He wanted
to meet with me.''

I could tell that Rodrigo was telling the truth.

"Did you know him?"

"No, no. I knew his family name. Margarita told me about doing his parents' house in Coral Gables. Anyway, I met him for coffee. He said he was sorry about Margarita's death, and that he had met her a few times when she was working on his parents' house. Then he said he had heard she was pregnant when she died."

"How did he know that?" I demanded. "It wasn't common knowledge at the time."

"I know. I was surprised." Rodrigo's shoulders slumped, and he watched my hands. "He said he found it out from his mother. Margarita's secretary, Leonora, called up Mariano's mother to tell her there were some fabric swatches left in the office. Since MMV was closing down, Leonora wanted to know if Mrs. Arango wanted them. Mariano said that Leonora started gossiping about Margarita."

I thought about Leonora—who was chatty to begin with—alone, depressed, closing up MMV. She probably called Isabel just to talk to someone, and ended up spilling secrets.

"Leonora let it slip that Margarita was pregnant," Rodrigo said. "And that I was filing a wrongful death suit against Dade County. Mariano then told me he felt an obligation to let me know that Margarita had been having an affair. He said he wanted to spare me the humiliation of having it come out in public that I might not be the father of her baby. He kept saying I had a 'high-profile' case, and that my life and Margarita's would be put under the public microscope."

Mariano was more of a shit than I had ever imagined. He was poison. I started to feel happy that I'd shot him. "He didn't seek you out just to be a good guy, did he?" I said.

Rodrigo shook his head and snorted. "Of course not! He said that for a percentage of the money I made from the lawsuit, he would make sure Margarita's lover didn't interfere."

"But you already knew the baby wasn't yours," I said. Rodrigo looked surprised for a second; then recognition played across his face. Margarita hadn't hidden everything from me.

"No, but I didn't know whose it was," Rodrigo said.

"So what did you think about all this?" I asked.

"Well, Mariano said he was having financial problems at the nursery," Rodrigo said. "But I think there was more to it. I could see it in the way he talked about Margarita—I think he loved her himself. And I think he was jealous of his own brother."

I didn't say anything. But I had to agree with Rodrigo, if only on this one little thing: the late Mariano Arango was a real piece of work.

"So you went along with this?" I asked.

"No, I told him I had to think about it for a while."

The next part didn't take much gray matter to figure out. "You went to your new best friend, Fernando Godoy, and told him about your visit from Mariano Arango."

"Lupe, you're a smart one." Rodrigo smiled at me; I was beyond disgusted with him.

"And Godoy told you he could find the lover without Mariano's help and without paying Mariano his percentage, but to keep all your bases covered you could keep Mariano strung along for a while. That's why he had Slattery follow me around—so that I would lead you to the lover."

I could see that I was right. "But why did Mariano's brother get beaten up?"

"He wasn't supposed to," Rodrigo said eagerly. "Slattery took it upon himself to rough Alonso junior up in case Alonso decided that he would come forward and volunteer that he was the father—to prevent me from getting the money. Mariano didn't know that was the plan. He didn't want his brother touched, but Slattery and Godoy got greedy. It got out of control." Rodrigo ran a hand through his hair. He looked exhausted, and no wonder—he had been busy lately. "And with you, well, you knew too much. That's why Godoy wanted you out of the way. But you have to believe me, Lupe, I had nothing to do with locking you in that jewelry store. Nothing!"

His eyes kept gravitating to my purse, probably looking

for a gun. "Then why didn't you come back to free me when the others had left, Rodrigo?" I demanded.

"I was going to, I swear. You were Margarita's best friend. I would never let anything happen to you, not in a million years."

I didn't know which was more disgusting, Rodrigo's lies or the begging tone with which he told them.

"Mariano was furious when he found out you got away," he said. "It was Godoy and Slattery's responsibility to make sure you stayed tied up in that closet until Mariano could figure out what to do with you."

Strange, I thought. Mariano was enraged that they had beaten his brother, but what seemed to push him over the edge was Godoy and Slattery's failure to keep me captive until he could kill me.

I had heard enough of this. "Rodrigo, I want you to shut up now," I said. "And listen to me, if you want to live. I'm going to leave you alone, and I'm not turning you in to the police—but only under one condition."

Rodrigo looked as though Christmas had come early. "Anything," he said. "Anything at all."

"As soon as you get back to your office, you will drop your lawsuit against Dade County," I said. "You'll have to get a new lawyer first, because yours will be fertilizing flowers in South Dade."

I looked into his eyes and opened my Chanel bag. "Otherwise . . ." He didn't move at all when I pressed the gun into his ribs.

"I promise, I swear," Rodrigo said, beginning to stutter. "I'll, I'll just get a lawyer out of the yellow pages."

"I'm only letting you go because of Margarita," I said. "She was my best friend, and I don't want her life dragged through the mud so you can make money. And I don't want you profiting over her corpse."

"I understand," Rodrigo whispered.

"You let her rest in peace," I hissed. "You're a shit, Rodrigo, a real bastard. You always were. But Margarita married you, and I have to respect that. Back off the case, and get on with your miserable life."

I pushed the gun harder into his ribs. His teeth started chattering.

I left him like that and got into my car. Hopefully, I would never see him again. He was scared enough of me to keep his promise, I knew. I could get him thrown in jail, or worse. I would be perfectly happy to carry out my threat. I had started the day a gun-averse investigator, and was ending it a female Rambo.

I was pleased to see the Mercedes parked in its usual spot back at the cottage. Bless Tommy, he always came through for me. And he would have to again—by proving what a great lawyer he was, and getting me out of all the messes I was in because of the Arango case.

My watch read precisely three o'clock when I parked Leonardo's Jeep. I had beaten my deadline by three hours.

FORTY-ONE

SAM ANSWERED THE phone, listened for a moment, and handed the receiver over to me without a word. This was the first call I had received in my six days in Key West. Sam and I had kept very busy—eating, sleeping, and drinking. My mind and body were restored to a semblance of what they had been before I heard the name Arango.

"Hi, Tommy," I said. "How are you?"

"I don't mean to interrupt your vacation," Tommy said. "But I thought you'd enjoy hearing this."

I had left careful instructions that I wasn't to be disturbed. Leonardo was taking care of things at the office, and Tommy was putting out my legal fires. I was in good hands.

"Before you say anything," I insisted, "tell me—am I in trouble?"

"Of course not," Tommy said. "I have everything worked out, and you're completely in the clear. That's what makes me the best. And I've told the police you're recuperating in an undisclosed location."

"Thanks, Tommy." I felt gratitude ooze from my every

pore. I watched the ceiling fan turn, and took a long sip of my margarita.

"I also heard through the grapevine that Aurora Santangelo, your old nemesis, is in Hialeah traffic court prosecuting speeders," he added. "Apparently her boss thought she was conducting her investigation as a personal vendetta against you."

"It's about time someone figured that out," I said.

"And guess who her new boss is, the guy responsible for her descent into hell? None other than your ex—Charlie Miliken!" Tommy chuckled under his breath. He loved giving me news like that.

I burst out laughing. I guessed Aurora wouldn't be needing the sign painter anytime soon. I thought about Charlie, probably awash in Jack Daniel's and Marlboros at that very moment.

"So what else did you have to tell me?" I asked, still laughing.

"I got Alonso senior out of the Stockade, for the time being," Tommy began. "And we reviewed everything that had happened in the case. He was embarrassed as hell. I had to ask him why he agreed to bring an investigator into the case when he and his family had so much to hide."

I had wondered that myself. "I'm on pins and needles, Tommy. What did he say?"

"The old man said that when he met you at the Stockade he figured I was sleeping with you. He thought I only wanted to hire you because you were my girlfriend, not because you were any good as an investigator."

"You're kidding." I had more of my margarita. I was too relaxed to be offended. "He was half right—only half, right?"

"I swear to you, that's what he said." Tommy barked out a raucous laugh. "He only agreed to hire you because he thought it would make me happy. He said he never thought a 'little girl' like you would find anything out."

Tommy laughed so hard he started choking. Soon I was

laughing with him. I drained the rest of my margarita, hung up the phone, and lay back, feeling the warm afternoon breeze.

Men! I said to myself. And I laughed some more.

"Gerry Boyle is the genuine article."
—Robert B. Parker

GERRY BOYLE

__LIFELINE   0-425-15688-5/$5.99

McMorrow senses a good story in Donna Marchant, an abused woman. But after the article is published and Donna is found murdered, he finds suspicion has fallen not only on her boyfriend, but on himself as well.

__BLOODLINE   0-425-15182-4/$5.99

Jack McMorrow returns to track down the killer of a local girl who was just starting to put her life back together after having an out-of-wedlock baby.

__DEADLINE   0-425-14637-5/$5.99

"A bone-cracking first novel."
—New York Times Book Review

Reporter Jack McMorrow leaves *The New York Times* to edit the weekly paper in Androscoggin, Maine. When his staff photographer is murdered, Jack learns small towns can be as cruel as big cities.